THE
SUNDERED
WORLD

SALWOWSKI '98

Also by Frank Ryan

—

Fiction

GOODBYE BABY BLUE

SWEET SUMMER

TIGER TIGER

—

Non-Fiction

TUBERCULOSIS:
THE GREATEST STORY NEVER TOLD

VIRUS X

THE
SUNDERED WORLD

—

BOOK ONE
TÍR

FRANK RYAN

SWIFT PUBLISHERS

A Swift Book

First published in Great Britain by Swift Publishers 1999

1 3 5 7 9 8 6 4 2

Copyright © Frank Ryan 1999

The author asserts the moral right to be identified as the author of this work.

A CIP catalogue record for this book is available from the British Library.

ISBN 1-874082-23-5

Typeset by ATG Design Communication, Huddersfield
Printed in Great Britain by Caledonian International Book
Manufacturing Ltd, Glasgow

Swift Publishers Ltd
PO Box 1436, Sheffield S17 3XP
Tel: 0114 2353344 Fax: 0114 2620148 email: swiftpublishers.com

ACKNOWLEDGEMENTS

Thanks a lot, John and Barbara, as much for your support through a difficult time as for your great patience and help with the typescript. Thanks also David Coen for your sensitive contribution to the editing.

—

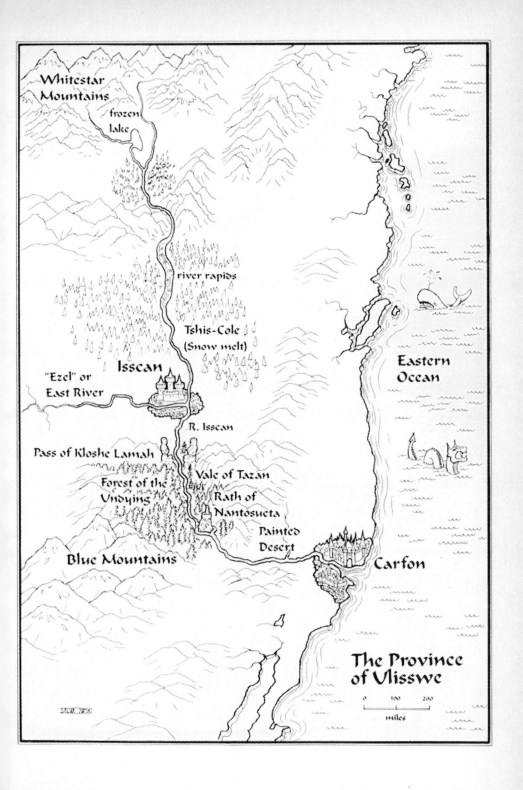

Whitestar
Mountains

frozen
lake

river rapids

Tshis-Cole
(Snow melt)

Isscan

"Ezel" or
East River

R. Isscan

Pass of Kloshe Lamah

Forest of the
Undying

Vale of Tazan

Rath of
Nantosueta

Painted
Desert

Blue Mountains

Eastern
Ocean

Carfon

The Province
of Vlisswe

0   100   200

miles

CONTENTS

For the friends I knew and
the adventures we shared long ago in the shadow
of Slievenamon.

—

In carfon there is a manual for rulers.
Page 1, line 1, reads: In the beginning it is wise to
assume that your enemy knows more than you.

—

WINTER

H E FELT BRUISED and broken in every bone and sinew. There was an agony beginning in the pit of his abdomen and spreading out in waves, a festering and dreadful wound. Vomit filled his mouth. For several minutes he hardly dared to move a muscle. He just lay there, struggling to open one eye to see. He thought his sight was gone until herealized that the right lens of his glasses was opaque, shattered into a spiderweb of splintered pieces. The left lens was splintered, if not quite shattered. Clumsily, through a curtain of pain, he dislodged the glasses from his nose and looked again with both eyes.

Snow!

It was not possible for Alan Duval to accept the fact that he was lying out in the open, in – he squinted his eyes open again for an instant – in a barren landscape in a blizzard.

He spat to clear his mouth, blinked, and looked again at a landscape of black rock and snow.

Of course this was not possible. All of his common sense denied the possibility of his being here. When he went to touch his face with his right hand, it was his left hand that moved, his left hand that now felt dominant, that palpated fevered skin, hard throbbing eyeballs under matted lids. He couldn't understand this. There was no understanding this.

Swallowing hard, he tasted blood mixed with the vomit. He remembered setting out to get food in London. Yeah – he remembered that. And he remembered the girl. But he didn't want to think about that. He didn't want to think too much about the girl.

It was madness – impossible. Whatever in the hell was it all supposed to mean?

Gasping with a new explosion of pain in the wound, he tried to remember how he had got here. The meaning of... of what he remembered – the impression of change, of incredible dislocation. The experience had seemed dreamlike, yet there was nothing imaginary about his surroundings.

He opened his throbbing eyes again, blinked them cautiously against pain, yet had to do so repeatedly in shock.

He could see better with his eyes narrowed. He could see perfectly into the distance through his left eye and without his glasses, which again was odd. His gaze faltered on huge shadows, which jerked into fitful focus in the gaps of a blizzard. He was surrounded by coal black mountains, caught in a blizzard.

Fright made him attempt to scramble to his feet, but he didn't succeed. Gasping again, attempting with deep breaths to break the stranglehold of pain over his movements, he lay still. While he rested, feeling was returning to the skin of his face; he could register the icy cold touch and the brittle feel of the snow crystals against his skin, the flapping of his disordered greatcoat in the wind.

He had to make some crude assessment of just how injured he was.

Pain seemed to rack every ligament, the root of every tooth, the tissues that held his eyeballs in their sockets, but at the same time his examination confirmed that he was intact. Then he began the scary business of testing movement. His left leg followed by his right. Everything worked, however reluctantly. His joints felt grotesquely swollen, massively disturbed. He had a vague recollection of a disordered spiralling through... through what?

Through time and space?

No – I can't believe that. There must be some alternative, some logical explanation.

Though he had no rational way of explaining it, that was how it had felt during the passage.

He tried once more to climb onto his hands and knees. Pain exploded in his abdomen. A giddy, swooning pain such as he had never known in his life before, coming up out of his belly, into his heart and lungs. His body shuddered with the heavy, sickening throbbing of it. Unable to control himself he twisted over onto his side and he retched.

He was only just coming to register the true fierceness of the cold. It was excoriating.

Think! Think through it to the logic behind it!

He did his best to think. The weight of sky, through the driving squalls of snow, appeared to suggest evening in an extreme northerly, or southerly, latitude. An involuntary scream came from his lungs as he tried to pull one leg under him – and failed. Moaning, he pulled the greatcoat a little tighter round his throat.

Blinking both his eyes, he registered that his right eye had been damaged by the same force that had shattered the lens of his glasses. The vision through it was so blurred as to be useless. He wiped his left eye with the snow-encrusted sleeve of his coat and blinked it through pain, blinked it more rapidly to try to dry it. Then he tried crawling, in an undignified scramble on tormented knees and wrists, like a soldier under a murderous bombardment. Even within the few minutes he had been conscious, the wind had reared into a new crescendo of howling. Jerking painfully sideways, to avoid what appeared to be a crag of rock, he eked out a slow but steady progress until he was sitting with his back against the crag. With nausea cramping his guts, he put his head round the edge of the rock and squinted once more into the howling storm.

Unbelievable!

Down a scree of ragged boulders and shale, and between those towering black ridges, a torrent of wind and snow fomented and roared, accelerating madly over the flatter scree, its moiling surface no more than twenty feet above the ground. Where it hit a stubbornly resisting rock, the impact created a vertical spume, sixty or seventy feet into the air, before rushing onward, like a river in spate.

He tried to think back: to those words that had just seemed to enter his mind. A woman's voice… something about an enemy that was evil incarnate!

Bloody hell!

Pressing his back into the crag, he gave up the struggle for explanations. He patted his left hip pocket and found the hard rectangular shape of the harmonica. The battered old harmonica had once belonged to his father – his alcoholic father who had taught him the blues. With a new thought, he patted higher up the greatcoat, searching for the three-quarters pint of Jameson's whisky in the silver flask that was his only other legacy from his father. Ignoring the pain, he bent his elbow to find the flask in the inside pocket of the greatcoat. He found it miraculously intact.

Thank you, father – thank you!

It was a small victory, yet the sweetness of it, the sheer bloody-minded exultation of that tiny victory, made him feel like shouting his defiance into the gale.

He exulted over the feel of the flask. He almost crooned over the shape of the bald eagle of his homeland. It was a manoeuvre to get the cap untwisted. He didn't bother to look at what he was doing. He just performed the action from touch, ignoring the pain as he brought the already ice-rimed silver to his lips, spilling whisky over his cheeks.

Oh, man!

He captured a gulp between numbed lips, swallowed it down, spluttering and gasping. Dropping his exhausted arm to his side, he gloated as the whisky coursed through his chest, warming his heart and numbing the pain.

This morning, for the first time in his life, he had sat down in a cold damp street in London and he had busked for the money to buy some food. It just didn't make any sense. Lifting the flask in that same shaky arc, he brought it once again to his lips.

Was it you, Kate? Was it really you, after all these years?

Not possible! He shook his head violently. No, he couldn't face that – it could not possibly be true.

Kate had... had disappeared. That had been the end of his real childhood, the cause of all the scandal and recriminations. Something mysterious had happened to Kate. Something terrible that had parted Duval from his closest friends. The end of everything.

He closed his lips around the neck of the flask. He drank again. He drank deeply, forcing the burning whisky between his chattering teeth.

Fear rose in him then, the fear that had haunted his life from that moment of losing Kate. Then, with his face screwed into a scowl of determination, he twisted his head from side to side, forcing it to move on the groaning joints of his neck, to shake his head. A howl of wind lashed his good eye back into the cave of its socket: it felt as if a single sharp barb of freezing steel had penetrated his eyeball, pinning the shredded flesh against the bone. Trying to shield his face from the cold with his frozen fingers, every shriek whistled through the gaps in his clothes, scourging his skin like fishhooks.

Dear God, give me strength!

Duval staggered to his feet, rising through nausea, wrenching pain and debilitating giddiness. Then, lurching around the lee of the crag, he exhaled in astonishment. He found himself inside what appeared to be a rough-hewn stone circle.

Leaning now, with his less bruised side against the inner face, he could not be mistaken about it. It looked as old as the mountains. Huge stones as large as those in the circles of Stonehenge or Avebury had been embedded in the bedrock, but the circle was smaller and complete. The stones jutted out of the restless snow in what felt like defiance, like the snarling fangs of some monster at bay.

Where could this be?

The skin of his face was being invaded by cold, until it felt as stiff as a mask. Breathing steam into the air, he noticed a rapid darkening in the sky, the wrack of clouds wheeling above, the light rising from the whited ground as if a black sun reigned in this blasted world and darkness instead of light was falling on the earth.

I am part way up a mountain.

He tried to consider that fact calmly, though his heart hammered beyond logical consideration. *I appear to be about a third of the way up an enormous valley.* Peering upwards, he could see those same fearsome ridges jutting rabidly into the sky for thousands of feet.

There was no doubt where he needed to go: that was down. Down into the valley.

No matter how impossible that seemed, no matter that the wound in his abdomen was gorging upon itself, like a filthy gangrene, that was definitely the way he needed to go. But he wouldn't be making his way down today. There couldn't be more than an hour or two of light left and the last thing he needed was to be caught in a blizzard. He would have to find some shelter to rest for tonight.

An overwhelming compulsion seemed to tether him here, in this circle of stones. Somehow there was a purpose here – though he wouldn't go so far as to call it hope. Duval staggered up onto his feet and stumbled, with gritted teeth, until he was standing in the centre of the circle of stones.

Was it his imagination, or did the force of the gale blow round and over the circle?

Standing shakily upright, he gazed up through the matted lids of his left eye into the darkening sky. His breath blew about his face – it was his breath that was freezing on the skin of his face, congealing as ice within every pore. But even that was revealing. His breath was not ripped away by the howling wind. There was peace here. A spindrift of snowflakes appeared to spiral downward into the circle. He was standing knee-deep in virgin snow.

He folded there in the snow, squatting down with his chin lowered to the surface. He wished he could have taken another warming swig of the whisky. If only he weren't so exhausted he'd have got himself good and drunk on the whisky. Under the blanket of snow, once more he searched out the shape of the harmonica in his side pocket. Its familiarity comforted him. He told himself he'd have played it too. He'd have entertained these black mountains with Sonny Boy Williams and Muddy Waters. If he weren't so worn out… so damned shattered.

— TWO —

LONDON

A FREEZING SMOG HAD lapped the streets earlier that morning as Duval had stopped playing his harmonica and folded up the cardboard sign that read *OUT OF WORK*. Slipping the whisky flask from his inside pocket, he took a small nip to ease the cold before pocketing the few pounds worth of coins from his hat. Then, rubbing the neuralgia induced by the cold from his legs, he climbed awkwardly to his feet, put his collection hat on his head and, walking stiffly as the circulation returned, he crossed through Berkeley Square, up Hay Street, and then Dover, past clubs with card-coded entrances through steel doors. Yet even this was more friendly than Selfridges, where private security guards stood between the pillars armed with submachine guns. The smog was as poisonous as the killers of the sixties. He coughed as he walked through streets as miserable and squalid as any that Dickens would have found familiar.

Turning left onto Piccadilly, the smog's dank breath curled down over the ice-laden gutters and roofs, merging poison with cold and filth. It was hard to believe the way things were going. A sort of social sickness had gone to ground in the inner-city ghettoes, spawning new depths of depravity and anarchy. It wasn't the best time to be out of work and hungry.

He stopped at the street newspaper stand, where he had been on nodding acquaintance with Sadiq Khan, the middle-aged Pakistani who had run it for the eighteen months or so that Duval had lived locally. Sadiq was always complaining about the misfortunes of Millwall football club. Duval didn't know if he had been murdered or he was hiding somewhere for his own protection. Murder was not so unlikely. Racism was an issue in these streets, especially at night. Stopping, ostensibly to cough into his hand, he sized up the rat-faced young man with a ponytail who had taken over the stand. He noticed the jerky cockiness and pasty-white face of the crack addict. He was selling pornography, sealed in brown paper bags, which was being pawed by a handful of men.

Crowds jostled him on Piccadilly. There was tension in their faces. Nobody looked you in the eyes anymore. He carried on walking. It was a mistake to do anything that made you stand out from the crowd.

Turning left off the Circus, he headed along winding older lanes for the dilapidated but surviving open market at Brewer Street. Here he haggled over fresh fruit, vegetables, bread, milk, two sausages – all at inflated prices. There were no women working the stalls. Even the men had that shifty dislocation, because they didn't want to make eye contact. Who would have believed that anything could have done away with the brassy Cockney humour that had once been London's pride?

So it was in a despondent mood that he ordered tea and a fry-up in Oggy's Café – one of the few still surviving around the markets district – taking a seat on a stool that was screwed to the floor.

Oggy pulled a stainless steel teapot down onto his working surface, he scoured it with steam, inserted the tea bag and then the boiling water. He slammed the teapot onto a small tray on the counter, added the tiny pot of milk and then the mug. Then he wiped sweat from his face, staring after Duval as he took his tray to an empty table hard up against the window.

It was warm in the café yet still Duval pulled his greatcoat tighter around his throat.

He couldn't believe that his hands were trembling. He was thirty-four years old, with a first-class degree in science from MIT, yet for the last two years he had been out of work. Out of work and out of money. With those trembling hands, he poured the milk into his mug, lifted the lid of the tiny teapot to stir the tea bag around, then poured the tea. He sipped despondently from the mug, peering out of the window. His own reflection, with its spiky black hair, gazed back at him against the steel mesh that protected the glass on the outside. Through it he saw the occasional body hurrying through the spoiled streets. He got lost for a while in his thoughts. Duval had been one of the brightest young stars in his field. Had he been foolish in coming here to work in London? Had he compounded that foolishness when he opposed his departmental line of work? Maybe he had gone crazy altogether in talking openly to the media about his conscientious objections to the new cusp of the scientific wave, the manipulation of the human chromosome?

Oggy's voice interrupted his ruminations, Oggy shouting out the order, sliding the enamel plate with the bacon, two eggs, and buttered bread onto the counter. Duval walked over and took the food back to the table, where he hunched down over it, making a sandwich with two slices of bacon and a fried egg. His eyes watered as he bit into it.

A sound: a faint rapping on the steel mesh beyond the glass, so close it seemed only inches from his mind. It startled him, focused his attention on somebody who was standing there, on the other side of that steamy window.

Black fingernails, like claws, withdrew from the mesh to be replaced by a spectre. A face was peering in at him, through the white lettering of HOT SANDWICHES that Oggy had painted on the window: tawny hair, filthy and matted, bunches tied into rat tails with rolled-up cylinders of silver foil. A girl – a young woman. She was leaning on the mesh looking in at him, a pointed face, pink tip of nose, a sharp little chin, and pink-heavy lids over green eyes that were now darting around his face. His heart was pounding as he shook his head, motioning her away.

He bolted what was left of his meal, wiped his mouth and

chin with the back of his hand. Emptying the remains of the milk into the mug, he added what was left in the teapot. He couldn't afford to let any of it go to waste. Hunching down over the table surface, he hid the way he was counting out the coins to pay for the meal. Grabbing the shopping, he went to the counter, where he slapped down the money, then he hurried to the door and slipped out of the warm café, with its comforting food smells, into the smoggy cold of the street.

Scanning the refuse-strewn pavement to left and right, he found no sign of the girl. Just a glimpse of movement at the corner of his eye, heading toward Oxford Street.

Duval felt such an irrational urge to catch the girl that he very nearly ran.

He half staggered through the filth and the averted faces, until he found himself in one of the junk markets. Within thirty yards, his heart leaped as he caught sight of her. The hair was unmistakable. She was peering back over her shoulder at him.

Even among the raggedy people, the girl looked out of place. Something about her ate at him though he couldn't remember seeing her before. But now that he was close to her he felt inhibited from just rushing up on her and asking questions.

He followed her, through the square of rickety stalls, with their secondhand rags, the shuffling feet and darting hands. Trampland. But these were more threatening than the tramps of old, who used to huddle under the bridges in their beds of newspaper. Those had maintained some kind of fellow under-standing. This new breed of hobos were as vicious as wolves.

Pretending to be interested in some rags that were draped over a line of broken-down tables, he kept his eyes on the girl.

She had stopped to look over the contents of a particular stall.

Edging closer, Duval saw the refuse of butchering. Lumps of bone, flecked with bloodied scraps of meat, or combinations of entrails were laid out over the rough planks like prime cuts. Yet there was longing in her eyes: as though she didn't have the few pence to buy bones.

It was a mistake to hang about here and he had made that mistake. When he tried to push his way through the shuffling crowd, he felt a sharp kick at his ankle. He turned to find two street thugs ogling him. One was about his height, with a long black overcoat and Doc Martens boots. The other was short, with mousy hair. The tall one was a skinhead, his face pocked with acne, a cigarette gripped in his teeth. His leering brown eyes squinted through the trickle of smoke. "Bleedin' rich tart! Give us a note or I'll kick yer bollocks into yer throat!"

Duval made a point of avoiding trouble. But the shorter one had blocked his escape. He was wearing a shiny bomber jacket, with badges sewn on down one arm.

The taller one had a lion – an emblem of some street gang – tattooed on the side of his neck. They shoved so hard against him, Duval could smell their body odour. Both wore stud earrings in their left ears and the smaller one had a ring through his right nostril, from which a scabby sore festered onto his lip.

The gangs were nearby, but they should have been sleeping by day. Maybe this pair had been sent out to hunt for food. Duval saw himself through their eyes: six-one and relatively fit-looking – strong enough to give them trouble. But they had probably seen him busking. When he turned to look, the girl had vanished.

"Damn!"

He sidled around the stall, but they followed him. It was likely that they would be carrying weapons. The skinhead backed into him. He saw the mousy-haired one grab his hat from his head, then drape it rakishly over his own head, horsing around with it. The other was groping at his pockets. Already he had stolen the few coins of change still left in the Duval's right hip pocket. Then he discovered the bulge of the harmonica. No way was he getting his hands on the harmonica. With all of his strength, Duval punched the skinhead in the centre of his face, giving him a bloody nose. Then he didn't hang around to wait for the reaction.

He tried to run but his injured ankle slowed him down. After making about a hundred yards, he slipped down a side street, kicking through the rotting planking of a derelict shop to get through into a back alley.

Backing into a shaded doorway, he stepped on something foul. He was startled by a rousing gallery of heads, filthy faces, missing teeth, mangy scalps, balding or capped with untended straggles of hair. Every crevice and doorway was taken up. A legion of tramps had taken over the alley. They had cannibalized most of the doors and frames for firewood and were sheltering from the weather in the holes in the walls. As one by one they got to their feet, he stumbled on, tripping over the jumble of legs, evoking an increasing chorus of curses.

Duval recoiled from these grotesque faces, the hatred in every eye, the overwhelming stench.

Then he heard them before he turned and saw them. They were walking down the alleyway toward him, with an insolent swagger. The skinhead, with his bloody nose, was slapping a lump of metal against his palm. The shorter of the two was swinging a pickaxe handle. He entertained the tramps with a display of legerdemain, tossing the handle into the air and catching it again. Then they parted to show that they were not alone. There was a third thug – it was with a shock that Duval registered his presence. He had the build of a heavyweight wrestler, with enormously over-developed muscles. The left side of his head was smooth-shaven, and tattooed with a parody of the Union Jack, the flapping standard capped by a skull and crossbones, dripping with blood.

In the hierarchy of the street gangs, he was a Scalpie, a hellish archangel. Sweat erupted over Duval's face, running in rivulets down his neck and back.

The Scalpie stood there for a few seconds, taking him in. From a pocket he took out some coke and he spread it in the groove between his thumb and the back of his hand, snorting it like water down a drain. His nose streamed as the other two kicked their way around the sea of tramps, creating a makeshift gladiatorial arena. The short thug passed a bottle of vodka to his partner and he took a swig before belching loudly. He grinned at Duval, wiping a furred tongue over his cracked lips.

The Scalpie was carrying a black casket. Kneeling on the ground, he placed it before him. Then he made a low, deep bow before opening it. From the casket he withdrew two gauntlets, made out of a matte black metal. He put them on. With his mailed hands he withdrew a dagger from the casket. The dagger was heavy and ornate and the Scalpie seemed to handle it reverentially, as if invoking some kind of a ritual. The blade was a tapering spiral that ended in a vicious-looking point. It too was black – darker it seemed than the mere absence of reflection – and the handle gleamed with inlaid silver. The three separated to block Duval's exit from what he already knew to be a cul-de-sac.

"If you walk onto the blade of your own free will," he said to Duval, "I'll make it quick."

"Fuck you!"

There was a tingling at the ends of Duval's fingers. Making fists, he opened and shut them several times. He could expect no assistance from the tramps. Looking for a piece of wood, or anything he might use as a weapon, he found nothing to hand.

Casually, the two thugs closed in on him from both sides. This time he concentrated on the one with the pickaxe handle, watching him out of the corner of his eye. Spinning round faster than the man expected, Duval kicked him hard on one knee. There was a satisfying crunch of boot against bone. The thug dropped back, limping and cursing. Duval was on the point of turning when he felt a heavy blow to his temple from the armoured fist of the Scalpie. A second blow hammered against his teeth. Half conscious, he couldn't stop himself sliding towards the side, with his shoulder and head thudding against the wall.

He thought, *What a miserable way to die.*

There was a movement through the ring of tramps and the feral girl was next to him. Incredibly she had taken on the skinhead. He was already down, dead or dying. Now she was facing the remaining two attackers, crouching like a wild animal, making snarling sounds. As Duval was struggling to get back onto his feet, the pickaxe wielder, still limping from Duval's first blow, darted in close.

She moved so quickly and silently, Duval was not aware even of her intention. He must have blinked, because already she was back in that defensive posture and the second thug was crumpling onto his knees, blood pumping from the side of his throat. Duval saw the blades of two stilettos extending from her clenched fists. The narrow blades moved about her fingers as if they were extensions of her arms.

She was already facing the Scalpie.

If she had astonished him too, he didn't show it. With a slick movement, he picked up the nearest tramp in his mailed fist, holding the cursing figure by the scruff of the neck, using him as a shield. He closed on the girl, crouching and hissing through clenched teeth. The girl made one of her lightning darts, but the Scalpie was quicker. The roar was Duval's. The spiral dagger had caught him a slashing blow, low down in the gut. Although the greatcoat had given him some protection, the Scalpie had inflicted a serious wound.

As he fell back against the slimy wall, Duval saw the tramp crumple, the blade of a stiletto brokenly protruding from the centre of his chest. The girl had withdrawn sharply but her right hand was bleeding, the handle dropping out of her injured fingers. The Scalpie laughed.

Throwing the tramp's corpse aside, he extended his reach, dagger in one hand and the mailed fist of the other, tightening his pincerlike trap about the crouching girl.

Duval worked out the avenue of the attack. Throwing himself in front of the girl, he took the mailed fist in the bleeding pit of his stomach. He retched from the force of it and felt weak from nausea. There was no time even to look toward the girl, only to hope that his intervention had given her time. Then he saw the Scalpie stagger backward, dragging Duval with him, into the tangle of squealing tramps. His face was so close to the man's that he was inhaling his rancid breath. A trickle of bloodied jelly was oozing from the Scalpie's right eye. With that eerie silence of movement, the girl finished him with a stab to the throat, expertly directed into the stem of his brain.

"Oh, shit!" Duval moaned, attempting to disentangle his injured body from the limbs of the dead Scalpie.

The girl made a nasal squeak, seeing how the blood was soaking into his clothes. She was trying to help him to his feet – pulling at him, as if to say they needed to get out of here. But there was no way he was getting to his feet right now. He pushed her hands away so he could probe the wound under the waistband of his trousers: he felt the gash, four or five inches long. His fingers were slipping in blood.

She ran her fingers over his skin, as if moulding the features of his cheeks, his nose, his brow and lips: as if the message she was trying so desperately to communicate was written in his face.

He studied her face. There was a translucency through which he could see blue veins marbling the porcelain thinness of chronic protein starvation. She had painted a thick blue circle around her left eye. A glance at her hair made him think she had lice. God alone knew what she had been through out there. Her right eye was surrounded by a yellowing map of bruising and her skin was a rash of healing cuts and abrasions. He didn't need to run his fingers down that starved skeleton to feel the lumps and bruises over those ribs. Duval reached out and touched her cheek with the back of his hand. Then, as if tormented by her growing frustration, she made a stuttering sound.

An excitement flickered in him as if she had touched a memory that lay deep and dormant.

He tried to speak, inducing a horrible spasm of retching. She used her sleeve to wipe blood from his face. With her own face a mask of concentration, she forced her throat to make a guttural croaking and whining, like somebody who had never learnt to speak.

"Aaah… Eeeurgghh!"

That was as far as they got with communication. Duval had to grit his teeth against the pain in his gut.

She made a stabbing movement: a twirling of one thin index finger, that suggested the spiral of the Scalpie's blade. What was she trying to tell him?

A sudden weakness swept over him. Consciousness wavered. His pulse flurried and a renewed sweat broke out over his face. Baffled, he shook his head.

Duval held both of his hands against the wound. He didn't think this wound was going to get better. There was a fevered throbbing to the edges of flesh that no longer felt like the cut of a clean blade. It felt putrid, as if a gangrene was already festering there, setting up a nauseating ache that was beginning to spread. Moment by moment, he felt the festering wound pulsate and send waves into his blood. Some sort of poison was spreading throughout his system, attacking his vital organs.

It seemed strange to him how the madness of the world had invaded his being.

Other figures were appearing in the street. Scalpies. There seemed to be dozens of them, heavily armed, gathering around them.

She was kneeling beside him on the filthy ground, holding his hand against her emaciated body, rocking gently. She took his hand and carried it to her face, fondling it against her cheek. She kissed it, then clasped it to her bony chest. "Aaah… eeaar-rgghhh!" She moaned again. She clung to him with such a fierce strength in those thin arms, held him to her, tried to force his face towards hers. His feeble resistance only made her more agitated and she forced her throat to make another guttural sound.

"Kaa-aate!"

He jerked in fright as another wave of debility shocked his system. It had sounded like a name: as if she were telling him that her name was Kate.

He spoke it in a whisper, "Kate!"

The Scalpies had formed a circle around them. Their mouths were moving, as if in the intonation of some dark hymn of triumph. His head fell back against the decaying red brick wall and blood trickled from his mouth.

He saw tears flood the eyes of the feral girl as she knealt by him, silent now, slumped in a final despair.

"Kate!" he whispered. "Dear God – is it you? Can it be you?"

No! Not possible! There was no way he could believe that such a thing could happen!

But he was in the grip of forces he no longer understood. His world was spinning out of control.

He wanted to explain to these forces that he wasn't a bum. He was a scientist. He belonged to a world of logic. But he had lost his voice. He heard a woman's voice, a calm, deep woman's voice, speaking strange words. The words entered his mind as if from a great distance, with the peculiar detachment of a dream.

You will not die. Your mission is too important. Remember then that your enemy is evil incarnate. Already his emissaries of malice have entered your world. Remember also that he fears the threat you pose to him. Beware the fact he will be expecting you.

Agony so universal he hardly recognized it as pain. Then a shock of dizziness, with a disorientating sense of extradimensional existence within it. He felt his consciousness become one with some terrible, almighty matrix. A rage of confusion.... Suddenly a second shock wave, as if his body had exploded, disassembled through time and space. His world disintegrated into motes of starlight. It surprised him that he remained conscious for so long. He wanted to vomit but he wasn't able; his limbs felt as if they were being torn from their sockets. He couldn't help but analyse what was happening to him before consciousness faded. A wheel of patterns, repetitive idiograms, as if he were translating new knowledge through a myriad of rainbows. A fierce keening in his ears. His reformed skin was erect with gooseflesh, as if frozen in its anticipation of things he did not understand.

THREE

THE CAVE OF MYSTERY

A FIGURE WAS STANDING over him, peering at him. The figure was the source of light that was dazzling him, the brilliance of the light obscuring the face that gazed down at him from above it.

Where am I?

He remembered the blizzard. Sitting down in the circle, the lancinating cold.

What's going on?

It was bewildering. He didn't know what was happening. All he could determine was the rough size of the creature, which was small, perhaps five feet or so, and the strikingly conical shape of its body, from a narrow tapering head to a wide, seemingly circular base, which appeared firmly fixed in rather than upon the ground. *The ground!* Suddenly there was a low-pitched snarl.

Fright made him attempt to sit up. But his limbs could only tremble and jerk fitfully. Darkness yawned about him, a terrifying abyss, that left him groaning and bathed in sweat.

"Arrrhhhggh – Duuuvaaallll!" He heard his name spoken, a rattling within his mind.

Nothing seemed to make sense.

He had been wounded in some squalid backstreet in London. Then he had woken up in an Arctic hell of snow and fury. He had stumbled into the stone circle, sat down in the centre. He remembered the never-ending fall of snow, covering him, drowning him in its lethal cocoon.

And now –

He was no longer exposed to the Arctic blizzard. That much was obvious. So somebody – or something – had found him, dragged him away from there. Some kind of a shelter, he thought. It was so maddeningly bizarre he wanted to scream. There was the impression that for some time he had been drifting in and out of coma. It was not possible. Nothing that was happening to him was remotely possible. He must have died in that filthy backstreet in London.

Lord God – I must be dead!

He lay still, helpless from the cold and the shock of mortal injury, while his uninjured left eye registered a sepulchral darkness. Even the darkest nights, with a heavy overcast of clouds, still allowed some faint illumination – a hint of moon or stars – but he could see nothing at all. He thought about that.

He also considered the fact that he could hear the howling of the wind, blowing that same blizzard, but he couldn't feel any gusting of the wind on his face. So the blizzard must be close – that Arctic landscape was nearby.

Trying to move his arms, they felt too weary to lift. Instead he blew air through pursed lips so that it registered on his nose, eyelids and cheeks. His face was not without sensation. There was a sickly, tumescent throbbing in his right eye and he could not part the lids. He explored the feeling in that eye, cautiously, by attempting first to blink it, then to open the eye. It felt bad, worse than before, when he had been exposed to the blizzard, a worsening injury. But he had felt his breath on his cheek. He still had normal feeling there. It confirmed that the wind was exterior. That he was somewhere inside, out of that blizzard. He must be in a natural shelter of some sort. It had to be a cave.

For a time he drifted again, lost track, resurfaced. Walking the streets of London… Oggy's Café… The feral girl. He saw her bruised face again. Her starved figure.

Terror caused another wave of sweat. It was so disorientating, so confusing.

Remaining still, hardly daring to breathe for fear of lapsing out of consciousness, he fought to analyse his situation.

His mind wasn't reliable. It was fogged by exhaustion, but he wasn't dreaming and he could think. His arms weren't paralysed. They were extremely weak but he could move them a little, even if it was only to lift them a fraction against gravity. *The snow – brought my temperature down.* In an ironic way, it had probably saved his life. The hypothermia that, over a longer period of time, would have killed him had in some shorter term eked out his survival. *The wound!* Although he had hardly been aware of the wound on first recovering consciousness, he could feel it now, the focus of sick, heavy waves of pain, from deep inside his abdomen.

If vital structures had not been damaged in the initial stabbing, the spread of the poison had ravaged them since. The wound felt really bad. It felt beyond hope.

He had been vomiting earlier. Whenever that had been. When?

Not so long ago. His instinct suggested it could not have been more than a day. He tried to focus on time and place. The stone circle wasn't very far away. If this was a cave, then it must open somewhere in the black tors.

Had he dragged himself here, in the extreme of injury and exhaustion? Not likely! Even the limited sensibility in his arms and legs told him that he was wrapped in some protective blanket under which he was wearing no clothes. That caused an irrational spurt of palpitation. Gently, hesitantly, he felt with the pulps of his fingers: the substance enveloping him like a quilt was natural, a soft material, like moss. Under him too – a bed of that same moss separated him from the dirt of the cave floor.

He was only coming round to the startling implications of this when he heard sounds approaching in the pitch dark, shuffling movements, yet regular and purposive, and without the benefit of light. His heart thudded again but he was so wearied he couldn't even lift his head in anticipation of what was coming.

Suddenly his left eye was blinded by illumination. Tears of irritation welled up into it and he was forced to close it. Even through his closed eyelids, he sensed how the light mellowed, faded. A greenish tinge settled over it and he squinted his eye open again, blinking.

That was when he first saw the extraordinary figure who was standing over him, peering down at him, and he heard that growling summons.

"Arrrhhhgggh – Duuuvaaalll!"

It sounded as dry as desert bones, yet so deeply pitched it demanded complete attention.

There was a muttering – it sounded more like a grumbling – in that same gravelly tone, as the figure poked at him with one index finger, armed with a talon of nail that projected like an auger from an incredibly wrinkled and filthy hand. The hand glowed with a startling phosphorescence.

Bloody hell!

He moaned again as the grimy nail scratched over his matted right eye. He writhed as it prodded at tendons, muscles, exquisitely swollen joints. He screamed as the finger found his genitals, then rose to dig into the livid and swollen abdomen.

"Maaannn – paaahhh!"

In the snarling twist of the creature as it wheeled away from him, eddies of air swirled and sparkled, as if ignited by its passage. He had glimpsed an impossibly ancient face. A female face – the most incredible old crone.

The afterimage of her face haunted him: skin of a brindled brown over silvery grey, like trout skin, with a thick, bedraggled mane of frost white hair that tumbled down over the filthiest collection of rags that had ever passed for clothes. Her build really was triangular, from the narrow, almost pointed top of her head, to the heavily sloping eyebrows, the widening nose, which protruded through a concatenation of folds and creases that moulded the complex landscape of her face. He could smell her, the odour of organic compost: as if he had taken a handful of mulched soil to his nostrils and inhaled deeply. Her smell seemed to follow him into another well of coma.

When he roused again, she was squatting on the floor no more than ten feet from him. A fire blazed between them. She was using her fingers to stir some unpleasant-looking ingredients into a bubbling clay pot over the fire.

Her poking had rekindled the pain in his guts. With the slightest movement, it radiated up into his chest, his jaw, out into his arms to the extremities of his fingers. For a moment, he was close to the abyss again, where another presence appeared to beckon him, a grim shadow cowled within darkness.

The old woman snarled what might have been a curse, causing the cowled shadow to shrink away, then she returned to her preoccupation with the pot, grumbling incessantly. In the glow of the fire, her hair was so long and matted that while she squatted there it cascaded about her onto the dirt of the floor.

Then, abruptly, she veered toward him and with a shock he registered her eyes. In a face that was as enfolded as a walnut, two solemn black eyes fixed upon him. There was no pupil or iris, no white. The eyes were all liquid black and as fiercely predatorial as an eagle's. And for a moment a distant memory came close to consciousness: the face of another woman with all-black eyes… and terror! The rise of terror overwhelmed him and his gaze fell from her eyes to the voluminous dark lace of her dress, which was not rags at all but something much stranger, something horribly organic in which diamonds of light seemed to sparkle and reflect the firelight. His heart was hammering like a hunted rabbit's, thrusting against the cage of his chest. She was addressing him, with her head down and her chin lost in the folds of her neck and upper chest. But even if the pounding of his heart had not expanded to fill his ears, he would not have understood a word.

He had recognized the true nature of her dress. It was woven from a myriad layers of cobwebs, the diamond lights that sparkled in its fenestrated depths were the bejewelled eyes of the spiders that spun its living matrix.

Her voice growled and crooned in hymnal cadences, or in litanies so obscure they belonged more to the grinding of pebbles against a rolling surf than the human throat. Her direct speech was as guttural as her mumblings, the strangest, darkest language he had ever heard. And in her ruminations, he seemed to catch that same word, *Quuuruuunnn*, again and again.

With a sudden pounce, she was upon him – she was gripping his face with one grimy hand, forcing that index finger of the other into his throat, the exploring probe wriggling ever deeper. He could taste the dirt of centuries upon that finger. He was choking, unable to breathe. He could see her nose was running, hear her breath crackling with phlegm. Suddenly, with a powerful flick of her wrist, she twisted his head on his neck, ignoring his moan of discomfort, and stared closely into his eyes.

Gagging, sweating with horror, his gaze was drawn into the midnight of those pupils, unable to resist the alien probing of his mind. In what seemed mere moments, she had reamed the contents, for she crooned loudly with triumph.

"Duuvaaalll – maaannn! Eeeeaaarrgh!"

"What are you doing? Where is this place?"

She wheeled about again, turned away from him towards the fire, whipping up clouds of dust with the wide hem of her skirts.

"Oh, shit!" His voice quavered like a single weak reed, his nostrils inhaled the excreta of insects and spiders, from the billowing dust. "Hey! Come back here! What in the name of hell are you?"

Without warning, she turned upon him once again, her heavy triangular head jutting forward, the grimy finger jerking aggressively into his face. "Duvaaaal aaassskkks – aaassskkks, yeeesss! Ssseeeesss nooo!"

His head jerked away from that finger, while his good eye continued to search desperately in the depths of those black eyes.

The finger, the eyes too, motioned to one side: he interpreted it as an indication of outside. Then a rattling sound from deep in her chest – an onomatopoeic sound. "Cha-teh-teh-teh-teh-teh!" That finger made darting signs at his heart.

"What are you trying to tell me?"

"Cha-teh-teh-teh-teh-teh!"

"Danger?" his instinct caught her meaning.

"Daaannngggerrr!" she affirmed, nodding, her voice if anything deeper, a growl that seemed to rise out of the very bowels of the earth.

Her eyes expanded expressively, the darkness in them glittering with portent.

Then she reached out and her finger appeared to enter his mind and peace overcame him. It was a wonderful feeling. All memory of the pain was gone. He was back in a beautiful morning in late July, early and quiet, before most people were awake. A sky of still glorious summer with scarcely a hint of cloud.

He recognized Clonmel – from the Celtic *Cluain Meala,* which meant the Vale of Honey – the Irish town, no more than eighteen miles from Waterford and the southern coastline, through which the waters of the Suir meandered towards the Atlantic Ocean. A vibrant town of perhaps fifteen thousand population, a small world within a larger small world that was rural Ireland. And a special day – the most special day in all the world…

So special, the fourteen-year-old boy, waiting astride his stationary bike, felt awed by it. So often had he dreamed about it and always it began right here, waiting outside the ivy-covered twin gates that led into the Doctor's House.

Alan Duval's fears centred on a mountain, now out of sight but looming ominously in the boy's imagination.

Slievenamon was the name of the mountain.

Beyond the town, over all its streets, the Main Guard and the decaying remnants of its medieval walls, the mountain soared, a breast of stone clouded in legend, two thousand three hundred and sixty-eight feet above the horizon. And there, on this fateful morning, lurked a secret so vast and brooding it chilled the blood in the boyish arteries....

The small door within the right half of the twin gates was opening. And even as his heart began to leap, he saw her eyes, the soft, calm green of an evening meadow.

Kate Shaunessy lived in the Doctor's House, with her widower father and a menagerie of dogs, cats, a tortoise, and a conservatory of exotic birds. She wore blue jeans, as they all did, loose fitting over worn trainers and her girlish breasts were hidden under a thick white sweater. This early in the morning, even at the end of a particularly hot summer, it would be cold. An inner voice was singing with joy as she drew close, because he had been uncertain until the last minute that she would come. Yet here she was, her smile as normal, carrying a plastic bag bulging with the rectangular shapes of sandwiches.

"What did you tell your father?"

"Nothing at all. Sure, he wouldn't have believed me anyway!"

The soft Clonmel accent... Kate so excited by the mission, she did not notice his own tremulousness.

He knew she had crept out through the first-floor lavatory window and climbed down the fall-pipe with its convenient bends, as she had before – because if she had left by the door the dogs downstairs would have barked her father awake. And he too had made his own furtive arrangements, tossing and turning through the night, with his bedroom window half open, unable to sleep – as his puffy face now testified – struggling to surface from that dreamlike state, and skating by the memory of poor Billy's screaming.

Then, the excitement no longer bearable, he did something he had never done before, something brave and wonderful.

He found himself awkwardly holding her against the lean of the bike. He was wrapping his arms around the slim warm life within her, his hands feeling her ribs through the muscles of her back, rising to marvel at the downy profusion of her hair, the feel of it running away between his fingers, with the silkiness of a bird's wing. He kissed her on the lips, feeling weightless with the ecstasy of the contact, the quickness of her surprise. He could not have functioned again until she, with the same blossoming of friendship into love, kissed him back, right there in the street.

He watched the deep flush invade her face, an expanding tide about the roots of her tawny curls and down into her throat above the white pullover, with its monogram from a capital letter of the Book of Kells.

Wordlessly, she sat sidesaddle on the bar of his bicycle, and he turned it round to face the town.

He was cycling now, his jittery legs rotating in their own inebriated motion, to the crossroads, with the slaughterhouse on the corner, where the animals bellowed in the big packed trucks going in and where the river tributary would later turn red with their blood.

Then they had already turned right, their course uninterrupted by traffic at this early hour of a Sunday morning, cycling by the hump of the second bridge – a frightening reminder of the bully, Flaherty, with its cracked coping stone in the lichen-encrusted limestone. And suddenly, as with every turn of the pedals the Comeragh Mountains loomed closer, time was running quickly. Time was racing through his fingers and it would never slow to normal again.

Their den was the disused dairy building at the rundown sawmill that belonged to Sean's father, Pádraig. Up the lane Alan had to stand on the pedals to cycle against the slope, doing his best to avoid the ruts and the humps of protruding stones. They rattled and swayed through the green-painted gateposts, past the blacksmith's forge, adjacent to what had once been stables and still contained horse boxes but now served as garaging for several rusting old vehicles. In front of the doors was the open-backed truck they intended to use, its hinged splats handpainted by Sean in camouflage shades of brown and green.

For today was the day of all days. Today the adventure was coming to its climax, a shared imagination that had begun in the final weeks of the long summer holiday the year before, when Alan had barely arrived in Clonmel and yet already he had lost his heart to this impulsive Irish girl who had let him kiss her, the first time in his life he had kissed a girl, and he had done it this very morning.

It was an adventure all through that wild summer that had already cost one life and had marked out the "gang" in the eyes of the townspeople.

And there was Liam Derby, the joker, waiting for them by the dairy door. Vaguely jealous already with the flush of both their faces, how meanly jealous Liam would have been had he known about the kiss. Liam, the black English boy, who had the sharpest wits. He who had explained to the po-faced Penny Burrows-Smith that shit was tapered at one end so your bum didn't close with a bang. Maureen Derby – Mo – was from London. She was Liam's adoptive sister, and Kate's pen pal. And Mo was waiting too, fidgeting with a diary she kept in her green-covered drawing book – Mo, who was so shy she scribbled her secret thoughts in a code of her own and drew her insects and wildflowers around the words in exquisite miniature.

This morning, as if seeing them for the first time, Alan noticed the increase in cobwebs. They were proliferating in every corner of the peeling blue-washed walls that sloped to a drain in the corner.

For weeks blue smoke had been rising from the chimney over the corrugated iron roof of the old forge at the bottom of the garden. Here, in the summer's heat, Sean had beaten a bar of solid iron, under Penny's incantations, then rasped and sanded it into shape, tempering its point in a bed of coke and polishing it until it gleamed – the spear of Lug. Alan could picture him learning the craft from his eccentric elderly father, who would light the stub of a cigarette from the red-glowing iron.

No time anymore – there was never any time.

They had come together in those long hot weeks of summer, like birds gathering to fly away upon a common calling. The weeks had merged together, all of a hurry.

And this morning there was little time for conversation, just the exchange of excited glances. Penny producing three battered-looking plastic drums, opaque and weightless, Penny kissing the stone talisman she had stolen from a sacred place, now hanging on its bootlace around her neck. Tall and angular Penny, her arm about Sean's neck, Sean who at fifteen was enormously tall, bigger than most men. Now it was Sean, his back bent and shoulders hunched to meet their faces, who was passing tiny glasses from hand to hand, each time adding a sip of the throat-burning poteen he helped his mad father to brew in a secret still in the woods behind the mill. The girls were gagging and complaining at the burning liquid as already, ignoring Liam's cackling laugh, Sean was proclaiming the toast:

"To Slievenamon!"

The answering chorus then with every heart throbbing crazily with anticipation – *to Slievenamon!*

FOUR

THE TRIANGLE OF POWER

T HERE WAS A pattern to it: restless sleep, punctuated by waking into a world of nightmare. He watched the old woman very carefully. He distrusted the look she would give him, the look she was now giving him, studying him from the edge of her fire. That prolonged stare, followed by a blink, before she shuffled over the floor to squat next to him.

"Duuuvaaalll – paaaiiinnn!"

Oh, sure – pain! That monosyllabic word, growled with the throaty cadences of a tiger. The pain came almost immediately.

She seemed to reach deep inside his body, to insert her black hands into the wound. Like ten red-hot irons, her fingers and thumbs roamed over the broken and poisoned edges of his flesh. Pain howled in an unbearable crescendo, causing his back to arch off the floor of the cave. In a final spark of strength, he lifted his fist against her, but his arm felt like macerated skin and bone. He thought the pain would drive him crazy, but then gradually, with what might have been the power of her guttural chants, it started to subside.

She's a healer!

It was that belief that kept him sane through the ordeal. And he could tell that his faith had not been misplaced. He had no idea how she performed the surgery, yet she had begun the healing of the poisoned tissues and organs.

He sensed the arterial blood no longer pulsing away from his gangrenous wound. He felt too the end of the throbbing of the poison that more than anything had robbed him of his vitality and strength.

Then he was content to feel the darkness rise up from the floor to engulf him.

He revived some time later to find her standing over him, as if inspecting every inch of his nakedness, under the fiercely burning torch. Then, without warning, she darted the fire-brand at his left hand.

He jerked his hand away from the flames, rubbing the singed flesh with his other hand.

As quick as lightning, she threatened his right eye. He howled, turning his face away from her with tears of rage in his eyes.

"Haaarrrggghhh!" She cackled with glee, her head thrown back and her tongue, green with mould, poked out between the liquorice black stumps of teeth.

As she shuffled back to the fire again, still cackling with merriment, and as his heart pounded at twice the normal rate, he realized that all four limbs felt stronger, that both his eyes were functioning, though the right eye still felt gritty and there was a residual halo about any object that strongly caught the light from her moving presence or the now dully glowing fire. It had been a brutal testing of his recovery.

Now she brought him some of the foul-smelling gruel she had been boiling in her pot, lifting it to his lips in a filthy clay bowl.

"SSSlllluuuurrrrppptltltl!" She made spittle-flecked sounds, while flicking her tongue over her lips, all the while studying him with a predatorial alertness. Trembling with revulsion, he brought his cracked and swollen lips to the edge of the cup. He gagged against drinking, overwhelmed by a wave of nausea.

"Duuuvaaalll – uuummmsssslllluuurrrpppp!" That tongue even more determinedly licking over black stumps of teeth. "Uuummmmhhh!" She forced the cup to his lips once more, making more of those repulsive lip-smacking sounds, inter-mixed with threatening growls. He tried again but was over-come with retching and coughing. He had to jerk his head away for fear of choking.

Her black eyes blinked at him, then held him in a belligerent confrontation with that finger reaching towards his mouth.

"No!" He gritted his teeth, shook his head violently.

"Aaaarrgghhh!" She whirled in a fury, darting away from him to vanish with impossible speed from the circle of firelight, but he could hear the echoes of her grumbles chasing one another along a maze of tunnels.

With his breath wheezy and over-rapid, he gazed about the cave, made visible by a sudden brightening of the fire. The vault was high, much higher than he would have imagined. In other circumstances he would have thought it awesomely beautiful. But he had a paranoia that he was not alone. There were sounds in the dark beyond the penumbra of firelight, faint hisses, sighs, cracklings, the dripping of water, the suggestions of whispers. He thought he glimpsed dark shapes out of the corners of his eyes, sinewy movements that seemed to glissade along walls or floor or ceiling, independent of gravity or the laws of nature.

Then suddenly he could smell her before he could see her. She was beside him, carrying his greatcoat over her arm. To the accompaniment of low-pitched garglings and burblings, her grimy hands were turning out the pockets.

"Huummmmphhh!" She discarded the harmonica, which he grabbed back. She was more interested in the half-empty flask of whisky.

Sniffing at the screw-top, she coddled its gleaming silver, chasing with her sensitive index finger the embossed outline of the American eagle. Abruptly, the cap was discarded and she had the flask to her nose; her tongue was lapping around the neck.

At the first taste of it, her eyes bulged out of her face.

"You like whisky, huh? Makes two of us!"

With a growl of satisfaction she had inverted it over her desiccated lips, her tongue making lapping sounds as she swallowed the contents in a single drink.

Disappointed with the now empty flask, she exclaimed a disgruntled "Paaarrrghhh!" – but now, as if captivated, she studied the brightly reflecting metal once more, holding the flask mere inches from her eyes.

Before he could follow what she was doing, there was a scurrying of movement back to the fire, then, with a shrill croak, she was swaying and crooning over the dancing flames, which had erupted, through no apparent mechanism, into a crackling furnace. Though her back was half turned to him, he could see that she had no fear of the fire, pressing her cupped hands deep into the flames. She was crooning happily, her body swaying from side to side, as she performed a moulding movement with her hands. In a mixture of dread and amazement, he watched her do something strange with the flask. The metal was coaxed and transformed, its elements spun and woven with the elements of fire, with added ingredients of charcoal and sand – and even her own spittle – until it was no longer a souvenir of an unhappy childhood but something remarkable, something entirely new.

A tiny eagle, as bright as the sun, beat its wings within the cradle of her widely spaced fingers.

Catching his breath, he watched the eagle settle with a gentle grace within the cage of her fingers. Then she cast her magic again, reforging its elements to become a goblet of glittering crystal, with a sinewy thick base; and, finally, with a circular friction of her finger that set up a melody of harmonics, she finished the bowl with a perfectly lipped edge.

"My God!"

Immersed in her act of creation, she warbled from deep within her chest before applying a final smoothing gloss by licking the goblet inside and out with her tongue. Then she held it aloft, revelling in the rainbow sparkle of its luminescence, a sudden brilliant glow of birth-light that coruscated over the walls and ceiling of her cave.

"Who, or what, are you?"

In her croon of triumph, he heard what sounded like a

name: "Graaannneee Ddddhuuu."

"Granny Ddhu – is that what I call you?"

"Duuuvaaalll!" She was mocking him again, in that gravelly voice, while polishing the goblet on the murky folds of her dress. "A biiirrrddd siiingggsss – Duuuvaaalll!"

Against the mockery of her reply, he felt foolish and ignorant, yet he attempted to divert her scorn.

"What kind of a place is this, Granny Ddhu? Where am I?"

A crinkle of mirth lifted the corners of her eyes at his use of her name. She thrust the still glowing goblet deep into the fermenting pot, elevating it brimming with the oily liquid, and then, in a whirl of uninterrupted movement, she brought it purposefully against his lips.

This time he drank greedily, ignoring any wash of nausea that still troubled him. The potion had a wilder, deeper taste than leaves or roots, or even herbs – a taste of fungi, with gristly bits, which seemed to inhabit his mouth with too lively a sense of movement for him to dare think about them. The healing power of the gruel tingled on his tongue, it appeared to crawl of its own volition down his throat, expanding to fill the emptiness of his gut.

Duval had no clear notion of how long he had spent in the cave. It might have been a week, it could have been much longer. The potions she administered to him contained a hypnotic ingredient, so that he slept for lengthy periods. But he knew he was recovering slowly.

His wakeful hours were fretful with danger. Shadows observed him, as if measuring his recovery against some hostile yardstick. He had died in London – or he had been wounded in some terrible way, so terrible that death had been inevitable. And then some force – he remembered the woman's voice in his mind – had brought him here.

Why? What the hell is expected of me?

Something to do with the group of children, Duval and his friends and their adventure in Clonmel? He sensed that. He sensed that so strongly, so terrifyingly, he hardly dared even to consider it.

It was no good asking the old woman. Communication with the old woman remained at the primal level of gesture and growl, laced with a cantankerous humour. His thoughts would return to the bleak landscape beyond the cave, to the black crags, the bitter cold and snow.

How would he ever get out of here – escape was the word that came to his mind – when he had no idea where he was or what lay outside the cave.

It was a time indistinguishable from many similar ones that she stirred him awake with a crack on his shins from a knobbly black stick. He roused to find that the fire was out and all of his clothes, including the greatcoat, were lying in the dust next to him. In her left hand she held a firebrand, with flames at least a foot high. Maybe at last he would get some explanations. He dressed hurriedly, though it was with a fearful anticipation.

She led him down a steep descent, step by step into the root of a mountain. She seemed to force their passage through solid rock that creaked and groaned in protest at their passage. That firebrand remained their only source of light. His ears caught the age-old murmuring of water deep underground, his nostrils sniffed the mustiness of organic damp, and increasingly, as they bored deeper, the acrid vapours of sulphur and brimstone. A passage, which looked like a natural cave, always seemed to open up before that squat conical figure, trailing her wild mane of frosted hair in the storm of her progress, as she scurried through her protesting underworld, rapping out her direction with her stick.

They rested from time to time, though it seemed to Duval that it was more for his benefit than her aged bones. He heard echoes, as if her snarls were being answered by forces within the mountain; at other times her shadow, cast by the torch, would expand to gigantic proportions, and her cackle, reverberating about the massive walls, would rumble in her wake like thunder.

It was easy to lose track of time and distance, yet he gauged they must have travelled deep into the earth. Here, at the centre of the labyrinth of caves, the old woman paused for a final rest, squatting before a lake of sulphurous lava. Duval was so exhausted, he flopped back against the cave wall, watching as she reached into the depths of those spider-infested garments and found the goblet she had fashioned from his father's silver flask.

Once again, in the cradle of her hands, the goblet changed back to the glowing eagle.

It was clear now that he was expected to watch – and he did so, in utter disbelief. Duval studied the tiny bird, the emblem of his homeland that had been created out of his father's flask. He watched it rise up out of the cage of her fingers, he watched its fluttering descent into the spitting and glowing lava. His horrified gaze followed the chase of the old woman's left hand into the yellow-spuming furnace. Then, with her right hand, she was beckoning impatiently, as if demanding that his own hand should join hers. He backed away, averting his gaze.

"Duuuvaaalll – paaahhh!" She reached out and took hold of his reluctant left hand, prying open his fingers and then dashing them into the sulphur.

Clenching teeth and eyes in anticipation of scorching heat, he was startled instead to encounter an icy cold. With amazement, he pulled his hand out again and gazed down upon his clenched fist. Light spilled out in rays and darts from between his fingers. When he opened them again, there was an oval ruby, as large as a pigeon's egg, in his palm. This was a new metamorphosis of his father's flask. She was growling incantations, ignoring his astonishment.

"Quuurrruuunnn!"

Duval stared in wonder at the glowing ruby, the light of which cast shapes and gyrations into the air about it, fathomless creations that melded and writhed in his vision, as if forever on the point of producing something even more remarkable. There was an associated feeling, a sense in which the ruby both influenced and was influenced by his mind as he held it in his hand. With a sudden snatch, she took the gemstone from him, squatting in the lava-lit dirt and manipulating it further. More deep-toned incantations, with their suggestion of sacred verse or litany, all of which he watched with mesmerized gaze as she spat and scratched with the talon of her index finger, hatching some new brood within herself.

He was the sole enraptured audience as, by some force of will, she transformed the ruby into a repository of her own energy. He saw how the features of her face, grotesquely exaggerated by the rays and spangles of light that burst through the ciborium of her clasped hands, turned colder and greyer as the ruby increased in power. The light grew even more brilliantly incandescent, transilluminating the bones of her hands. His eyes were dazzled by it.

Blinking in confusion, he was led by the old woman past the cave of lava, which now appeared to be an antechamber, leading into an enormous second cave.

"Duuuvaaalll aaassskkks – nooo! Duuuvaaalll seees!"

Granny Ddhu had collapsed onto her knees, yet still she progressed in this humiliating posture, holding the incandescent ruby aloft to guide them into a vastly widening chamber. As if catching fire from the ruby's spark, light, brilliant and multicoloured, swept through the chamber in a billion motes, that spiralled and flickered like starlight throughout its great spaces. The coloured motes seemed to encompass a wider spectrum than the rainbow and they ignited in their turn a Milky Way of flickering reflections in the walls, in the quartzite floor and the kaleidoscope of ceiling.

In their progress, they brushed by straw stalactites, as delicate as ivory hair, glittering with diamantine refractions. From the floor giant stalagmites sprung up, in beautiful reds and oranges, some striated and polished like marble. He marvelled at the dazzle of hues and tints, as if he were privileged to see beyond the human range of vision. For Duval, the scientist, it was as intoxicating as it was beyond reason. As if in answer to his incredulity, the glitter of iron pyrites seemed to metamorphose into the glory of a peacock. Recoiling at the extravagant impossibility of it, Duval saw the bird move, as if for a moment it had come to life, and then it reverted to false gold. At another turn, what might have been a shower of rose quartz crystals became the delight of a red-breasted robin.

How in the hell –

Still the forms spiralled and shimmered in the dazzle of energy and light about him. He had time to inspect the newly created feathers, an eye, a proliferation of petals or leaves. He did not doubt that if he had the facilities to study their biological infrastructure he would have found every detail intact, all functioning perfectly. It was as if he had entered a world where life could be struck from some utterly different mould, overwhelming beyond any human sense of logic, and exquisite beyond any sense of loveliness.

Duuuvaaalll aaassskkks – nooo! Duuuvaaalll seees!

A lesson then? If that was what he was being treated to it was a lesson that went beyond his capacity to understand. He sensed forces, powers that bordered on the infinite, and could not accept it: to do so would have meant the abandoning of his scientific education, his culture and civilization.

There was sound too, a tintinnabulation of musical chimes and harmonies, as if the labyrinth were vying in song with the beauty of vision. Duval smelled the scents of spring in his nostrils. A wave of his hand evoked a cloud of damselflies, metamorphosing into being from crystalline motes; a second wave brought into life a hummingbird, with its whirring hover, the fall of silver dust became the glory of a leaping salmon, with full-bellied arc through the rainbowed spray of a mountain torrent.

It was as if he had strayed into a fairy-tale world whose creation arose from the wonder of imagination instead of the red tooth and claw of evolution.

Of course, it could not derive from reality.

Yet, desperately, urgently, the human heart in him wanted to believe, while the scientist saw only illusions, a magician's phantasmagoria to delight the senses.

Even as he held his breath, the brilliance that seemed to exude from the very molecules of air was extinguished and he was being directed toward a single focus. In the glow of the ruby, still held aloft in the hand of the crawling woman, he was drawn through the entrance into a third cave. This was smaller, more intimate, and dominated by what appeared to be a circle of stalagmites. Yet as he approached it, the stalagmites took on the appearance of petrified trees. Closer still, he saw they were carved out of crystal: some trees had the distinctive bark of oak, with typical leaves and acorns, others were identified by beech leaves and nuts, or the distinctive flat fruit of elm, the prickly edges of holly, the smooth bark of birch or the ashlike leaves and berry of rowan.

And standing in the centre, at the cynosure of this strange power and beauty, was a single stone column, vaguely humanoid, as if a cowled and shawled figure brooded there.

As he came closer the figure loomed, blue-black in density and flickering in its depths, as if dormant with inner life.

With haggard patience, the old woman inched her way forward, entering the circle of petrified trees, her face downturned and averted. At last she reached the central pillar and he could see that she was anointing a face on the stone with what appeared to be a sacramental chrism. How respectful her hands had become! Those coarse and taloned fingers now traced the delicate lines of that face with real devotion in the whispered incantations. Abruptly her task was finished. She drew back from the pillar, fell onto the dusty floor with her face still averted, skulking into the background. But Duval was compelled to turn his attention from Granny Ddhu, for there was a force drawing him to the stone figure.

Conflicting emotions swept through his heart and mind: a wave of immense power, great weariness, the potential for almighty malice.

He felt he might have stood there, just sensing communion on this vast scale for eternity, but then hands he recognized, grimy and taloned, took hold of his elbows and propelled him forward, into the maelstrom of power. Her words, harshly rasping words, growled in his ears, the hiss of veneration: "Quuuruuunnn".

Into the spinning vortex, those gnarled hands guided him.

"Daaannngerrr, Duuuvaaalll!"

The whispering of other names, *Qurun Bave*. Had her words been leaves, they would already have dried and decayed to powder in his mind. And then even in her voice there was a hint of terror. *Qurun Macha*.

Could Qurun mean 'queen'?

A face in the stone seemed to come alive, a feminine presence. Granny Ddhu had anointed that face. In that care she had taken, in the quaver of dread in that old voice, he felt a powerful reinforcement of her warnings.

He was aware of the old woman dragging herself back a pace from him, still hugging the ground, on her age-old knees. Duval realized that he no longer needed the light of the crystal. He was standing between two members of the petrified circle, the upstanding trunks and branches lambent with an inner radiance. His guide appeared to urge him deeper, yet she withheld herself with hisses and moans. Studying the stone figure at the heart of it, he saw how its surface was deeply etched with sulci, as if hands of knowledge from ages past had scored some forbidding runes over its surface. Compelled by forces he was unable to resist, he stepped closer to the cowled figure.

"Daaannngerrr!" Again he heard the old woman's feral whisper, as if she were reading his mind.

He glimpsed her at the margin of his vision, frantic with worry, scurrying about herself, dragging her finger in the damp earth, drawing at a furious rate, faster than he could register. *Matching the runes!*

A bridling terror caused him to wheel about, to stretch his arm toward her, as if reaching for the crystal; but she cringed back, withheld it from him.

Yet she did not seem convincing in her efforts. She seemed to compel herself to come a yard closer again, to follow his progress, however reluctantly, her lips moving in that deep and sonorous mantra – then suddenly, with her eyes widely staring, she thrust her hand through the fringe of trees, pressing the ruby against his forehead, abandoning it there, her lips writhing against each other, as if both an immense duty and most grievous sacrifice had been completed.

Pain exploded in Duval's head. For a moment, his senses swooned and dimmed.

He was flung back against the trees, his eyes wide and staring, his heart hammering. A great and potent force was assuming form in the pillar before him. In place of the cowled figure he saw a spiritual being, composed of an irrefragable matrix of dark and light.

Compulsion overcame dread, forcing him to stagger forward again until his outstretched hand could caress the deep carved surface of the luminescent figure. He pressed his finger over the runes – like fingerprints on a hand of time. Consciously he could not read them but unconsciously he sensed the force of them and it impressed the charge of their message on the memory of his trembling fingers.

The old woman hung upon his progress from outside the circle, murmuring, incanting, despairing at his ignorance in the presence of the powers that held him in their thrall.

"Duvaaaalll, abide! Harken! The test – *the test!*"

Real words at last – why should he suddenly understand her meaning? But there was no time to wonder as he turned from the inner faces to the spiritual being that seemed to grow ever more threatening and powerful at the absolute dead centre. He sensed a fulcrum of more than the circle, more even than a world. For the obelisk, as he approached it, had several faces, over a body that was a conflagration of glowing runes.

Falteringly, struggling as through a gale of power and dread, he pressed closer to the obelisk. He heard the old woman's hiss of alarm. Standing before the being, he forced his arms through the blizzard of force, so that he embraced its glowing outline. Distantly he registered the shriek of outrage as the old woman, who had been trying to wrestle him back, was herself thrown backward, forced to prostrate herself once more two paces beyond the circle. His brow, with its implanted ruby, was in intimate contact with the anointed head. He could smell the aromatic oils of the chrism.

He could feel the area of contact condense to form a triangle. An inverted triangle, for reasons that seemed at once obscure yet unarguable.

The sensation of fusion was so agonizing that for a moment he blacked out, but the strength of attachment would not allow him to fall. Without understanding why he did so, he kissed the lips, tasting the old woman's earth-encrusted fingers, the burning, cloyingly sweet aromatic oils.

A new shock of union rippled through him, ramifying throughout his nervous system like an electrical discharge, thrilling to the very tips of his fingers and toes. A deep, animal part of him exulted in this oneness with a female entity so powerful he was overwhelmed in its embrace. His vision was swept up in a momentary light of revelation that expanded in all directions to infinity.

A whisper entranced his mind. He was aware that it entered through the burning triangle in his forehead, though he was no longer in contact with the face of the being.

So the De Danaan blasphemy is begun. Yet is such an ordeal warranted? Are you worthy?

"What ordeal? What blasphemy?" The rational core of his mind struggled to question.

Such was and should be the fate of worlds. As the power withers and returns to the Maker, so the cycle returns to the chaos of beginnings.

The words barely penetrated his mind: they were too vague, too fantastic, for his comprehension.

Though understanding still eluded him, Duval felt a shock

of fright: there was no air in his lungs as, with clumsy fingers, he palpated once more the runes under the face of his approach, a stern yet not unkindly face. His mind opened still, as if, however timidly, to question. But the voice of Granny Ddhu was no longer in his ears but in his head – he was hearing her through the ruby triangle on his brow – cautioning him, growling at him, to move around the obelisk, as if explanations could be yet more dangerous, to hesitate equally dangerous.

He was allowed mere moments to confront a second face: a much younger, playful omnipotence, with lips parted in the lubricious smile of sensual love. This being aroused him sexually with the merest wisp of touch, then shimmered away through dimensions of time and space, as if reacting to his presence with a fluttering mocking laughter. A whispered name, like a sigh against his ear.

Seduced by the voice, he could not resist the kiss upon those second lips.

Then, as if in a moment, a throng of nubile succubi had surrounded him and were playing tricks with him. A family of lovesome shadows danced and gyrated about him, brushing against his flesh, sighing and whispering, as if he only had to free his will, to lose himself in pleasure beyond imagining… *She is the One, we are the Others.* These Others seemed younger, in competition with one another for winsome seductiveness. *Come sport with us and you will know paradise.* Sibilant peals of laughter, a myriad enfolding and stroking about his groin, a thrill about his prick so erotic it sprang to agonizing erectness.

"Duuuvaaalll – heeed!"

That old voice was in his mind, crackling, quavering, at the same time her head was bowed to the floor – and her hand was reaching down, slowly, carefully, to throw upon the second face a cooling handful of soil.

"Now, Duuuvaaalll, foolish maaannn – back!"

Only with an immense force of will could he tear his flesh from their blissful embraces, the temptresses that melted from about him and faded into the sighing figure. He stumbled around on muscles of lead to the third face, hidden from the light of the atrium in shadows so dark it seemed that it could not even be illuminated by the ruby's glow. His palpating fingers recoiled in dread. The third face was smoother than glass, colder than the voids of space – this was the ivory of bone, caverns for eyes as dark as the void that prefaced creation. Teeth bared in a dreadful rictus.

Terror threw him back against the ring of trees, his jaws chattering, his limbs weak and trembling.

Then, through a mist of dread, he realized it was the old woman speaking. Her words addressed the third entity, whose lipless mouth he had refused to kiss.

"No, Mo-rí-gán. Stay your white mane over this frail coracle. Else the fall of creation will subsume all. What was asked of him has begun. Though he knows nothing and understands less. What was profaned yet is. What will be has yet to be determined. Grant him the chance to redeem the apostacy of the De Danaan. Soon enough failure or success will condemn or succour him through the great peril that lies before him."

Grant him the chance to redeem the apostacy of the De Danaan.

What did it mean? A riddle.

He felt certain that it was from this dreadful countenance that the shadows crept, to wheel and gyrate, as if in consideration, over the walls of the cave.

Then, abruptly, it was another voice, a more humanly caring voice, that his heart reached out towards, and in his need he had become the lonely child, the son of the loving hobo father, reaching out for the arms of his mother.

Alan is afraid. Alan has been afraid for a very long time. Yet he will assume the powers of True Believer and then he will discover the purpose of my will.

With his heartbeat roaring in his ears, he heard the voice of the second face, more musical than before, yet still laden with erotic seductiveness. *Does he not understand that something which so terrifies him in ignorance will become a much greater terror through understanding?* In this strange existence, when he sensed the suspension of time and space, he sensed a purpose so awesome it was beyond considerations of individual love or suffering.

"Why am I here?"

In answer there was only silence, echoing in what seemed this cavern of knowing.

"Will none of you answer me? What is this True Believer you talk about?"

Again there was only silence, broken by the urgent caution of Granny Ddhu. "Bewaaare – Duvaaalll! Have patience!"

As if wishing to comfort him where forces greater than her own prevailed, the eyes of that voice of suffering were clearer now. He perceived them as if they were crystallizing out of the mists of memory. With a shock he saw that they were all-black, like those of Granny Ddhu, but infinitely kinder, more sympathetic. There could be no doubt that hers was the voice of suffering. Yet still she pitied him enough to deflect the wrath of the others.

He shook his head. It seemed that his life had been saved so that he could fulfill some bizarre and extraordinary purpose. But how was he to fulfil this purpose when he did not understand what was expected of him. When he didn't understand any of this? Pausing to allow the shockwave of contact to recede, his heartbeat to fall from an enfeebling crescendo, he asked again:

He turned to question the spirit behind the eyes of suffering. "Why am I here? I have been brought here against my will, to this – this incredible world. I am told that I have an enemy – that my enemy is evil incarnate. If I am to fight this evil as you seem to demand of me, I must be given a clear understanding of my quest."

Tír is no delusion, to be dismissed as a nightmare after waking. It is as real as your world and as capable of misfortune. Its misery has been to suffer the ravages of a global war for a thousand years.

Tír, he thought: as resentment flared in him, a fierce and burning anger that nobody had bothered to discuss it with him, that his opinion, his will, appeared not to matter.

You are angry. You will need your anger. Use it to survive. Fight death so you may find the strength and purpose to reach Carfon. This is the first step in the most perilous of quests.

"What are you? Why have I been chosen in this way?"

With his teeth gritted bitterly together, he turned his impassioned gaze full into that vision of power.

But the sympathy of the voice of suffering was abruptly terminated. His mind was thrown open to terrible visions. He heard the frenzied growling of Granny Ddhu but he could not avert his vision from these dreadful revelations. He saw a future overwhelmed by horror and malice. He witnessed the end of his own species in the perversion of innocence and pitiless slaughter.

A different voice spoke to him, the voice of the first face, with a force of reason that was enough to make Duval groan aloud.

To avert such a fate did the apostate burden you!

Was this vision what had to be or what only might yet be?

Duval shrank from those horrifying insights only to find the succubi waiting for him in the shadows. In his weakened state, they easily beguiled him. Naked arms of many races beckoned him to a white chamber, carpeted with arum lilies. Emboldened by his despair, they brushed his face with pointed breasts, breathed the perfume of intoxicated abandonment into his nostrils, caressed his prick, evoking pleasures he had never imagined possible. In this dreamlike arbor, he allowed himself to be seduced by them.

He sank from fear into the delight of their embraces, the whispered promises of love, gentle and passionate, carnal and profane. So, with their coquettish sighs, erotic touches, and gossamer kisses, they prepared him for the second face, on her bed of surrender. As he moved to a rapid and irresistible climax, those sybaritic lips drew back on sharp canines, the mouth gaping on a voluptuous grin of triumph. At that ultimate moment, the spell was invaded by the growling roar:

"Beware the love of the daughters of Mab! Daaanggerr, Duvaaall! Peril – peril for all worlds, all futures!"

Recoiling in shock, he saw how they would devour him, as cruel hunters might kill an innocent beast for its musk or the small pleasure of its ivory. Tottering once more within the circle of crystal trees, he saw that the first face was waiting for him, her patient, sentient gaze reasserting primacy. He sensed her light expanding in stature and anger, like a fury.

He heard a screech, then felt a hand pull at his hair, clawing him back from the storm of force, even as it had begun to swirl and turn. Still he retained a glimpse of things to come, of the present and the future as a road more perilous than he could endure.

Like a whiplash in his mind, he heard also the caution of that awful maelstrom of power:

The De Danaan had the greatest wisdom of her age. You have seen what she foresaw, a dreadful future in which darkness will triumph over all creation. In her desperation she searched for hope. Only in innocence did she see the flickering candle of that small hope.

Confusion still. He didn't understand her. His need to understand was a roaring in his head. He sighed, his voice a croak.

"Quests and riddles! I'm not some knight on a white horse – I'm a scientist!"

There is much that you must learn before understanding is possible. A fearful quest awaits you. Yet the De Danaan would not have placed this burden upon such frail shoulders unless she saw in you some quality and strength. Think therefore upon that. Discover that wisdom within yourself, Duval. For the fates of Tír and Earth are intertwined – as well they might be, since they are mirror worlds, born of the same seed. If Tír falls, then Earth will surely follow.

"Tell me then what I am supposed to do. What do you expect of me?"

Let there be no uncertainty of what is expected of you. You must find a way to destroy your enemy. Yet this will be no easy quest. For your enemy is the darkest malignancy that was ever spawned from the foul pits of eternity. On Tír he is known as the Tyrant of the Wastelands. Use the powers that are given to you. Discover through the pain of experience how in you and none other these very powers must bear fruit. And do not fail, Duval of Earth, True Believer. For upon your shoulders rests the fate of worlds.

The madness of such expectations of him caused Duval to groan aloud. A sickening despair was growing in the pit of his stomach.

"Damnation! I need to know more than that." But the old woman was pulling him by his hair, back from the circle of trees with all of her might. Her strength was ferocious and he fought against her, half wishing himself to be drawn back towards that sweet womb of erotic and fatal sacrifice. Still he shouted his anguish back at the first face. "For the sake of my sanity, tell me at least where I go from here?"

"*The first step in your quest is merely to survive. Survive but to enter the gates of Carfon. There you will find the answers you seek. But have a care. In great danger, you will think to call upon me. Yet it may be my sisters who come to your beckoning!*

Already they were moving back in a fearful hurry out of the cave with the petrified circle. He heard the words of Granny Ddhu echoing in his mind, that scornful voice with which she seemed to despise his ignorance:

"No more questions! Have you no sense of abomination! Have pity on creation, foolish maaannn!"

FIVE

THE THREAT IN THE WILDERNESS

H E WAS CROUCHING at the edge of a cleft in the rock, looking down at the harmonica in his hands. It felt wrong somehow. He didn't know why. Behind him, the old woman had lit a fire from what appeared to be chips of stone. For a moment, his concentration faltered – his stomach reminded him that he was starving – smelling that mushroomy, by now almost addictive, smell of the soup she was making. He tried running a few riffs past his lips. It sounded wrong too. It sounded so clumsy he didn't feel like playing it anymore. And that baffled him so that, shaking his head in bewilderment, he put it back into his left hip pocket.

They were resting after two days of relentless hurrying. He recalled her face as she had dragged him from the stone circle; the all-black eyes protruding out of their parchment folds with a desperate urgency.

"Hurry, Duvaaaal!"

Her voice had been quieter, grave with urgency as she helped him to his feet, then pulled him in a furious hurry, leading him through a new labyrinth to escape from the caves.

In that headlong rush, without sleep or rest, she had taken him through the heart of the mountains to emerge some distance lower down the glacial valley. Now, looking about himself into that terrifying panorama, a prickling erupted over his face that would have been sweat in temperatures above zero.

First light had broken only minutes before. The sun was hidden above a low, dark sky heavy with snow. Even without the gale blowing, there was still a wind squalling and the temperature must have been ten degrees below. It would plummet a further twenty degrees at night. Squinting down the slope, he estimated ten miles of snow and ice with hidden crevasses before they reached more level ground. How could she possibly intend to walk down there with nothing on her feet? What slender hope had either of them for survival?

Her eagle eyes met his as she handed him a clay bowl full of steaming gruel.

Cradling its warmth back with him to the mouth of the fissure, he stared once more at the desolate terrain that lay in wait for them.

You could almost kid yourself that you were gazing down a river valley. What looked like a river valley, in between the squalls of snow, even if the river was an unrelenting moraine, the debris of fallout from the mountains. In the distance he could see a fuzz of grey on the lower hillsides. He hoped that this might mean scrub, any kind of vegetational growth at all. He prayed for trees.

He felt surprisingly revived after the gruel. His arms and legs braced to get on with it. Then, with fingers that were numbed, he searched his pockets for his handkerchief. He wrapped it around his mouth and nose so he could take some of the sting from the cold air he was breathing.

Eyes slitted and head down, he forced himself out of the shelter of the cave and into the blustering wind, grimacing with the sting of the cold on his face.

The old woman looked out of place in the snow. The hard, light flakes, spinning and eddying, seemed attracted to her, like iron filings to a magnet. The dusty matrix of her cloak was white within a few minutes. When her jet eyes turned to look back at him, he detected something pensive in them – he could not bring himself to associate dread with that quirky personality – before she turned back again and quickened her pace. He followed the prints of her bare feet, small and curiously wide, with a splay between the great toe and the rest.

After they had travelled two or three miles, he had a better idea of their bearings.

He estimated they were more than half of the way down from the soaring black peaks. Below them, zigzagging through the snow-blanketed valley were alternate moraines of boulders and shale, or mixtures of both, blasted clear of snow by the frequent gales.

At first he kept his eyes on that distant grey but as it seemed to recede with each step he stopped looking into the distance. It was impossible to move more quickly than a steady walk. The exposed ground was iron hard, with sharp outcrops that would have snapped an ankle. At other times he was up to his knees in drifts of snow; or worse still it was ice, slippery enough to take his feet from under him. They made no more than a mile in hours. They rested that first evening in a snow-cave. She didn't speak at all and seemed unwilling to light even a small fire, so he curled up and tried to sleep.

He woke in the middle of the night, too cold to sleep. In the near dark, he tried to figure out if she was awake. He found no sign of her in the cave so he moved to the entrance hole, poked his head out, snow buffeting his face. The mountains were shadowy outlines against the inky dark of night, the snow-covered ground a more pallid shade of grey. She was squatting thirty yards away, that conical shape, strangely dense and compact, like a sculpture in stone.

He wondered if she never slept. He wondered what was really expected of him?

He thought about those strange words of advice that had been given to him in the cave. *You will need your anger. Use it to survive. Fight death so you may find the strength and purpose to reach Carfon.*

"Carfon!" he muttered to himself, blowing onto his hands to warm them. His hand reached up and touched the sore triangle in his brow.

The first step in the most perilous of quests.

He pondered the significance of what had happened in the

cave, the horror of those dreadful revelations of the future. He could not pretend to understand it. For the moment he would have to live with the fact he did not understand it. The following day his mind began to play tricks on him.

He had left the snow-cave and was walking, with no memory of the time in between sleeping the previous night and this moment when he found himself walking. All he could focus on was the rhythm in his feet. They reached the shale by midday.

He had been looking forward to it as a break from the snow-drifts. He had imagined the friction of walking on it, the warming effect on his frozen feet. But appearances were deceptive.

A hard patina of ice had fused with the surface of the stone. Although the shale was glued by that same black ice to the layers underneath, here and there the glue was not strong enough to bear his weight. The stones under his feet were as slippery as ballbearings. No matter how carefully he moved, no matter that he kept his feet widely spaced, the ground would slide from under him. He would lose his balance, fall onto his bottom, or his outstretched hands, or his side, before picking himself up and moving even more tentatively onward.

He had crossed half a mile of its treacherous surface when he lost the grip of his feet. Suddenly he was tumbling, turning over and over, down a broad, deep fissure, pain macerating his entire right side. After several minutes of jarring descent, he came to a halt in the frozen bed below. His hands were too numb to feel for injuries. He had to hope that he hadn't broken any bones. The dark, squat shape of Granny Ddhu peered down at him from a good hundred feet up the slope.

Slowly, ignoring the hurt from his bruised side, he pulled himself back up the fissure on frozen hands and feet.

Injury and exhaustion forced them to stop that day in the mid afternoon.

With that arcane dexterity that defied any logic she constructed a shelter out of that same treacherous shale. He watched her with a mixture of discomfort and fascination. It was as if the very elements that threatened him were aids to her. Resting then, trying to sleep, he hated this malevolent land-scape.

He was sitting at the mouth of a snow-cave, staring bemusedly into the clearing sky, with his numbed hands threaded dis-tractedly through his hair. He had lost track of the number of days they had been walking. The background went through pallid green to olive, and then the constellations appeared. He looked up at those stars coldly glittering in the dark. He continued to stare at the heavens until his eyes were blurry, unable to come to terms with what he was seeing.

The familiar constellations were there, the big and small dippers, Orion, even the tiny diamond cluster known as the Pleiades. But they were a mirror image of what he would have seen from Earth. It was like looking at a sky that was turned back to front.

He recalled that he was now left-handed, the improvement in the vision of his eyes. He took the harmonica out of his pocket and looked at it again. He turned it around so that right was left and left was right. Then, though his hands and lips were numb with cold, he tried to play it. He fumbled his way through the opening riff of Howlin' Wolf's "When I Laid Down I Was Troubled". It felt a little awkward at first, but not overly so and not for long. Soon he was playing with confidence in spite of his numbed lips and fingers. He was playing the great blues number whorling and moving through his lips and fin-gers – as good as he had ever played it in his life.

"Hssst!" she growled, returning to scold him from where she had been squatting in the snow. "Be silent, Duvaaal – even the sky has ears!"

He stopped playing, looking up into that listening sky with its alien stars. There was no doubt about it: the chirality was reversed. The sky of Tír was a mirror image of the sky of Earth.

Suddenly, as if to confirm her warning, he heard the distant howling of a wolf. The sound was utterly terrifying, cutting through the silence. Duval wondered what a wolf would hunt at these high altitudes.

He was puzzled that she was no longer leaving tracks in the snow. How was it possible that where there had once been prints of her bare feet – which he could easily follow – now there was no impression to mark her passing. He peered forward at her leading figure, shaking his head in bewilderment.

Something about Granny Ddhu had changed, was continuing to change.

Though her conical shape was encrusted with snow, she seemed less robust, somehow less substantial. *No footprints!* He wondered how she could leave no footprints.

They continued all that same day without eating or drinking. He kept her in view at all times now, that bent figure, battling the elements several paces ahead of him. He wondered if the journey was killing her.

She ate nothing – she gave him all of the gruel. He couldn't bear the thought that she might die as a result of helping him.

A sudden start in his forehead, a stab of pain and then a spreading sense of burning. It was so intense, he felt sick with it. He could feel the sensation spread over every inch of skin, as if his face had erupted into flame. He could trace the source to the triangle in his brow. A terrific throbbing.

They trudged on into a wilderness in which there was not a single flicker of life, not a plant scratching out a precarious existence in the crevices in the rock, not even the verdigris of lichen. At last the mountains were losing some of their fanglike sharpness. They were flattening out. Black slabs of more worn appearance were shouldering out of the snow and ice. Then that pain again, with a dizzying sense of turning, as if he could sense the very motion of the world beneath his feet.

The pain was so severe it brought him to his knees. *What's happening? What's happening to me?*

The weariness of a stage beyond exhaustion hung upon him, mentally and physically, as they arrived at the first evidence of ice-melt. Duval stared down the ice-bound valley and he thought he saw trees. Distant trees. He was so stupid with exhaustion that he could not point out the trees to the small, dense figure that had stopped beside him, camouflaged under her mantle of snow.

Night fell but he didn't know if he was still walking or he was dreaming. Then once more he heard the howling of the wolf.

The dreadful sound seemed closer. Suddenly, out of the grey shadows, he saw its dark shape snuffling the snow four hundred yards ahead of them. As he watched it, the figure came closer, as if in a single bound. Its heavy head swung this way and that. He could see no clear animal shape, just a matrix of darkness with two pinpoints of red that were its eyes.

Duval's mouth went dry and his legs stopped walking.

The phantasm sprang again. It seemed that in just a few bounds it had come to within a couple of hundred yards of them. Whatever it was, it was not a wolf. It was hardly an animal at all in outline, more a grotesque shadow, yet still it was crouching as if on all fours, its head swivelling. To Duval's nostrils came a horrible sulphurous smell. Fear rose up into his mouth.

"Legun!" he heard Granny Ddhu whisper.

Gazing now at his protector, her hair a ghostly nimbus in the near dark, he wondered just what malign forces she was protecting him against. *Remember then that your enemy is evil incarnate…. Beware the fact he will be expecting you.* It was not necessary for her to explain. The wolflike creature was hunting him!

Suddenly she had taken hold of his hair and she was forcing him down into the snow.

Her strength was immense. He was aware of a change in the air about them. A torpid vapour was spilling toward them across the snow. Black tentacles curled forward over the shadowed ground, as if probing their smell. With widespread arms, she made a protective screen of herself about him. A seething wave of malice struck the protective shield and swept above and around it. Terror squeezed his heart, like a claw.

He was suffocating. He did not dare to breathe. He had to hold his breath and wait with his lungs bursting. He forced a fistful of snow into his mouth, to keep holding his breath, the cold freezing his lips to his teeth.

Though he could no longer see it, he felt the baleful approach of that monstrous head – the pitiless searching of those dreadful eyes.

With his heart pounding and his lungs screaming for air, he felt its rancorous presence hesitate close by them – and then, after a pause that seemed to stretch on and on, it leaped again, passing on by them.

"Do not bemoan the wind and snow, Duvaaal. They confuse its senses so that it cannot easily find us. And it is still hunting."

Her words were understandable now: a low clear voice – but he couldn't afford to dwell on this new revelation.

But with every mile the old woman was further exhausting herself. Still, when he placed his hand on her shoulder to slow her down, her determination was like iron under his fingers.

By morning of the following day they had come to the river, which in its centre melt seemed impassable. They were forced to stop. Then she signalled to him to climb upon her shoulders. Duval refused. He got angry with her, a sudden strengthening swell of anger. He gathered her up about his own shoulders and waded the ice and freezing stream. When he put her down on the far bank, she sighed deeply, squatting on the shingle, sinking into herself, her eyes shrinking to mere slivers of jet in their beds of wrinkles.

The confrontation with the Legun had taken all of her remaining strength. When he wrapped his arms around her, she felt colder than the ice yet adamantine in her composure, her squatting posture like the craggy top of a mountain appearing through sea or soil.

He said, softly, "You won't live another day if you go on like this."

She was too feeble to argue with him, her chest quivering with her struggle for breath.

Slowly, with careful deliberation, he rubbed the tiny icicles out of his eyelids, his movement a slow motion because his fingers were solid at their joints. A sheer cliff face soared to one side and the river to the other, with ice only a foot beneath the new-fallen snow. Yet it was magnificent. If you had to die some-where, then this was as good a place as any.

"Are you mortal then, Granny Ddhu?" He had returned to warm her cold squat form again.

"Duvaaal asks but still he does not see."

He looked closely at her, saw some reluctant emotion flicker for a moment in the slit of eyes.

"I don't know how it looks to you. But to me it looks like the end of my quest before it has even begun."

Irritability rallied her. "Has your quest not already begun? Is it not in your nature to question what you see?"

He forced a little water, made from blowing through snow in the cup of his hands, into her mouth. She was breathing faintly, her eyes closed. Her skin was pale as ash, her face so withered she seemed little more than a ghost: if she were to stand between him and the sun, he wondered if he would see through her. He tested his strength against her weight. "In London I met a strange young woman. She saved my life." He tried lifting her once more onto his shoulders. But he was weakened himself, since crossing the stream. He put her back down, waiting for the race of his heartbeat to settle. "She had green eyes… the same eyes as a girl I once knew."

Then he caught her under her arms, placed his feet apart for balance. "Her name was… both their names… were Kate."

He paused, blowing steam, took a deep breath, threw her onto his back. It must have shaken her old bones to the marrow but he was too numbed to be gentle.

"Although it seems… impossible… she was my Kate. From all those years ago."

But he heard no words – only registered the resistance from

her mind to his. He had begun walking. "The same name.... The same green eyes."

"Foolish maaan. Your prattle tells of the great nothing that is all that you know. Now!" Her voice had become quietly insistent. "Put me down."

"No way... put you down. So you can stop hindering.... and damnwell help me."

Then she seemed to accept it. He felt her redistribute her weight like a bird that was settling on a nest for the night. There was a weird sensation of union, as if she were melting into him. He felt a wimple embrace his head and shoulders. It was as if her bizarre dress were creeping over him. Even as he got into his stride, the living edge expanded, mandibles and spinnarets creating it, so it was growing as a living lace. It grew warmer from his body heat and it itched and squirmed over his head and neck until he was cowled in that same cobwebby material, and although he could breathe through it, he had to use his fingers to poke holes for his eyes.

He felt strangely lighter, as if the fusion of their two beings had the opposite effect on gravity. And already the snow was settling on his new coverings, creating the perfect camouflage.

Walking again, with Granny Ddhu perched upon his back: walking on and on until she seemed to meld entirely with him, being into being. He conversed with her in broken phrases, thinking the words as his exhausted legs carried on the rhythm.

"Who are you... tell me... Granny Ddhu?"

"In my spring," said she, her voice a burbling stream in his mind, "the young men... called me Nimue Guinevere."

Even in this strange symbiosis of fusion, her being seemed to gasp for breath, as if the flesh were dissolving from her bones. "I... I was beautiful then."

He saw her for a moment as she willed him to see her. A diaphanous sprite, with the breasts of puberty, on the back of a king of stags, racing through a wood of spring birch, pussy willow, and alder catkins.

He heard a throaty gurgle, that might have been an attempt

at a laugh. "You asked and… now I answer. I am the only one. Even before the evil one came into the Wastelands. The only one… to remember the Arünn."

There was an important clue here but his mind was numbed. He was no longer conscious of walking through the snow. In his mind he was the fourteen-year-old boy again, sitting with friends around the battered old table at the sawmill, drinking the toast to Slievenamon…

They had all plotted and lied for this. Before Billy Foran's death it had been exciting, a little scary maybe, but still an adventure. Since then a cold outrage had galvanized their planning.

"Right then," cried Penny. "Let's put all we've got into one pool. I hope you have all managed to find some money since last night?"

Dutifully they all emptied their pockets, even Liam. Alan was surprised they had managed to gather more than twenty pounds between them. They gazed at it in awe on the middle of the brown-stained and chipped table surface. More than anything, that small pool of money was the evidence of their resolve to face the terror. In that cluster of Irish coins, and two crumpled five-pound notes, the last excuse had been abandoned.

Liam could not resist clowning, grabbing Alan's harmonica and pretending to play it until Alan snatched it back from his mouth.

Sean added his father's cigarette roller to the pile, though none was a smoker and even Sean only possessed papers and no tobacco to put in the middle. Kate was the only one to have brought sandwiches. Most of the money would go in diesel. What to do with the rest was put to the vote. The first priority was two large bottles of Coke. The rest, after a few minutes deliberation, would buy tobacco for Sean's roller. They had seen how battle-hardened marines would smoke a final cigarette before going into danger.

So here they were at last, all getting ready for the adventure to begin.

Kate, the tomboy, so comfortable in her blue jeans, and Penny, whom Liam would call "Penny from Heaven" or "Penny for It", meaning a smile, because she never smiled at his jokes. At once bossy and mysterious, Penny's bright yellow shirt was only marginally yellower than her strawblonde hair. Mo, with her freckled skin and her haystack of red hair about her blue-eyed face, was the quickest to smile or to frown. And Liam, already telling farty jokes. Liam, moody and changeable – Liam, the only black face in Clonmel, who had pissed into Flaherty's trainers when the bully had left them to go skinny-dipping up where the riverside was called the Green.

Liam had already clambered aboard the truck into the residue of pinechips and the smell of resin. A glimpse of Mo patting his hand as she joined him. The three five-litre plastic drums were already in the back, washed clean of their original liquid soap contents.

It was Alan who had thought of mixing the water from the three rivers to invoke the triple goddess of the Celts. And they had accepted his idea, as they always did, because he was the ideas guy, their leader in this adventure.

Now Alan was helping Kate to climb the dropped tailboard. Then they were in the truck, sitting opposite Liam and Mo, and he caught Liam's wink, mocking at the way Kate squeezed his hand. Penny slammed the door as she climbed into the passenger seat of the cab, sitting next to big Sean, their driver, so proud of his stubble he had left it unshaved for a week.

The sound of the revving engine, the backs of Penny's and Sean's heads, through the cracked window into the cab, the stench of diesel: then the four of them staring at one another in the back, bouncing about on sacks laid over the bare boards as the truck lurched and swayed down the slope of the rutted track and onto the singing tarmac of the main road. Too early as yet for the few Sunday shops to be open, they trundled down Irishtown, where the houses hugged one another in pastel-washed single-storied terraces, until the bulk of the West Gate straddled the road. They cheered as they passed under the gate and down O'Connell Street, the Narrow Street, past the Main Guard and by the Old Bridge.

All the time it loomed over them. Slievenamon. Though the mountain was still twenty miles distant, it was visible now, towering over the graveyard where his grandfather was buried.

A secret lurked in the shape of the mountain. A secret so immense, so terrible…

How Alan's heart surged. It beat so hard in his chest that his breath caught when he tried to inhale deeply.

A final stop, at the filling station on the Carrick Road. Then they had left the town, running along the tree-lined banks of the river Suir, that joined waters with its two sisters, the Nore and Barrow, meeting, like the fabled Celtic trinity, the Trídédana, at the great estuary of Waterford Harbour. It had been one of old Pádraig's stories that had first suggested it to Alan: that there was magic in the meeting of these waters. And his idea had set his imagination aflame. Now the river Suir coursed by them, mile after mile of slow-moving current, a dazzle of whorling eddies and reflections about its deceptive surface. At least once a year still somebody would drown in its waters: a careless child, or even an experienced swimmer, underestimating its flows and currents – like a steady sacrifice to its darkling majesty.

The truck pulled creakingly to a halt about half a mile after a bridge and not far from Carrick. Young willows with their drooping summer leaves overhung the river, dappling the glare of the surface reflections.

Alan helped Mo through a gap in the hawthorn hedge and then he walked with her through a field mined with cattle droppings. He watched her as she slipped down the bank, the bobbing of her carroty hair in the shadows of the trees. He saw how, as she pressed the neck of the container below the surface, Mo turned for a moment and looked fearfully over her shoulder. He saw the expression on her face, the shock of fright in her pale blue eyes, the pupils large.

For a moment, as he leaned down the slope to pull her back, he shared her fear, a shadow crossing the mind, as if a darker mass was moving in the shade of the trees.

Then as they reached the hedge, looking back to the distant bridge, they both saw the figure, silhouetted against the sky.

Mo abandoned him with the bulk of the container as she tore through the hedge, screaming a warning to the others. A creeping horror prickled Alan's skin as he paused to take a second look at what appeared to be a black hood and cloak. The formless malice within the hood seemed to reach out as if to close the distance between them, and the thrill of fright was so strong he almost abandoned the water in his panic to run back to the truck.

In clouds of diesel smoke, Sean accelerated along the Carrick road. Alan reached out and took Kate's hand. It felt cold and damp, the fingers bony, like the legs of a crab.

"Do you think that... that yoke has been following us all summer?" Mo demanded, the Irish expression all mixed up in her London English accent, the freckles prominent on her ashen face.

Nobody answered, or contradicted her.

The watcher had appeared from time to time and followed them like a dank mist that froze the blood in your veins.

They had all encountered it in recent weeks. They had dreamed about it in their nightmares, ever since poor Billy Foran had followed them into the bamboo grove at Saint Patrick's Well. Billy had got lost. They had heard him screaming, over and over. They had followed the sound of his screaming but they had not been able to find him. All the police had discovered was his blood on the grass. They had told the police this story when they came to interview each of them in turn, but the police had just dismissed it. The shadow of the watcher, the screaming, and the blood were linked. All six of them knew this but nobody else would believe them. Now everybody in the town was talking about it and Mo's parents were planning to take her and Liam back to London.

It was as they entered Carrick that Liam, in his Donald Duck voice, was telling them a new joke about what Adam said when Eve asked him if she could look at his and she would let him look at hers.

He was so clever with his jokes and his voices that everybody except Penny laughed.

In some ways, Liam was the toughest of them. Almost as tall as Alan, but stockier, his daring found an ally in Penny. Penny never laughed at one of Liam's jokes but she listened carefully as he told them, as if studying him with an eye to reforming him. Penny was not English at all but Australian. She just happened to be going to the same school as Mo in London.

"Do you think that Pádraig is really a druid?" Mo demanded as the truck started off again, heading north. Her voice was trembling slightly. "I mean, it all began with your dreams. Don't you remember, Alan. Then it was mind-blowing when we found we were all dreaming the same dreams."

Alan remembered all right.

And Pádraig was a druid. Thinking that Pádraig's son was driving the truck, that the mop of dark brown hair visible through the cracked glass was a druid's son, gave him a sense of inner comfort. And maybe that was the link, because druids were somehow linked to dreams. And Mo was right. That shared dream had been so mind-blowing, so skin-tinglingly awesome, it had welded them together, closer than mere friends.

Still it had been Alan himself who had recognised the summons to Slievenamon and the blood ties of the mountain to the three rivers, and they had all accepted the wisdom of that.

Liam interrupted his musings, looking behind him with wildly staring eyes and crying out – "The watcher, the watcher!"

Alan's eyes widened with fright but he could see nothing, only a dark cloud swelling over the western horizon, a cloud of strange shapes, now a mushroom shape erupting into the sunshine, now a hand raised, a hand as hard as a claw, that might have been cloaked with a black cassock.

And then... then... he was playing his harmonica, playing the *Batman* theme, playing it as loud as he could play, causing them all to break down into hysterical laughter.

Walking on and on. It was as if he had been walking for eternity. There was no longer a burden on his shoulders, no weight at all. The pain in his brow had cleared and in its place was a realm of dreams.

Snow gusted about him, in his eyes, in his flared nostrils and his gaping mouth. The sense of snow, the awareness of it, penetrated to every molecule of his being. It no longer troubled him. Anger – *anger* was the force that drove him on. Anger at them all, a raw swell of violent anger at the world, at the crass stupidity of it. His exhausted legs seemed to find a new tiny reserve of strength, another step, another ten, a hundred yards. A series of hundred-yard intervals and it was another mile.

He knew there could be no more resting. If he stopped, he would die on his feet.

He tried to remember who he was, the reasons for things: he could not focus anymore. Hunger – he thought of hunger. But he was beyond hunger.

A pulsation in his brow beat time with his legs. The pulsation was a metronome, its tingling swell coursing through him from the triangular focus in his head. He felt himself pitch headlong into snow – deep snow, like falling into a cloud in a dream. Still he was pulling himself up, sitting first, resting on his arms, then onto his haunches, then climbing his legs to stand. Snow enveloping him. Too much of it. The snow was striking him about his head and shoulders, in heavy solid blows. His eyes were swivelling upward. Green patches where the snow was falling from. Pine needles.

He had reached the trees. He was tottering for support against a sapling and had shaken the snow from its needles.

Onward again. His legs just kept on walking, step after step, the air blowing from his lungs like bellows, his frozen breath making a solid mask of the cobwebby matrix over his cheeks and chin.

It seemed that he had wandered into the sea.

The sea and the snow had become one. As if in the slow motion of a dream, he was entering a sea of snow in which dark shapes were floating. Boats. Wooden boats. They were sailing on this sea of snow, wheeling and spiralling about him. And a man's face was peering into his.

SIX

THE CHILDREN OF
THE SEA

HE COULD SEE people, dressed in thick-furred animal hides sewn with leather thongs. Their weather-browned faces were moving in and out of his spiralling vision. He tried to talk but no sound emerged from his frozen lips and tongue. "People," he insisted mentally, his legs still propelling him forward, in stumbles and staggers.

A man abandoned his repair of fishing nets to walk alongside him, inspecting him as if he were some exotic animal. The man's face was dirty and unkempt and his hair was ragged. His eyes were a dark brown, padded against the extreme weather. He might have come from the Mongolian steppes.

More and more people were arriving to look at him. They were coming out of boats, built out of stout cedar planks, with decks and timbers peeping out from under their burdens of snow.

Duval staggered under the stern of a massive ship: what appeared to be a great galleon, with timbers of black and fissured oak soaring above his head. He was still tottering forward, unable to feel his legs moving. Then a man appeared to be walking backward in front of him, a man who wore a wide-brimmed indigo hat of a stiff felt, like a Pilgrim hat, with an upturned brim. He appeared to have huge strength in his broad shoulders. His chest was as stout as a barrel and his face, with its broad black moustache, as round as the full moon. It was this man who stopped Duval walking. He grasped him solidly by his upper arms and stared at him in amazement. His fingers poked through the icy mask, widening the holes for eyes, then tearing it away from his mouth and nostrils.

The man's lips were moving. Duval caught a single word, "Hul-o-i-ma!"

The cry was taken up by the other people, who clustered around him in the snow.

"Huloima! Huloima!" Men and women were calling out to him – the children too, all dressed in the same thick furs. An entire village of boats was disgorging its human cargo to come and stare at him, their communal breath making clouds in the air.

When he lifted his head it stunned them into silence.

Duval attempted to ask them for help, but the words would not come. Then another man helped the big man, gripping Duval under his arms as he sank to his knees. Their voices muted to piping sounds. The people were still shouting but the removal of his protective cowl seemed to have frozen his eardrums. The men were dragging him through the snow.

Duval thought about Granny Ddhu. Why were they not lifting her from his shoulders? Where was she? How could she have left him?

Two other men were taking hold of his stiffly frozen legs. They were picking him up bodily, carrying him into a central area, where the boats were drawn in a circle about the central focus of the galleon. Another face was blocking out his vision. This man was thin, weasel-faced with eyes that were almost black. There was a calculating cruelty in those eyes now scrutinizing Duval. What remained of the mantle of cobwebs was ripped from his shoulders and trunk. Again he tried to speak but the muscles of his lips and tongue would not move. Then, abruptly, a third man confronted him. This new face was the oldest of all, wrinkled and weathered, with eyes in which senility had so invaded the brown that they appeared like silver discs. His left eye was completely clouded over by blindness and he hobbled on a withered leg on that same side as he knelt by Duval's side to study him, peering first with his head inclined one way and then the other.

At a signal from the old man, they carried him up a gangway, through a leather-hinged door, and into the gloom of one of the boats. Duval could smell fish and burning charcoal. He winced with pain as they deposited him onto some hide-covered planks. His senses swam in the strange aromas of the cabin, and when he opened his eyes again all had departed except for the old man.

"Al-ah mika chak-ko!"

The man spoke in a questioning voice. But Duval heard him only distantly, as if through water.

There were other words spoken with that same passion: words he could not understand, though he heard that key expression again, "Hul-o-i-ma".

That was the last Duval remembered, the old man's wizened and lined face, his slightly quavering voice, his limping movements about the lamplit interior.

It was daybreak, judging from the wintry light diffusing into the room from the opened doorway. A gangling youth was standing by the side of Duval's bier. The youth had fed him something hot to drink. Now he was rearranging a bearskin rug over Duval. They must have removed his greatcoat and over-clothes while he was stuporose. It had been the sudden blast of icy air from the door that had woken him. Now, squirming away onto his aching side, Duval drew the thick rug tighter around his throat. The boy stood there just watching him for a while before pulling the door closed behind him. Sleep fell over Duval like a shadow.

In the middle of the second night he was woken by the light of a lantern. The man with the cruel eyes was clawing his face. There was a stabbing pain, as the man dug his fingernail into his brow, and then Duval came fully awake to the sound of his own shouting.

There was no return to restful sleep after the visit of the thin man.

He drowsed fitfully, aware that strange faces were coming and going, peering at him where he lay. He listened to the alien patterns of their speech, the tones of their voices, friendly or unfriendly. He struggled when the old man with the silver eyes spooned an oily gruel down his throat. It was lukewarm and contained solid fragments of fish.

He came to recognise the old man's approach. He could tell from the clump of his lame left leg on the bare wooden floor. This was the old man's boat. The Shaman!

The gangling youth who had brought the bearskin worked closely with the Shaman. He brought him back his fire-dried shirt and trousers and an additional undercoat made out of fur-lined sealskin. By degrees they improved the comfort of the wooden bier and they kept a brazier burning all through the night. The youth would bring in fresh charcoal at daybreak, throwing open the door to the wintry world, and squatting in front of the stone crucible he would scrape away the white ash onto a wooden shovel. He would light it again with fresh charcoal, blowing it aglow with long gentle puffs, before departing again, leaving Duval to the warmth and illumination of the brazier.

At first, Duval would search the shadows for the conical outline of Granny Ddhu. It was his impression that she was still here, very close to him. But there was no visible substance to his imaginings.

Then, it might have been the third or fourth day, the youth brought him a jug of steaming water and a bowl. Duval stood before the bowl, washing his face and chest, then drying himself with a fleece. The youth produced a small container of an aromatic oil, indicating that Duval should rub it into his bruised limbs.

Duval studied the youth as he made ready to leave him again, the jerky movements of his limbs – yet there was nothing awkward about his intelligence. He put his hand on the young man's shoulder, pointed to himself and spoke – "Duval."

The boy recoiled from him, his eyes wide.

The following day the youth returned with Duval's great-coat and boots. The coat had been washed clean and dried. The tear caused by the dagger had been repaired and even his leather boots had been waxed. Duval nodded his thanks and immediately put on his greatcoat, over the fur-lined undercoat, and he tried out the laced-up boots for comfort. Soon after leaving him, the youth returned with some smoked fish and a hot cob of corn, greener and smaller than Duval was familiar with. Duval's hunger had returned and the simple food was welcome. As he was leaving, the youth grinned tremulously, tapping his chest as he cried out a single word, "Tur-kay-a", before slamming the door behind him.

It was several moments before Duval realized that it must be his name. Turkaya!

After massaging the oil into his aching muscles and eating the food, Duval felt more cheerful, stronger. The old Shaman had been treating him with herbal brews, which seemed to help him recover from exhaustion.

That same day Turkaya returned in the company of the Shaman. They walked him out through the thick-planked doorway onto the deck and down some steps onto the ice-field, in which he saw that the entire fleet was becalmed. The sky was the colour of grey slate and the temperature well below freezing. The wind was so cold he could hardly keep his eyes open more than slits. Frozen snow crunched under his boots, like splintered glass. As they walked him around, he examined this village of sturdy boats, each about thirty feet long, with a single mast for an oblong leather sail. The living quarters were struck from the same adze-carved cedar as the keels, although many were painted with bright, cheerful colours, reds and yellows and greens.

His first impression had been an accurate one. These were fishing people.

Each boat housed a family, and the fleet was becalmed in a frozen lake to one side of a meandering bend of a great river. At the heart of the village was the galleon he had seen on his arrival. A massive ship, triple-masted and built of oak so ancient it was as black as ebony. Duval's eyes were drawn to it in astonishment, where it towered over the simple fishing boats, as incongruous in its majesty as a medieval cathedral towering over the ramshackle streets of its builders.

The following morning, he was woken by the Shaman, who gripped his shoulders and stared at him with impassioned eyes.

The old man's voice was once again tense with emotion, but Duval did not understand anything he said.

"Chahko kloshe!" He opened his hands, indicating Duval's body, as if in admonition that Duval was now well. Then, "Kah mika chahko?" Desperation was flaring in his single good eye. "Hyas Dia-ub!" The expression was accompanied by a mixed look of fear and hatred.

The Shaman pointed to Duval's brow, then made a sign with his fingers over his lips.

Duval did not understand. But later, wondering about the old man's gesture, he felt at his forehead, the triangular depression that still seemed exquisitely sensitive. His fingers moved over a surface as smooth as glass, then jerked away with something like an electrical shock.

Studying his reflection in the bowl of water by the light of the door, there was a smooth triangle in the centre of his forehead, each side about an inch in length and inverted so its point was downward. In colour it was a deep, polished ruby. In its depths he could make out a faint metamorphosing matrix.

Blinking in shock, he went and sat down on his bier.

He carried the bearskin across the floor to the brazier and pulled it around him, sitting cross-legged, palpating the triangle again. There was that same shiver of electrical tingling.

A wave of gooseflesh swept over him. It felt as if the device in his brow had pulsated. As if it were linked in some way to his biological chemistry, to the throb of his life itself.

A device that in some way extended the power of his thoughts?

There is much that you must learn before understanding is possible.... Yet the De Danaan would not have placed this burden upon such frail shoulders unless she saw in you some quality and strength.

He shook his head, incredulously.

If some source of power was linked to his mind, then the capacity to respond lay in his mind. All he had to do was find it.

For many hours he attempted to focus his thoughts onto his brow. He was aware of discomfort there, but nothing more. You couldn't make it work by just ordering it to do so.

What if it worked as some kind of additional sense? Like a sixth sense?

What if he just accepted its presence and let it use him? He attempted relaxation, he did his best to remove every other thought from his mind and waited to see what happened. Nothing happened. Pulling up the bearskin still tighter around him, he moved onto the deck of the boat and there he sat for hours, observing the ordinary activities of the people in their icebound world. He watched them as they trudged from one home to another, or met and chatted in the trampled channels between their boats, some going down and coming back from the river a hundred yards distant.

The river was deep and wide enough to have allowed the fleet to sail here: in full flow it must cut a broad swathe through the landscape. Already, with some early melt, a considerable stream of water was flowing in mid-channel between the ice that extended outwards from either bank.

These people must have arrived here before it froze over.

So this must be their winter resting ground, where they survived by catching fish through the ice or hunted for meat amongst the pine forests.

The great galleon in the centre of the frozen lake was less easily understood. Its timbers seemed too ancient and ornamental for the simple needs of these fisher people. By now Duval knew that the Shaman spent most of his day within the floating cathedral.

His mind wandering in such reflections, Duval was shocked to realize that he was hearing a man's thoughts.

The man, a fisherman, was walking by, oblivious to his attentions; yet, though the structure of the language within the man's head was alien to Duval, he understood the essence of what he was thinking. The fisherman had struggled through a miserable morning and caught only a single fish. There was a word that described the fish, which was "Lekye". Duval played about with this word on his lips and then he realized with delight that he saw its image in his mind: a "winter salmon".

That was the beginning.

Clumsily at first, but with a growing confidence, he found he could enter the minds of any of these people, to learn their names, a little of their hopes and fears. He could hardly wait for dusk when the limping figure of the Shaman would return from the floating cathedral.

Duval waited until the old man was rubbing his reddened hands over the embers before he murmured, through the power in his brow, "Nah sikhs, Kemtuk Lapeep!"

He laughed heartily at the look on the Shaman's face.

Over the succeeding hours, and with a shared excitement, Duval and Kemtuk Lapeep – for this was the old man's name – experimented with language and understanding. Duval discovered that Kemtuk's people were the Tilikum Olhyiu, which meant the Children of the Sea.

Kemtuk was a great deal more than a medicine man to his village. He was the historian and philosopher for his tribe, a people widely scattered about the entire northeastern shoreline. And there was a hint or two, cautiously touched upon, that he also had other knowledge, a deeper and more arcane wisdom, that was passed down from loremaster to pupil. Turkaya was not only the Shaman's apprentice, he was also the son of the tribal chief, whose name was Siam – and Siam was the barrel-shaped man who had confronted Duval on his arrival. When Kemtuk, with a laugh, first spoke Siam's name,

Duval saw the image of a growling bear.

He did not need to learn the Olhyiu language. His understanding, through the triangle, seemed to come naturally from the minds of others.

The old man had many questions and Duval attempted to answer them honestly.

"How is it that you, bearer of the Soul-Eye of the Trídédana, have come amongst us? Why was it that you seemed to carry the burden of the world on your shoulders when you arrived? How is it that you come at the time another Hul-o-ima comes amongst us."

So "Huloima" meant stranger.

Duval was interested to hear of another stranger in the village, a girl from an unknown tribe – the emotion she evoked in the Shaman inferred a ferality or wildness that was a painful reminder for Duval of Kate in London. This girl had been found in an empty camp of the occupying soldiers, who were called the Leloo Kwale, or Storm Wolves. Hunters from the village had found her trapped in a pit, where she had been abandoned to die. Kemtuk's descriptions suggested that she was much younger than Kate yet still the awakening of that memory evoked a bitter pang of regret.

Duval attempted to explain all that had happened to him, his arrival into this world from the despoiled streets of London. How he had been dying in the snow when his life was saved by Granny Ddhu, who had implanted the triangle in his brow.

The old man fell to his knees, muttering incantations. Without daring to look Duval in the face, he sprinkled pollen grains into the embers of the crucible, his face visibly awed in the sudden flare of sparks and flames.

"It is as I had not dared to hope. Even when I saw with my own eyes and could not believe – ! Oh, I offer thanks! I praise the powers of fallen Ossierel for what and who you are. For truly you are our saviour."

Duval had to shake the kneeling figure into listening to him. "I am nobody's saviour."

But Kemtuk persisted in his astonishment. "Even the simplest child would see in the mark upon your brow that you were the one we have so long awaited – the stranger who would come out of the wilderness. The mark of a great Mage. Only the Mage Lord of legends could carry such power."

"Will you stop bowing and listen to me," Duval groaned. "I'm no hero. I'm just an ordinary guy. In my world, I was a scientist. I went to work – or at least I did before the London University made me redundant. I searched for the secrets that lie at the very heart of life."

"Perhaps," the Shaman continued, "if I judge your words correctly, you have not yet learnt how to use your power. But in you is the seed of great and terrible potential. You are surely a Lord amongst Mages, Al-an Du-val. There are many who will envy you such power – they would kill you for it if they had the opportunity. Ah, such portents!"

Duval was bewildered by the thoughts reeling through the Shaman's mind.

"There is a great deal I don't understand, Kemtuk. So much I need to know about myself and how I came to be here. Tell me more about yourself and your people."

"I am nothing," insisted the Shaman. "Oh, Mage Lord, we have such little time. Since the fall of Ossierel, evil has taken a firm hold over all the land. We, the proud Olhyiu, are in thrall as all others to the accursed Storm Wolves of Hyas Di-aub, the Tyrant of the Wastelands. The Children of the Sea are forbidden to fish in the Eastern Ocean, even to gather the simple fruits of its shores. We must fish only in these northern rivers and our entire harvest goes to fatten the troops in Isscan. My people are slowly dying here, on this icy rack. Shamen such as I are forbidden to practice our art. We are forbidden to call upon A-kol-i, the Creator, even to succour the sick or wounded."

"Then you have already broken these laws in helping me?"

"These are wicked laws, contrary to natural goodness. But we pass time in conversation when there are things I must do.

And so little possibility for preparation. I must work indirectly, for I cannot be seen to help you in the trial that lies ahead. There is one amongst us, a cousin to our chief, Siam, called Snakoil Kawkaw – rightly named, Kwapsala, the deceiving crow! He is too cunning to show himself for what he is, a cruel usurper, who robs his own people while pretending to promote safety in his influence with the Storm Wolves. It is he who is already plotting to betray you."

"You spoke of a trial?"

"I must make haste to protect you. To protect you is to protect my people. Oh, I see it clearly. For you are our only hope."

"Hey – I've already told you, Kemtuk, that I am just a man, like yourself – a confused stranger."

"Do not trifle with me. Did you not tell me in the very innocence of your words that you are the One. Such was the blasphemy of the last High Architect, Ussha De Danaan. Yet though all revile her, the knowledgeable few have suspected the greatest wisdom in her laying down her oracular powers and abandoning Ossierel to rape and plunder. Did she not cast the prophecy in her dying breath, an omen so profound as to make the earth tremble! So the true amongst us, those who knew the greatness of the De Danaan, have refused to believe her capable of cowardice. And that faith has kept a single hope alive. A stranger, or so it is said, who would come out of the wilderness to redeem all Monisle from persecution."

Duval remembered the words in the cave of creation. *Only in innocence did she see the flickering candle of that small hope.* Everything seemed to link him back to the memories of his childhood in Ireland. The answer to every riddle seemed to lie there – in that strange adventure of the six children. Those glimpses of memory were the key: the memories of himself as a fourteen-year-old boy. But what did it mean? What had they done?

It was madness – as incomprehensible as ever. He clawed a hand through his hair in frustration.

"No!" he shook his head.

Kemtuk lifted his face to look into Duval's, clutching at his shoulders with desperate hands.

"Rest a while. Gather your thoughts. For time, of which we have long had too much, is suddenly more precious than the blood of life. I am all of a tremble – so my mind will not tell me what to do. First – I must hurry to the Temple Ship and call a grand meeting. It must be done tonight, for that pestilential crow will have found a way of informing our enemies that you are here."

A short while after the Shaman left a great bell pealed over the icebound lake. The door to the chamber was flung open and three men rushed in. They herded him out into the cold, leading him to where the great galleon stood imprisoned in its lake of ice. They prodded him up the steep gangplank, crossed with well-worn laths to give a purchase. Judging from the trampled footprints on the ship's decks, a great many people had entered here before him.

Duval looked around in a mixture of anger and wonder.

The ship was at least sixty feet in breadth with balustraded upper decks fore and aft, and a dense spiderweb of rigging.

They pushed him through a massive arch astern of the quarterdeck, under a great bell tower that soared into the snow-laden sky. The doors were rebated into a complex geometry of carved jambs, adorned above their lintel with a circular carving. A sperm whale leaped out of the ocean over two crossed harpoons: he assumed it must be the symbol of the Olhyiu people.

The more he saw of the great ship, the less he believed that these unsophisticated people could have built it.

Where the other boats were functional vessels, masted for a single sail, this leviathan, towering over the surrounding forest, stirred feelings of wonder and awe in him. Piloted by a great wheel and driven by a complexity of sail that demanded great navigational skill, every square foot of the superstructure was exquisitely carved. Artful birds and butterflies preened and fluttered their wings. Shoals of fish darted through a labyrinth of coral and seaweed. Other panels depicted forests, with a vista of mountains and great trees. Yet in the complexity there was a balance, a natural delight and wholeness, that seduced the imagination.

He knew from reading the minds of his captors that they called it the Temple Ship, their cathedral dedicated to A-kol-i, the Creator, which they pronounced in their guttural stopped syllables, and which was also their word for the sperm whale.

Through the doors, he was bundled down a narrow staircase to enter a great chamber with a low ceiling, warmed by free-standing braziers. The room was so dark it needed the additional illumination of oil lamps, which reflected in the sweat on many faces. In the murky light, he made out a broad space, following the shape of the ship's basic design.

Every member of the village was here, even to the babes in arms. His arrival threw them into an excited tumult.

Most of them were sitting cross-legged on the bare planks of the floor. The crowding was so dense the near company could have reached out and touched him. Amongst the rows of people he noticed that the older men and women were gathered closer to the front, presumably the elders of the tribe. The walls, between gigantic murals, were festooned with carved oars, ornamental maces and clubs. As his eyes grew more accustomed to the gloom, he saw that the murals depicted the history of the people. Whale hunts he recognized, from boats similar to those around the frozen lake. Yet the great mammal was revered as a deity. He could see that in better times their lives had depended on it: for the oil that burned in their lamps, for meat – for the very furniture that supported the braziers was constructed from its bones.

Yet here was no cruel overfishing of these great and gentle creatures, for a single whale would have kept the village alive, through meat and oil, for an entire winter. One of the murals showed a community on its knees, praying by the carcass of a sperm whale in what was obviously a vigil of atonement.

You did not fish for whales in rivers. Whales inhabited the deepest oceans. And now he wondered if Carfon, the city of his quest, might lie on the shores of that ocean.

His captors had waited until the excitement settled. Now he was pushed into the small semicircle below a dais, on which a committee of three men were sitting before a wooden table. Duval recognized their leader as the thick-set man with the broad black moustache and moonshaped face – the man who had gripped his arms when he had first stumbled into the village. This must be Siam, chief of the tribe, and Turkaya's father. The Shaman, Kemtuk Lapeep, was seated to Siam's left.

Behind the table, and running almost the length of the wall, was an enormous lance. The blade and neck, of pitted steel, was four feet long and the heavy weathered shaft, twice that. Attached to the neck with twisted leather thongs were two huge floats, made out of the inflated skins of seals.

Duval assumed it was a whaling harpoon.

He saw the chief in a different light: the stout man, balancing barefoot in the prow of a seagoing canoe, pitching and tossed by the elements, the massive blade hefted in both his hands. The fierce courage it implied!

His guards took up a position behind and to either side of Duval, while, in front of him, and to Siam's right, sat the thin man, Snakoil Kawkaw, who stared at him with open hatred in his scheming black eyes.

Siam brought the proceedings to order. Raising his voice above the shuffling and coughing, he addressed Duval in a clear and heavy voice.

"I am assured that you understand these words I speak to you. Then understand this, Hol-o-ima. It is unique for a stranger such as you to be allowed entry into the Temple Ship. For this honour you may thank the sage of this tribe, Kemtuk Lapeep."

The big man paused, as if studying Duval's reaction.

"For a stranger to arrive amongst us in such times! These are days of the gravest peril. We demand that you give an account of yourself and your arrival amongst the Tilikum Olhyiu."

Then, abruptly, urgently, Kemtuk's voice called out to the people to be silent and allow the stranger to speak.

There was a wide-eyed urgency in his gaze as it fell upon Duval. There was no mistaking his look. This was a court that would decide if he lived or died.

Duval summarized once more the events that had brought him here. He described the attack by the Scalpie, the feral girl who had saved his life, and the disorientating vortex of the crossing into this world.

There was a renewed outbreak of murmuring, with loud cries of derision.

The chief silenced them again, with a slap of his open hand upon the table. "Hul-o-ima, you speak of strange and disquieting things. I am a simple fisherman. Who, I ask myself, would wish to come here to these starveling lands? A stranger, with no purpose? Such an arrival might herald mischief. We have no food to spare. Our children run wild in the woods, scratching for pine nuts to fill the emptiness in their bellies. I demand that you stop this lying and confess the truth. What is the real reason you have come here amongst us?"

Duval controlled his own anger, remembering the words of caution from the Shaman.

"You are right – I am a stranger to your world. I didn't ask for the quest that has brought me here."

"Yet you speak of this quest – and your words imply a purpose to your coming. How then did you survive in the wilderness? What was the nature of those strange coverings you wore when first you arrived amongst us?"

Duval explained the cave and the attentions of the strange old woman, who had both healed his wound and put the triangle on his brow.

Siam appeared to stiffen with apprehension. He fell back into his chair and wiped his face with his hands. It was Kemtuk, quietly spoken, who continued the interrogation.

"What was the nature of this old woman, with coats of

spiderweb, who took it upon herself to save the life of a stranger?"

"When she spoke her name it sounded to me like Granny Ddhu. Yet I –" He could not avoid the hesitation. "I can't pretend to understand the things she did. To me it looked like magic. I can't explain these things to you when I myself don't know what to believe."

From behind him Duval could hear raucous shouts. When he turned to look at them, he saw people shaking their heads, with anger in their faces.

He turned once more to address the three behind the table. "Everything I have told you is the truth. I owe my life to this old woman, though I don't know who or what she represents to you. I suspect that she saved my life not once but twice. First when she treated my injury and for a second time when we encountered a wolflike creature in the mountains – she called that creature a Legun."

The uproar exploded to panic behind him, yet he held his ground. It seemed to be the moment that Snakoil Kawkaw had been waiting for.

Suddenly he was on his feet, a bony finger extended toward Duval's face. "Now we know the extent of this treachery! Not only does he bring danger of reprisal from the Leloo Kwale amongst us, but he profanes the faith of the people."

Snakoil made a sudden movement to rush at Duval, but was restrained by the powerful arm of the chief.

It took all of the authority of Kemtuk to impose calm upon the murmuring and gesticulating crowd.

The Shaman held up his right hand and there was a quiet gravity in his words. "Would it not be reasonable to ask evidence of this visitor for the worrisome events he describes? Perhaps we should ask this man, Al-an Du-val, for such proof to be brought forth before condemning him for his very life?"

"What proof can lies and treachery offer!" scoffed Snakoil.

Kemtuk demanded, "Did he not learn to speak our language in the few days he has spent with us?"

"What spy would not acquire some use of our language when preparing himself to come amongst us? Is it not, on the contrary, evidence of the most perfidious planning. Have a care, Kemtuk Lapeep, that you do not find yourself tainted. For we have seen how readily you profane the old ways in bringing him within these hallowed walls, this hol-o-ima you have been so assiduously attending in your boat!"

A roar invaded the voices behind him as one man broke through the guards and Duval felt a burly arm take hold of him around his neck. Kemtuk, with a look of fury, dashed forward to free him and then he brought them back to order. "Are we so broken on the yoke of the Death Legion that we cannot see the truth? All this time our people have been hungry and humiliated in this desert of snow and ice. Have we not prayed every day for a redeemer?"

"Redeemer!" screamed Snakoil. "He will prove your damnation!"

The Shaman spoke quietly, but firmly.

"Does he not bear the Soul-Eye of the Trídédana upon his brow? Have you not all felt the wind of change during his stay amongst us? Are you so consumed with fear you do not recognize the time of your deliverance?"

But Kemtuk's wisdom was no proof against the anger and terror that was growing amongst the people now milling around Duval.

With a clatter, the great harpoon fell from the wall. Suddenly the bulky Siam sprang to his feet, compelling his advisers to left and right to sit down, with a hand on either shoulder. Then he picked up the harpoon, tore the steel head from its wooden shaft and, grasping the heavy metal as his mace, hammered it upon the resounding table. In the palpitating silence that followed he addressed himself to Duval with a growl.

"You come out of the wilderness, bent over – as if you bore the weight of a world upon your back. Your speech is strange to our ears. Your eyes are blue, like the Geltigi of the Western Mountains. Your bearing is humble but your words belie it. For the last time I demand it of you. Where have you come from? Why are you amongst us? Do you not realize the dangers that oppress the Olhyiu from all sides? Yet if only the words of the Shaman be true! Prove it then! Do as he asks of you. Prove that what you say is the truth or we will be obliged to kill you before the accursed Leloo Kwale descend upon us."

Duval was dumbstruck for several seconds. He was no redeemer. Yet the pleading in Kemtuk's eyes made him hesitate to say so. Duval looked up into the glowering face of Snakoil Kawkaw and the triangle flared in his brow.

"I know nothing about these Storm Wolves, or the suffering they have inflicted on your people. But using this thing – what Kemtuk has called the Soul-Eye – I can see what is hidden in the minds of others. While you have been debating what to do with me, I have been reaching into the mind of this man, Snakoil Kawkaw. What I have observed there is selfishness and greed – and a willingness to cheat and profit from the sufferings of his own people."

"Serpent's-tongued hogsturd!" Snakoil broke free of the grasp of the chief and hurled himself toward Duval.

But he never reached him. A sudden flare of anger from Duval's own mind reached into his own and he stopped short, his hands clawed no more than inches from Duval's eyes.

Duval's voice was deliberately calm as he continued. "If you want proof, search under the floor of his sleeping quarters. You'll find the evidence of his treachery."

All of a sudden the tumult behind Duval fell to a breathless hush. The chief glowered at Duval in shock, while Snakoil's face was livid, a scream of outrage on his lips. But Siam silenced him with a great blow of the lance-head upon the table. Two men took Snakoil's arms and held him where he stood.

Siam's voice was a guttural whisper: "The stranger has been allowed his rope. Let us see if it hangs him."

"It sickens me to put into words what I find in this man's mind," Duval continued. "I see a party of women taken prisoner by men in armour. I see an elegant woman and a girl I presume to be her daughter, with a golden clasp in her hair. They appear with other hostages taken from you by soldiers of this army of occupation."

"Have a care, hol-o-ima! For Kehloke, as you describe her, is my wife and Loloba my daughter," the headman growled, with his features dark and dangerous. "You provoke me. Yet I must hear what you know of this?"

"All these hostages were put to death within a day of their taking. In the mind of this man I see him gloating over their suffering, as if it were not enough for him that they were killed."

Duval described the courage of Kehloke to Siam, her regal bearing facing the certainty of her death. Kehloke's only concern had been for her daughter, Loloba. He spoke, of how the Storm Wolves had indulged in a ritual of execution. The soldiers had torn the clasp from Loloba's hair. He recited, into the gathered silence, Kehloke's prayer to the great whale and its journey of joyous rebirth as, in a final act of courageous defiance, she had comforted her terrified daughter.

Siam interrupted Duval's recitation of the prayer and intoned the remainder himself, with his elbows propped upon the table surface and his face in his hands. Then, abruptly, Turkaya was by his side, the headman's son throwing his arms about his father.

Duval did not go into details of the terrible scenes that followed, pitiless torments of disembowelling and beheading, which he saw in the memory of the evil man, who squirmed and spat hate at him. After a pause to shake off the disgust he felt from such visions, Duval addressed himself once more to Siam, his eyes compassionate yet never faltering.

"The hostages are all dead. Their deaths were the price demanded by this man for his treachery. Some were abused by Snakoil himself before being put to death by his allies. Their deaths were offered as a sacrifice to the Tyrant of the Wastelands, the one you call Hyas Di-aub."

"Stop! Do not say more. I know that Snakoil once coveted

Kehloke and he was jealous that she chose me. But if I find that you have lied to me about such things!"

"Among the things he has stolen from your people you will find Kehloke's necklace, together with the gold clasp from your daughter's hair."

It took no more than minutes for a party of men to search Snakoil's boat and return, their hands laden with the evidence of the cruel man's treachery.

Siam called out for men to take hold of the traitor. "In Ghork-Mega," he intoned, his eyes black with grief, "the Death Legion render their female slaves barren by cruel surgery, such is their hatred of women."

The chief growled to the restraining men, "Lay him in the circle so all can see." They tore away his clothes and splayed the man's limbs and the headman jabbed the blade of his great harpoon into the red-hot embers of one of the crucibles.

"No!" Snakoil snarled in terror, screwing his head with gritted teeth from face to face.

"You murdered my wife and daughter. Now I shall first make you into a woman before I cut your heart out."

Kemtuk spoke to the traitor as the perspiring chief stripped to the waist, then took the red-glowing blade from the crucible. "At least confess your crimes and give us the information that might yet save some lives."

"Fools!" he shrieked. "How I relished my fun with your women – I relive it now, in every exquisite moment. It is my turn to be tormented today – but it will be your turn tomorrow. And the Storm Wolves are your masters in inflicting pain."

Siam struck the man in the mouth with the head of the lance, silencing his mocking tongue. Then in the fury and despair of his grief and loss, he lifted the blade as if to plunge it into Snakoil's heart.

"Wait!" Duval raised his hand to restrain the chief, then squatted by the shivering Snakoil.

"How much time do we have?" he pressed him.

Snakoil bared his bloody mouth, but held his silence, his eyes still glaring a hateful defiance. Then Turkaya was on the floor to the other side of him, a sharp knife directed into the spy's face. "Speak up, traitor. Or I'll cut out your eyes!"

"I cannot be certain," he slobbered. I… I sent a message. But I did not call for urgency. You have days, perhaps a week."

"He's lying." Duval gazed away from Snakoil, towards the chief. "We have no more than a day."

The Shaman put his hand on the chief's sweat-drenched shoulder and advised him to keep Snakoil alive. He might still prove a source of information in the difficult hours to come.

At nightfall, with Kemtuk in ceremonial robes by his side, Siam prayed for his dead wife, Kehloke, and for his daughter, Loloba, and the other women and children who had been taken as hostages from the village. Siam recalled Loloba's birth, and the wisdom of his dead wife, whose guardian was the swan. He extolled her virtues, contrasting them with his own clumsiness and stupidity. Then Kemtuk Lapeep, with his eyes to the heavens, guided their tormented souls to the refuge and sanctuary they should find there.

Duval followed the Shaman's gaze up at the once familiar constellation of Orion, its image reversed in the moonless sky.

Kemtuk put a comforting hand upon the shoulder of the chief, stiff with grief.

"It was not for wisdom but for your courage that Kehloke chose you. Now your people have need of that strength. Take us away from this place of hunger. Make haste, brave Siam. Though our path may be one of great danger, yet it is not our lives that matter. There is one amongst us whose safety greatly outweighs our own. He will assist our escape to Carfon. This chosen one, the Mage Lord Al-an Du-val, from another world."

SEVEN

FLIGHT

Thunderheads were massing in the sky, invading from the north. Even as his skin prickled with the charge of wind scouring and gambolling over the people gathering around him, Duval could smell burning. The air whistled and tossed as if the elements were one with the passion of the Shaman.

"Kemtuk!" he called out hoarsely.

But the Shaman's eyes were distant. His face had become a mask of concentration. Duval felt a flickering alarm clutch at his bowels.

Morning light had been just breaking when Duval had awoken several hours earlier on Kemtuk's boat. He had thrown open the door onto a scene of frenzied activity. Bands of men were hurrying back from the pinewoods, dragging bundles of brushwood on blankets fashioned out of sail leather. Others were heaping great piles of brushwood upon the ice. He watched them drenching the piles with lamp oil. Looking for the limping figure of Kemtuk Lapeep, he could see no sign of him. The Shaman must be within the Temple Ship.

Suddenly Duval sensed a great feeling of sadness. It was such an unbearable anguish he reeled in confusion for several moments before he could lift his head again and focus upon an individual's thoughts here and there. In the spirit of the people there was fear at the prospect of a mass evacuation. The oil-soaked brushwood was being laid out in a broad path linking the boats to the river and beyond its banks out along the frozen stream into the central melt, where the first thaw rushed its waters southward.

It was a desperate measure, intended to soften the ice enough to create a passage.

Stroking his beard, which was several weeks old, Duval returned to the cabin and dressed hurriedly. Then he descended from the boat to find the Shaman on the quarterdeck of the Temple Ship, standing erect before the rail. He was dressed in a formal regalia Duval had not seen before. On his brow he wore the skull of an eagle and over his shoulders a heavy necklace of whale's teeth. In his right hand he held the pointed lance of a narwhal and under his left hand he cradled a human skull. His eyes were glazed, his attention focused inward so that he was oblivious of Duval's presence. He intoned a prayer, deep and powerfully worded.

As his nostrils caught the first pungent aroma of the burning brush and oil, Duval lifted his eyes above the Shaman into the gathering thunderheads. Suddenly the force of sadness struck him again. Such despair that it felt like a physical blow.

He shouted for the Shaman again – "Kemtuk!"

But the Shaman did not respond. There was a fierce glow in his one good eye as he extolled the visions that had been forbidden for all the long years his people had been held in captivity.

Now, even as he heard Kemtuk's spoken words, Duval was forced to probe Kemtuk's mind to discover the thoughts that lay behind the words. Immediately the hairs upon Duval's neck stood up in awe.

In the Shaman's mind Duval found himself gazing out on a vision of creation, at a time when there was but one existence, and his name was A-kol-i, the Creator.

"In that time he was in the form of the great spirit. In one day he created the world, lifting up the lofty peaks of the mountains and cloaking their shoulders with snow. Then he forced apart the mountains and into the deeps between he blew the moisture of his breath and created the oceans. Henceforth, these would become his spirit home."

It was more than a communication of voice, more than the incantation of a story drawn from myth or memory: Duval felt the cataclysms as the mountains reared up out of the land. He shook with the earthquake as their vastness was cleaved apart and, through the turbulent upheaval, a titanic gust of wind and rain surged and swelled through the birth of continents to become the storm-tossed oceans. Through the Shaman's words and vision, Duval tasted the bitter-damp mulch of the new-born earth upon his tongue, his nostrils shrank from the sulphurous breath of the first lifeless atmosphere, he stood on the brink of spuming calderas, a moment later disintegrating in the catastrophic eruptions of boiling lava that would fashion and refashion the primal landscape in the dawn of time.

"Then the leviathan, A-kol-i, he that would henceforth be known as the Creator, took form in the eternal chaos of the deeps. From there he rose against the howling of beginnings, for then he came as the moon and as the fury of the storm. With wind and cloud he filled the skies and the world below, and then he wept dew so that the rain of his passion might make fertile the land and his joy would become the rainbow. Finally, A-kol-i sang and it was with the music that makes the tides and the wind that rolls the clouds upon the air. He called together the mountains and the sky above, the stars and the planets that live within the sky, and he told the heavens: Let there be night and day. He made the golden sun and bid it wander over the sky. He made the silver moon and had it swell as a woman with child each month. So sun and moon would rule the mysteries of creation as they made their journeys from the sea to the sky and back again."

Duval studied the Shaman. The right eye that was still unfocused, the maelstrom of emotional energy that whirled about him, flapping his clothes and lifting his white hair in a startling nimbus.

"Then, guarded by the thunder of the heavens and the icy

roar of the north winds, he bade the storms to clear over the land and there, upon the first great shore, he ordered a new place of gentle beginnings.

"Here, hidden from the weather spirits by a veil of mists, he brought to being the fruits of the sea and shore. Then, in a mighty leap on high, A-kol-i gazed down upon the deep, and everywhere his gaze fell life was born, from the leaping dolphin to the silver flash of the herring and the joyous leap of the spring salmon."

Duval's eyes moved from the Shaman to the men with the brushwood.

"A-kol-i, the Leviathan, leaped over the oceans he had made with the flash of the rainbow. Then, tired from his labours, he pulled about him the blanket of the icy peaks and closing his eyes, he rested there."

People were having difficulty keeping to their feet in the fury of the wind. Still they continued to lay the path of fire directly to the ancient timbers of the Temple Ship itself. They were piling the brushwood against the massive outcurved hull. They would melt the ice to free the other boats by burning the very repository of their spiritual inheritance. They intended to burn the great ship down.

"Kemtuk – stop!"

The activity around the floating cathedral to A-kol-i was the source of sadness, as if in their intended immolation the Olhyiu had had to come to terms with an irredeemable despair of sacrilege.

"Kemtuk – you must stop the incantation!"

But Kemtuk's prayer had begun again, his face like ravaged stone and his voice deeper, more urgent still, the words boiling up out of his tormented spirit.

"When A-kol-i, our creator, first ventured from the deep, he came as the storm and lightning. He brought forth his fury and let it boil over into the world below. The Leviathan was troubled because he saw that he was lonely. So, after many eons of sadness, he awoke again, as the mountains broke apart once more and they gushed forth molten rock and fire."

Only now did Duval notice the standing crucible behind the old man, a small stone altar of whorled carvings, as ancient as the Temple Ship itself, an altar upon which he had heated a crystalline drug, the vapours of which were pungently aromatic.

Duval felt the awe of new visions, of the first rainstorms that brought alive the green shoots of life on the land, extending that spring of life into the sea about the wakening shores.

The thunderheads were erupting with lightning. He could smell ozone in the charged air. How was it possible that the Shaman could draw such forces? In a sudden violent swell, Duval was blown backward, staggered, almost lost his footing. Whirling about himself on the trampled snow, he realized that there was a great force at work here. But just as he attempted to discover it with his own oracular ability, it was extinguished… as if it had detected his probing and snuffed itself out.

As Duval clambered back onto his feet, Kemtuk had roused himself from the spell that had gripped him. His eyes were gentle once more and he was addressing the people directly.

Soon there was an irregular drumming.

It came from long iron-tipped poles, whaling harpoons, that were in the hands of the men and women on the boats. They were hammering the ice around the boats with the tips of the harpoons.

The drumming of harpoons on the ice mounted to a steady rhythm. Duval pushed his way through the gathering throng to reach Kemtuk, who had raised the lance of the narwhal in anticipation of the man who stood before the bonfires about the great ship.

"Stop!"

Still Kemtuk could not hear him above the general pande-monium. The Shaman's face was set like rock and his mind was closed on the words of command. Duval had no option but to force his way up onto the quarterdeck and to confront Kemtuk before the gathering of the people.

"You must not burn the Temple Ship." Then, descending again among their resentful faces, he ran to the men with the firebrands. He snatched the flaming bundles from their hands and threw them away into the snow.

"What is it, Mage Lord?" they cried out to him. "We need the heat of the burning ship to break the grip of the ice."

"No!"

Duval whirled among them, his dismay showing on his face.

"It's wrong. You mustn't burn it. Move the brushwood from around it and use it elsewhere. Add it to the piles you have already gathered over there!" He pointed to an area thirty or forty yards away, yet still somewhere close to the centre of the ice-trapped village.

Kemtuk, looking angry, had descended from the deck and was now standing before Duval with a glare of challenge in his silvery eyes.

"In the night, the traitor Snakoil slipped his bonds, taking the lives of the two good men who guarded him. Though it grieves us, we must sacrifice the Temple Ship. The enemy is near. They will spare no one. We must flee, however dear the cost."

Duval was shocked to hear of Snakoil's escape. But this was not the time to dwell on it. "We can't burn the ship, Kemtuk! It feels wrong – a price we cannot afford to pay."

"What is it, Mage Lord? What vision do you see that so alarms you?"

"I can't explain how I know it, other than to tell you that I feel it here – here in my mind, through this mark you call the Soul-Eye. You must help me – tell the people to do as I say."

Duval felt dizzy with the burden of prescience. There was a sense of inevitability so dreadful it could not be violated.

Then, as if labouring under a dreadful burden, he staggered up onto the deck to join Kemtuk.

"You told me, earlier – another stranger. Another hol-o-ima. You mentioned a girl. Ask Siam to find her. Ask him to bring her here to me. And tell him to hurry! There is no time for explanations."

Duval's ears were full of the crackle of flames, his nostrils choked by the tarry smell of the burning brushwood.

Distant figures were attacking the ice where it had already been softened by heating, using mallets to drive staves of cedar into it at intervals in order to crack it open. But a glance confirmed what he had already suspected: in spite of their efforts the thickness and extent of ice would prove too much for them. Even the burning of the great ship would have taken a day or more to create enough heat to enable the flotilla to break through to the river. And with the renegade Snakoil somewhere close on the approaches, ready to direct his murderous allies, there was no time for the villagers to make their escape.

The morning had turned dark under the towering thunderheads.

Duval listened to the crackling of the melting ice, to the oaths and grunts of the men carried on the wind, to the steady hammering of the women with their iron tipped harpoons. He gazed down at the frightened masses of elderly and children about the bottom of the gangway, and nearby the men who had not yet taken to their own boats.

On their faces, he saw a growing panic as they also realized the impossibility of escape.

And then he sensed her coming even before he saw her. A group of villagers accompanied the chief to the gangway. They were looking up at him in anticipation. He sensed the dread in their minds.

Pressed to the fore, with the hand of the burly Siam resting on her shoulder, was a girl with hollowed cheeks and with black hair unbrushed and awry. It was clear from her face that she had been weeping. When Duval first set eyes on her, there was a curious sensation, like a flash of light that blurred his vision. He blinked his eyes clear before looking more closely at her. She looked no more than ten or eleven years old, of a slim build, more oval-faced than the Olhyiu.

The crowd had swelled as the exhausted men returned from their brush burning. There were more than fifty people clustered about the gangway, wide-eyed and murmuring, all eyes on Duval. The girl had halted halfway up the gangway, where she had been propelled by Siam. She was looking up at Duval with an unblinking stare. His voice was gentle as he addressed her through the triangle.

"Who are you?"

"I am Mira."

She pronounced her name with equal emphasis on each of the two syllables: Mee-rah. Duval was surprised by the clear, intelligent speech of the child, curiously accented and pipingly high-pitched, like birdsong.

Walking down the gangway to where she stood, he squatted down so his face was on a level with hers. She intrigued him. Her build looked less and less like that of the Olhyiu people. Her limbs were long and delicate, with bones that seemed too prominent for health. From close up, her head too was drawn back – like that of an Egyptian pharaoh – with a face as delicate as a bird's, and deep brown eyes, almost black. He could see the throbbing of the fine arteries in her temples.

"What frightens you, Mira?"

"I have lost my mother and father."

She spoke the tragic news hesitantly, her face contorted by distress, but then, as if in an effort at self-control, her eyes cleared and she asked him, "Are you the True Believer?"

Duval jerked back, startled by her address.

Not even Kemtuk had called him that – nobody had called him that, except the voice in the cave.

"I am just a man. My name is Alan Duval."

"Al-an!" That same difficulty they all seemed to experience on first hearing his name.

And now, as he indicated to her that she should ascend the rest of the gangway with him, she held back and her pupils grew blacker and larger.

Then, feeling that resistance still, he went back down on one knee to bring his face to her level once more. "What happened to your parents, Mira?"

"They were k-killed by the soldiers."

"I'm sorry," he consoled her. "How old are you?"

"I am eleven years old."

She gazed at him, that curious assessing gaze again, her eyes more lustrous than any he had ever seen. She seemed to search for some recognition in his eyes.

Duval felt overwhelmed with that sense of great sadness again, so overcome he had to close his eyes while her term for him, the True Believer, reverberated inside his head. He would have pressed the girl for more explanation but she had begun to cry. Still on one knee before her, he brushed the tears from her cheeks with his fingers. How could these soldiers torment such innocents? What was gained by it? There was so much he did not understand about this world.

And yet, during those few moments of overwhelming sadness, an idea had crept into his head, an impossible, crazy notion.

While he was leading her back to the quarterdeck, there was a nearby crackling of fire. Siam had ignited the pyre not twenty yards away, at the centre of the ice. Duval could see the burly man, swaying slightly as if he were drunk, but showing the way to the others, applying a firebrand to a second place in the crackling pile of tinder. The chief tottered back as the flames sprang as high as the mastheads on the lesser boats.

Still that feeling of constriction about Duval's chest. An impossible idea.... And the dark-eyed girl appeared to know more than she should.

He asked her, "Do you believe the soldiers are looking for me?"

"Perhaps."

How intelligent she seemed. There was a precocity in her demeanour and expression. He gazed down into her eyes again.

"I am no redeemer, Mira. I am just an ordinary man, though I come from a different world."

"They w-will not believe you."

"Do you believe me?"

Again those eyes in looking up at him carried that strange appeal, yet a look that seemed to contradict the certainty in her reply.

"I believe you are the True Believer."

An idea took possession of his mind. He called out to Siam over the heads of the crowd below. Tell your people to prepare the boats. Do it now, Siam. Ask them to make ready to raise their sails to the wind. But you must come on board the Temple Ship with sufficient sailors to man it. And you too, Kemtuk!" he addressed the silent but watchful Shaman beside him. "Stay here. Here by me. Have somebody take care of your boat. I need you both on the deck with me."

Kemtuk gazed at him for several moments appraisingly, but he could volunteer no further information.

Siam, who was tottering a little still, had approached the lower gangway and he was shaking his head.

"How can I make the people listen when we give them no reason for hope?"

But Duval was already remote, no longer communicating.

Kemtuk made a signal to Siam, who began shouting out to the men, calling them about him, wiping his brow with his wide-brimmed hat before struggling to find the words to address them.

"I am not a clever man, and you all know that. But I loved my wife, Kehloke, and I loved my daughter, Loloba." He wept openly, took a deep breath. "It is true that I got drunk with those accursed abominations, the Storm Wolves, many times, when they came to our village. I would get drunk with them now, even after they have murdered my wife and my daughter, if I thought that it would save you, my people. So these are the words of a very stupid man. Maybe I am too stupid to lead the Tilikum Olhyiu."

He crumpled his hat between his hands while a new squall of snow blustered about his bare head.

"But I remember with pride when we, the Children of the Sea, were hunters. We did not fear the deep. No more do we fear these abominations of men who would rob us of our pride. Perhaps they underestimate us when they think we have forgotten the ways of battle. Now, as death threatens us, it is time we blew alive the embers of those who once were warriors."

Siam walked out to where the brushwood was burning. He picked up some glowing embers in his copper-skinned hands and – oblivious to the scorching of his flesh – he walked among his people, with his cupped hands held out before him.

"Blow upon these embers and bring our hearts alive. Punish with fire this oaf whose stupidity knows no bounds."

When none would rekindle the embers, Siam wiped the ash over his weeping face. "I am a stupid man who looks at death and still asks for a sign. But the gods have sent us a sign. Great A-kol-i! You have sent us this Mage Lord, Alan Duval. The Shaman, Kemtuk Lapeep, tells us his life is important.

"Yes, he is the one who will lead us. He will help us to escape to the sanctuary of Carfon by the Eastern Ocean.

"Now, though the fates may fail us, go every man and woman to your icebound ships. Go now, my friends and kinsfolk, and prepare your sails to catch the coming gale. We have no swords but we have harpoons and the skill to use them. If we die, we die as warriors."

There was a renewed outbreak of shouting, then the sight of many people running here and there, against the crackling of the flames.

Kemtuk had descended onto the ice to grip the shoulders of the impassioned chief and escort him back on board the Temple Ship. But once aboard, the Shaman himself stayed at the head of the oak gangway, gazing not at Duval but outwards, to the periphery of the flat ice of the lake, his head tilted as if listening.

Duval, a protective arm about the silent child, also narrowed his eyes in that direction.

The lake was much wider than the Olhyiu settlement. It extended for at least three miles to where it ended at a scrabble of snow-covered pine trees. Then Duval heard a sound in the far distance, a metallic tinkling, like the chiming of bells.

He turned to Siam, who waited with his head bowed. "What is that?"

Leloo!" was all that the pensive chief would reply.

Duval frowned, his attention drawn to a family who were struggling with a small heap of belongings, carrying them bodily up the rickety ladders into their boat. Then he guessed. The sound suggested dogsleds. Yet the sound did not carry the image of dogs in the chief's mind, only fear and hatred.

Kemtuk stood apart from him before the rail, next to Siam. He wiped away the ashes that still clung to the burnt hands of the chief. Then, taking a handful of pollen from a pouch before his heart, he sprinkled it in a sweeping arc over the boats of his people, blessing them as he did so. That completed, the old man stood gravely, his sparse frame silhouetted against the smoke and flames.

Siam also stood brave and silent, as did every Olhyiu elder, man and woman, on all of the boats.

Duval sensed their waiting upon him for a sign. He glanced away a moment, caught a glimpse of movement now, a gathering flurry of snow between the trees at the edges of the ice.

Suddenly the nature of the Leloo was all too apparent. A deep-throated howling rent the air. Wolves! The sleds of the Storm Wolves were pulled by real wolves.

Now the howling carried for miles as the harnesses pulling the teams sent a twinkling light across the ice. While a group stood back and waited at the edge of the ice, at least thirty sleds had invaded the frozen lake. And to be able to see them, to make out the vague outlines of the beasts that pulled them from such a distance, suggested great size. Already they were moving much faster than Duval could have anticipated.

He heard the lick of metal on snow, even the laboured

panting of the beasts that pulled them as they consumed the ground between them and the ice-locked boats.

Mira was terrified. Her hand gripped Duval's own and her weeping eyes swivelled from the approaching danger to look up into his.

Suddenly, the thunderheads above them spurted lightning. Duval had to take hold of the rail with his free hand to remain standing under the brooding immensity of the forces that were gathering there. How had Kemtuk harnessed the power to attract such forces? The sky itself seemed to whisper to him, in a voice that filled his mind with violent notions.

Is that your voice, Granny Ddhu? Are you still here with me?

But he did not think so: the violence of the communication was not hers.

The Leloo were easily visible now, no more than a mile distant. Duval soon caught his first clear sight of the Storm Wolves themselves, powerful shapes of men under their surcoats of bearskin, with black helmets that devoured the morning light. As they came closer the air carried their curses and the cracks of their whips, the snarling beasts driven to a frenzied galloping under the lashes of the drivers, with perhaps ten or so of the soldiers astride every sled. Into his mind came Kemtuk's vision of the approaching beasts: with bright yellow eyes, rippling shoulders, and big splayed feet, fur-padded against the cold and through which curved talons scored the ice under its covering of snow. They hardly resembled wolves at all but looked much larger and more ferocious: like snow tigers.

The brute menace of them took Duval's breath away.

Siam had taken hold of his shoulder and was shaking it violently. "Help us, Lord! Help us, now! Or all is lost before ever we begin our journey!"

Yet he waited until they were no more than two thirds of a mile distant from the boats before he growled the instruction to Siam.

"Tell your people to raise their sails!"

Siam blew a single loud tone on a horn at his waist. Over the little cluster of boats, the waxed leathers climbed the masts.

He heard the final blessing of Kemtuk: "Grant us your protection in this peril, as you protected our fathers before us through many perils. Whether into death or salvation, yet your will be done, O great A-kol-i."

Duval turned his face up towards the spuming furnace of sky. Mira still clung to his right hand.

Tentatively, behaving from instinct so he hardly understood what he was doing, he raised his left arm, his hand splayed, a funnel made of his straining fingers and thumb, directed into the fury of those whirling masses. He remembered the parting words of the first face in the cave. It felt as if an instinct buried deep within him had taken charge of his actions.

Help me now, whatever forces you really are! Give me the power to save these innocent people from slaughter.

Fashioning the command within his mind, entering the wheeling thunderheads just as he had entered the minds of people, reading the forces there as he had earlier read human thoughts, he opened the power of the triangle to the gathering storm.

Flickering tongues of lightning were tumbling from cloud to cloud.

Duval could hear and see, smell and sense it all, though his mind remained detached from it. The fury on the faces of the Storm Wolves, the bloodlust in the slavering jaws of their beasts, the flash of steel over snow, the levelling of weapons on board the sleds. He heard the sharp detonation of their weapons, audible, even from half a mile's distance. A terrible explosion of green fire ravaged the sail and superstructure of one of the boats. He heard the screams of the dying on the deck, as they were consumed by the living furnace.

All of his life he had been a quiet man, a man who avoided trouble. But now a great anger rose in him. Through the triangle, Duval entered the immensity of the elements. He recoiled in shock at the power for destruction that had been placed at his command.

With renewed concentration, he forced his being into the communication.

His understanding followed a single flickering river of lightning, that played over the black underbelly of the tempest, and as his mind found the mark, one river of lightning joined another, until they coalesced to become a single great cataract of force, and the cataract itself began to twist and turn about the point of his focus.

A second boat barely escaped the discharge of foul green fire. Still the Olhyiu women maintained a furious hammering over the snow along the radial lines from the fire where Siam had ignited the first bonfires. The men on deck levelled their harpoons at the approaching threat.

Duval held his position as the wrack of tempest wheeled and moiled over the dreadful scene.

"Now!" Duval hissed the command through gritted teeth, his focus never faltering upon that centre of seething energy in the sky. His eyes followed the leading cluster of sleds, with their slavering beasts and the weapons of the troops now directed at the Temple Ship itself.

His left arm tensed against the sky and his fingers closed to a white-knuckled fist. Abruptly, he brought it down and with a splay of his fingers he directed all of his fury at the approaching enemy.

The bolt of lightning struck the ice with a great explosion. Where the army of sleds had been speeding toward them, a fountain now erupted, spuming a gigantic mushroom of bloodied ice and fragmented bodies against the slate of sky. From the boats a roar of triumph arose as the entire surface of the frozen lake shattered into a *craquelure* of fragments, the boats tossing and bucking, but nonetheless freed. The entire fleet was breaking clear of the ice, the tempest billowing sails as their ears were filled by the roars of animals and the shouts of drowning men against the gale.

Siam was organizing his sailors aboard the Temple Ship, as

the three great masts were bending before the wind.

And there, for a split moment, Duval's eyes met the good eye of Kemtuk. He understood the emotion he encountered there.

The Shaman had seen the power of destruction invade Duval's eyes. And now he feared him.

Yet there were more pressing concerns for the moment. Not every Storm Wolf had been destroyed. Some had stayed at the edge of the lake. They would regroup. And they would follow the fleet, lusting for vengeance.

EIGHT

THE SNOW-MELT RIVER

IN THE MELT current, with sails billowed by the following winds, they left the icebound lake behind them. The sky was black with storm clouds and the reflected snow illuminated the waves that spread from the prows of the small fleet, with the Temple Ship forging the way. Standing on the foredeck, his hair and beard tossed by the wind, Duval found himself back in that Arctic landscape of snow and bitter cold. The use of power had exhausted him and he stood pensively on the deck, a fur cloak wrapped tightly round him.

Mists coiled over the water so that it seemed that they were entering an eerie world of cloud and light.

This was the great Tshis-Cole, the Snow-Melt River. By degrees the free channel widened so that by late afternoon of the first day the ice had receded to either bank. Still the mists swirled about them, blurring the snowy bank sides. At times snow fell so heavily that they could not see the way ahead. The near trees were grey shadows against the milky haze of light. The individual branches held frozen ice in their beards of lichen and, seen in gaps in the mist, the giant conifers at the forest edge were so heavy with snow they resembled a great cliff wall.

On the first night of their journey the mists lifted and there was a cry of excitement from the women. One of them saw the spirits of her ancestors standing among the trees, observing the ship's passage. And peering through snow-grimed lashes into the shadows of dappled greys and silvers, Duval's ancestors might also have been standing there, the parents he had lost in a poor and difficult childhood in America, a country he realized he might never see again.

He woke about midday on the second day in an unfamiliar chamber aboard the ship.

He was lying on a pallet of rushes, enclosed by walls of black oak. By his side was a stone crucible that had burnt its way down to white ashes. He washed his face in a basin of freezing water, then climbed a coiling staircase to emerge onto a swaying deck that smelled of wood smoke.

Snow gusted like a frozen breath over the riverbanks. Glancing astern, he saw the following boats as insubstantial as ghosts. He returned to his watch in the prow, his ears lulled with the rush of water and his eyes filled with those haunting woods against the backdrop of high white mountains.

Thinking back, the play of forces at the icebound lake was more bizarre than anything that had preceded it.

In all that had gone before, he had been no more than a passive ingredient. But he had influenced the storm over the lake. He had raised his fist and… and controlled the lightning that had struck the enemy in that tempest of destruction. He had sensed the power to do so as if it had been an extraordinary expansion of understanding in his mind. How could such a thing be possible? With his eyes narrowed against the biting wind, he watched the snowy banks give way to rock and shingle, moist with a scum of yellow-green algae.

Duval needed to understand what was happening to him. He needed to discuss it with Kemtuk. It had been the old man who had invoked the gathering of the storm clouds. If anyone could begin the process of explaining these strange events it would be the Shaman.

He found Kemtuk on watch beside Siam, both men alert for every whim of the wind or weather. Already it seemed they were fearful of an attack from either bank. He didn't want to reveal his bafflement under the scrutiny of the chief.

Instead he asked Siam, "Why not an attack by water?"

Siam shook his head, his eyes probing Duval's own for a moment, as if reading the confusion there before returning his attention to the river and its mist-shrouded banks.

"Here," he replied, "we are the masters. The attack will come from land – and at a time that disadvantages us and favours their malengins. Not for nothing are they called Storm Wolves."

Tell me more about them – these Storm Wolves."

"They are legionary soldiers, renowned for their cruelty. Trained to live and fight in these wastelands, they are the most northerly of the Tyrant's army of occupation, which calls itself the Death Legion."

While absorbing this, Duval noticed how Kemtuk's eyes were avoiding his.

The Shaman had grown frightened of him since his bringing the lightning bolt down onto the lake. Duval realized that the old man was not to be persuaded or hurried. He would bide his time for a more suitable moment.

It was with a continuing apprehension that he noticed Mira nearby, happier now that they had made their escape. Her face was less drawn about the hollowed cheeks and even a childish joy was visible in those dark eyes as she played games with a small wooden doll. He squatted on the deck beside her as she played.

What he had taken to be a doll was an elaborately carved manikin – it looked like a Native American kachina, made out of bright-coloured wood and feathers.

There was no mystery then as to who had made the toy for her.

Duval's eyes glanced toward the Shaman who was still en-grossed in his tactical conference with Siam. Mira seemed happy in her play with this symbol of tribal lore and – he could not avoid the word that sprang to mind – superstition. She seemed so childishly innocent in her absorption that it was difficult to recall the mystery Duval had previously remarked in her dark eyes. He relaxed for a while with her, helping her invent adventures for the manikin while watching at the edge of his vision the continuing thaw in the wilderness that was gliding by.

Black tors still filled the gaps between the trees, shoulder pressed against shoulder, crushing the light from two thirds of the sky. Shags posed on the frosted crags of rock under the shadows of the banks and they disappeared, with barely a ripple, into the surface stream.

There was food in this wilderness for its resident birds but little comfort for hungry people.

Always on the threshold of starvation in the icebound lake, the Olhyiu were already dangerously low on food. They were limited to two frugal meals a day consisting of nothing more than salted fish washed down by a bowl of warmed gruel.

On the evening of the fourth day, after they had made a rapid passage with long hours of sailing, they felt safe enough to draw up the keels against a bank of shingle. Hunters made preparations to enter the forest in search of meat. Some of the elders disembarked with the hunters to sit about fires on the snow-covered shore.

Duval joined the Shaman's group around one of the camp-fires.

Inland the ash white barks of birch trees faded into wraiths and shadows, while to the waterside, under a quarter moon, the bleached forms of the boats were aglimmer with moonlight.

Duval welcomed a bowl containing an alcoholic fermentation, warmed in the embers about the edge of the fire. Sipping it gratefully, with his shoulders hunched against the night and cold, he watched the Shaman's wrinkled face, the glitter in the pupil of his good eye. The old man was deeply thoughtful, his pipe aglow. Duval had grown fond of Kemtuk and he was reluctant to intrude upon the privacy of his reflections. Waiting until the Shaman was filling a new pipe, he broached the mystery of the Temple Ship.

"As you suggest, such a wonder was not constructed by the Olhyiu – nor by any people known to us. Its origins date from before the age of the wandering."

"How far back is that?"

For a moment or two, Kemtuk Lapeep sucked in a thinking silence against the glowing bowl of his pipe.

"Older than we might dream. From the days of legend. From the time of Ahn-kut-te. In that ancient time the Tilikum Olhyiu were spread three thousand miles along the coast from Carfon in the south to this northern world of the Whitestar Mountains. Yet there are tales that suggest it was ancient even then." Kemtuk shrugged. "But what is a world without mystery? Is it not a body without a soul!"

Duval nodded, shivering with the cold. It was obvious that Kemtuk had nothing more to say, since his eyes had closed in contemplation. Duval's own eyes darted about him, at the red reflection that played about the shining faces of the other elders over the thick fur of their capes and trousered legs.

He saw, with a sudden fearful clarity, another fireside rising out of the depths of memory, the same smell, the reflected light on anxious faces, surrounded by terrible danger… *the children.*

It felt as if inside his mind that closed shell, long concealed within the darkest labyrinths, was once more cracking open.

Somewhere along the open farmland between Kilkenny and Carlow, Sean had pulled the truck off the road onto a grassy track that led down into a disused quarry.

Here, screened from the world in a bowl of shadow, they gathered about their flimsy fire of brushwood, talking in hushed voices as they remembered their hunger, eating the sandwiches and drinking the first of the two bottles of Coke. Sean rolled a cigarette with tobacco he had bought at the service station, and all except Penny had a few puffs at it while over the rim of the quarry the tiny curl of smoke rose toward the gathering clouds of mid afternoon.

"One river – one sister – gathered. Two to go!"

Penny's voice. Her words issuing out of tight-pressed lips, as she kept glancing down at the scrap of limestone she called her talisman. Taking his clumsy puff of a second cigarette, Alan watched the intensity of her focus on the stone in the palm of her hand, and her fingers opening and closing with a gentle, even rhythm over it. He remembered how, on the day Billy Foran had died, Penny had pocketed the piece of stone from the tumbledown wall of the ancient chapel at Saint Patrick's Well.

The chapel had Celtic runes about the preserved fragments of its ancient alter. Now Penny was holding the piece of stone in her hand. She was praying over it. Though what the prayer might be, whether Christian or invoking some Celtic goddess, he didn't want to know.

Back on the roads north of Carrick, they kept to the smaller lanes. In places these were so overhung by trees that they were driving through dark tunnels. The sky that had been so limpid earlier had given way to clouds, and though they would sometimes emerge from shade into sparkling sunshine it was never long before the brooding shadows would loom up and swallow them again. Sean knew these lanes well from helping his father to deliver loads, but Alan quickly lost track of their wanderings through narrow and winding roads, at times no more than muddy lanes.

An hour or more passed, weaving through flat farmland, with scattered grey-walled cottages, surrounded by fields of sugar beet or the golden acres of ripening wheat.

Then a shout from Penny announced that they had arrived at the second of the Three Sisters. More eerie than the Suir, they had reached the Nore close to its headwaters. Here it was little more than a stream below gentle rapids, where white spray flecked the currents about shiny black rocks.

This time it was Kate's turn to fetch the water. But no one volunteered to go with her.

They found their reasons. Liam had climbed onto the roof of the cab as lookout, shading his eyes from a rare appearance of the sun. And Sean, even though the spear was his, waited by the wheel with the engine running. Penny was organizing the expedition at the side of the road. There was a toughness about Penny, who saw rules in their games where nobody else bothered even to try. Alan had to brush past her tall figure to help Kate with the second of the containers, down a slope of tussocky grasses and birch saplings toward the river. Yellow starworts grew in the culvert. A bearded reedling watched them, motionless, from its perch among the reeds. Tall bullrushes and cotton grasses hung trembling in the dankly humid air.

Kate too was trembling as she jammed the neck of the container into the stream.

It took longer to fill in this shallow water and the Nore hissed softly, as if warning them to hurry. Alan was darting fearful glances back over his shoulder into every shadow under the small trees.

The shadow overwhelmed them as the sun went in. He had an awful sense of a cold shroud spreading over the landscape, prowling about them, discovering their scent. The hairs on the back of his neck stood up. He was pressing his lips into a taut white line. "Quickly, Kate – *hurry!*"

The jittering hand of Kate reached up and joined his equally trembling fingers. Clammy tentacles were wrapping themselves around his legs, as if to hamper any escape.

Breathing deeply, wildly, yanking her upward, he took the weight of the container from her hand and he ran after the flashing alternation of her jean-covered calves. Lungs bursting, they reached the barbed wire at the top of the slope, struggling between the strands that Penny was holding apart for them. He could hear the sounds of the truck starting to move. And the hoarse shouting from Liam and Mo, urging them to run, as, bleeding from multiple tiny scratches, they threw themselves frantically into the back.

NINE

THE RACE OF DEATH

D UVAL SURFACED, PULLING his collar tighter about his throat. His memories had been interrupted by a sudden row from the direction of the beached canoes. Siam was hitting Turkaya about the head with his broad-rimmed hat. The big man's face was red and flustered. Kemtuk made a gesture of non-interference, shaking his head.

"Turkaya wants to join the hunters. The forest is in his blood and he can read a trail even by night. But his father makes him stay.

While Kemtuk once more puffed at his pipe, Duval watched the sullen youth stalk back to the boats. Duval thought he understood Siam. The chief had lost his wife and daughter: he didn't want to lose his son. Duval's gaze returned to the shadows, where the hunters were just departing. He saw their forms fading from sight among the wraiths of trees.

A distinct aura of evil had stayed with him since the interrupted memory. Now he sensed danger here. From time to time, though it might have been his heightened imagination, he felt eyes watching them from the darks of the trees. Peering into the dark, he was unable to stop his eyes flickering from one ghostly form to another. For a moment, the Shaman also seemed to sense it. He stopped puffing at his pipe to rub unconsciously at his wasted leg, overwrapped with sealskin, and laced with thick thongs that reached almost to his knee.

There was no comfort in resting around the fire for either man, not anymore.

The hunters returned at dawn with bundles of wood pigeon and half a dozen white hares. The women took them to the waterside, skinning and gutting them with razor-sharp knives, sprinkling the snow with blood. Then they were pressing the bows once more into the stream.

On the second week they lost the first of their company, an old woman who had given up the will to live. She slipped away during a hunting stop to die ashore. A party of men, led by Turkaya, followed her track for a few hundred yards among the rushes and sedges of the bank until they found her. They left her frozen body there, erecting a small mound of stones over it.

The old woman's death increased the gloom, and fearful eyes peered more anxiously at the snowbound forest as they moved out again into the increasingly turbulent river. The landscape was unchanging, that frighteningly stark contrast between the snowy ground and the indigo of the trees.

Duval did his best to keep track of the days.

Today was two weeks and six days since they had first sailed out from their icebound captivity. He estimated they were travelling from twenty to fifty miles each day, depending on the difficulty they experienced with navigating the river. And those difficulties were mounting.

That same morning they came to a complete stop while steersmen passed out ropes to men standing on the bank. They had to edge each boat past treacherous rapids, while people pressed with poles from the decks. The Temple Ship became a major undertaking. The steam of breath surrounded their heads like haloes and on the banks thick reeds, coated with hoarfrost, crackled like gunshots under the feet of the men as they heaved and tugged on ropes attached to the prows. Hearts faltered when one of the fishing boats ran aground on a trap of breakers. With anxious eyes scanning the trees, this family home was finally saved by cantilevering it over the rocks using fulcrums hacked out of young tree trunks and lubricated by slippery inner bark.

But they had lost an entire day negotiating a few miles of water. The sense of menace increased as the food reserves were dwindling. The meat caught by the hunters had long run out, and even their stores of fish and oil were almost spent. Duval's heart fell with the plaintive sound of children wailing from hunger.

That night, sitting around another fire on the bank, Duval heard a loud flapping in the air, a leathery sound, like great wings beating. Craning his eyes through the dark, he saw nothing more than shadows. But he remembered his earlier sense of eyes spying on them from the trees. And to his nostrils came a foul stench, left on the air in the wake of the wings. Shivering involuntarily as he peered into the forest, blue-black against the virgin white of the snow, Duval thought about his father, whose life had seemed a similar journey through an alien landscape.

In that life-ravaged face he remembered moments of humour, a kindness not of touch or declared affection but of being with him, a shyness about the eyes, which extended even to his only son. It was as if there were a tangible guilt there, the guilt of mere existence in his eyes. He remembered with gratitude the small comforts his father had been able to provide for him after the death of his mother. The fact he had never abandoned him, not even during the aimless drifting from state to state. He remembered the comfort of cheap alcohol in those final days, tormented by illness, when those nicotine-stained hands could still extract a wonderful magic from their manipulation of the battered old harmonica.

Love, the love he had longed for most of his life, burned like an acid in his chest.

That night he slept by the fireside. At dawn he didn't hear Turkaya come up beside him. The youth's voice cut like a knife through sleep, waking him. "I worry about the journey ahead, Mage Lord."

Duval stood up and stretched and then they walked along

the shore, staring into the wintry landscape together. "Call me Duval."

The boy had a quick intelligence. Duval knew that he had been profoundly affected by the loss of his mother and sister. "What's worrying you, Turkaya?"

"There are great hazards in the river close ahead. The water will boil over the Race of Death."

Duval sighed, digesting this information, sharing the thick cloud of steam of their breaths. He considered Turkaya for several seconds, reflectively. "Tell me – are all the tribes like you, the Olhyiu?"

"Few live as we do. Once our people left the ancestral lands to live about the cities. We toiled upon the land as farmers. But my grandfather's grandfather's people could not settle there. They rediscovered their wild hearts."

Duval stiffened with surprise: he had to adjust mentally to this information.

Hunger was so pressing that no matter how worried he was about the delays, Siam was forced to spend this additional morning with the ships' keels drawn up against the shore of sloping stone. He had selected the spot, where high cliffs reared on either bank, making ambush difficult, while within the undergrowth of the narrow river valley were bushes laden with winter berries. As the hunting parties set out on a brief foray, the women and children gathered the berries. Soon happy cries sounded out as stomachs were filled for the first time in days.

Duval held back as Turkaya left him by the forest edge, aware that the Shaman was close to him. The old man had a distinctive smell of pipe tobacco even when his pipe was unlit.

Refreshing his face with a handful of snow, he spoke as he turned to face him. "You are watching me while avoiding me, Kemtuk. There's no need for that. You and I should be friends."

A flicker of assessment in that silvery eye. When the old man spoke, it was with a voice husky with anxiety. "If I am afraid, it is for my people. The Storm Wolves are great warriors and cunning, for all that we despise them. I have felt hostile eyes upon us these last few days."

Duval was shocked. How could Kemtuk stand there so calmly, knowing what he did?

"Then we must get the people back into the boats. We must hurry – risk travel by night!"

"Do not distress yourself. Siam knows. That hunting party is also a scouting party."

Duval's eyes darted about him for Mira. How vulnerable the girl seemed, so often around him that her presence trailed him like a shadow. Yet she could disappear, as now, like a will-o'-the-wisp, as if into nowhere.

They walked back together to join a circle of elders, who were rekindling the ashes of the fires. Duval sat down with them, the river mere yards behind their backs, and he could not avoid a fretful backward glance to where phantoms of mist were rising from its surface. In full daylight the wilderness seemed even more bitter. The vastness of the landscape dwarfed their presence. They were utterly insignificant here, desolate and vulnerable.

Lost in his brooding, his boots buried in fresh-fallen snow, Duval was hardly aware that he had pulled the harmonica from his pocket. He was already playing one of his father's favourites, not a blues number at all but the tune he would play for Duval's mother, "Cajun Girl", before he noticed the squealing response about him. A small group of children had come up close and they were dancing to the music. He continued to play the Cajun tune, putting more life into it, entranced by their natural rhythms, these little ones with their lips split and their faces black with cold, their hair poking out from fur caps and bonnets. Steam from his breath bathed his face after he had finished, returning their glances and stroking his beard to clear it of snow.

A little girl – they called her Amote – darted up close and grabbed his beard before she ran away squealing. Duval laughed too, gazing after the little girl, who had bright red poppies painted over her cheeks.

After the children had gone back to their mothers, he spoke urgently to Kemtuk, not caring that many of the elders were close and listening.

"I know what you have sensed for days. Eyes are watching us even as we speak." Duval tapped the triangle in his brow. "I need to understand this – what it is and how it works."

He hesitated before adding, "I am puzzled, Kemtuk. Once before, as a child, I took part in a kind of adventure with five other children. They were my closest friends. I sense that whatever happened to us then is crucially linked to what is happening now. But I have no memory of what followed.

"I need to know what happened. Is there a way that you could help me regain my memory of this."

There was a prickling silence and then a murmuring of muted voices among the elders, who glanced from one to another under lowered brows. The Shaman puffed at intervals on his freshly lit pipe, so that Duval began to wonder if he would answer at all. But eventually he spoke.

"My friend, all can read your troubles in your shoulders and in your eyes. But I cannot help you in the way you seek." The old man took his pipe from his mouth and tapped the bowl against a stone, while looking towards the nearby river. "I would help if I could. But I do not have the power to do so. Only one mage in all the land has such power, or so legend has it. He lives in Isscan, where we are headed. He is known as the Mage of Dreams."

The following day Duval heard the murmur of the rapids Turkaya had called the Race of Death. An hour closer and the murmur was a roaring.

The valley sides became jagged cliffs, like sinews of iron tethering the mountains about the swollen river. Between them the torrent was squeezed between a narrow pass, whipped into a frenzy by the speed of its passage. The current broke into heaving waves, seething where it struck the sharp edges of submerged boulders.

The sails were down but still the boats raced among the breakers and pole-wielding men and women were hard-pressed to keep their keels clear of the rocks. He saw how their protective poles bent with the pressure of water alone, and from time to time one of the spars splintered against a reef, the crack lost against the background thunder.

Beside him, Duval heard Kemtuk groan aloud: "A madness has invaded the pass!"

Jagged teeth gnashed at the keels. Siam was hoarse from shouting to the sailors on board the Temple Ship, the sails furled and every hand pressing their long poles against the rocks. Just moments later the whole ship shuddered as it crashed against a reef. The decks shelved and an immense wave swept over them, before the great ship righted herself again. From the boat closest to them, a small child was torn from its mother's arms and flung, with a single heartrending scream, into the maelstrom. The child's father fought off the grappling arms of his family to hurl himself after his child and was lost within seconds.

With a pole clenched in his own hands, Duval pushed against the rocks. Mira was curled up under the rail close to him. She had her eyes squeezed shut and her hands over her eyes as the ship bucked and twisted in the snarl of the current.

In the eye of the storm, Duval felt it again: that soul-devouring grief. It came from the ship.

Suddenly the prow caught on another reef. There was a great shudder, as the stern jerked high out of the water, weightless as a twig in the grip of such forces, and another foaming torrent rushed over the deck. In that same moment he saw Mira's face, her mouth wide open: but against the roar of the water he could not hear her scream. As if a giant hand had taken hold of her, she was thrown aloft, then carried away into the seething water.

Terror! His mind was flooded with the sensations in the child's brain.

Duval threw himself after her, caught at once by the tumult

of current, crashed against ship and boulders, yet struggling to search with open eyes in the pandemonium beneath the surface. He was dazed from where his head had cracked against the stern. Shaking the confusion from his mind, he struck upward, his legs and arms flailing until his face broke the surface. But he could see nothing. The girl was nowhere near him.

"Mira!" he shouted, his voice torn from his lips and lost in the background thunder.

He reached out his inner voice and pressed the urgency of his call through the triangle. *Mira!* In answer there was the faintest whimper. They were communicating through thought alone. He saw through her own eyes the frenzied race of water, of black stone and whirling current. She must be under the surface. Still alive, but drowning. He tried to shake off his boots but they were too firmly laced. His greatcoat, heavy with water, was dragging him under. But his fingers were too numbed to unfasten it. There was no time. Her terror was overwhelming him. Her mental screams had become an explosion in his brain. But where was she? She couldn't be far from him.

Think, Mira – think!

But only panic lunged at him from that small frightened mind. The terror was so great, no rational message could penetrate it.

Duval's body had been thrown close to the ship again and his flailing hand clutched a guardrail that ran just above the waterline. He held on there, rising and falling with the heaving timber, his head plunging in and out of the moiling surface. His eyes scanned the river ahead, saw a great boulder which bisected the stream. If Mira could survive long enough to reach that boulder, he would be able to locate her. Pushing desperately with his boots against the hull, he swam away from the sanctuary of the rail and into the raging water.

He forced all awareness from his mind, tethering everything to that flickering mote of life.

Mira! he called again, desperately, with every ounce of

strength through the triangle.

Believer! Believer! Believer!

She was answering at last, as if the oxygen deprivation of drowning had numbed her terror. Yet how powerful still was the communication from that weakening mind. His own mind felt overwhelmed by the signal of her need.

In that brief communication, strange memories brushed against his perception. Extraordinary visions. A glimpse as if he were looking through a universal window, where great knowledge had come into focus for a moment. It was a mad, impossible notion, as if… as if through the dying mind of the child he were privileged to perceive great mysteries. Then he saw the rock. The dark shape of it flashed across his vision, as if through the open eyes of the unconscious girl.

Diving under the surface currents, almost immediately he saw her. The small body, bent and limp, was brought up against the black surface of the rock, held against it by the force of the river. There was no thought there anymore. He didn't know if she was unconscious or dead. Thrusting out with his own lungs bursting, he caught hold of her and lunged to the surface.

He broke into air with his right arm wrapped under her chest. His breath came in gasps. After a few seconds of rising panic, he drove away from the rock.

Thrashing out against the current, his mind could not grasp the horror as it lifted one of the boats clear out of the water, dripping spume and spray, then broke its back upon a black anvil of rock. He heard the screams of the family on board, as they were dashed against the boulder.

He held more tightly to the girl, forcing her unconscious face above the pulling waters. He communicated to her, mind to mind, urgently:

"Hold on!"

Even as he did so, an arc of livid green cut through the spray and another boat exploded into flame.

The Storm Wolves had timed their attack to perfection. The harpoons of the Olhyiu were useless here. There would be no counterattack with thunder and lightning here.

Struggling to stay alive in the boiling tumult, he lifted the body of the girl against his chest, cupping her face in his palm. Mira's eyes opened wide with terror, before she clutched weakly at his exhausted arms.

Swim! A strange voice entered his mind. It was a command. The voice was a deep contralto, calm and measured, devoid of fear.

"Where?" he gasped.

He was so drained he could barely float, let alone swim. The air was full of oaths and curses as more arcs of the sinister green cut through the storm-tossed air to find their defenceless targets. An impression of fierce conflict close to the bank – then a huge armoured figure plunged into the water not twenty feet away from him. "Blasphemer's brat!" He heard the hate-filled growl. "My Master would relish your pious heart."

Desperately, Duval found a small remaining reserve of strength. Still clinging to the girl, he attempted to move away from the bank into deeper water but within moments a mailed fist had gripped his hair. A brutal strength was plunging him back under the surface. Duval's eyes opened under water, saw the soldier's other hand reach to his submerged waist and extract a dagger. His head dragged up, clear of the surface – he reeled, from the blow of the dagger's pommel. But even as he struggled to fight back, hampered by Mira's body, the soldier's own head parted company with his body and fell, trailing mire, spinning and dancing into the current before Duval's failing vision.

Struggling back to the surface, Duval's hand never relinquished his hold on Mira. Bloodied, exhausted, his head still reeling from the blow of the dagger's pommel, he lifted her face above the surface.

They were tumbling over a race of smaller boulders, descending through the jarring impacts into a white-frothed cauldron. His body was numb. He was suffocating again, his face below the deluge. Then, suddenly, the storm was over. The water, beyond the cauldron of mist and spume, was fast-running but there were no longer any rocks.

He felt the weight of his burden increase and realized that his feet were touching bottom. He was staggering towards the bank, though his numbed feet could hardly register it.

Shoving Mira out of the water onto a crumbly shelf by the water's edge, he was too worn to climb out himself. He remained submerged up to chest level, holding on to the shelf, which sloped gently up to the forest floor. His ears were filled by the sounds of continuing attack. His vision caught the flickering green light of the Storm Wolves' weaponry. In moments several mailed arms took hold of him and he was dragged out of the water and onto the sloping shingle. Blows rained down onto his head and shoulders.

TEN

TAKEN BY THE STORM WOLVES

H E WAS ONLY vaguely aware of the hoarse shouts and curses in an alien language. All he knew was the fact that Mira was gone. Storm Wolves had dragged her away. And with it a darkness had invaded Duval's mind.

Guttural commands, accompanied by jabs of weapons and kicks, issued from faces hidden behind masks of fur-covered hide. The effect was to make the Storm Wolves seem more animal than human. The helmets that capped their burly heads were constructed of a metal alloy that resembled matte black steel. Black bearskin surcoats dressed their trunks and limbs under chain mail bodices of the same black alloy. Their booted feet were also fur-lined, and their hands were protected by leathery mittens that seemed extensions of the fur tunic, designed for combat in the extreme cold.

Reviving Mira had taken his last reserves of strength, and Duval could not resist their dragging him up the bank of snow-covered shale. At the top, they beat him again until he was al-most unconscious. Their attack was ferocious. His nose and mouth filled with blood. As he fell onto his hands and knees, he caught their derogatory reference to him, "homunculus". It suggested, although it made no sense, that their language was a bastardized Latin. A single thought remained and that was somehow to protect Mira.

Where was she? Where had they taken her?

A group of Storm Wolves came running back out of the trees. They carried two sinewy poles, still covered by bark. They tore off his soaked greatcoat, his boots, and the fur-lined undercoat. Then they made a cross by tethering the springy poles at their centres before bending each pole into a bow, lashing his wrists and ankles to their extremities with leather thongs. The effect was to stretch him, the tension in the bowed poles tearing at every joint and sinew. A gag of filthy leather was rammed between his teeth before they cast him, face down, on the trampled snow and shingle. Those visions, of the terrible fate of Siam's wife and daughter, left him in no doubt of his own fate.

A huge legionary – the rank of Centurion entered Duval's mind – leaned down to poke at his bonds. His fur-mittened hands had sharp nails, filed into claws, so that the probing left him gouged and bleeding.

The pain in his limbs was agonizing. His teeth were chattering. His exposed body was shivering with cold. A darkness extended over his mind, like a malevolent vapour, draining his will.

As minutes passed, the physical agony of his stretched limbs grew steadily worse. It was impossible to think beyond the pain. Yet he had to think. He had to focus his mind. A battle nearby... Who was fighting the Storm Wolves? If he could just focus on that, on the sounds of battle: sense through the triangle what was happening and where.

Fight against it! Use the pain!

He concentrated on the tormented bones and swelling joints, accepting the agony, bringing it into focus in his mind.

Then, through his pain came the memory of that disarticulated head. He saw the head falling. He felt its weight strike his thigh, he followed its mirey trail in the water, he could almost taste the blood on his tongue.... No Olhyiu could have attacked that legionary from the bank. His life had been saved by... by whom? What were the forces involved in this terrible battle that raged around him.

Sounds of heavy feet hurrying nearby... then six or seven Storm Wolves burst out of the undergrowth to join the small party holding him prisoner. One was carrying a body about his shoulders, which he cast down as mercilessly as a sack of fire-wood onto the trampled snow next to him. Duval struggled to turn his face to see who his fellow prisoner might be, hoping it might be Mira.

"Snakoil!" he hissed, inside his gag.

It was with difficulty that he recognized the traitor. Snakoil's face was bloodied and swollen. His neck was choked by a leather thong, tethered to his shackled feet so it arched his body backwards. His overlords had punished him for leading them into the trap on the ice-bound lake. Even now, the guard that had thrown him onto the hard ground gave the emaciated body a bone-crunching kick. Duval heard the slobbering sound that came from the broken lips.

"Snakoil!" he hissed again, forced the communication through the triangle.

The shock of hearing his name caused the figure to stop moaning. He twisted his neck in Duval's direction, his eyes madly staring. Grasping with difficulty the possibility of this mind-to-mind communication.

Snakoil's mind, through the weakened triangle, was a cauldron of fear and pain – yet it retained the spite and cunning of old. As if fallen back upon the very dregs of the human soul, hatred had become an inspiration for this most depraved of men. And in the traitor's mind Duval confirmed the fate that lay in store for them both.

Ritual sacrifice!

Torture and death was the way of life in the brutal existence of these legionaries. Cruelty was their pleasure, the reward they coveted for their work of oppression and killing.

The Centurion had returned. Snakoil kicked in his limited way at Duval to make him aware of something, though he couldn't read what it was on that face, contorted as it was with pain.

"What is it? What are you trying to say?" He heard Snakoil's words aloud in his mind.

In the struggle within Snakoil's maddened brain, he also saw a desperate use for him. "I am accursed… a renegade amongst my own kind."

"Through your own greed and betrayal!"

"So it may be. Yet I spit upon it!" That ravaged face twisted into a snarl again as he twisted around his constrained neck, so he was squinting at Duval from the corners of his eyes. "Siam, the stupid! Who could make such a man leader in place of me. I had the guile of a leader. As to that shambling dogsturd, Kemtuk. What Shaman would shackle the soul of his people into such servility and bondage. If I betrayed them, it was from contempt because they had betrayed themselves. Theirs was the bigger betrayal. What was left for me but to gather the crumbs before even they were taken from them."

One of the guards appeared to sense the communication between them. He ran at Duval and kicked him viciously in the ribs. It was several minutes before Duval could focus his thoughts again. He kept his head averted from Snakoil as he attempted communication again.

"What are they waiting for?"

"The service of their god," Snakoil laughed in a broken cackle, as a man in suffering might derive comfort in the agony of another.

Duval remembered the macabre scene he had read earlier in Snakoil's mind, that grotesque ritual when the legionaries had murdered Siam's wife and daughter.

"What god?"

"That slime of offal that is their leader."

This caused Duval to forget his caution of just moments before and he turned his widely staring eyes upon the traitor.

"Help me, Snakoil. Now you have a chance for redemption – atonement!"

Hatred contorted the face of the traitor, even the muscles of his neck. "I shit on your atonement!"

"I know you want to help me. I can sense it in your miserable brain."

"Those rabble who thought themselves my people! Ah but I

relish their doom, as they forced my own upon me. No! These abominations for men will exterminate them as they will see me off, and soon. I don't give a damn that they will kill me. I have had enough of suffering. But you – if you can but live! You might be the tool of my vengeance upon these abominations."

"But how? When I'm as doomed as you are!"

"Harken to the battle – fool! Who do you think attacks these excremental scum with such deadly earnest? Not those fish-gutters."

Duval struggled to grasp what Snakoil was talking about. He had to force his mind to think against the agony in his limbs.

"Who then?"

"Those self-abasing witches!"

The witches? In Snakoil's mind the derogative term was accompanied by a vision of tall and fierce-looking women. But there was no time to question him about this because the Centurion was back, blowing steam in a rage. He stamped down hard on the crossed poles, causing a new agony to rack Duval's spine. Duval cursed him back from a crimson mist of semiconsciousness. Then, abruptly, he found a respite. Snakoil had kicked out with both tethered feet at the genitals of their tormentor – in spite of the pain it must have caused his tethered throat, the traitor was distracting attention from Duval to himself.

The respite bought by Snakoil's diversion saved Duval further torment. But he had no time to feel gratitude. He needed that respite to return to his previous thought.

The tall, fierce women - who were they? In Snakoil's mind they evoked not only the image of Amazons – they also evoked fear. Could it have been one of their weapons that had decapitated the Storm Wolf while Duval was being forced under the icy water? The calm voice that had made contact during his struggle in the river... *Swim!*

That communication had been authoritative, certain. The voice that spoke it understood the communicating triangle in his brow. If so, its owner might have answers to questions that had baffled him since his arrival here. It had been a distinctly female voice, if very deep – and not the voice of Granny Ddhu. If this unknown female was still nearby, there was a chance she would hear him call for help in the same way that she had been able to communicate to him when he was in the water. Now the call burst from his tormented mind, cutting through the surrounding shadows of forest.

Hope restored his concern for Mira.

Snakoil's scream returned Duval to the reality of his position.

With horror he watched the Centurion tighten the noose about Snakoil's throat as he writhed on the ground. The other legionaries gathered to watch this, with a sadistic glitter in their eyes.

Snakoil's face was black against the snow. His split and fissured lips began to bleed; yet still his eyes were staring with a white intensity at Duval....

"Beware... Isscan." His thoughts came in gasps from the remorseless strangling. "If you live to see it... beware the treachery of Isscan."

An enormous legionary grabbed hold of Duval's hair to lift his face and inspect the triangle. More of the debased Latin, declaiming the sorcery of witches.

Through a storm of pain, Duval kept his focus on his tortured companion. Two of them had taken hold of Snakoil by his upper arms, as two more brought up a leash of the beasts that pulled their sleds. Seen from close quarters, they were even more dreadful than Duval remembered, with jaws slavering at the prospect of blood. The Centurion laughed as he shoved Snakoil's face into the snow to restore full consciousness.

Urgently, Duval projected his thoughts: "I will tell your people of your final courage, if I survive to meet them again!"

"Spare me... such sentimental slobberings!"

"Tell me – what have they done with the girl?"

For a long moment, as they forced the spitting and snarling man into a kneeling posture, there was only silence in response.

But hatred so dominated the soul of the traitor that it revived him for a final defiance. "Nature's abominations... ah, such pain!" Two of the legionaries had cut his bonds and were stretching out his arms to right and left of him – forcing his head forward so it was no more than a foot above the frozen ground – and the Centurion was bracing his posture to wield his sword.

Even then the traitor's eyes squirmed Duval's way. Duval saw there a remarkable if malevolent courage as Snakoil uttered, "They... they suspect... the girl!"

Those were Snakoil's last conscious words as the Centurion brought the gleaming blade down, not upon his neck but upon his right arm, cleaving it midway between the elbow and the shoulder. Blood spurted in arterial throbs out over the snow.

The group of legionaries threw back their heads and howled, as if some deep lust for blood were being satisfied. The sound was utterly inhuman, so spitefully evil, that loathing for them combined with rage in Duval's heart. Then the snarling beasts were unleashed, taking up the howling from their masters as they fought one another over the discarded arm.

Duval used what force was left in the triangle to probe the surrounding forest. Along the river, northward, he picked up the cries and the fury of battle, but there was no impression of anybody coming to help him.

The respite was brief.

Snakoil's stump of arm was bound with a thong to preserve him for more torture. Then it was Duval's turn. The legionaries tossed him over in the snow, so his body lay stretched above the crossed poles. One of them pulled his head back by the hair. The circle of helmeted heads gathered about him, eyes closed as they intoned some propitiation of their foul leader, in those corrupted Latin cadences. The Centurion lifted his sword, still scarlet with Snakoil's blood.

But the strike was averted as a new presence materialized from the shadows close by Duval.

A stranger had lifted his hand to stay the Centurion. Duval

squinted up at a small man with a thin face under a black cowl, a face so drawn and emaciated as to appear cadaveric, with eyes that were red-veined with malice. A miasma of evil descended over Duval from his proximity. He could smell the dankness of the thin man's breath as he bent close enough to inspect the triangle. Fury, and even a little fear, contorted those emaciated features as from his side he slipped out a dagger with a black blade. There was a dreadful familiarity to that blade, serpent-like in its spiral evolution to its cruelly sharp tip. It was identical to the dagger that had wounded him in London.

A ritual blade.

It was a link, a frightening confirmation of some commonality between Earth and Tír. *Already his emissaries of malice have entered your world.* And this creature needed no gauntlets to protect himself from the dark power of the blade. From the legionaries' common minds came a term of fearful respect: *Preceptor.*

The Preceptor lifted the dagger, holding it lovingly before him, to kiss the grip with wormlike lips that writhed together in blasphemous supplication. Duval caught a clear glimpse of the symbol that fashioned the entire handle, the triple circle of an extended infinity, cast in a loathsome white-silver that sparkled with awful power. As the Preceptor held its point against the triangle, the hateful oppression of it invaded Duval's mind.

His heart stopped, then beat falteringly and slow. His mind drowned in a nauseous darkness. Duval felt the effluvium of force leaking from the triangle, as if his own life force were ebbing away.

The terrible irregularity of his heartbeat went on in a dread slow motion…boom…boom…boom. The will of that cowled figure so crackled with wickedness, so contrary to all joy and hope, that Duval felt closer to drowning in its darkness than he had felt in the turmoil of the river. A final spurt of denial, of anger, rose in him, and as if that faint spark of goodness took seed within his spirit, the force of its rejection flashed back from the triangle and struck against the Preceptor's blade. He saw it flash through the enveloping miasma of darkness like a bolt of lightning, casting the evil man down onto the bloodied ground.

But the Preceptor was much too powerful to be damaged by this weakened force.

With a hiss, he urged the Centurion back. "This one is dangerous. Kill him quickly. I want his head and the bauble on it!"

As if from a disembodied distance, Duval saw the Centurion raise his sword aloft, rearing onto his toes to strike. The howling began again, as the legionaries threw back their heads in celebration of their lust for blood. He thought: *If I die now every hope is lost.* He saw again the three faces in the cave, the First Power, the Power of the Earth, the Second Power, of carnal creation, and the Third Power, the dreadful countenance he had refused to kiss, grimmer than the voids of space. And he remembered the parting caution of the Trídédana in the cave: But have a care. *In great danger, you will think to call upon me. Yet it may be my sisters who come to your beckoning!* Faintly, as if from a great distance, he heard the gravelly voice: *Duvaaal, heed! Daaannngerrr!* But Duval no longer cared about the danger. A conflagration of rage was already blazing in him. A rage of hatred for them, for their wickedness and cruelty, that expanded within a single heartbeat until he became that rage: rage became his being.

For a fraction of a moment, there was self-awareness. He perceived himself as he now appeared before their eyes: a figure at once freed and standing upright, as brilliant as a sun but as cold as starlight. There was no humanity in that figure, tall and lean and masked with horror. Its eyes were furies.

The blade of the Centurion did not fall. The roar of Duval's fury tore through the shackling malignancy of the Preceptor and reached out mercilessly from mind to mind. Already the Centurion's brain boiled within its skull and his eyes turned white. In that terrible moment of metamorphosis, the others had no time to register their danger. Spirits took substance in the snowy air: sylphlike shapes with the whisper of voices. The succubi of the Second Power, were shimmering into existence. He heard their whisperings, like a tide of longing, dancing and gyrating about him, fanning out among the Storm Wolves, brushing spirit against flesh, sighing, as if each man had only had to free his will, to lose himself in pleasure beyond imagining....

With the oraculum blazing more fiercely still, Duval scattered the bewildered legionaries to the right and left of him, while the daughters of Mab whirled and spread, and at every contract a frenzy erupted. A madness of lust rippled out among the armoured soldiers. With wild eyes, the Preceptor tried to stab at Duval with his dagger. In a flash of lightning from the oraculum, the evil man was lifted into the air, thrown down before Duval, smashing into the bewildered legionaries like a human battering ram.

The succubi were transforming within the disordered ranks of the Storm Wolves. Voluptuous lips drew back on razorine fangs, their mouths gaping. They had begun feeding, springing from one lust-bewildered man to another.

Rage wheeled more furiously still, turned in the spiritual matrix of Duval's being. Figures in front of him burst asunder, as bolt after bolt of lightning spread from his brow. Only the Preceptor had the strength and the wits to flee. Every other mouth had time only to gape with horror as the twin furies of the two Powers struck them.

A mist like blood was raining about Duval, as if the spirit of death were cooling the skin of his face, dimming the vision in his eyes. He was drowning in the taste and the smell of blood.

Although it seemed that an eternity separated that moment of dimming vision from the return of consciousness, it was probably no more than minutes. On the ground nearby were the poles that had tethered him, reduced to a white residue of ash. He saw, as if from a distance, that tall figures were entering the clearing, their swords drawn and flashing a strange actinic green. But there was nobody left for them to fight.

He was standing in a circle of dead legionaries and Leloo, their carcasses still oozing blood into the frozen ground. But the Preceptor was not among them. Duval registered this as he was struggling to recover control of his limbs. Snakoil was the only other survivor within the clearing, though he was mercifully unconscious. Duval ignored him, grinding his teeth at the agony of release from more than the mere bonds that had tethered him to the poles.

But the shock of recovery was so debilitating, he couldn't walk. He felt utterly exhausted. The agony had returned to his limbs. He had to defer the search for his greatcoat and boots.

"Mira!"

He lifted his head to look directly into the eyes of the statuesque, bronze-skinned woman, who was gazing back at him with deep brown eyes in an expressive if exhausted face.

"Save your strength," she addressed him in a strangely accented contralto voice, indicating to one of her companions to put a bearskin rug over his shoulders. For a moment her eyes darted about the clearing, as if baffled by the slaughter.

Then, with the help of one of the others, she was offering him a sip from a turquoise flask containing a honey-coloured elixir.

"Drink, Duval. This is Niyave, from the Guhttan Mountains, the homeland of the Shee." In her mind Duval sensed both life and health. "It will help you to recover your strength."

The elixir burnt his mouth, like strong alcohol. It worked quickly, the weakness subsiding and the pain lessening in his limbs. A strange chanting began in the distance, somewhere behind the line of trees. It raised the hackles on his neck.

He made a conscious effort to calm down. Glancing past the woman, he eyed her astonishing companions. None other than the first woman had spoken a word: not even to one another.

"Mira!" he murmured again.

Urgently, he took hold of the woman's arm. He glanced away into the forest, in the direction of the chanting.

ELEVEN

THE SHEE

"WHO ARE YOU?" He turned back to address the bronze-skinned woman, his voice still croaky but now with much less pain.

"I am failing in my diplomacy." She allowed him a second sip of the honey-coloured elixir – though she still did so sparingly, as if it were very precious. "You are Duval! Forgive my lack of diplomacy, borne out of dread that we might not find you alive."

The woman's words implied a familiarity he did not understand. The tall women standing in the background wore long capes that gave them camouflage. He could see swords attached to their belts. *Women armed with swords!*

The spokeswoman's eyes had never left his since her arrival. Her voice had become urgent. "We have come in great haste from Carfon. Permit me to introduce myself and my company." She stood self-consciously erect, grimacing as if her duty pained her. "My name is Milish Essyne Xhosa. My matrilineage is that of a Princess of Laña. I was until recently a stateswoman of the Council in Exile of Continental Monisle. But needs demand honesty between us. No council edict has sanctioned our coming here. Yet still you might regard me as an ambassador for my world."

Even without the headdress, she must have been six feet tall. Her companions were much taller. Although he was an inch above six feet, they towered over him.

The face of Milish was haughty, a patrician mask, perfectly

proportioned even to the deep shadows below the high cheek-bones. His eyes darted past her once again, drawn beyond belief to the armed giantesses watching him from the background.

"My companions are Shee, bred for war since ancient times. Ainé" – she pronounced it "Eye-nay" – "bears the Oraculum of Brí upon her brow. It is the mark of hereditary leadership."

"Oraculum?" He looked up at the brow of the most ferocious looking of the Amazonian women, Ainé. He observed a puckering of scar tissue there, broken veins about a flat oval set, like his own triangle, centrally into her forehead. It looked as if a piece of wafer-thin jade, perhaps an inch long by two thirds of an inch across, had been welded to her skull. Its surface was as smooth as a pearl's, yet there was an impression of patterning there, like moiréed silk.

"Ainé is the Kyra of all the Shee. Her companions are Muîrne, the teacher, and, by her side the warrior-in-noviciate, Valéra. If you cheat death on the road that lies before you, this will be your debt to them."

Although there were other Shee present, Milish had no time to name them. Duval interrupted her. "Listen to me – listen carefully, all of you. There was a girl with me. Her name is Mira. The Storm Wolves have taken her. We must save her."

The Kyra returned his gaze with a calm appraisal.

She appeared to be astonishingly tall, perhaps seven and a half feet, with hair the dull red of old copper, coiled into a braid that was fastened over her left shoulder with a silver pin. But there was nothing romantic about her: she looked more like a bloodied survivor from the battle of Stalingrad.

It was the Kyra who answered him. "Hers is but one life."

He recognized that deep, authoritative voice. It was the voice that had called out to him in the river. She spoke again, directly to him. "A cloud of blood hangs over the entire province of Ulisswe. Word has spread of the arrival of the Mage Lord Duval, the Redeemer of the Olhyiu, bearing the Oraculum of the Holy Sisters. The hearts and souls of the oppressed have been set aflame. Already rumours are spreading of the destruction of an entire platoon of Storm Wolves in the icy north. Such hopes have been stirred by the flight of the Temple Ship, heading south to confront the Council in Exile at Carfon."

She had called the triangle in Duval's own brow the Oraculum of the Holy Sisters – the Trídédana! He shook his head at the lack of opportunity for explanations. "We have to save this girl."

"Why do you worry about this girl. All the armies of the Death Legion have taken to war. They are fanning out over all the occupied lands. Rebellion is in the air. Many villages and towns are in open insurrection. They will be put down in an ocean of blood. It was this rumour of the Mage Lord that led us to you. It is also the reason why so few of the Storm Wolves could be diverted to this ambush. The Shee too are moving eastward from the Guhttan Mountains in such numbers as have not been seen since the fall of Ossierel, though they are too distant yet to assist us."

"Mira is not Olhyiu. I believe she may be important to my purpose. She called me the True Believer."

Milish joined the Kyra in confronting him. Her face had paled and her pupils had expanded until they almost filled her mahogany irises.

Duval ignored their astonishment. "There's a thin man among the Storm Wolves armed with a black-bladed dagger. A man they call a Preceptor. I sensed an aura of great evil about him. Find him and we find Mira."

Milish made no attempt to hide her alarm. "We spend too much time in discussion." She whirled to confer with the Kyra, Ainé, who had a linear scar running from the left brow down onto the cheek, like a coup-de-sabre. Words were exchanged between them. Duval's eyes caught a flickering of light, as if some force had activated in the oraculum of the Kyra.

Then, as if in a moment, the Kyra was gone. She had melted away, silently, as if under her cloak of invisibility, into the surrounding forest.

As soon as she was gone, the remaining Shee formed a guard around him. They included the novice, Valéra, who had golden blonde hair fastened with a silver pin, and Muîrne, the stoutest and perhaps most matronly of them, who had white hair, as snowy as an albino, that contrasted markedly with her dark brown, shrewdly assessing eyes.

Under Milish's direction, they led him, still wrapped in the heavy bearskin, through the trees. Their movements, for such gigantic people, were silent, so lithely graceful they might have been great cats. Under their camouflage cloaks, which fell to mid-calf, they wore loose-fitting trousers of an olive green cotton, tied at mid calf over the cross-lacing of leggings and above boots of the same material as the cloaks. The only ornamentation was a clasp of silver upon the right shoulder, which fastened the cloak. Their naked arms were tattooed with a fantastic imagery of animals and foliage.

In the gaps of sky Duval saw that it was not as late as he would have assumed: only mid-afternoon. They emerged onto a gravelly beach upriver of where Duval had been dragged ashore, and here he saw several long canoes that had been beached in a hurry.

These, he assumed, were the vessels that had carried the Shee into the battle zone. They were powerful craft, adzed from whole trunks of cedar, their prows uplifted six feet out of the water, Y-shaped in end section. Sleek in design, they contained packs that Duval realized must belong to the Shee – but the lead canoe also contained a trunk of polished ebony, inlaid with silver, from which Milish refilled her flask of Niyave. Duval could find no trace of the Olhyiu boats, not even of the Temple Ship.

Above the shingle, a series of tracks led away into the forest.

There was more time, as they waited here for word from Ainé, for Duval to study Milish more closely.

Her hair was the lustrous blue-black of Asia. The black strands were parted centrally over her forehead, swept down in careful arcs over her temples, with folds that hid the upper third of her fleshily lobed ears, then swept backward, to be brought together and lifted over her head in a plume of silver filigree at least nine inches high. The plume was kept in place by a heavy clasp of that same antique silver. It was a beautiful creation, encircled at the base by bottle green and copper blue enamelwork of intertwined foliage and blossoms in a sybaritic fantasy that extended halfway up the plume.

"You mentioned Carfon – you talked as if you were expecting me? You know of my quest?"

"Duval – Mage Lord – all of Monisle has been expecting you for a generation."

"Then maybe you can give me some answers to so many questions. Like why the hell am I here? Why me? Why was I chosen?"

"Is it possible that you remember nothing of the quest that was entrusted to you? Are you not the chosen one of the last High Architect of Ossierel, Ussha De Danaan – falsely scorned as the Great Blasphemer?"

Duval shook his head, then fell silent for several moments.

"I don't know what to believe. I can't remember anything of what you are telling me."

Then, suddenly, Milish was holding his face in an embrace of passion. Her eyes roamed his features in what appeared to be wonderment.

"Oh, believe it, Duval! There can be no mistaking the Oraculum of the Holy Trídédana! It is true! You are the hope of an entire world!"

Shaking his head in confusion, there were other questions he would have liked to ask Milish. But this was not the time. Ainé had reappeared out of the gloom of the trees.

"Come quickly!" she ordered.

She led them back into the forest, away from the river and in a new direction, until they arrived at a clearing that had obviously served the main body of Storm Wolves as an encampment. Here, in the filmy light of winter, Duval hung back in amazement at an arcane ritual of warfare.

Two dozen Shee, now led by Ainé, had spread out to encircle a similar number of Storm Wolves, who had assumed a close-knit trapezoidal battle formation. Peering about the clearing, he could see no sign of Mira. Then the chanting began again. It was the Shee who were chanting, a deep-throated battle-hymn, then, suddenly, as if goaded into fighting, the ranks of Storm Wolves appeared to dissolve, the huge legionaries were among the encircling Shee, in a fury of hand-to-hand combat.

Duval had never seen hand-to-hand fighting move with such speed. The Shee too were darting and weaving about him. He saw that flashing green of their sword blades, eerily luminescent. And with every arc and thrust, another body was falling in its cataract of gore. But the battle was not one-sided. There was a maniacal exultancy to the savagery with which the Storm Wolves fought back, glad, it seemed, of this opportunity of killing Shee. Duval saw one of the Shee stagger and fall, the speed of movement of the legionary's blade so swift her head was disarticulated even in the act of falling.

It was brutal and short. Suddenly, with the same lightning change as it had begun, the surviving legionaries had fallen back into the trapezoidal formation again and the Shee were closing ranks to reform the encirclement.

Duval studied the shields of the Storm Wolves. They were long and rectangular, decorated with the same symbol he had seen on the handle of the Preceptor's dagger, a triple looped infinity. The symbol provoked a sense of fright in him: as if it had touched upon some fearful memory that lay locked away within the vaults of his mind. Wiping sweat from his face, he noticed that the shields were curved in their transverse section, and that they appeared to slot together along their long sides to form an impregnable wall. Others carried their shields aloft, creating a defensive dome.

Yet it made Duval wonder why, given that the soldiers equalled the Shee in numbers, they adopted such a defensive posture. Nothing in his brief experience of the Storm Wolves had suggested caution.

Even from this distance, he sensed the same darkness that had recently enveloped him, an overwhelming power of evil. The Preceptor was among them.

"Mira is here, Milish. They are holding her at the heart of the battle formation."

Ainé must also have figured this out. It explained why the Shee were not attacking.

The soldiers were performing another battle strategy, with a harsh, guttural chanting. A smoky emanescence curled from the fissures between the shields and then coalesced over them, to envelop the shield-wall, as if welding them together in a power-charged unity.

The calculation involved in this strange warfare, the rhythms and formalities of it, interested Duval.

The Shee were passing items from one woman to another. Duval glimpsed a jade green glow, like the colour of Ainé's oraculum. It looked as if the Kyra was charging the points of arrows and the blades of swords, touching crystals that were carried on each of the women against her oraculum. For several minutes nothing happened other than a repeat of the ritualistic chanting. Yet the women were tensing as if with a tangible expectancy. Then sporadic fire, with long plumes of white smoke, broke out of the shell of shields, and with the erratic volley the Shee were a blur of movement, dodging the smoking trails.

Whatever weapon the soldiers were using, it passed out through their own defensive shield to streak through the air, trailing a putrescent green glow. He remembered the green fire during the attack at the frozen lake – and more recently in the attack on the river. Observing another volley, there was also a distinct odour coming from the burning missiles, a chancrous smell.

There was a groan, as one of the Shee was hit. In a final defiance, she hurled her sword into the glistening force of the shield wall, but it rebounded where it struck, incapable of penetrating it. There was something crawling over the sword. What appeared to be a living growth of some sort. A horrible glistening material, that crawled and proliferated, as if attempting to devour the living flesh it came into contact with.

Biological weapons?

Even the fallen giantess was being consumed by the same living poison of the legionaries' weapon. It invaded every organ and tissue with horrible speed and malignancy. Duval saw how the charnel green was already glowing in the woman's eyes.

"What's happening, Milish? Why will nothing get through their shields?"

"Such is the power of their malengin."

A malengin: studying the shield wall, he noticed a resemblance to a glassy prism, in the way it refracted the light in a rainbow sheen of colours. It was also distorting or bending the light waves emerging from it, so that the figures wavered beneath it, or seemed distorted, like a view of something under water.

"Quickly, Milish. Explain this malengin."

"The Tyrant uses the enslaved people of the Daemos to plunder the Wastelands to find the malignancy that exists in the dark side of nature. The Preceptor among them has the ability to project it thus."

Even as he was considering this, a glowing fragment hissed between him and Milish, igniting the trunk of the tree behind them and showering them with malodorous smoke. It forced them back, coughing, their eyes watering.

"If this continues, Milish, the Shee will be annihilated."

"If they die, they will die with honour."

Wheeling around, he addressed Ainé through thought alone, from oraculum to oraculum. "If I can breach the malengin, can you attack through the breach while still keeping the girl alive?"

In moments, he found himself looking into the questioning eyes of both Ainé and Milish.

Duval knelt down by the mouldering remains of the dead Shee, while Milish and Ainé stood back, repulsed by the sight and charnel stench of the brightly glowing corruption that still devoured the flesh of the courageous warrior.

"They must be using some type of biological weapon. The livid glow can only derive from plague bacteria that are multiplying within her flesh. The light and the stench are the by-products of their accelerated chemistry."

"We do not understand such terms. Tell us only what we must do."

"It means that there is a logical explanation to this. Maybe we can turn their weaponry against them."

Duval straightened, his eyes meeting those of Ainé. "Can you find me a javelin – shafted with wood but with a good strong point."

Then, handed the javelin, he studied the tip.

The point resembled no substance he was familiar with. It might have been a curious amalgam of bronze and a crystalline substance, a natural stone, like flint. He closed his eyes, focused on the point through the oraculum. He felt his imagination expand. Through the oraculum he sensed an additional ingredient: a spiritual essence within the point. The observation was utterly bizarre to his training as a scientist. No scientist, that he was aware of, had ever tried to measure spirituality. There was a hint here of the very different evolution of two worlds. And he sensed that force, he sensed it so powerfully, he could not be mistaken about its presence.

Was this the charge the Kyra was infusing into their blades?

He recalled the feeling he had had in the presence of the Preceptor: that had also been spiritual, if one of a dark malignancy. As if the Preceptor were some malign priest among the Storm Wolves.

When he spoke, his voice was husky from his own realization: "I believe I can help you to penetrate the wall of force around their shields."

In the dirt, Duval drew a dome, representing the shield wall. "Here," he declared, jabbing his finger into the precise apex, "is both its binding strength and its weakness. It is a little like the keystone in an arch." Under the horrified eyes of Milish and Ainé, Duval dipped the tip of the javelin in the putrefying flesh. Probing it again through the vision of the oraculum, he sensed the dark force that now inhabited the tip, before he overwhelmed that force with a spiritual infusion of his own. The red glow from his oraculum burned intensely to a white heat, to make sure that the plague bacilli no longer lived in the transformed javelin head. He didn't want to harm Mira.

"I believe it will now penetrate their shield wall." He turned his sweat-soaked face toward Ainé. "Cast it carefully, so it impacts precisely at the centre of the dome. Then have your Shee ready for an immediate attack."

He watched as Ainé bent her gigantic frame, then cast the javelin. He heard the screeching sound as it arced through the air, striking the precise point of maximal weakness of the malengin. He saw it explode on impact. A stellate web of brighter green spread over the shield wall. Then the Storm Wolves began to howl. The force of the impact invaded the shields and further, to the arms that were steadying them. The dome of the malengin burst asunder and the powerful frames of the legionaries pitched and tumbled, in torment and panic, over a ground that was already proliferating with that vile green.

Duval had not anticipated the release of their own biological weapon, which must have been thrown down carelessly in their panic. In spite of all of his precautions, Mira was in grave danger. The attacking Shee darted cautiously among them, killing with a deadly efficiency while searching the core before the mutated plague could spread inwards from the perimeter.

Over the ground the web of lividity was still spreading, subtly metamorphosing about its edges, as if the deadly force of the plague weapon were actively mutating. Duval picked his own careful way through the confusion of bodies. He saw many dead enemies but he found no sign of the Preceptor or the girl.

The Shee left the battle zone and began probing the encircling forest.

Milish helped Duval to search for Mira, with fresh snow matting in individual large flakes in her hair.

"Over here!" It was Ainé's voice from some distance away, and Duval hurried toward her.

The evil man was still alive. Without Aine's cry, Duval's nostrils might have led him to him. The deathly luminescence leached into his gibbous features, causing him to shrink back for support against the bole of a great tree.

Hate contorted his face and with one clawlike hand he clutched Mira about her temples. His other hand pressed the black-bladed dagger against her throat.

Duval was astonished and relieved to see that Mira was clear of infection. There was a mystery here but he had no time to ponder it. The cadaveric features suddenly wrinkled with glee, a gurgling obscenity within his throat. A mist of green vapour exuded from his stinking flesh and the foul glow was in his eyes. Dark blood trickled between his gritted teeth, dribbling down onto Mira's head as he clutched her more savagely against his chest. All the while those hate-filled eyes stared deeply into Duval's own, as if daring him to come and rescue her.

The Preceptor's voice was rasping, as if it issued from a throat that was already partially consumed.

"Witches obsequium! Chance has favoured you today but it will not long save you. Stand back! The merest prick of my blade and the insect-spawn dies in torment."

Duval searched the scarlet-veined eyes within that evil face. He spoke grimly, urgently. "Let the child go and we will end your suffering."

The thin man cackled again, that dreadful gurgling. "Decide then which death is dearer to you? Is it to be this insect's, or are you so foolish you would exchange your life for hers?"

"No, Duval!" Ainé had taken a restraining hold of his arm. "Beware the scheming nature of this creature. Though weakened, he retains power beyond your comprehension."

Duval's pulse had risen to a steady fast pattering. How close was the Preceptor to death? The spreading malignancy burned more fiercely by the moment in his tormented flesh. If he could delay the dagger mere seconds longer...!

"How do I know," Duval demanded, "that you will release the girl if I volunteer to take her place?"

"How does he know?" The reply was orgasmic with rancour. "I have no concern to reassure this witches' brat. I...." He paused, as if to gasp with the mere contemplation of it. "I am no more than the instrument of my master's will. Yet for that honour, I would sacrifice an infinity of insects such as this."

Duval used the oraculum to probe the Preceptor's state of mind. Here he discovered no resemblance to the human envy and malice of Snakoil. This was a mind of utter darkness. And the brooding malevolence was not entirely spent. It attacked him back as he entered that mind, strong enough in grim defiance to gain a hold over his will. Duval's limbs were stiffening again in that creeping paralysis.

The Preceptor had anticipated his move. Duval knew that the dagger was extending toward his own throat. Waves of shock reeled through his mind. But even as that skeletal hand lunged forward, he wondered why the Preceptor had not simply killed the girl. There was a puzzle here: a puzzle as baffling as Mira's immunity to the green plague. Even as he thought this he registered furious movement. Faster it seemed than thought itself, he felt his body being pushed aside, and in that twinkling of time his mind was released.

"No!" Duval's shout was a second too late.

In that distracted moment, the Preceptor with blade extended, was pulled violently away from Duval, his body crashing backward against the tree. Still the knuckles enclosing the black-bladed dagger were white with tension. "Infidelus!" that cackling voice now hissed.

Powerful arms encircled the Preceptor from behind. It was Valéra – her arms long enough to encircle the entire bole of the tree and still squeeze the life from the man's throat. But the evil man was not defeated. With a lightning reflex, he turned the dagger about, plunging it repeatedly back at the Shee.

Duval had taken hold of Mira's dress. He pulled her back toward him, his eyes still following the struggle about the Preceptor. He could see the marbled decay in the gibbous face, the eyes aglow with the green death, the poisoned blood that flecked the rictus of teeth.

"Valéra!"

The cry exploded from his throat, but it was too late. Even as the Shee's fierce hold crushed the throat of the Tyrant's priest, Duval saw the sinuous blade thrust to the hilt into Valéra's abdomen.

TWELVE

THE IMMORTALITY OF THE SHEE

A FIRE OF BRUSHWOOD flickered by the head of the dying Valéra, as Ainé and Muîrne sat cross-legged on either side of their wounded companion, under a rough bower of pine branches. The remaining Shee had withdrawn to the forest, leaving these two to tend her through the night. The only concession to the presence of Milish was the acceptance of Niyave from her hands, yet even this they insisted on administering themselves in the privacy of the bower.

It had been snowing gently all night, and dawn of the following day broke with a violaceous sky, heavy with foreboding.

During the intervals when Muîrne left the sickbed to fetch more brushwood, Duval caught glimpses of Ainé, her cloak enfolding her sagging shoulders, her great frame rocking slowly, with the litany of her nightlong lament.

His boots, undercoat and greatcoat had been found at the main encampment of the Storm Wolves and the sleepless night had allowed him to dry them before a well-banked fire. Putting them back on, he was thankful for the anticipation of Turkaya, whose waxing had kept the boots supple in spite of their soaking. With the dawn, Milish arrived by the fireside to break-fast with him and Mira and then she made a signal to draw him away from the scene of tragedy.

"There is a great deal I still don't understand," he shook his head at her as they were walking into the pine-woods. "Other Shee have died – and there was less grieving over them. And Valéra's condition – surely more could have been done. You and I – we each have knowledge that might help her. We could help to ease her suffering."

"There is a deeper injury to Valéra than a mortal wound, even from the blade of the Storm Wolves." The eyes of the Ambassador caught Duval's and he saw in them some additional grief he did not understand. "There are mysteries to the death of a Shee that are best left to their own ministrations."

Duval watched Milish reach out to fondle the head of the girl, Mira. He hadn't been aware that Mira was following in their footsteps, her presence had been so silent. Yet here she was, another mystery to him, beautiful – almost etiolated, like a lovely flower grown weak and pale because it had been cut off for too long from the life-giving sun. Yet for all of her delicacy, Mira had resisted contamination with the living poison. Duval wondered how she had survived such close contact with the infected Preceptor. He studied Mira's eyes, the way they moved in that solemn, thoughtful way from Milish to himself, recovered already it seemed from the near-drowning and the terror of her captivity. After a tender hug, Milish ushered Mira back, ostensibly to keep watch over the activities of the Shee, but Duval assumed that they might talk in greater depth alone. Watching her reluctant departure, the grace with which she appeared almost to float over the snow-dappled forest floor, he was reminded of that fantastic vision she had communicated as she was drowning – as if, for the briefest of moments, he had glimpsed the mysteries of the cosmos.

Milish had to shake his shoulder, to bring him back to full attention.

"The sacrifice has been great, nevertheless all that has happened has been worthwhile. Be mindful always of how precious she is. Oh, Duval – promise me that you will protect her." Her fingers brushed his brow to either side of the triangular crystal, a supplicatory gesture, yet so intense was the look that accompanied it he was taken by surprise.

So Milish felt it too, that aura of wonder about the girl! Duval shook his head, returning to the suffering of Valéra.

"These mysteries you talked about in relation to the Shee – are they so important that we can't even try to help Valéra?"

She hung her head, walking hurriedly onward, as if deliberately leading him still further from the scene of lamentation. They emerged from the trees into the smaller battle arena, where the bodies of seven or eight Storm Wolves still lay in the scatter of their deaths, their eyes burnt white with cataracts and their spilled blood still frozen to the bitter ground. Only now did he remember Snakoil. He scanned the ground for his body but he did not find it. He found the leather thongs that had bound the traitor's feet, but they were neatly cut, as if manoeuvred against the edge of a fallen blade.

How likely was it that the spiteful man, exhausted and so grotesquely maimed, would have survived the night in this bitter landscape?

Duval shook his head without knowing the answer. In the drama of Valéra's nightlong suffering, he hadn't given a thought to Snakoil - or the Storm Wolves. But now found himself gazing around at the horror of his own rage.

The larger group, whose bodies had fallen close to the bower where Valéra lay wounded, had been unsuitable for close examination. The plague bacilli had continued to feast upon their shrivelling flesh until even the bones were consumed. But this smaller group of soldiers had died from a fury Duval did not want to think about. Now, in the light of dawn, he wanted to take a closer look at their bodies.

It was difficult work since their limbs were stiffened by *rigor mortis* and their armour was welded to their flesh by the cold. Some of their insignia, upon epaulettes and over the right breast of the matte-black chest armour of the Centurion, must signify military rank. On every helmet, constructed of that same matte-black metal, he found the malevolent symbol of the triple infinity.

"What does this mean, Milish?" he asked the Ambassador, who, standing always to one side with that regal bearing, watched him as closely as he studied the dead enemy.

"It is the symbol of the Tyrant. Every foul division of his army of occupation – aptly named the Death Legion – wear this accursed mark. Though what subtlety it might mean in his perverted reasoning, I do not know."

Bending over the Centurion's body, he examined the face he had exposed after removing the helmet. Duval withdrew in shock.

The black fur was not a mask. Although most of the fur had been scorched, there was enough of it intact, on the trunk and limbs, to confirm that the man's whole body had been covered in that thick pelt. Other than the fact it was black rather than white, the fur over the torso was so luxuriant he might have been inspecting the winter pelt of a real wolf.

His fingertips found a heavy crest running down the centre of the skull from front to back and ridges over the eyes that were as robust as you might find on a gorilla. But these were intelligent humans, not primitives. The prominent bony ridges were the anchor areas for massive muscles. Even in death there was an unrelenting fierceness about the eyes of the Centurion.

He said nothing, gazing down in shock.

"Such is the tragedy," Milish spoke softly. "The Tyrant does not permit such unfortunates to be reared as any normal child might be, in family or village. The soldiery are selectively culled from the Daemos."

"Who are these Daemos?"

"There are the many strange and barbarous peoples who populate the vast regions of Wastelands across the Eastern Ocean. From a time beyond written history the Tyrant's over-lords have harvested these people as a breeder might select dogs – or wolves."

Climbing back onto his feet, Duval remained silent for several moments. What kind of world was this? A world, it seemed, in which strange beings and even stranger forces, spiritual forces, whether for good or evil, were accepted as normal. It had begun to snow again, hard dry flakes, as large as petals. There was a new chill in the air that made Duval shiver.

"Why does the Tyrant do these monstrous things? Why has he fought this war with you for a thousand years? What interest could he possibly have with my world?"

"I do not have the wisdom of a High Architect." Milish's voice was tired, but her eyes belied it as they returned his gaze. "Yet it seems to me that in the wonder of existence there is dark and there is light. In those long ages following the creation, all manner of choices might have been made. The impulse that attracted one spirit toward the light might have led another to a darker, more desperate path?" She hesitated, shook her head. "The Tyrant has escaped the bonds of natural control. Has he not lived for a thousand years – and perhaps a great deal longer even than that! Surely he has ways unfamiliar to the probe of reason. Speak to Ainé of this, if you wish to learn more of it. But choose your moment carefully, for the Kyra does not care to be reminded of her trials as a child in the great arena of Ghork-Mega."

"What you imply is hard for me to believe!"

"Yet it is true that for all of written history on Tír, every advance in truth and understanding on Monisle has been opposed in war and subterfuge by the Tyrant and his malice. Even this last thousand-year war is just the most recent of many. Mine is a world that has never known peace."

She nodded toward the dead legionaries. "And through these troubled histories, their people have been no more than the pawns of his will." Then she hesitated before she asked him, bitterly. "Do you pity them now?"

Duval looked around at the bizarre corpses, still shaking his head in disbelief. Of course there was a second, unasked, question in her eyes: how had he killed them? But she did not put voice to this. Sensing perhaps that he didn't wish to talk of it. The truth was he didn't even want to think about it. There would come a time when he would have to think about it – but not yet. That flicker of alarm moved in his bowels again. But there was no opportunity to reflect upon it because Mira had come running:

"Come quickly, Believer. The Kyra, Ainé, is calling for you."

They hurried back to the clearing, where Ainé stood outside the bower, her downcast face evidence enough of Valéra's progress.

"My sister-in-arms is dying," she stated bluntly. Then, lifting her eyes to look directly into Duval's own, she added tersely. "I have tormented myself through wondering why you, a man and from another world, should be granted the power of the oraculum of the Trídédana. Why so — unless, through a grace that I, a mere warrior, am not given to understand — " She checked herself, inhaled deeply. "Were you not chosen by the De Danaan herself, a sisterly lineage close in blood to my own? Yet in asking assistance of you, what I ask I dread, for it is anathema to my race."

Then, her eyes sweeping across to the snow-encrusted bower, where Valéra lay dying, she continued. "I know that it is beyond any hope to save Valéra, but you might yet grant her peace by saving the immortality of her lineage."

Duval turned in amazement toward Milish, who watched him from a few yards away, her eyes clouded in her anxious face.

Looking back once more into the direct gaze of the Kyra, he said simply, "Valéra took the wound that was intended for me."

He entered the oval enclosure of the snow-encrusted bower, where the embers of the overnight fire still burned, the flame scented with ferns and other potions. Valéra tossed in a stupor on her bed of rushes. Her beautiful hair had been freed in a sweat-soaked nimbus about her face and the blue eyes that had once smiled at him now stared blindly out of their orbits.

"I need to examine her wound," he spoke quietly, though waiting for permission from the Kyra before proceeding.

For a moment resentment darkened the face of Ainé, an acknowledgment of the blasphemy she was permitting. Then, with a heavy sigh, she took her place opposite Muîrne, both Shee exchanging heavy-lidded glances. "You must inspect the wound as you see fit and then you will understand the nature of our despair."

Before he removed the dressing from the abdominal wound, he asked Ainé if Mira could also attend the examination.

"I doubt, Duval, that even you with all of your powers realize how profoundly Mira is already in attendance." Ainé closed her eyes as she replied, and then, with her great head fallen and her arms folded about her chest, she resigned herself to the profanity. Duval hoped that somebody else was also in attendance: the greatest healer of all, whose spirit had been incorporated into his own. Milish took her place by Valéra's fevered brow and Mira stood just inside the entrance. Then, gently, he lifted aside the packing cloths to examine her wounds.

There were several defensive wounds to her arms, which he ignored. The mortal wound was to the right of her abdomen, low down, barely above the pelvic bone.

It was almost a foot long, ragged and livid about its edges. He had seen the black and twisted blade plunge to its hilt so he knew it would prove deep. The rank odour of poisoned flesh pervaded the enclosed space. Valéra's abdomen close to the wound was swollen and festering. Prising the edges slightly apart, and eliciting a tormented moan, Duval could not see into the still darker inner cavity. But inserting his fingers, he could feel how the dagger had lacerated everywhere as it had penetrated. The muscles and delicate membranes that lined the pelvic cavity had been cut open, internal organs punctured. Although the attacking blade had struck deep and hacked wide, yet the attentions of Muîrne had staunched the bleeding. It was not until Duval pressed his fingers deeper still into the ravaged flesh that he encountered the shock of the venom that had been implanted there.

"My God!" he hissed in agony.

An icy cold froze his fingers, a cold deeper than any he had experienced even in the bitter world of his arrival in the blizzard-swept mountains.

The cold gnawed into the marrow of his bones. The physical shock of pain caused him to wrench his hand from the wound and to stagger back, clutching fingers that were already a livid purple.

"Milish?"

"The blade of a Preceptor carries more than just a physical poison. It is infused with the malice of the Tyrant's own darkness. The Preceptor discharged the evil of his life force through that debased weapon before he died."

Duval clenched his teeth against the agony that was ascending into his wrist from the contaminated fingers. He tottered back against the makeshift wall, feeling the structure sway. He heard the patter of the snow over its exterior, the drip-drip of meltwater within its walls, saw the anguish in the faces of Ainé and Muîrne, and the crestfallen look of Milish. The only eyes that still regarded him calmly were those in the pallid face of Mira. "The True Believer must use the oraculum."

Mira was right. But how could he relax his mind sufficiently when the bones of his fingers screamed in torment? *Don't think about your own pain. Think of Valéra – how she has suffered all through the night!* He remembered London. The agony of his own wound. He remembered Granny Ddhu. How the healing had taken place. Forcing his fingers back into the wound, he pushed them deeper than before, as deep as they would go. Then a more profound sorrow swept over him, a horror that shocked his unprepared mind. Valéra was pregnant.

Though Duval was puzzled about the pregnancy, the pregnancy itself was now obvious – it was the point of everything.

Her giant frame had concealed the gravid womb, which lay hidden in the broad bowl of her pelvis. Valéra's womb was swollen to full term with the curled-up burden of what Duval instinctively knew to be a daughter. This was the focus of Valéra's torment and it was the grief that had so demoralized Ainé and Muîrne.

Putting aside his own agony, and the questions he might have asked about the pregnancy itself, Duval focused upon the threat to Valéra's baby. The point of the Preceptor's blade had not caused such an assault randomly, but in a pattern of search. The blade had gone close to penetrating the muscular wall of the womb. Even now the pulsations of the great arteries were erratic under the deadly assault of the poison, as the heart of the Shee faltered. Duval withdrew his hand and he almost fell to his knees by the sickbed.

Milish took hold of his shoulder, an anguished look in her eyes.

Tearing himself from the diplomat's hold, Duval blundered out of the bower and into a gathering storm. Icy snow blinded his eyes, the bitter wind flayed his skin, like a swarm of stinging wasps. He searched in the fury of the storm for the memory of how he might help the dying Shee. His face was turned toward the north. Hunching forward against the force of the storm, he saw himself back in the tempest when confronting the elemental forces that buffeted the stone circle. Again, with great urgency, he called out her name.

"Granny Ddhu!"

The sound was whipped from his lips by the spite of the wind.

He stood up erect against the driving snow, his head fallen, his arms adrift by his side, with his hands thrown open.

He was so exhausted with his own fever, and the cold was so bitter, that within moments his mind was wandering. It seemed as if in a dream he had abandoned the snowy landscape to find himself standing in a flat wilderness, devoid of life or contour, that stretched to the horizon in every direction. A presence hovered before him. Though the presence assumed a human form, it remained as insubstantial as a reflection upon a dancing sea, glimmering and sparkling, as if brought to existence in the wonder of its own awareness.

"What are you?"

I am not the one you call yet I might have the answers you seek.

The voice was calm, gentle, but he heard it with the utmost clarity. He hesitated, peering into the region where eyes might be. "I'm tired of riddles. I need more explanation than anybody appears willing or able to give me."

You must continue to seek the truth. In such knowledge lies the answer to your quest.

"Where is this place?"

It is all places and all times and therefore nowhere and time-less. To some it does not exist while to others it is the only reason for existing. But take care – for those of good heart are not the only True Believers.

In exasperation he called out: "What does that expression mean? What is a True Believer?"

One who may enter here.

"Why in hell won't you answer my questions! I need to understand where this quest is leading me. I need to understand how I got here."

You ask too much in this place and this time. Such under-standing awaits you at Carfon.

"Carfon – *Carfon!* Everything always seems to point to Carfon!"

No anger on his part seemed capable of fracturing the calm of that answering voice. *Be patient in your search for answers. These are dangerous times. The understanding you seek is power unlimited. In Carfon it stands at the very Gates of Eternity.*

"What are you talking about? What is the nature of this power unlimited?"

I warn you again. Do not question such things in this un-guarded moment. It is enough that it holds all truths, including the truth of Dromenon.

"Dromenon?"

Here you stand upon its exalted plane. You are not entirely un-familiar with it, for it was through Dromenon that you entered Tír from Earth.

He seized upon this. "What are you saying? Are you saying that I can return to Earth? I can use this – this Dromenon – to go back to my world?"

Your will is your blade, though you must discover through trial how best to wield it.

Duval hesitated, considering this. When he spoke again, he did so thoughtfully: "What is the importance of this place you call Dromenon to the Shee, Valéra?"

She knows it as Cuan na Hanam, *which is the Harbour of Souls. At this moment she lies at its* Doras Vawish, *which is the portal of death.*

"Does that mean that Valéra must die? That nothing can save her?"

Silence only in answer.

Then it seemed that something in his own grief triggered the metamorphosis: the being became brilliantly incandescent so that it flooded his senses with wonder, as though he had passed through a universal window to witness the birth of a star.

"Are you in some way linked to the child, Mira?"

The reply, which followed after a momentary pause, appeared to enter his consciousness through all of his senses, like a symphony of sound, light, feeling, taste, and touch: *I am a part of she, as she is part of me. She is the* Léanov Fashakk, *the Heralded One. Yet I perceive that one mystery is merely replaced by another in your mind. So I will give you a guide to what you seek. All wisdom is contained within the* Fáil. *Yet such wisdom is perilous beyond your understanding.*

For a moment, Duval sensed how the storm seemed to heighten round them, as the voice continued: *Be warned, therefore! Prepare yourself well before you confront such power – if you survive even to your journey's end.*

While Duval's mind reeled once more with the perplexity of this communication, the being metamorphosed to the human figure it had first adopted, though the voice echoed as if it had divided into many voices within his mind. *The future is shrouded in uncertainty. The dark seed of chaos, long dormant, has come into flower.*

"Don't confuse me with any more riddles. If you care at all, help me to understand Valéra's sickness so I can save her child."

In a moment the spirit of the fair-haired Shee stood before him. She appeared without the terrible wound, her form transparent, a pale shimmering, barely visible in the light of the glowing luminosity of the first presence. Then, Duval noticed that what he was seeing was not a single figure but two. Before the towering shape of Valéra was a much smaller body, so slender and delicate as to be almost invisible, yet also standing quite still, no higher than her knees. The two shapes seemed almost to mingle as if identical in spirit, as Valéra cradled her unborn child.

Duval's voice was deepened by emotion. "Valéra's daughter is born from her alone? There is no father, only the Shee as mother?"

She is, in her language, the Inion-Baha, *which is the sister-child of Valéra's lineage. Thus do you witness the mystery of* Neevrashvahar, *which you would call her immortality.*

The full realization of Ainé's words was clear now to Duval. And it was astonishing.

The Shee were born not through the blending of paternal and maternal genes but through parthenogenesis – the cloning of their mother's egg alone. It presupposed an entirely matrilinear line, every mother replaced by her perfectly identical daughter. A sister-mother gave birth to a sister-child. Although it conferred an absolute resistance to change, yet it was truly a form of immortality.

It was little wonder that the sharing of such knowledge was considered blasphemy by Ainé and her race.

In spite of the revelation, the poison still attacked the vital organs of the mother in its efforts to kill her daughter. And brave Valéra, who had withstood the blood-borne venom all night long, was approaching death.

Groaning with the pain of another transformation, he found himself back within the snowy landscape. The storm had heightened, as if the dark forces that opposed him fulminated against his intention. Duval was so blinded by the snow and wind he found it difficult to see his hand before his eyes, but he could struggle through it, feeling his way through the oraculum. *Your will is your blade....* He hoped he understood what that meant.

Though the poison had attacked him with even greater malignancy than when he was wounded in London, he was immune to it, thanks to the previous intercession of Granny Ddhu. His body must have developed its own immunity – perhaps a kind of spiritual immunity.

He already had a plan of what he must do. He was only mildly surprised when a small hand grasped his and he was aware that Mira was beside him. In more ways than one, Mira's slight form was his anchor. She was holding something in her other hand, as if she too had forecast his need. She had braved the fury of the storm to collect it for him and she gave it to him, without ceremony, on his return. Duval felt it pressed into his hand, a coil of hollow reed, as delicate as the finest glass, yet as supple as the wind.

In the eye of the storm, he activated the oraculum. He felt the healing power of Granny Ddhu invade his arms at the same time he saw flickering motes of starlight about the head of the girl. He touched Mira's hand, a momentary gesture of affection, already smiling to hear the gravelly voice berate him in his mind, piercing through the howling of the elements. *Duuuvaaalll aaassskkks – yeeesss! Duuuvaaalll seeesss – yeeesss!*

Struggling back through the entrance of the bower, he stripped and cut back the reed so it became a tube about eighteen inches long. Under the watchful eyes of Mira, he sucked a thin stream of Niyave through it, to lubricate its inner walls and prevent the blood from clotting within it. Then, shaping the ends into sharp bevels, and kneeling by the arm of the dying Shee, he used a dagger to cut a small slit in the vein of his left arm and inserted one tip of the reed into the vein. For a second or two, he watched his blood engorge the reed and then trickle onto the ground. Next he cut a similar slit in a vein in the arm of the Shee and he thrust the pumping end of the reed deep within it.

Now, as Ainé averted her face at the profanity and as the fretful Milish watched in amazement, his blood coursed into the circulation of the dying Shee.

Valéra's need was great and Duval gave generously of his blood. His heart pumped the precious gift of immunity into her, so that, minute by minute, he weakened and she strengthened. But Valéra's condition was too advanced for any hope of a cure and by degrees even Duval drifted into a physical stupor so that he was unaware of the moment when Milish, alarmed at his pallor and thready pulse, tore away the blood-darkened reed that connected him still to Valéra's arm. Then they lay side by side, on the bed of sweat-soaked rushes, covered by the cloaks of Ainé and Muîrne, while Milish, frantic with worry, busied herself with administering the Niyave.

Duval had only a vague awareness of the two days he lay in stupor, though his memory retained the unmistakable cry of a newborn baby, deeper and more powerful than any he had heard on Earth.

The only other memory he would recall was the litany of lamentation that made him aware that the tragedy of death had accompanied the first anguished beat of a newborn heart within that bower, buffeted and tossed by the fury of gale and snow.

THIRTEEN

BLOOD ON THE GRASS

Duval lay in an exhausted stupor, in which he was back as the fourteen-year-old boy in Clonmel, sharing the truck journey with his friends. He heard the sound of its engine droning through the twisting lanes, the crash of Sean's inexpert changing through the grinding gears.

But now, hurry as they might toward the third and last of the Three Sisters – the Barrow in its upper waters between Carlow and High Athy – the shadow stalked them, never losing them. The quiet lanes seemed more lonely than secure.

In the deepening shadows of late afternoon, Sean pulled to a halt over a slope of marshy ground and scattered scrub. The road and river had parted and they were dismayed at the distance between them and the distant river down a sloping field. Penny, with that light of determination in her eyes, snatched the third container from the back of the truck. Sean needed to sit in the truck with the engine running. A pensive Liam was already standing on the cab roof. Sean's brow was contracted into a worried frown as he pressed the spear of Lug into Alan's hands.

"After her then, ya amadawn!"

Penny was already part way down the slope, in a loping stride. He had to break into a run to catch up with her, using the fresh-smelling wooden shaft of the spear here and there as a prop against the boggy ground. The slope levelled onto a flood plain of clinging mud, with fouled rushes and giant weeds. Penny had to pick her way carefully now, doing her best to keep to the firmer ground. Alan saw how her left hand gripped her talisman so the knuckles showed white, while she used the empty container in places to stop herself falling into the mud.

Entering the dense shrub of pussy willow and overgrown oaks and alders by the riverside, Alan was startled by the brooding silence. Other than the merest whispering of the water over slimy stones, there was none of the chatter of nature. No birds declared their territory here, or pecked at the seed-heads among the grasses. As then, deep in the shadows, Penny slithered down a final slight slope to reach out with her long arm and force the neck into the black water, Alan saw in the foliage above her an empty nest that had once been home to a family of wagtails.

The bowl of the nest was broken. The ruined nest was littered with feathers.

With a prickling flush about his face and neck, Alan noticed other small clusters of feathers still attached to some fragments of wing and splinter of bone, scattered about the ground close to his feet.

Blood on the ground.

A stab of panic transfixed his heart. His lungs seemed waterlogged.

He was back again, searching for Billy Foran in the thick coppice of bamboo at Saint Patrick's Well. He could hear the screaming. He knew it was Billy's voice, Billy who had wanted to join their gang, but they had thought it too dangerous. And Billy had followed them. He had got lost in the thick coppice and fear had overtaken his senses.

Now, with the dread of knowing, Alan's eyes lifted to the shadows between the trees.

The hooded figure was only yards away and stiller than the stones. Its eyes were fixed on Penny. Those eyes had the un-blinking stare of a pike. He saw with a horrible clarity the cold wavering discs of quicksilver that were the irises, the imperfect pupils, black without reflection, opening on a pitiless void.

With a whisper as hoarse as a rattle, he moaned, "Oh, Penny! Don't look up. Just pick up the container and hand it to me. Then run!"

But the embankment was much harder to climb up than it had been to slither down. There was no time to place their feet and they sank to-mid calf in the clinging mud. Penny moved faster than he could, weighed down with the water-filled container.

With mounting dread, he watched the long-limbed Penny extend her lead on him, a third of the way up the field already, while, twisting and turning, jabbing at the foul ground with the shaft of the spear, he struggled to follow her.

"Go on – warn the others!" he shouted, his voice high-pitched, almost a shriek. "I'll delay it with the spear."

He had reached about midslope. From what seemed a long way above him he could hear the shouts of Liam and Sean, the screams of Kate and Mo, willing him faster. He felt the mantle of suffocating darkness close about him. He could run no further. He stopped and wheeled about him, hoping he was wrong, hoping it had just been a trick of his overheated imagination. But it had not been his imagination. The eyes were close, gloating in their evil. Though he jabbed at them with the spear, his heart seemed to stop and he felt his legs buckle under him.

In moments the darkness was lapping about him. The eyes were ten feet above him, louring over him.

"Come on, Alan!" Penny had come back for him. She was pulling violently at his arm. "The spear alone will do nothing to stop it."

What did Penny know?

In a flash of insight, Alan remembered how much time Penny had spent that summer at the sawmill with Sean… with Sean and Pádraig, his druid father.

Now Penny, with her eyes squeezed tight, was holding her talisman aloft, and Alan could see it had been carved into a female figure, with three heads. He heard her strange incantations. The monstrous presence seemed to recoil a little, the pike eyes wavering as if they had lost some of their substance.

"Now run, you idiot! Run till your heart bursts!"

In that strange suspension of time and distance, the slope, with its boggy ground, became a treadmill of pounding heart and rasping breath. A red mist invaded his eyes. His feet sunk in the ground and tore themselves free in a wild desperation. With the spear tearing at the ground ahead of him, his flailing legs were clockwork extensions of his terror. Yet, though it howled and screamed about them, the foul mantle held back a little, as if less certain of itself. And then he felt Sean take the container from his hand. Sean on one side and Liam on the other, they were pulling him over the top of the field, onto the dirt road.

Then they were in the back of the truck and the engine was rattling.

"Nassty – *nassty!* We hates ol' fish-eyes – yesss, my precious. Nassty ol' fissh-eyes, yesss!"

Liam's Gollum voice, croaking, "Slievenamon!" Liam's face grinning sickly at him, his arm resting on the third container, held in the space between him and the ashen-faced Maureen.

A hand was shaking him out of the dream. A voice he did not recognize, was calling to him.

"Slievenamon… *Slievenamon…*" he muttered, his hand reaching out, clutching, as his mind clutched at the fading memory, desperate to stay there with the only friends he had ever known in his young life.

For a time after Milish's hand had shaken him awake, he still did not know where he was, in what world or reality. The memory of Clonmel was so strong, so powerful – it felt as if he were abandoning his friends at that moment of terrible danger. He heard Milish's voice continuing to talk to him, he heard her reassuring words. He could smell the river. A different river, in an alien world. He was in one of the great canoes of the Shee. He could hear the soft splash of the oars cutting through the water.…

It was in a distracted mood that he watched the steady rhythm of the arms of Ainé and her companions, as the canoe carried them southward, leading the others down the ink black waters of the Tshis Cole River.

Snow still gusted from the darkness overhead and nobody spoke again for many a mile, aware of the danger of spies on either bank.

During those long hours of silence, Duval remembered with sadness the fair-haired Shee who had saved his life. He saw again the great funeral pyre, with its orange flame, as it had engulfed Valéra and her dead companions, their heads positioned so that they faced southwest, across the great landmass of Monisle toward their ancestral home in the Guhttan mountains. And now, in this same canoe, Muîrne cradled the sleeping crescent of the sister-child, so startlingly reminiscent of her mother, with the first wispy tresses of flaxen hair and the eyes a more summery blue than the brightest flag irises.

So hope had been born out of despair in this strange and frightening world.

At daybreak, when they pulled in the canoes and rested, he had a little time to talk with Milish. He learnt that only noviciates among the Shee carried their daughters in the womb. The mature warriors, such as Muîrne, had long ago given birth. The young Shee were taken back to the Guhttan Mountains, to be schooled in their history and trained in arms.

Duval wondered if Ainé too had a daughter, back in the Guhttan Mountains. But Milish seemed to avoid talking about this. In the Kyra's brooding silence Duval now sensed a tragic secret, although he thought better than to enquire further.

Still physically weakened by his torture and blood loss, Duval felt a growing apprehension. He still wondered what had really happened in Clonmel, as he lay down to get some sleep. But even his dreams were laden with foreboding so that he woke frequently, fighting shadows.

Then on the third night, the southern sky was increasingly aglow – the reflection of the night lamps of Isscan.

A few hours before dawn, as they pulled the canoes under the shadows of some riverside trees, Milish told him the history of the city states of Monisle and that of Isscan in particular, this great inland port and market centre from the days when it was a walled city of ancient tradition. But a shake of her head and the fall of her eyes suggested that things had changed since the coming of the Death Legion. As they whispered together, Ainé and Muîrne were casting a roof of pine branches over an already shadowed hollow, so that they could sleep a few hours before entering the city.

Duval felt guilty about the fact that he concealed from Milish the real focus of his thoughts and hopes. He didn't tell her about the warning of Snakoil. No more did he mention talking around the fireside with Kemtuk, or the Shaman's belief that a great mage lived here: a mage more ancient than any other and whose art could probe the labyrinths of the mind. The Shaman had called him the Mage of Dreams.

FOURTEEN

ISSCAN

A S THE PARTY of three emerged from their hiding place, disguised as a merchant woman with her male and child servants, Milish concealed her worries with a jaunty step. Duval, looking the part with his soiled and tattered great-coat, followed with Mira, a discreet pace or two behind her. For many a mile they walked through farm lanes, surrounded by winter pasture. They passed few people at this early hour and those they saw ignored them, as if it were prudent to avoid strangers. But one farmer, a bald-headed man, leaned on a wall of unmasoned stone and watched them pass, his expression surly and suspicious.

Milish wished him good morning, without even a momentary pause in her step.

Once past the man, however, she fell back abreast of Duval to murmur: "A farmer with the face of a townsman – if I am not mistaken, we have encountered the first spy of the Death Legion."

Why, Duval now wondered, had the Death Legion not destroyed Isscan? Having witnessed their brutality, it could only mean that the city was useful to them. The Storm Wolves were only a minority of the main army of Death Legion in continental Monisle, which in Ainé's reckoning numbered two million. An army that size must need its belly fed. And these farms would provide an important source of grain and meat.

The ramshackle outer city gathered itself about them as they came near, the dispersed farmsteads condensing into villages –

pits of gossip, as Milish took care to warn him – then dirt-lined streets, their meanderings more the result of organic growth than any architect's quill.

Duval felt oppressed by these vast slum-warrens, devoid of clean water or sanitation, where desperation bred greed, cruelty, and disease.

There was no longer any possibility of being ignored. Sharp eyes in unwashed faces watched them at every step. More intrusive still were the outstretched hands of beggars, the sight of deliberately blinded and maimed children.

They had to pass a gauntlet of offerings, unwholesome sweetmeats and alcoholic drinks, trinkets, often gaudy and increasingly vulgar. In one section, where the proliferating shanties hung back in the shadow of the massive city walls, the offerings were lubriciously obscene. Here, in the frames of rickety doorways, the most perverse of sexual fantasies were openly advertised. Sadistic deviations of pain and pleasure and orgiastic cavortings, regardless of age or gender, were enacted before their eyes.

"Stop and indulge your wildest dreams!" a man with gold-capped teeth wheedled, running among and about them. "What could be more tasty than these fruits of the secret passions?"

"None, I grant you." Milish smiled at his obscene play-acting and sly grimacing. "And perhaps we shall have time to dally after our business is done."

Most dispiriting of all, in the open air of the poorest alleys the vilest activities were paraded before them on the despoiled snow. The naked and bleeding displays were so shocking, Duval struck out at the clawing hands, or the beckoning fingers, but Milish, with a squeeze of his arm, maintained her calm. "Hurry – always hurry!" was her whispered insistence. Despite the most vile or debased appeals, she showed not the slightest irritation or displeasure.

Then they arrived at the most sickening sight of all: the miserable faces of children for sale into slavery – or worse.

Mira trembled with terror at every step through this distressing gauntlet, with so many ravenous eyes ogling her unspoiled face and elfin figure. The pervasive wickedness was so unsettling that Duval found himself thinking back to a few hours earlier and to memories of innocence.

It had been a curious moment, as the canoe was being hidden, when he had noticed a subtlety on the part of Ainé, the merest touch upon the brow of Valéra's baby. But during that momentary caress the oraculum in Ainé's forehead had pulsed, a single intense throb from deep within the matrix.

What had it meant?

As they had made final preparations for this journey, Duval had not been able to resist curious glances at Muîrne. What clandestine role did this quiet older Shee play?

In this most discreet of warriors, he had noticed a maternal concern for Valéra's baby. How strange it now seemed that Valéra had not died. She was already reborn. In those final minutes of preparation, he had seen no evidence of anyone other than Muîrne tending the sister-child. In particular he hadn't seen anybody feed her. Yet there were no signs of hunger in that innocent face, with its wisps of golden curls. It seemed that Muîrne might even be breast-feeding the infant.

His present ruminations were interrupted by Milish, who was whispering last-minute advice to Duval as they neared the gates.

"Take care, Duval. Isscan holds many perils. The occupation has encouraged abominable practices. They have already erected one of their accursed arenas within the city walls. We have no desire to become the entertainment."

Before setting out, Milish had encouraged Duval to wear a broad-brimmed yokel's hat, which Mira had woven for him out of reeds. "Even if your face isn't known, the oraculum is too easy a beacon. You must keep both your face and brow well shaded."

No amount of disguise would conceal the stature of the Shee so it had been decided that they could not accompany them into the city. The Kyra was far from happy about this. Furious debate had taken place during the hours of darkness until they had arrived at an uncomfortable compromise. Should the need prove desperate they had agreed a meeting place: the old harbour under the city walls. Here, provided the Olhyiu had sufficient of their boats in working order, an escape downstream lay open to them.

Now, walking in the shadow of the walls, as they were approaching the confluence of two great rivers, Duval was astonished by the architecture. Masoned from huge blocks of granite, the walls towered a hundred feet high on their aprons, and another twenty feet where hexagonal towers buttressed their angles. The ramparts sloped in from their base to about two thirds of their ascent, after which the summits cantilevered out again to form a hanging collar that would have made attack by scaling virtually impossible.

Their circumference was awesome. Within its walls, Isscan was greater in area than any medieval walled capital that Duval could remember from Earth's history. It would have required a vast army to defend, or encircle, it. Then again, he saw no evidence of a breach – so he had to assume that the city had been captured by more stealthy means.

In the distance, unapproachable by road from this northern direction, he glimpsed the masts and cranes that marked the docks. The North Gate, which had once pierced the walls, had been torn from its hinges so that the shanties, stalls and booths abutted against the massive portals themselves, with their sculpted coat of arms and foliate decoration. Approaching them, Duval made out two sheaves of corn crossed and a fish leaping over the balances that symbolized its once proud trading status.

It was strange that no soldiery guarded this northern entrance.

Once inside, the lanes were carpeted by a thick settling of dung, wetted to a foul effluvium by snow. This was churned to spray by the traffic of carts pulled by short, stout ponies, their passage spattering the walls about them. Other riders, on grander horses, wore greatcoats of velvet, embroidered in stitching of gold and silver with geometrical patterns. The farmers had their horses and flat-bottomed carts, loaded with provisions to sell in the markets.

Here was a bustle Duval felt more comfortable with.

Children went running and shrieking. Men and women jostled one another, warmly wrapped in long coats, or dresses, that reached to their laced leather boots. It was like peering into a well of history.

In some of the side-alleys the houses overhung the pavements, like Tudor shambles, the windows oak-mullioned and glazed with leaded panes of different patterns, diamond or squared, oblong or naturalistic. It was the first time that Duval had seen glazed windows in this world. The panes were distorted with dimples or bull's eyes, suggesting they were hand poured. And between the alleyways he saw charnel houses and brothels. At every corner he found a multitude of beggars, their dishevelled forms caked in mud.

In Isscan every day was a market day, so that despite the snow and the cold there was a bustle of activity, with music, entertainers, hawkers, and peddlers.

Open stalls were selling a variety of vegetables and bloody joints of butchered meat. In one cobbled area, where heat blasted their eyes from an open hearth, an entire pig carcass was being turned on a spit. The scent of burning wood mingled with the smell of the roast meat, with glowing braziers reflected in the red cheeks of the men and women who tended them. Some of the braziers had griddles over them, where they cooked flat pancakes of corn. Others served soup in chunky bowls, so hot they had to be held in straw mats.

All three of them were hungry and the savoury smells made their mouths water.

A boy with a running nose ran beside them, pestering them to buy the carcasses of small birds, roasted on sticks. In response to Milish's refusal, he cursed them, screeching obscenities in their wake.

With legs already wearied, they were trudging at last along cobbled inner-city streets, over walkways lined with timeworn paving stones.

Begrimed buildings of two, three, and even four stories hung over them, constructed of rough-masoned stone courses, some built around stout oak frames. Had danger not been so overpressing, Duval would have taken more time to inspect the ancient city. He saw a mason's love of ornament on jambs and lintels: a mastery of carving, with organic tracery, that reminded him, though of much poorer quality, of the Temple Ship. Then, emerging from the side streets in the heart of the city, he was awestruck.

Confronting them was a great boulevard with a tree-flanked highway enclosing a central island.

The island must once have been magnificent. It had been densely planted with decorative trees, now irregularly hacked down to fuel fires in the shanties. Bisected by a paved causeway, it widened at its seaward end to enclose a central plaza, cobbled with granite and with a raised platform that was reached by climbing ornately carved steps. It looked like a stage for important speeches or where, in a more enlightened age, open entertainments might have been performed.

Riverward, two great horns embraced the plaza, which was completed by a three-sided buttress upon the harbour walls. Great bronze cannons extended out over the masts of the ships. From this elevated platform, high above the moored ships and gantries, the eye was drawn to the confluence of the two rivers below, which had dictated the shape of the plaza and after which the city had derived its name.

Isscan, as Milish now explained, meant the "marrying of waters", where the Ezel, or Green River, made a spectacular consummation with the Tshis-Cole, whose snowmelt waters had carried them southward from the frozen peaks of the

Whitestar Mountains.

From here a great new river took the city's name as far as the mountainous Pass of Kloshe Lamah.

"There it meanders," she whispered, as if she were in fear of it, "through forbidden forests, to emerge as the Carfon River, running southeast to the greatest city state in all of Monisle – fair Carfon, on the shores of the Eastern Ocean."

It seemed that the plaza, with its stepped platform, celebrated two thousand years of mercantile achievement. But today, as they neared the pentagonal meeting place under a leaden sky, the multitude gathered about its steps were celebrants of a darker kind.

"My God!"

Duval recognized the obscene carnival of a public execution. And not of a single prisoner, but of a long series of men and women, and even children, who were being lashed and tormented as they waited in chains under an armed guard.

"Mask your aversion," hissed Milish. "Notice only how grief follows in the wake of the Death Legion, as flies follow the reek of corruption. In times to come, remember this tragic lesson of Isscan, where the rule of darkness usurps justice and the light."

With nausea rising from the pit of his stomach, Duval made out the distant figure of a white-robed priest, who was presiding over the executions. After the beheading, he collected the blood in a glittering chalice and was elevating this before the exultant mob. At a roar from the crowd, the tall figure brought the chalice to his lips and drank. Milish had to take a fierce hold of his arm to distract his anger from the horror, while Mira clutched his right hand, each tugging at him to keep moving, despite the compulsion to watch and pity.

Milish led them away from the grand boulevard, though her gait was less certain. "Damn the Tyrant!" she muttered. "Damn him and his minions to the pits of eternity!"

Duval had no stomach to admire the city further. In that depraved scene he saw the omen of their own fate, and that of the Olhyiu, if their luck did not hold.

Quickening their steps, Milish led them to a street that was still grand with its three-story buildings of finely masoned stone. Midway along this street she stopped by an entrance with windows guarded by spiked embrasures and the door head bedecked with hieroglyphs. It appeared to house some of the civic offices. The gap-toothed man who answered Milish's knock eyed them with suspicion – but Milish was persuasive enough to get them past the threshold, where the doorkeeper told them to wait. He brought his mistress, a squat civil servant, who eyed them up and down with a contemptuous stare.

She led them to a wide and high-ceilinged chamber where other men and women, busy at desks or tables, glanced up curiously at them from their ledgers. Duval gathered from the ongoing conversation between Milish and the woman that the Olhyiu were seen as backwoodsmen by the more sophisticated townspeople. Still business was business in this mercantile economy and now he witnessed how business was done.

The woman took a seat in a padded mahogany chair, leaning her fleshy arms on a desk of similar wood while listening to Milish's prevarications.

There had been a flood caused by an untimely spring, as Milish explained, modulating her voice to a more earthy accent. This had forced a village of fisher people to abandon their allotted winter quarters to seek sanctuary in Isscan. Among these simple people, as Milish confessed, somewhat shamefacedly, was her brother by marriage. She begged this good lady, busy as she was with her public duty, to assist them. Was not Isscan's reputation for shelter famous throughout Monisle! Perhaps this councilwoman might have heard word of some new arrivals that fitted Milish's description?

The woman, with a yawn, made it clear that she had no interest in homeless rabble.

Milish produced a purse that jingled with coins, which she now tipped onto the desk. It was the first time since his arrival in Tír that Duval had seen money. The coinage was gold, of different sizes and geometric patterns, some triangular, square, or hexagonal. Each denomination was decorated with a symbol from nature: corn, flowers, animals, birds, and insects. Duval saw how greed invaded the eyes of the official. "*Aurum singulum!*" In her mind he heard the Latin words as a gloating whisper, though she still affected a superficial disdain.

Milish scooped the coins back into her purse and held it firmly. "It is important that we find them as soon as we can. We are wearied by our search for them. We would be pleased to share what simple refuge they might have found."

The barter lasted several more minutes, during which the squat official tested Milish, greedy to be sure there was no more gold to be extracted. Only then, taking the purse and dismissing them with a peremptory nod, did she bark an instruction to the doorkeeper, who was instructed to lead them.

Once back in the streets he was equally cunning in extracting Milish's last triangular gold coin from her before he would lead them more than a block from his mistress's offices.

They soon left the grander streets to enter a labyrinth of shambling alleys, lined by raucous taverns. In the yards of some of the larger taverns were sunken arenas that looked like bear pits. From time to time, Duval thought that their guide was attempting to probe his identity under the low brim of his hat. But confronted in the act, the man would jerk his eyes away with a half leer, hurrying them on. Meanwhile their journey took them in the direction of the waterfront, through a low gate set into the massive city walls.

The end of their search was a wooden building on the wharfside, sunken at one corner into the foul-smelling mud, where the piles that sustained it had rotted away. Its weatherboarding was splintered and peeling and many of the deformed planks had sprung their nails at the corners. Here, their gap-toothed guide bowed before them with a mocking flourish as he kicked open the rickety door.

They were assaulted by a strong medley of odours that suggested the building had seen recent use for fish gutting and as a distribution warehouse.

Inside, after Gaptooth had deserted them for the taverns, they woke a drunken Siam, whose face was bruised and scabby. The chief was so astonished at their arrival he babbled incoherently and then jumped up to welcome Duval, lifting him off his feet in a drunken embrace. Duval was relieved to see Kemtuk among the astonished faces that peered at him from the shadows.

"My friend!" the old man exclaimed, stumbling on his lame leg over the irregular floor to come and clasp his hands, trembling with relief.

"I was afraid I had lost you too." Duval put his arm about the Shaman's shoulders, intending to introduce him to Milish but first he had to wait for Siam to let her go – the burly Chief, with scant regard to dignity, was hugging and twirling her around in intoxicated excitement.

"But tell me quietly," Duval whispered in Kemtuk's ear while they waited, "how many were lost?"

"Sixteen." Tears welled out of the old man's eyes. "Two whole families and one or two each from other families. But it would have been worse if the fierce women of Guhtte had not arrived to divert the attack and save us."

Wiping his eyes upon his sleeve, the Shaman stood back a foot to look in amazement from Duval to Mira – he had last seen her go over the side of the ship.

"The danger is hardly over." Duval gritted his teeth in anger. "This city –"

The Shaman nodded his head in agreement. "Since our arrival, I have been pressing Siam to make plans for immediate departure. How it grieves me to see how the Hyas Di-aub has corrupted the once generous heart of Isscan!"

"We need to make plans – and urgently, Kemtuk."

"Talk we must," interrupted Siam, his brawny arm about Duval's shoulders. "But first we must show our guests a little of the traditional Olhyiu courtesies. Food and shelter we do possess, though the quality of both is meagre."

In a swirl of bonhomie, in which Duval sensed the underlying despair of the big-hearted man, the newcomers were taken on a tour of the accommodation.

The surviving Olhyiu, numbering perhaps a hundred and forty adults and children, occupied three barnlike attic rooms, with pallets made up from grimy old sacks distributed about the floor. The ground floor was a single huge chamber, its ceiling supported by beams fashioned from whole trunks of trees, many still retaining the bark. In the riverside wall, twin doors opened onto a staircase that led down to a rat-infested jetty. The ground-floor chamber was thick with dust, old packing cases, and piles of the moth-eaten sacks. At least the plentiful supply of packing cases fuelled a grate, in a great brick fireplace.

Impulsively, with a spin of his body and a wave of both his arms, Siam called for a celebration.

"The Mage Lord has come back to give us purpose! Gather more timber to feed the fire. Let them come close to warm their weary bones. And then we shall feast as best we can. Dance – and music! Let these poor walls shake and the roof lift with the joy that springs from the deliverance of our friend, Alan Duval, who came to us from another world, and who will lead the Olhyiu to Carfon and freedom!"

The women made preparations for the impoverished feast, while Kemtuk and Duval shared information on their recent adventures. A common foreboding hung over both men as the day drew on toward evening.

But there was no repressing Siam's welcome and soon there was a refreshing singsong of children's voices, warming more than their hands before the flames.

Seated around the fire, on boxes, or on rags laid out over the grimy floor, Siam described how they had been forced to pawn precious objects to buy vegetables and corn from the market, always with the certainty they were being cheated. "Every little coin or trinket is gone. They have robbed us of the very wedding motés, which are the gifts from husbands to their wives on the first night of their marriage."

Duval remembered tiny jewels that had decorated the women's throats.

Clearly for Siam this had been the single greatest act of betrayal by these corrupted city people. Yet with agreement to share their catch, the fishermen had borrowed some small canoes down in the harbour, and, working out on the river all day, they had netted enough fish to guarantee their supper, which tonight would accompany a thick soup of vegetables in which to soften their corn bread. Most notable of their small victories had been Siam's own, with a local tavern keeper, when he had won a bare-knuckle fight in one of the bear pits. His prize had been half a dozen stoppered earthenware jars containing a powerful corn liquor. It explained Siam's battered features and his drunken state on their arrival.

Duval was puzzled by what Siam had remarked about fishing. Surely the Olhyiu had the use of their boats?

A scowl contorted Siam's face. "All confiscated, from the moment of our arrival in the harbour!"

"Confiscated?" questioned Milish sharply. "For what transgression?"

"For no transgression other than to make us join the legions of beggars." It was Kemtuk who replied on behalf of the furious Siam. "Even the Temple Ship itself. They call us 'Malvus' – people who cannot be trusted. We, the Olhyiu! All our boats lie chained and guarded, pending the decision of the High Preband of the City."

Duval turned to Milish, whose look of anxiety reflected his own. Mira's face was a mask of shadows at the periphery of the semicircle.

With nightfall, as a cold wind rattled the wooden walls of the warehouse, carrying a bitter hard snow, Duval was entertained by a dance of three young men in the centre of the floor.

Turkaya organized the music, which sounded a little like pan pipes but was played on strange pots, shaped like fat carrots. He could hardly fail to notice the three young women who hung back, shy in their demeanour, yet with eyes excited by the dancing of the youths. He realized the significance of the dance. Three families had perished and three couples were being bonded. While they had young men to dance and young brides to be seduced by their dancing, death would have no hegemony over the Olhyiu people.

The dance ended with the young men carrying away their brides and it was followed by great merriment and playmaking. Milish, with one hand cupping Duval's ear, begged him not to judge the evening on appearances, for appearances might not be as they seemed.

"Let these people enjoy their night of release," she whispered. "And do not think less of your friend, the ambassador, if she appears to join them."

Siam was the natural ringmaster, as with jokes and suggestive movements of his hands and body he circulated among the people, a jar in his hand. And frequently, when their eyes met, the chief would hold the jar aloft, with liquor still trickling from his laughing cheeks, before downing some more of the contents in one swallow, then belching loudly.

Duval accepted an earthenware cup from a woman close to him, raised his hand in acknowledgment, then took a small swig of the strong liquor.

As the merrymaking increased, Duval watched Kemtuk Lapeep, who kept his distance from the crowds. It intrigued Duval that, after the completion of the music and dancing, the gangling Turkaya was nowhere to be seen. Mira was also missing – Mira who was developing a friendship with Turkaya. Another long and thunderous belch and Siam had Milish in the fold of his arm, turning her in a drunken pantomime of dance, with another half-consumed jar aloft in his other hand. Duval watched in amazement as Milish allowed the chief to fondle her cheek and neck, even to cup her shapely breasts. Milish did not react other than to pinch the battered face of the chief before accepting the jar from his drunken hand.

But in spite of the fun, Duval sensed a step-wise increase in the general tension.

The townspeople had lent the Olhyiu this miserable roof over their heads, but it had hardly been a friendly act. And there was an ominous purpose behind the impounding of their boats.

In a moment, Milish was by his side, her usual elegance overcome by the effects of the liquor. She was drinking from a ceramic pot with a circular base. Her actions were a little un-coordinated, her speech slurred, but her eyes were sober, even as she pressed the bowl into his hands. "Drink, Duval – and let any watching eyes observe you."

Duval brought the bowl to his lips, noticing it was nothing more than water. He made a play of taking a hearty swig. "Siam?" he enquired.

In a show of wantonness, Milish put an arm about his neck and kissed him. "None," she whispered, "are quite so drunk as they appear."

She laughed then, with a seductive pout of those full lips. "Your presence here is known, for there are forces that would detect the oraculum." She placed a second lingering kiss upon his lips. "The town and the surrounding district has more legionaries than a rotting tree has termites. Members from every division of the Death Legion have been arriving at the harbour. Some, Siam thinks, have travelled southwards – large numbers by land and river. It can only mean that they intend to breach the power that guards the ancient Vale of Tazan, with its forbidden forests. If they succeed, Carfon will be vulnerable to attack. And if Carfon falls, so ends all our hopes."

"Tell me more about Carfon," he asked, making a play of brushing her throat with his lips. "I'm interested in this Council in Exile you have mentioned."

"There will be opportunity enough for the politics of Carfon if we succeed in passing through the Vale of Tazan ourselves," she murmured, her lips in turn brushing his ear. "Suffice it to say that our mission to save you was an act of rebellion, contradicted by the orders of the Pretender herself. In such times, danger bides where you least expect it."

A large-framed and drunken man staggered out of the melee of celebrating and Duval recognized Topgal, Siam's brother-in-law. Topgal was in too bitter a humour for celebration. He blamed Siam for the deaths of his niece and sister and now he turned his anger on Milish.

"Where are your allies, the witch warriors of the Western Mountains? Why have they abandoned the Olhyiu to their fate in this godforsaken city?"

Milish hushed him with soft-spoken words. But he would not be placated.

"Mark my words – the Olhyiu will never leave this accursed place. They will end as blood and bones, entertaining the crowds on the profanity of the plaza."

A furious Siam pulled his brother-in-law back. But Topgal's words only deepened the prevailing worry. Milish left Duval to move among the people, quelling the alarm provoked by Topgal's outburst. She whispered in many ears, touched arms and shoulders, patted the heads of fretful children.

The very warmth of the fire seemed no more than a false cloak drawn about one's shoulders against impending treachery.

Not needing to feign exhaustion, Duval sat down on a sack by the fireside, where through the plank floor he could hear rats squeaking and scurrying about the half-sunken wharf below.

Minutes later he heard a scuffling outside the entrance and several men rushed in, led by Turkaya, who was holding a knife against the throat of a beggar. "Caught him peering through the cracks in the wall. He has been spying on us through the night."

The beggar was on his knees in the dirt, his hands outstretched, his voice shrieking. Siam took him by the scruff of the neck and exposed his features to the light of a firebrand.

Duval recognized the cringing face.

"This is the servant who led us here."

"Save me, Mage Lord!" the man whined, his forehead dashed against Duval's feet. "I do not come to spy but to serve you. I bear a message from one who would offer you counsel."

"What treachery is this!" Siam demanded.

"No treachery, I swear upon my honour."

"You have no honour." Siam took the hunting knife from Turkaya and he pressed its point against the spy's scrawny throat. "Search him for his bribe."

They stripped the man of his beggar's cloak to discover ordinary street clothes beneath. In one pocket they discovered a dagger. But they found no change from the gold coin he had haggled from them earlier. His beery breath suggested how that had been spent. They also found a flattened oval of jade as big as a fist, which was inscribed on both surfaces with intricate carving. Milish took the jade from the searcher's hands and marvelled at the art of it.

"It would demand skill indeed to inscribe runes on such an unyielding surface!"

She studied the runes and then she passed the talisman to Duval, who weighed the heavy runestone in his hand, his eyes unable to read its message.

"What does it tell you, Milish?"

Milish hesitated, as if her instincts were torn by contradictions. "It is an invitation, from one who calls himself the Mage of Dreams."

"This is true, Mage Lord," the man whined, the blade of Siam drawing a bead of blood from the cords of his throat. "The Mage of Dreams is greatly venerated in this city. Though with the perils of these dark times, his chamber must be hidden from the eyes of the merely curious. I have been bidden to take you to him."

"The choice of emissary is evidence enough of treachery," growled Siam. "I say kill the spy and make haste to the harbour."

"Master, I beg you – were not my father and his father true friends to the fisher people? I would not wish upon you the fate that beckons if you tried to cut free your boats. Read the message in full, Mage Lord. Its truth is sealed within the rune-stone."

Kemtuk, who had been observing the drama closely, took the jade from Duval's hand. He crossed to the fireside, where he spent many minutes running his fingers over its surfaces, even sniffing at it – exploring it through every sense before he returned.

"This is indeed a talisman of power from the Mage of Dreams, the great Qwenqwo Cuatzel himself. And there is a message concealed within the runestone, though what that message might say, I cannot tell. The art of the Mage of Dreams overwhelms my humble learning. Though, as far as I can tell, danger does not lurk within. Perhaps the message may truly be a personal one, meant only for the one to whom it is addressed."

Duval accepted the heavy runestone and he moved across to kneel in the firelight, where he could transilluminate its jade in the cradle of his hands. He watched how the subtle veining of its crystalline core glittered and shifted even when he held it still. Then, closing his eyes, he probed it with the oraculum, as delicately as he would have entered a human mind. Astonishment shook him as he saw a face imprisoned there.

Like a ghostly spectre, the features of the feral girl peered back at him, that passion in Kate's eyes as she struggled to tell him her name.

A shiver of regret passed through him, crushing his spirit and robbing him of strength.

He could hear the voices of Milish and Kemtuk, though they might have been a thousand miles away. It took the touch of Mira's fingers against his cheek, as fine as the flutter of a butterfly's wing, to bring his senses back to him. Duval exhaled slowly, before climbing back onto his feet.

"Tell me why you anticipate treachery, Kemtuk?"

"I always expect it. Yet this talisman confuses me. The Legion know where we are. They allowed us entry to this town by open river or, as you tell me, through unguarded gates. They spy on all we do, even from moment to moment. Yet still they withhold their attack. I would wager that they fear you, Duval. Perhaps they sit in counsel even now, considering a way in which they might test your power before they are prepared to attack."

"It is as I have dreaded every hour since entering this fallen citadel," said Milish with a shudder.

"Yet if such be the threat," murmured the Shaman, "there is but a narrow window of opportunity for our escape from this corrupted place."

"Thank you, all of you, for your concern. But I'm determined to take whatever risk is necessary to meet this Mage of Dreams. My purpose, not to mention all of our lives, may depend upon such a meeting."

"It must be alone, Mage Lord," insisted Gaptooth, his eyes squinting with a sudden cunning. But he winced again as Siam jabbed the blade harder against his throat. Still the cowed man insisted. "Entry to the Mage's chamber is forbidden except to those he has invited."

Kemtuk took Duval's arm to draw him out of earshot of the untrustworthy guide.

"Let me offer my protection. For the lore of such a mage will be powerful indeed. I will follow your path tonight and will be nearby if danger threatens."

FIFTEEN

THE MAGE OF DREAMS

A BITTER WIND SCOURED the streets, blowing sleet as cutting as ice against Duval's face, as Gaptooth took him on a circuitous perambulation, as if deliberately clouding any sense of direction. They passed the night's drunks, lurching between hostelries in the meaner streets, with wooden houses almost meeting as they fell toward one another in their upper stories across the vile-smelling cobbled passages.

On and on they weaved, through a decrepit labyrinth that seemed to extend for miles, arriving at a district of tall and rickety buildings closely gathered about iced-over walkways of ochre cobbles. Here, they entered an inner maze, ascending and descending staircases of age-worn stone, moving through hunched arches and poorly lit avenues, far from the light of sun or moon.

At length his guide opened a gate concealed in an ivy-shrouded wall of irregular and deeply shadowed boulders, close enough to the waterfront for Duval's ears to pick up the creaking of rigging and for his nose to pick up the ordure of polluted brine. The Mage's chamber was a few hundred yards further of twist and turn in what was now a maze in three dimensions. It was Duval's impression that they had entered the fabric of the ancient city walls. He was unaware of having entered a dwelling, so confusing was the approach through tunnels and portals, yet immediately he bristled with a sense of numinous power as they arrived at an antechamber with a narrow window, looking down eighty feet onto the masts of ships. There was no time for him to see if the tall triple mast of the Temple Ship was among them.

A figure was waiting by the window, his white-cowled face in shadow, as if impatient for his arrival. Duval spotted Gaptooth's furtive hand return the runestone to its master.

With his guide melting away through the closing doorway, Duval saw the cowl drawn back upon a face harrowed with age and bent forward over a frame as spare and fragile as the bones of a heron. This man was taller than most of the people Duval had met in the city, several inches taller than himself, though he was bent over the staff he held in his right hand. He seemed old beyond the threshold where one bothers to count the decades. His locks of hair, thinning over the front and crown of his head, fell down over his neck and shoulders in a cataract of white, as fine as silk. As Duval's left hand was taken in the withered fingers of the Mage, a dwarf with strikingly red hair appeared from a gothic doorway, swaying in his hesitation as if drunk. The dwarf made a guttural sound, as if he had lost his tongue, then a clumsy bow, leading them down a sloping passage with damp walls and into a long and narrow chamber where a fire sparked and roared in a corbelled fireplace.

As he left, the dwarf appeared to totter against the wall of the entrance passage, causing a flicker of amusement to cross the eyes of the Mage.

"Forgive my servant, who cannot help an unfortunate habit. I retain him through fealty." The Mage waved the nuisance away. "Perhaps you will indulge an old man in his amusements. In this poor dungeon, I nourish them for the brief candles of their beauty."

With a clap of the Mage's hands, clouds of brilliant colour filled the air between them, dazzling and shimmering. They spiralled and fluttered until they filled the chamber, like the fall of beautiful blossom in a breeze. Duval gasped, realizing they were butterflies. Several, all a perfect sapphire, alighted about the Mage's eyes to create the illusion of a mask about their gentler blue. Duval could not help gazing into those gentle eyes in wonder. He sensed a great power there. From the fire a fragrant incense cloaked a reek that Duval assumed must be rising out of the harbour.

For a moment, in the poor light of a chandelier and the flames of the fire, the Mage put aside his staff to stand erect before Duval and, intertwining the fingers of his hands, as if in a passion, gazed even more deeply into Duval's eyes. "These are troubled times. Yet such determination and courage do I read in your character!"

Those gentle eyes had dense circles of white invading the blue, concentric circles from the periphery inward: for a moment Duval felt a dizziness pass over him but it quickly cleared. The Mage's voice, even in Duval's oracular interpretation, carried a tenor of refinement that suggested prodigious intelligence and learning.

"Well now, young sir!" Those skeletal hands, dappled with liver spots, waved him to a comfortable old leather armchair by the fireside, while the Mage took his seat in an identical one opposite, with a low round table in between. "A gentleman is a gentleman in all worlds – and it is such a pleasure these days to meet one. And the bearer of the Triangulum potenti – known to the ignorant as the oraculum of the three witches. You grace a lonely hermit with the courtesy of visiting me here, in these reduced circumstances. Perhaps you would like some refreshment?"

The Mage's blue eyes twinkled with merriment as he picked up a tiny silver handbell and tinkled it above his head. Only four of his teeth still survived, all canines, which gave his smile the look of an old cat yawning. His nose, as if with the emotion of their meeting, had begun to run with a clear mucus and its tip had turned a bright scarlet. With the forgetfulness of an old man, he wiped his nose on his pendulous sleeve, as silkily white as his hair, and interwoven with cabbalistic symbols in a scarlet thread. Then, with a flourish of his hand, he waved to the door which was opening cautiously.

"Ah!" he cried. "A noggin, my dear Zoda. A refreshing philtre that will aid our guest unburden his apprehensions." Then, as the servant hesitated, those aged eyes fell upon Duval and the thick brows arched in a moment's sharp contemplation.

"Forgive my boldness, yet I already know the reason you have come. I have been expecting you for many a day."

"How do you know of me?"

"How? He is the direct one, is he not, Zoda?"

Inclining his head, the rheumy eyes widened with a mischievous amusement. "Of course some of we adept – should I boast the more erudite – have long awaited your coming. You, my dear young man, are a prophecy of future history, so to speak. But enough of this for the moment. A solitary life has made me forgetful of the common courtesies. Zoda! Have I not called for refreshment!"

Duval was a little uncomfortable with the obsequious tone of the Mage. He nodded his appreciation while his voice remained firm.

"I am too pressed, Qwenqwo Cuatzel, to waste our time in pleasantries. I would rather you were direct with me. There are questions I must ask you. I would be grateful if you would tell me the simple truth."

A more knowing smile crinkled the corners of the Mage's withered mouth at the mention of his name, for he had not volunteered it during his courtesies. "Is truth ever simple? Ah, were it so, what knowledge might then illuminate the dreams of old age. But surely we can unlock a part of such an elusive whole – at least if each of us is prepared to share a secret or two with the other?"

"I have no money –"

"Money! Hark at the gentleman! Money, he declares. Are you not a doctor of wisdom in your world? Can one sage not aid another from benevolence rather than his purse? My dear young man, I assure you that if it is within this poor Mage's compass to minister such afflictions as oppress you, I shall not hesitate to do so. But first, a little information from you in return. Your companions. A warrior of the Western Mountains, a leader who bears a stone upon her brow – and a child with enquiring eyes?"

Duval tried to conceal his surprise. How could the Mage have discovered this information. He had no awareness of his mind being probed. But he had no wish to talk of Ainé or Mira with a stranger, however benevolent.

He studied the old man a moment, wondering if he dared to use the oraculum to penetrate the learning that lay behind the rheumy blue eyes. Even as he considered this the dwarf re-entered the chamber. Duval accepted a goblet, of heavy silver and brightcut with arcane symbols. The dwarf filled the goblet almost to the brim with a clear, thick liqueur, poured from an ornate ewer of a glowing turquoise crystal. Duval took a sip to find that it tasted sweet and strong. His senses reeled from an immediate intoxication.

"I understand my quest – which is to oppose the Tyrant and his evil. I am told that I must discover my potential for myself. I am given powers but the scope of those powers are a mystery to me. I sense great fear – as if terror is blocking important memories from my mind."

The Mage of Dreams accepted a similar goblet and he took a delicate sip from its contents before replying. "Great fear – terror – you say? My dear young sir!" As if in celebration of Duval's honesty, he took a second, more noisy, swig. "You have a rare perceptiveness. There is indeed a source of such a... such a power as you have acquired. A source... Ah – hmm! But the witches are careful to conceal it, and how right they are too. Have you by chance witnessed such an exalted presence, a being of universal light?"

"No," Duval lied, from a sudden instinct.

"Ah – pity! Yet without a full and powerful use... such promise will atrophy, like a flower that is locked away from the white flame of the sun. But drink up, my friend. For the philtre will relax your mind and help me to help you in your need. Yes, that's it – that's the way!" He waited until Duval had taken a second, deeper sup of the powerful liqueur. "How my old bones envy your youthful quest. Yes… um! Yet can it be true that you have witnessed nothing at all?"

"I have imagined I have seen something on one occasion, a nimbus of lights, a myriad of stars that seem somehow alive, and… sentient."

"Sentient? Indeed? Ummm! Oh, dear – but this is truly fascinating. And such a burden has been placed upon your troubled mind. But do not worry. I am confident that such burdens can be lightened." He clapped his hands and the sad-looking dwarf appeared, avoiding, as before, eye contact with Duval. "More refreshment, Zoda! Let us not strain the courtesies for such an important visitor. Another drink, clumsy servant!" The Mage reached out and struck the dwarf a blow across his face. The dwarf tottered back, striking the wall with a wince of pain.

"Ah!" the Mage dismissed the cringing servant to take a rasping slurp at his upturned goblet, draining its contents.

"How should I put it – you have spent too much time in the company of women."

Duval was startled a second time at the grimace that accompanied the old man's derogation. "Yes, young sir. I wonder if women have been telling you lies? Oh, you will think me overly suspicious no doubt, but my experience in a long and eventful life has made me wonder if that gender are not born with forked tongues. Oh dear – I see now that I have offended you. Yet is it not conceivable that at the very least you have been misled by them? Has the thought even strayed across your mind that they have led you a merry dance. These women who call themselves your friends have broken the edicts of their own High Council."

The Mage's tone had taken on a quaver of indignation and his brow split into a web of pallid wrinkles.

"And what else stands between the Tyrant and ultimate victory in Monisle except the common strength of that wisdom in fair Carfon. My good young man, you must ask yourself that simple question, as indeed have I. Why break the edict of their own Council? Have a care and consider all that has befallen you since you first arrived in this blighted land."

"Perhaps I should invite these women here, so you could confront them yourself, Qwenqwo Cuatzel?"

The Mage waited, with ill-concealed impatience, for the frightened dwarf to refill both goblets. Then, recovering his composure with what seemed an effort, the old eyes gathered all of the power that Duval had first glimpsed in the sapphire mask of the butterflies. He stared at Duval as if in intense speculation. A covetous look flickered within his eyes, quelling what appeared a momentary confusion within their rheumy depths, before he replied to Duval's invitation with a calmer voice.

"Ah – my dear fellow! Is it likely they would sacrifice an hour of their busy day to meet me? If only, perhaps, to reassure an old man of the foolishness of his suspicions?"

The face of the old man appeared to wrinkle even more, as his lips drew back thin and wide, to drain in a single swallow the entire contents of the refilled goblet. His shoulders seemed to fill out and hunch still rounder about his neck, as if embracing a secret desire. "Perhaps I could help them also in their direction. In aiding them, would it not indirectly further whatever would appear to be your quest in Tír?"

Duval felt the creeping invasion of his mind by an alien force. It was as if the Mage were attempting to control his thoughts. He resisted it with all of his might.

"You spoke of – of this?" He brushed his oraculum with his left index finger.

"Indeed – the mark is most certainly that of the fabled Triangulum potenti, uh, um." He stretched enormously long arms, as if to reach out to touch it, then concealed the intention with a suppressed yawn, after which he widened his eyes, shook his head. "The first power you appear to have discovered... Oh, I can see that, without doubt. You derive an inner strength from it... difficult to... to overcome. All who meet you must see how it graces the brow of great intelligence, as befits the noble mind that dwells therein. Such a mind as befits the conferment of.... Dear me, yes! And a brief taste of the Third Power. I can see how it must have alarmed your timid.... Ah, my – yes! So much that puzzled is now revealed. The coveted.... Oh that damned porta of the... of the.... Confound that witches trinity!"

A hateful glee transfigured his face before he could conceal it. Consternation now flickered over the Mage's restored face. His expression seemed to vary from moment to moment.

"How very fascinating. Umm – intricate. Cunningly creative, for ever the Blasphemer of Ossierel was cunning, and in many senses indeed. Never have I seen it, though of course every adept – speaking in terms of Magi, of course – is familiar with its powers."

Duval was sweating freely in the effort at resisting the mental probing. "Are you well, Mage?"

"Well? Am I sick perhaps – sick? he asks. How could the Mage of Dreams be...."

"I don't understand what you are trying to say. You were explaining the powers of this oraculum?"

With an immense struggle, tranquillity again cloaked the features, though the eyes stared suspiciously into Duval's own. "I believe you have already discovered the first part. Through one entrance lies an atrium to many – and the choosing of which thereafter, as you, young Sir, have already discovered, may be a trial as much as a blessing. For nobody could carry the mark – Ah, confound the witches! Carry the mark without discovering its burden. Oh, for the feebleminded, fecundity, the lore of dull creativity. Of the plants and the earth, the beasts and the air, if I am not mistaken, uh, um...."

"You seem to be ill... confused?"

"Confused? Don't you bandy powers with me! Foolish manling! Oh, devour the witches! Lick their blood!" Those bony fingers scratched at the ancient brow, the overly long nails gouged the skin to either side of his wrinkled face. "How deviously they have misled you. Perhaps the witch of the Guhttan hills has… undone. I am being undone. Uh, umm – well, umm – they hate to talk about it. Superstitions, women, secretive, they need to be – though a man of nobility such as yourself should anticipate such." Duval had noticed how, with every sip of his drink, the scarlet of the old man's nose had spread in a butterfly over the face. "Pain cleanses. Oh, the sly perfidity of that gender. Pain," he seethed, barely above a whisper, inwardly, "is the delight of it not in the very nature of woman? Does she not cry out in the ecstasy of it as she resents, oh, so bitterly does she resent, the very birth of life itself out of her foul cloaca." The eyes peered out of their enfolding wrinkles with the hard glitter of polished jet.

"What are you saying?"

"Ah, drink – why do you not drink! Zoda, you scabrous excrement! Fill the goblets – fill them up, I say!"

Duval no longer wanted to drink what the withered old Mage was offering him. He attempted to stop himself drinking but that sense of compulsion had strengthened in his mind. He was unable to resist picking up the glittering silver goblet, unable to resist drinking deep again, though his senses swooned. And the Mage with lip-smacking relish, drained his own in another noisy slurp.

"Think you not, my naive young friend – yet, I'll warrant, is not that gender the very epiphany of suffering? Oh, yes, indeed!" The Mage's hands had tightened about the gibbous swelling that formed the head of his stick, fingers arched about it like claws over a skull.

"Cries," he warbled, "oh, even in torment, how their cries have a certain cadence and sibilance, a music of their very own.…"

Duval was no longer in control of his will. His growing horror must have shown. "I see.…" He struggled to formulate his thoughts. "I see no difference in quality or dignity between men and women."

"Ah, hark at the fool! Think you that I am ignorant of your world. How can you deny the ecstasy that transmogrifies a little sacrifice now and then. Could you but witness each sublime moment, behold each flicker of pain so close your lips are virtually touching it, your mouth salivating with the taste of each and every drop of spilt blood. Oh, what a poor rival you have proved in truth – I would have relished a more vigorous joust with you."

Through his increasingly clouded senses, Duval felt a stab of panic. He remembered the tall and lean, white-robed figure lifting the bloody chalice to his lips before the exultant crowd in the plaza. He had been too distant to see that figure's face. But now he knew who that figure must have been. With an immense effort of will he used the oraculum to enter the mind behind the curtain of those rheumy eyes.

And in so doing, he confronted the intelligence there, dreadful and ominous, an intelligence that knew exactly what he was doing and permitted Duval to perceive only what it wished him to perceive. The drinks must have been poisoned. He turned the oraculum inward, struggling to discover the chemistry of the poison within him, determined to nullify it – but he found nothing, not an alien spark or a chemical he could oppose. The Mage had so outwitted him. All of his will and purpose was draining from his mind even as a dreadful malevolence reached out and undermined him in his chair. Fear and revulsion shrank his skin. A dank sweat oozed out of his brow and plastered his hair to his head. Duval could not prevent the taloned finger that reached out to his brow, that touched with a contemptuous ivory point the recoiling matrix of the oraculum.

"Ah," weened the voice, now deeper pitched and crackling with glee, "terror it was that troubled you? Terror the cloak over memories you wished to resurrect to your miserable brain? But perhaps the information you require is in the possession of my master. Surely then it is my master you would like to meet...."

A black vapour materialized over the table that stood between them. It solidified as a perfect pentagon. Though it seemed smoother than still black water, not a glister of reflection showed upon its surface. In its depths he perceived an expanding matrix of awesome power. With that twinkling smile once again on his malleable features, the Mage had taken a blood-red stone from a pocket in his capacious robe and was dangling it over the centre of the pentagon.

Suddenly the bloodstone was spinning rapidly about all of its axes, and the Mage's cackle had become distant and hypnotic.

"You desired enlightenment. Well, meet him then – for this Clef will enter the most secret labyrinths, my foolish young friend."

The withered Mage was eclipsed by a third presence, a more formidable figure by far, dark in outline, its features shadowed within a still darker cowl. The light in the chamber had fallen to the deepest charcoal, yet it pained Duval's eyes. He was unable to blink. Slowly the cowled head lifted and he saw there a being of utter darkness, more ominous than the gibbous mask of death. The figure appeared to will him closer and his limbs ached to comply with that instruction, though his mind resisted with all of its might.

"No withholding. All will must be surrendered," the voice of the Mage of Dreams echoed within his skull.

Then, abruptly, his mind was penetrated as sharply as if a blade had entered it and Duval was gazing down upon the group of six children, three boys and three girls. Though he knew the scene so well, Duval felt a strange, cold sensation of detachment. The children were gathered about a tumulus of stone. Under the dreadful sky that wheeled about them, he saw the expression on every face... that look of absolute horror.

"A pernicious little cabal!" exclaimed the Mage. "Perhaps you might even remember their names?"

Duval struggled to resist that question. Yet the compulsion to answer it overwhelmed his mind. He had to fight it with every ounce of his will.

"Surely my young friend has not imbibed enough. Another

drink, Zoda — a token of trust!"

Though he did not know the nature of the Mage's poison, his mind spun with its intoxication already. Fighting with every fibre of his soul, he searched again: scoured his blood for evidence of the chemical nature of the poison, so he could fight it. But still he found nothing. A thought struck him with the suddenness of revelation: he remembered the spiritual essence that had charged the weaponry of the Kyra in the riverside battle. He felt certain that the Mage had infused a darkly spiritual poison into the drinks, a chalice of evil that had no effect on the Mage but was undermining his own spirit. Sweat erupted from every pore as Duval, paralysed where he sat, resisted the force of compulsion that rose again within him. As the dwarf once more brought the glittering goblet to his lips, a darkness deeper than the blackest midnight enclosed him, as if to physically devour him.

A glimpse alone and Duval almost died from the horror of it: a vision as through the pupil of a monstrous eye that enclosed an entire universe of darkness. And the deep and dreadful voice that addressed him was no longer that of the Mage but his master.

So we meet! And thou, miserable whelp of a self-indulgent species — imagining thyself my adversary — hast dared to question, what am I?

Why, I go by many names in many worlds. Suffice it to say I am the other side of grace, the left hand of darkness. My power is infinite. Yet such is my appetite, is it not a wonder that I still relish the tiniest spill of blood, the merest blanch of pain of a brat under its mother's hand, the death of a hungry sparrow in winter. All is mine, even as the ultimate sweet savour of the destruction of the things that crawl or burrow, that pitter-patter upon the scum of soil or that dare to stand up on their two hind feet and think they understand their own existence. Such, crackled a voice, as laden with doom as the friction of lava over a wretched landscape, *is the despair of thy challenge!*

Duval shrank back into his chair by the fire, its flames now cold as tombstones, his limbs withering with a growing paralysis, aware only of his hands writhing uselessly over one another, until the knuckles crackled and the stretched skin over his contorted face turned white as ashes.

That figure was gesticulating with a single ebony talon, its cowled head so close it could have stretched out and touched him. He was gagging on its foetid breath.

He saw, as if through a pitiless eye, the children again. Duval's gaze could not move from the children, from the expressions frozen upon those terrified faces. A gigantic shadow was bisecting the sky. In his eyes the orange of flames, in his ears the howl of battle. The howling condensed, in a moment, to become a bell that was pealing, distant in his mind. Yet he ignored it in his struggle to comprehend the terrible significance of what he was beginning to witness through the portal even as the figure extended an arm of absolute darkness out of the cavern of its sleeve. The claw on the end of a stygian finger was reaching toward his brow....

"No!" Though his heartbeat faltered, like the irregular pealing of his own doom, he found the inner strength to resist it for one final moment.

In that same moment, a clatter woke him from his entranced horror. The dwarf, who had refilled their goblets, stumbled as he left the chamber through the door that now seemed more the gothic portal to a crypt. The clatter was the ewer shattering against the floor, a confusion of energy as elemental forces released from the ewer flashed and exploded about the chamber.

A howl of wrath filled Duval's ears as the dwarf bowed repeatedly in a profuse apology, while collecting the fragments in his hands.

The black pentagon had melted away.

"Clumsy spawn of grotesque lineage – I shall take pleasure in the hundredfold multiplication of your pain!"

The voice of the Mage was a snarl, issuing in slurring cadences through grotesquely elongating lips.

Duval was horrified still by the memory of that figure of darkness, yet he knew he had to deflect that terrible wrath from the dwarf. He intoned not through speech alone but subtly, through the mind's eye of the oraculum, fawning over the Beast's head that now capped the figure of the Mage, a spectre with slavering jaws from which protruded a serpent's fangs.

"Surely anger does not become such a sublime mind," he suggested to the Mage. "In all of this troubled land I have never encountered any other with such a force of reason as you. Not even, I daresay, the Tyrant himself!"

"Never, you say?" the voice preened itself in a sudden pat of hubris. It rose to a gloating shriek. "Not even the Great One – not even He!" And in that moment the dwarf was signalling to him. He made a drinking motion, then shook his head. Then wildly, with a face laden with significance, he pointed with his two index fingers to his own wide-staring eyes. The gestures lasted but a moment before he scuttled away with head bowed through the door.

A conflict of rage and flattery fought within the grotesquely metamorphosing figure opposite Duval. For a moment, the old man dominated. "But you flatter me, surely?"

Duval struggled to interpret the dwarf's signals. "Would you not detect such flattery in an instant, since yours is the superior intellect in all that is ignoble."

"Ah – the wonder even of such a possibility – ah!" The eyes, now yellow, fissured with red, were positively reptilian as they bulged in leering self-admiration. The power of the Mage – the entrancement – was not solely located in the drink. There was a second and even greater danger. That seemed to be what the dwarf had been communicating. The drink was intended to weaken his will and allow entry to this far greater danger. And what he was warning Duval was that the greater peril of entrancement lay in the eyes. *The eyes!* Suddenly he understood how he had been taken in: from the very first trick with the butterflies.

Duval broke eye contact, pretending to examine his silver

goblet, as if in admiration.

"Yes –" the voice hissed. "We must partake of the civilities. Yeeesss!"

A contemptuous gloating gurgled at the back of a lengthening throat, edged by fangs. The eyes flickered as if considering a return to the hypnotic blue, the blue eyes, with their concentric circles of senile white, within their mask of butterflies.

Yet, it seemed to consider, was not the foolish wretch still held in its entrancement?

"I can see how you might adore the likes of me, even at the delicious moment your life is forfeit. Sup your last, spawn of Earth. Savour, if you can, your eclipse by no small captain of darkness. I will join you in the toast before I partake of your mind, in the flesh as it were...."

A muscular tongue, glistening blue-black and forked on its tip, darted from between the fangs in the gaping maw of the Beast, as it licked the circumference of its stretched lips before swigging its drink in a single gulp.

Duval watched with horror the monstrous changes that continued to invade that frame of benign pretence. The Mage was rising out of his chair. All semblance to the wizened old man was abandoned and in its place a darkling shape sprang to its hind legs, hardly human in outline anymore, but elongating into a tail and gaping snout. From its paw sprang three huge claws as it reached out toward Duval's brow.

The dwarf was suddenly back in the chamber. His face was contorted as if in an agony of effort. He was holding something in his outstretched hand – the oval of polished jade. By some sleight of hand – or will, perhaps – during the confusion of the dropped ewer, he had stolen the runestone from the Mage: now he was pressing it forward with an extended arm, fighting every inch through a resisting force that caused the veins on his temples to bulge and knot... reaching toward Duval's brow.

Still the distance that separated them, though mere inches, was too much for him.

The dwarf's face was grotesque with effort. A fire of scarlet ignited his features. But he was losing his struggle.

Duval felt an overwhelming impulse to help the little man. He turned his head, as if to move. The claws, like iron pincers, had caught hold of his hair. They twisted and turned, attempting to bring his face closer to the Beast's slavering maw. Duval tried to tear himself loose with his faltering hands. He focused his desperation through his mind, focused the greatly weakened First Power through the oraculum in his brow. There was a thunder clap, a flash of lightning, that caused the Beast merely to stagger off balance. But its strength was enormous. The outstretched paw slackened, but did not release him.

Instead, the claws tore deeper, twisting wildly, as powerfully as a hawser shackling his head.

Duval forced himself an inch closer to the runestone, feeling blood start to trickle under his hair. He stretched his scalp, forcing his skull to move against it, to scream through the hurricane of pain, another inch closer to the jade. The Beast roared, already fully recovered from the shock of lightning, retightening its grip. Its head was lolling from side to side with the force of its struggle to pull him toward it. The jaws were gaping, the tongue flicking from side to side, through and around the slavering fangs. The agony mounted until Duval could no longer see the dwarf, he could hear nothing but the roaring of the Beast's fury, its ravening lust almost touching his face.

Then, abruptly, he felt the oraculum make contact with the jade and a great force, like an ocean freed by a breaking dam, flowed from him and into the runestone.

The chamber exploded with a continuous fury of thunder and lightning.

Duval found himself on hands and knees on the flagstones, in front of the extinguished fire. The storm raged about him, hurling the table and chairs against the walls and ceiling. The dwarf had been thrown down on the floor beside him, still managing to hold the runestone aloft. Its matrix exfulgerating a hurricane of power against the shadow of the cowering Beast.

He struggled to think. Struggled to conclude that in some way his oraculum had awoken great power in the runestone and the dwarf had known how to use it. But there was no time to dwell on this. Suddenly the stone was extinguished, pressed into some inner pocket of the small man's tattered clothes, and Duval was helping him to his feet, taking hold of his face between his hands, rubbing the pallid skin, slapping him on either cheek to hasten his recovery.

Opposite him the monster flickered uncertainly between metamorphoses, yet a single open eye, alternately blue and dreadful yellow, still watched him, the blue-black tongue lolling over the fangs of teeth.

"Go! Get out!" the reviving dwarf murmured. "The spell of the runestone will not hold it for long."

"Did you see – ?" Duval's voice was a croak, torn from a throat still husky with horror.

"Yes, I saw. His respect for you must be great for the Tyrant to challenge you in person. But quickly now. We must escape this prison while there is time."

Shaking his head, Duval was only gathering his own senses as the dwarf, no longer needing his support, took his arm to lead him away from the Mage's chamber.

They staggered into a run. "Thank you, whoever you are – for helping me!" Duval gasped, as they arrived at the gate in the wall of boulders.

All of a sudden, the dwarf stamped his foot and, seizing Duval's arm in a fierce clasp, his face scowled and their eyes met. "Whoever I am?" In the half-light of daybreak, Duval was confronted by two bright green eyes that blazed with pride. The dwarf struck his chest with a gnarly fist and stretched to his full height, his rage making him seem a foot taller than his diminutive stature. "I am the true Qwenqwo Cuatzel, the Mage of Dreams."

"Then who – what was he?"

"An imposter. A warlock from the realms of chaos. Do you

imagine that he alone would have had power enough to usurp me. None other than the Tyrant himself could have cast me down! And this he did in the time of despair, after the fall of Ossierel. I was forced to be the amanuensis and slave to that hypocrite and liar, my tongue sealed while his evil shadow grew and spread. But enough of explanations! Hurry now! Every moment, the danger increases."

He led Duval in a shambling run through the labyrinth of shadows, to where Kemtuk hovered in the shade of a doorway, his face racked with contrition.

"Mage Lord, I followed through the most difficult of tracks to this point, when an ague came over my mind. I awoke only minutes ago with Mira's hand upon my shoulder, convinced in my dread that we had lost you."

"Mira," Duval shook the old Shaman harder than he intended. "You brought Mira to such danger, Kemtuk? She's here?"

Then Mira stood out of the shadows behind the old man, her hollowed smile gentle with concern. "Do not criticize the Shaman, for I followed in his footsteps as he followed you, without his knowing."

Duval held her shoulders a moment, unable to believe a being so vulnerable could survive in this land of darkness. But the dwarf's grip on his arm was unrelenting, his upwardly directed breath hot on Duval's face. "There is nothing left for me here, in this fallen city. I shall join you in your escape."

"But I have people with me."

"You must take them all with you. Anyone who is left will be hunted down. Those fighting witches will not save you."

Duval was shocked at this disrespectful reference to the Shee and he studied Qwenqwo's face a moment. "But how? The boats of the Olhyiu are confiscated and guarded."

"The Temple Ship is our only hope. All other boats will have to be sacrificed. We must flee downriver to the Vale of Tazan. The Legion will follow but we may yet evade them. I know that for all their boasting, they have not yet defeated the power of the Forbidden Forest beyond the gates of Kloshe Lamah. If only we can pass through that dreaded valley, sanctuary awaits us in Carfon."

The dwarf twisted his neck a moment, as if he had heard a distant growl on the night air, his twisted back hunched and gnarled as an old tree root. Then he looked up at Duval once more, his emerald eyes full of urgency.

"Take this and treasure it, if I do not survive to assist you." He pressed the runestone into Duval's hands.

"Go and gather your people. In two hours, I shall meet you at the harbour. Take only what food and provisions you can carry. Two hours – and not a minute longer."

SIXTEEN

THE ARK OF THE ARÜNN

I T SEEMED AN impossible task to move an entire village of men, women, and children, out of a town in the first light of morning and not attract attention. But these were people skilled in the art of moving silently. And fear gave an added urgency to their feet.

With their bundles of possessions carried on their heads, or strapped to their backs, they followed the meaner streets, cutting through the yards of closed and derelict buildings where locked gates held no problem for the nimble fingers of Turkaya. The morning sun had barely risen, its insipid light obscured by the haze of smoke from wood-burning fires in a city of open hearths as the Olhyiu made steady progress toward the harbour. Then, on the upper wharfside and no more than half a mile from their destination, a company of black-garbed men sprang from the shadows to confront them.

The platoon from the city watch, though outnumbered by the villagers, was better trained and armed. In a contemptuous voice, the officer-at-arms demanded an explanation of this dawn plague of rats. A heavyset man with a bully's face, he pretended to quake so much from fear of them that he had difficulty withdrawing his sword from its scabbard. With a pretence at bravado, he whirled the blade in a feint and parry before plunging it into the throat of a man, shielding his wife and children.

"Squeak now, vermin – but what is that you say? I can't hear you!"

The brutality of the attack shocked Duval, still weary from the earlier horror.

The Olhyiu drew what weapons they had to make something of a fight of it. But the thirty or so soldiers had already spread out among the women, elderly, and children, selecting the most vulnerable in order to humiliate the men, bantering them into a one-sided sport. The oraculum blazed in Duval's brow as the bugler lifted his horn to blow for reinforcements.

But there was no need for Duval to intervene. The note was cut short on the bugler's lips as those lips rolled, along with his head, over the stone quay and into the freezing water.

Tall shapes were materializing out of the dawn mists. Duval caught the actinic flash of green blades. Ainé had kept her vigil. And she had brought other Shee although Duval noticed that Muîrne was no longer with her. He assumed that she had taken Valéra's baby with her, back to their homeland in the Guhttan Mountains. Now the swirling movement of Ainé's warriors made it difficult for Duval to count their numbers, though there were more of them than he had left at the edge of the trees, perhaps a few dozen. The skirmish was over in less than a minute – they were looking down on a scene of carnage while still keeping an eerie silence.

Duval and Milish took their cue from the silence of the Shee and with fingers to lips they picked up the dead body of the Olhyiu, hurrying onward, with the whispering of many feet into the awakening morning.

At the harbour, wreathed in a heavy mist that was rising out of the confluence of the two rivers, Duval heard his name spoken in an urgent whisper. He would have walked by a high white wall, faintly luminescent in the pearly light, had he not heard the urgent summons.

"Here, Duval, is your destination!"

Swivelling his head upwards in astonishment, he realised that the white wall was the hull of the Temple Ship.

Through gaps in the whirling mist, he glimpsed a towering superstructure, aglow with a strange lambency, dressed in a wraithlike maze of rope-ladders and rigging that ascended into the murky air. The Temple Ship appeared ghostly, as if a diffuse pale light flickered and danced in the essence of its existence. What had happened to the black timbers, so fissured and worn with time and weather? What metamorphosis had overcome the decaying superstructure or had extended and swollen its already great mass into this spectral monolith?

The summoning voice was that of Qwenqwo Cuatzel is-. suing from somewhere above them, over the rails of this eerie transformation.

"This is no time to stand in astonishment," Milish hissed at his elbow. "We must make haste to climb aboard while the mist it has wrought from the deep still cloaks our passage!"

Her words sounded strange in his mind even as he caught a glimpse of her ornate trunk being carried aboard in the hands of two of the Olhyiu men. Duval assumed it had arrived with the Shee. It seemed that even fear of death would not distract the Ambassador from her finery. Others carried the body of the dead man aloft, so that when opportunity presented they could bury him with time for grieving and a proper dignity.

As the rush of feet scrambled up several gangways, and without the help of anyone on board, the ship appeared to judder and move. Duval felt more and more in awe of the strange transformation. A crackling force shook its massive timbers. Climbing up onto the deck, he spun around, marvelling at the changes that continued to grow and pervade the creaking and groaning superstructure. He thought that minute by minute the ship glowed brighter, a light that seemed hardly to reflect the dawn but to exude from every timber and line of the vessel, as if the ship itself had become the cradle of light. Ainé, with an expression of wary incredulity, reached out to touch a glowing rail and withdrew her hand sharply, as if she had received an electric shock.

Siam, with his eyes wide with astonishment, ordered the raising of the gangways. Assuming mastery of the vessel, he shouted orders to his men. Already the great sails were rising.

Ainé called out to the Shee, to take up defensive positions on the port side, where they faced the battlemented walls. Duval, now probing with his oraculum, sensed even more powerfully the immense and mysterious charge of energy that surrounded them.

"The chains!" Siam roared, his alarm too urgent for whispers.

Running along the deck in Ainé's wake, Duval found the Kyra with legs astride a massive retaining chain. Each individual link was a foot in diameter and cast of the same matte-black metal as the armour of the Storm Wolves. The chains manacled the ship to the huge iron capstans of the dock. With jaws clenched in warlike incantation, Ainé raised her sword to its extremity and crashed its green-bright blade against a single link, causing an explosion of brilliant sparks but barely making a mark on its surface. Milish placed a cautionary hand on the upper arm of the Shee. The blade of the Kyra was not indestructible and they might have great need of it in days to come.

With an oath, Ainé sheathed her sword and glared with rage at this shackling of their escape.

Duval was equally appalled by the massive girth of the chains.

Powerful and strange as the Temple Ship appeared to have become, there would be no escape without first breaking through these constraints. And no weapon could possibly sever them.

A sudden shout from above caused the Olhyiu to crouch down on the deck, already rolling and shuddering as the power of the unfurled sails battered against the obstruction. An army of Death Legion was proliferating on the walls above the dockside. They had the advantage of the harbour side of the great plaza, which brought them high above the level of the groaning deck. Others among them were swinging cannons into position so they could direct them at the Temple Ship. Duval caught a glimpse of black mail, of helmets glittering with the hated sigil of the triple infinity. Then suddenly, the first thunder of green flame and smoke. The discharge of that same foul weaponry struck the superstructure about the mainmast, and a conflagration of sparks exploded in the rigging.

Duval recoiled, gagging, from the green fire, noticing how an answering force upon the deck smothered the flames, causing them to splutter and die.

The Shee were hurling javelins at the Death Legion on the harbour walls. Bodies were tumbling down onto the quayside. But there appeared to be no shortage of reinforcements.

Confronting the chains, Duval focused on them through the power of the oraculum. The red glow from his brow caused the people to shrink away from him. From above two more cannons were being pulled into position, their muzzles turning around until they were trained directly into the faces of the wailing clusters of Olhyiu on the deck. Ainé's voice of command sounded out like a clarion call, exhorting the Shee to greater battle. A fierce flare from the oraculum caught a single link in the chain and within moments it glowed red. Sparks of hot metal began to crackle from its incandescent surface. But the massive strength of it resisted the force of his rage. Several more detonations of green fire descended upon them from above: the burning conflagration and foul stench of one of them struck no more than yards from Duval. More deaths among these people he thought of as friends: his ears were filled by the screams of the injured.

Suddenly the dwarf, Qwenqwo Cuatzel, was by his side. A scowl of rage contorted his features as he held his two arms into the air, as if invoking the assistance of the elements. Duval felt a gale of wind rise about him, he felt it catch in the heaving rigging.

A roar of triumph fell upon him from above as a gigantic cannon was dragged into place.

The Legion had to ram it through the stone wall of the parapet to enable them to direct it downward. And now they were wheeling it back again to load its muzzle, before training it onto the great central mast of the ship.

Duval stood rigidly still, his legs parted on either side of the chain, his brow cast down, furrowed with the intensity of his concentration. The desperation of need consumed him: there was an almighty flare from his brow and the link blazed white. A cataract of brilliant white sparks erupted into the air from the blazing link.

He heard the passionate voice of Ainé ringing out, concentrating a deadly fire onto those commanding the huge cannon. The fierce dwarf seemed to be howling at the wind.

With all of his remaining strength Duval focused even more desperately on the link that tethered them to this deadly harbour.

Suddenly there was a massive lurch, as if the ship itself were coming to his assistance. The sails swelled in the gathering wind, a shuddering jerk as the restless ship crashed against its restraints, and then, with an almighty crack, the chains sundered. Duval watched, unblinking, as the splintered edges tore apart, dripping showers of molten metal. He watched them still as the fractured links slipped out from between his stiffened legs, tumbling over the decks, hissing deep into the storm-whipped water. From above, and rapidly receding, rage-filled faces howled as they watched the great ship pull away from its moorings with sails billowing on its towering masts, the tallest complete with a crow's nest in which Turkaya was shrieking his triumph.

In a blinding conflagration of force and light the Temple Ship forced a reluctant passage through the hindering maze of other vessels in the harbour, battering a path through into clear water, and throwing up a mountainous wave of spray across its bow as it approached the pincers of the harbour mouth.

"Danger! Beware!" screamed the voice of Turkaya, from the top of the mainmast. His hand was pointing into the river, straight ahead.

Peering out over the prow, Duval saw the massive iron teeth that loomed suddenly out of the depths, about fifty yards ahead. A trap for the unwary, they spanned the entire harbour mouth.

Running to the stern of the ship, the oraculum had burst into brilliant red flare before he got there. He leaned forward against the stern rail, his fists raised, his eyes glazed. He heard the screams and shouts from the prow, as they approached to within twenty-five yards of the trap. Then he brought his fists down, invoking the First Power, directing the force of it deep into the turbulent water. In moments a great sea-spout whirled into the sky, raising a tidal wave that lifted the great ship high on its crest, carrying it, bucking and heaving, over the danger.

Once clear, the ship drummed in its depths and sang in its rigging, so that from instinct every man and woman on the decks joined the ship in this hymn of liberation, sharing in their hearts the pure, sweet joy of the freed leviathan, as it struck a majestic course into the central channels of the great river.

The thrust of wind in those proud sails was so perfectly balanced that the waters surged by with scarcely a rhythm of resistance. Although the thunder of cannons still cracked and boomed behind them, they were already out of range of the batteries on the walls.

Siam was aft, gaining confidence at the new helm, and the dwarf, Qwenqwo Cuatzel, stood upon the prow, his enraptured face lifted up into the sky and the wind. He shouted encouragement back to Siam.

Duval watched Qwenqwo closely, wondering about the real nature of the little man.

Ten miles south of Isscan, the mist had blown away, and Duval saw that no boats had been fast enough to give chase from the harbour. No more could he see any sign of organized pursuit on either bank. Still an echo of his horror in the Mage's chamber haunted him: he remembered the overwhelming malignancy of the Tyrant and he wondered how he could possibly defeat him. After the transient happiness of liberation, a pall of dread now hung over the liberated company and a frown had deepened over the face of the Kyra, as if an unseen menace oppressed her from the land to east and west. They were sailing in full majesty through a hinterland of devastated nature.

Kemtuk arrived to stand by Duval, dismayed at the sight of such wanton destruction.

"When an Olhyiu fells a cedar to construct his boat, he keeps vigil for a night and a day to ask forgiveness of the spirit of the forest for his act of need. So, until the coming of darkness, all of the people of this eastwards province of Ulisswe cherished the gifts of A-kol-i, the Creator. Yet today you see no repentance, only a malice of greed that might cause an entire forest to fall. The hearts of the people of Isscan have become as stone under the brutal overlordship of the Tyrant."

Duval clasped the shoulder of the Shaman.

A ravaged land it certainly appeared: what must recently have been a great forest of pine and cedar had been reduced by axe and fire to a wasteland.

Although they must have travelled thirty miles or more since Isscan, not a single stand of trees had survived the destruction. In places the rape of nature had been so recent that smoke still rose from the smouldering ruins of black charcoal and sepulchral ash.

He paced the length of the deck to stand by the sombre Siam, whose eyes were ever watchful over the elements and river currents and whose hands were steady on the wheel, his feet planted firmly upon the quarterdeck.

"You still anticipate danger?"

Siam lifted his face to the south, where mountains of grey, bronze-tipped in the morning sun, soared from the distant blue-green mantle of surviving forests. Row after row of scarps and jagged peaks lay directly ahead.

"To my people," Siam confided, "these are the foothills of the Blue Mountains. To another in our company they are the Mountains of Mourning. Great passions and tragedy ravaged this country in times long past. Ahead, in the Vale of Tazan, it is rumoured that warring armies called for assistance from all of the warrior people of Monisle. The warriors who fought the forces of darkness in those far-off days encountered dangers even from the very elements. Though they had courage and strength beyond any that are known today, still they could not prevail over the darker arts of the dark Queen, Nantosueta."

Siam's voice fell to a whisper and he caught hold of Duval's arm to bring him closer.

"It is rumoured that the Shee were a different race in those times: women such as any others, who knew men. But they allied themselves with the Dark Queen and it was she who changed them."

The chief fell silent for many minutes, staring into the distances ahead, as if reluctant to expand on such matters. At length it was in a voice more husky still that he seemed to force himself to continue.

"It is Nantosueta who from her ancient rath upon the island fortress still casts her shadow over the valley through which we must pass. There the great river, fully a league wide, narrows and deepens as it enters the mountains, a slow and twisting course called in our language Kiwa Hahn, which means the crooked throat."

"Many and strange are the tales that warn men against entering the Vale of Tazan. You ask of danger, Duval. I must caution you that after the guardians of the pass are behind us, and within the long and winding valley, the river passes through a blighted land in which an ancient and forbidden forest has long endured. The trees of this forest are such as are not seen anywhere else upon the face of Tír. You might laugh at such foolishness. But I have met hard and life-worn men who told me tales as we sat around the campfires of winter – tales that speak of ghosts of human origin, warriors who were sacrificed for the vanity of eternity. Other legends claim they are not ghosts of warriors but the first people, the human animals created by the Earth Mother to please A-kol-i after his great slumber. Fearful for their survival at the hands of their children's children, who threatened them with fire, they took the long and weary journey to that valley, to preserve the old ways.

"Who knows," murmured Siam, "where truth lies in the Vale

of Tazan. But great are the powers of that forest. And the spirits that guard it must sense in this wanton killing of trees a reminder of its bitter past. If I appear to dread, it is because death itself is said to have taken pity upon them there and has since protected their sanctuary with accursed powers."

"None dare enter that forest, not even the Death Legion. Such has been the protection of Carfon from the degradation we have witnessed in Isscan."

Siam paused and his fretful gaze flickered about him, over the altered timbers, with their pearly glow.

"Believe me, Mage Lord, that when even we, the Olhyiu people – who are the most experienced mariners in all of the land – must pass through this accursed vale, we dare not delay in those strange shadows or gaze long at the temples of stone that lie abandoned among the roots but keep our prows steady in the centre stream."

Then Siam's eyes darted aloft to where the red-haired Qwenqwo was visible high above: the dwarf had taken Turkaya's place in the crow's nest atop the mainmast. And Duval was startled to follow Siam's gaze higher still, where the widespread wings of a great bird followed exactly the course of the ship.

"How far are we, Siam, from this pass?"

"A hundred leagues."

Duval shook his head, profound in thought: a league was three miles – *three hundred miles!*

He thought about the dwarf. The Mage of Dreams was certainly a strange man. Duval remembered his derogatory remark concerning the Shee and now he noticed how he stayed well clear of contact with the female warriors. Duval reached into his pocket and withdrew the runestone given to him as he had left the Mage's chamber. Holding it against the pearly sky, he saw deeper than the etchings over the polished surface the symbol of an emerald eye. Even as he held the stone to the light, the image of the eye fell onto the deck at Siam's feet, as if projected through a prism. The Olhyiu chief cursed and dropped the helm to run, roaring, along the deck.

Ainé dashed forward and, with her face averted from the green eye, she seized the runestone and hurled it far out over the water.

A shout exploded in the air above the mainmast and the dwarf hurled himself into the rigging, tumbling and sliding down the ratlines. Yet even as the furious figure descended, another moved faster still, a cruciate shape of grey, mantled with white, swooping in the arc of the falling runestone. The speed of movement was swifter than the eye, though there was a keening of wings and a glimpse of ferocious beak and talons. Duval barely had time to recognize the eagle that had been monitoring their passage before, in one great swoop of its taloned feet, it snatched the runestone as it struck the surface of the water, perhaps a hundred yards distant from the ship, and with a shriek of triumph it arced through the air to drop it upon the deck at the dwarf's feet.

He had no more than blinked before Qwenqwo Cuatzel confronted him on the heaving deck, his eyes no longer green but a burning crimson, consumed it seemed with that same rage as the eagle.

The runestone was clutched in a hand that had taken on a resemblance to the eagle's claw.

In the same moment Ainé had withdrawn her sword from its scabbard. The blade was glittering a fearsome green and the oraculum of the Kyra was pulsating powerfully. "Poison arrives in small bottles, Mage Lord!"

"Perhaps," hissed the dwarf, stretching to his full height, at which he barely reached the Kyra's waist, "this witch would prove less arrogant if her legs were reduced to the level of her knees."

Duval reached out and took the stone from Qwenqwo's hand and he wrapped both his own hands about it. Closing his eyes he held it in the focus of his oraculum. Though his spirit became invaded by a sense of unassuagable grief, he could detect no evil. Opening his eyes and gazing deeply into the dwarf's, no more did he witness treachery there. If anything the shadow that hung behind the eyes shared a common tragedy with the sadness he had sensed within the stone. As he looked still into the eyes of Qwenqwo Cuatzel, their anger dissolved and faded from blazing crimson to the quiet green of that inner grief.

Duval passed the runestone back to its master. He would have to talk with Qwenqwo again, at a time when emotions had calmed down. For the moment he turned to question Ainé. "Why did you throw away the runestone?"

Ainé refused to reply, staring over all their heads toward the distant pass in the Blue Mountains.

The dwarf's face blushed scarlet. "Ask the witch to talk of mendacity and slaughter – ask of treachery in the Undying Forest!"

"Ainé!" Duval spoke urgently to the silent Shee, whose sword had returned to its scabbard. "What has happened in the past to cause you to hate one another?"

Neither dwarf nor Shee seemed prepared to enlighten him but continued to stand apart in equal fury of posture and gaze. Even as the anger still charged the air between them, there was a delighted cry further back along the deck. Duval's gaze turned to a small cluster of women, gathered about the stern, who were urging their men to cast their nets into the water. All hurried to join them, where a shoal of silvery salmon leaped and flashed in the ship's white wake. The fish followed them, keeping up speed for speed, like a living cloud, glittering and sparkling, intent it seemed upon offering themselves.

Duval's eyes were drawn to Mira, standing quietly to one side, a look of entrancement about her features, and at her side the solemn-faced Turkaya. Their closeness, their rapt expressions and the apposite timing of the bounty, he committed to memory, before turning to Siam.

"Can you find nets? We are short of food and we should take advantage of this good luck."

Many hours later, and with the welcome store of fresh food

on board, it was Qwenqwo Cuatzel, placated by time and Duval's efforts at friendship, who satisfied the curiosity of all on board with a story that might throw light on the history of the Temple Ship.

Sharing a pipe of tobacco with Kemtuk Lapeep, the Mage of Dreams joined the Shaman in sitting cross-legged on the deck, joined in their inner circle by Duval and the tribal elders. Ainé refused to join the circle but stood apart, while making no secret of the fact that she too was listening.

"Oracula," confided the dwarf, "are not to be found solely upon the brow. The runestone is also a portal of power. Though it was no threat to the Mage Lord, the Kyra, with her suspicious nature, misunderstood its purpose. To some it might appear to threaten, as a doubter might question fealty." Qwenqwo's eyes were once again veiled in the sadness Duval had noticed earlier and he guessed that on another day and in more private conversation the dwarf might be induced to explain rather more.

"I was deceived, as you know, by a spirit more powerful and malevolent than any that might be defeated by mortal wisdom. It was then, during my enslavement over many years, that I concealed what I could of the power and wisdom of my people in the eye of truth that you see in this runestone. The eye looks into the heart of those who possess it, searching there for good or malice."

"And did the heart pass its test?" Duval asked, with the hint of a smile.

"Your heart is good. You saw for yourself how the eye glowed. If it had discovered evil in you, it would have darkened to jet and even beyond, for in the closing of its eye it would have become a consumer of the light."

Their gazes met again and Duval wondered, without asking, if there was a reason why Qwenqwo might have found it necessary to test him.

"Perhaps," said the red-haired dwarf in a brighter voice, "I should explain how profoundly moved in spirit I have been since first setting eyes upon the Temple Ship. And that reminds me of a story – loath as I am ever to tell old stories!"

There was general laughter about the dwarf as he puffed on his pipe and his green eyes twinkled.

"But now I see that there are too many curious faces in this company to be disappointed. So I will share a little of what I know. For I am acquainted with a legend that tells of a very ancient people, of what the Olhyiu might call First Man and First Woman. Now, if you believe the legends, this man was known as Ará and the first woman as Quorínn and these people were henceforth known as the Quorínn – and others among us who are less inclined to fireside legend, such as the Shee and the Council Woman, Milish, will know them as Arünn.

"Whatever the accuracy of the legends, all people who now live in Monisle know them in some shape or form, whether by different names or in their stories of beginnings, for these were the first people to gather the fruits of land and shore. Some stories suggest they came here from another world in a great ship, which is known as the Ark of the Arünn, for the vessel, which was later embellished with foolish notions of gold and precious gems, had powers bequeathed to it by the Changers themselves.

"The Ark responded, sense for sense, with the power that derived from their hands and eyes. It was beyond the comprehension of ordinary senses, for it was one thing and all things to those who travelled within it. Some believed that it retained the capacity to swim through the air, with great wings beating, like the black-headed swan. Others that it could transform its substance, according to the instruction of its masters, even as the creatures, whether of myth or fact I cannot tell, known as changelings."

The eyes of the dwarf caught Duval's fleetingly and a sparkle at their very pinpoints seemed for a moment to tantalize him before Qwenqwo blinked and then smiled, puffing contentedly on his borrowed pipe.

"Stranger still are the stories of the Arünn themselves. For it appears that above all they venerated knowledge. So obsessed did they become with their understanding of things that they coveted the immortality of the gods – and such, if the legends are to be believed, became their downfall."

On the sixth day after leaving Isscan, the wind blew from the north and its chilly breath whipped about the decks and rigging. Winter howled in Duval's ears and men and women passed by in his vision as dark silhouettes, bent into their furs with cold. The night landscape was showered with snow and the bitter squalls cleared all but the essential mariners from the deck. Although they passed copses of evergreens, often in clefts of hills, or rills where greedy feet would have had difficulty entering, it was a great distance out of Isscan before they came upon the surviving forest that had once covered the land from the Whitestar Mountains in the north to the Vale of Tazan. Great trees overhung the water and sparks of light glittered in the green-black depths of their shadows.

Here, in a more respectful ground, they buried their dead, prayed over by Kemtuk, who was wearing his eagle's skull headdress and holding the skull and the narwhal's lance. A dark shadow still brooded over Duval's spirit since his encounter with the Tyrant in the Mage's chamber. It haunted his attempts at sleep.

In the hours of darkness, sleeplessly prowling the decks and avoiding the company of the guard of Shee or the Olhyiu sailors, Duval overheard snatches of their conversations.

"Is the Mage Lord Duval a demon?"

He recognized the voice of Topgal, the brother-in-law of Siam. Topgal never seemed to speak without a deep and abiding bitterness.

It seemed that they alternated in thinking he might be a demon or a god but never a man. He had never felt so alone in the world as he felt that night, listening to these honest and bewildered people talk about him. He welcomed the piercing barbs of snow that whipped his face in the bitter wind. He ignored the pain as his lips cracked and his ears went numb. He ate his meals alone, or occasionally in the company of Milish or Kemtuk. His growing alienation found him once more disbelieving his very presence here, peering at the wintry landscape through the unshuttered porthole in a small room below decks that he had taken as his cabin.

Sitting cross-legged on the floor and imagining he was a little drunk on Irish, he played the old numbers to himself on the harmonica. He didn't notice any knock on the door as Qwenqwo and Turkaya let themselves in. The dwarf appeared to have read his mind, because he had brought a flask of powerful alcohol, which he must have hidden in the ship before they arrived at the harbour, and Turkaya had brought two of his strange musical instruments, shaped like bulging sweet potatoes with holes. The big ones, he informed Duval, were called pootapoos and the small ones piwis. They listened to Duval singing his songs and playing his harmonica and they soon attempted to join in.

Turkaya had a lovely, high tenor voice in which he, just beginning to sprout whiskers, sang a song of his own about a foolish young man who fell in love with a seal. Qwenqwo, half drunk before he even arrived, had the best gravelly singing voice of them all. He was a natural for the songs of Howlin' Wolf, while Duval accompanied him on the harmonica.

"What," slurred Qwenqwo, "is this sweet music we play together?"

Duval slurred back, "It's called the blues."

"What a strange world you come from," piped up Turkaya, who was disgustingly lively still, as he was turning over Duval's harmonica in his hands. "A world where music has a colour!"

This started Duval laughing. "You think my world strange!" Soon he was laughing a good deal more. He was laughing until there were tears in his eyes at the antics of this improbable band.

"Yeah," he sighed, wiping tears from his eyes, "it's a colour. But it's also a celebration of the troubles of life – a celebration of how people survive through the worst of their troubles."

"And this?" Turkaya blew a disjointed few rills on the harmonica.

"My father had more than his share of troubles. But he left me two gifts after he died. He left me the harmonica, which was once played by Howlin' Wolf, at a club – a kind of an inn – called Sylvio's in Chicago. And he gave me a liking for Irish whisky, drunk neat from the neck of his silver flask. That battered old harmonica is all I have left to remember him by."

On the following day, the weather warmed above freezing, yet wraiths of icy mist ran among the great trees, like hunting wolves. By nightfall it had thickened to a bank as dense as smoke, rolling over the uplands to either side of the river, obscuring all sense of geography and distance before merging with the low dome of sky. Then the sigh of the water under the bows seemed to rise to comfort the weary travellers – the hiss of the bow-wave, spreading out in great ripples to the black shingle of the banks.

The land to either side of them seemed ever to rise in scarps, capped by plateaus, hills and valleys, gripped in the white thrall of winter.

Nobody wanted a new night to fall, for a deep and brooding menace was gathering in those black rocks, as if the angry earth were showing through its sparse cover of mist and snow. The last they saw of the sky was its massing clouds, their edges shrouding the caps of the mountains so that the darkling sky became one with the shoulders of rock and the coiling mists rising from the river.

They were drawing closer to the jaws of the pass, through which they would enter a valley where new dangers awaited them. That night his sleep was tormented by nightmares. Duval found himself only half awake at first light, his whole body drenched in sweat.

He was back in his memories – back again among his young friends, heading for a mountain.

SEVENTEEN

SLIEVENAMON

FOR THE FOURTEEN-YEAR-OLD Alan Duval, fear of the mountain had grown so powerful, it was as if his mind could not register the journey, though it must have lasted an hour, along the main road southwest from Carlow, through the open streets of Kilkenny, past the ruins of the ancient castle.

Then, as the truck was rumbling noisily, turning right off the main Kilkenny-to-Clonmel road, he heard Kate exclaim, "We're here!"

He saw the sign for Nine Mile House and soon the final village, Kilcash, with its fading baskets of flowers outside the post office.

Sean took them as close to the slope as the small lane would allow, then stopped and cut the engine.

"Slievenamon!" Penny looked up at it with round eyes, her voice a whisper.

In Celtic it meant the Mountain of Women. The mountain looked different from here, flatter, yet still breast-shaped. The nipple outline was the cairn of stones upon the peak. They all stood for a minute or so and gazed up at it, swathed in the heather of late summer. Nobody spoke another word. There was such a prickling of awe, such a thrill of excitement mixed with a sickening proximity of danger, Alan felt the hairs stand up on the nape of his neck.

The boys took a container each as in single file the six friends began the long climb through the blackberries and ragged trees about the lower slopes.

Before they had even reached the trees, the sky grew heavily overcast about them. A solitary blackbird sounded out its warning, as if the power of Slievenamon was declaring its intention to fight the darkness that gathered about it.

Alan pulled alongside Sean, who was once more carrying the spear of Lug upright in his hand, his face held in a perpetual frown. Sean had grown enormously tall in this last year. Soon he would be forced to bend his head to get through a door, especially so when he took to wearing his father's knee-length forester's boots. The weapon sat naturally in his hand. As they pressed upward, growing hotter in their faces, Alan felt such a current of friendship for them all, for the way in which they had come to know and understand one another, their strengths and weaknesses, loving each other all the more for the weaknesses.

They were the only true friends he had ever known.

The boys had carried their burdens beyond the point of mere tiredness. Wordlessly, the girls took the containers from hands in which the handles had cut impressions deep into the flesh, bearing them upward another few hundred yards until even their exhausted arms forced them to a halt and the boys took over again. So it continued, ever upward, under the black race of cloud wheeling over the sky. A charge of static electricity lifted the hair on their heads as, too exhausted to cheer, they crested the summit. Clonmel was visible in the haze of distance, its outline ghostly in the smoky plumes of its chimneys.

They had run out of Coke so they drank water from the containers, lying down to rest on the bracken under the leaden weight of the sky.

Change was in the world about them, a galvanizing excitement that tingled upon the skin, a numbness ascending through their bodies from the charge of the mountain. Suddenly, Alan's heart was pumping madly, a cry rising to his lips. The clouds were devouring the evening sky.

But Penny had beaten him to it. Penny had shrieked, though

not through sharing his alarm at the gathering darkness but in an excitement of her own. Turning in confusion, they all saw the focus of her eyes. Penny was already running toward it. Then they were all running in that same direction – toward the place all of them had seen many times in their dreams.

It was no more than a hundred yards distant, a collection of dark grey boulders shaped like a table. But even as Alan joined the other boys in struggling with the water, he could not resist a glance over his right shoulder, toward the west, where a dreadful darkness was blanking out the light.

Penny was already exploring the stones before any of the others could catch up with her. In a flushed but silent excitement, she dashed about the ancient tumulus, peering into clefts and touching the rough, lichen-encrusted surfaces.

Could none of them see what he could see: the deepening shadow that was devouring the world? But they couldn't see it as he could see it. They were all too intoxicated.

"What is it, Penny? What are you looking for?"

"Here – *here!*"

She was waving them all to join her on a stony ledge, five feet above the ground.

Alan sensed what she wanted, for suddenly he was shouting to all the others to stand well clear. Then, with his eyes bulging and the veins and muscles in his neck and face standing out, he pulled fiercely at an irregular boulder that sat on the higher table, tugged at it so fiercely that blood was squeezing around the whites of his flattened fingernails. At last, he made the rock begin to move. Big Sean sprang up to help him until, with a low-pitched rumble, the rock slid sufficiently for the two of them to get their fingers beneath it and then to lever it over the edge of the stone table, sending it crashing into the heather.

"What is it?" They were all clambering up now, onto a rough but serviceable ledge on which the flat table of stone stood, at about waist level.

Their amazed eyes fell upon a circular depression in the table, perhaps two feet in diameter, its floor a perfect half sphere. About its rim, deeply inscribed into the hard edge of the stone, were inscribed lines and angles – runes, clusters of them, running over and into the bowl.

"What does it mean – will somebody tell me what it means?"

It was Sean who answered, Sean, the druid's son – whose voice had suddenly become more knowing. "Do you realise what we are doing. Nobody has looked on this altar for thousands of years. We are standing at the entrance to *Sidhe ar Feimhim*. Ah, you omadawns of history – it means the gate. We are knocking on the Gate to the Other World."

Sean was standing side by side with Penny, the tall pair triumphantly erect.

"The gateway," intoned Penny, "the gateway that has been calling us!"

Still it seemed that only Alan was aware of the gathering danger.

Clonmel was no longer visible. All the sky was being consumed by darkness. Even as he watched, the daylight was extinguished. The black clouds seemed to lower down upon them until they were a mere stone's throw above them. And with that, everybody sensed it, that dreadful feeling of evil, stronger by far than they had ever felt it before. Penny could no longer see the runes that ran about the bowl in the rock.

Duvaaalll!

"Oh, Mother of God – what was that?"

Kate's quavering voice sounded up close to him. Kate's left hand upon his shoulder, her other hand crossing herself over and over.

Kate had heard it too. His surname – it wasn't just the whisper of nightmare in his head.

The sound of splashing water now, the gurgling noise it made when it came out of the neck of the first container too quickly and sucked in the sides. All of a sudden there was a faint pink glow coming out of the font in the stone and Penny's face was outlined by it, ghostlike in its reflection.

"Everybody!" She addressed them urgently, her voice muted

by the dark about them. "Take off your shoes."

"Take them off – what for?"

"Do as I say – do it, quickly!"

Alan set the example, sitting down between Mo and Kate, tearing his trainers off, throwing them down onto the ground. "Come on, do as Penny tells you. Our bare feet on the stone."

Suddenly the air was too gloomy to breathe, as if the individual molecules were turning chill. Terror sprang into every heart. Then they were hurrying, ripping off their shoes.

"The second container of water – quickly!" Penny's voice sounded out, quavering but still authoritative above them.

They had to jump back down to the ground, scrambling about, unable in the dark to make out the outline of the containers anymore. Alan tried to help but every movement of his limbs had become leaden, as if he were floundering under the weight of an ocean. Then he heard it again, that same horrible rasping voice, a rancorous breath out of the enveloping miasma.

I am coming, Duvaaalll!

"Come on – come on! Two more. The Suir and the Barrow. Come on, all of you. Alan – Sean, get them up to me. Oh, God – quickly! Quickly!"

Shouts now – Sean's groaning breath as panting and cursing he heaved the heavy burden of the second container up onto the ledge, more grunts as he heaved it up further onto the table and into her waiting hands. A splash of light, the fall of the water was silver in the dark. A spiral of vapour was rising, illuminating Penny's face but not the ground.

"One more!" Her contorted mouth was screaming it. "Up with it now – before we run out of time!"

Alan was back on the ground, his shaking hands discovering the bulk of the container. His hands seemed drawn to its cool, firm outline. He sensed that it was the water of the river Suir itself. It was his own frantic effort that hoisted it onto the ledge, and then, grunting himself, struggling to climb after it, he hoisted it to the table. He felt its weight taken from his hands by Penny. Her eyes were liquid reflections of the furnace that fumed and spiralled within the black outline of the stone. Alan saw how her hands tore off the cap, then, leaning her weight against his own, she tipped its gurgling contents to join the others.

A rush of foul air enveloped them. He heard the sound of Mo's terrified screaming.

Green cataracts of putrefying luminescence descended in an irregular shower all about Slievenamon, devouring the life-giving molecules of air.

"Up here! Quickly, Kate – Mo – Liam!" It was his own voice, shouting.

As Liam helped the terrified Mo into Alan's grasp, Alan could hear Liam muttering over and over: "Oh shit! Oh shit! Oh shit! Oh shit!" Kate was picked up in a single quick lift by Sean. With a scramble, Liam had joined them, all six now gathered in a circle about the white-glowing circumference of the table of stone. About them a vast malignancy spitted green fire. The sanctuary of the rock altar would not long save them.

Penny's face was lifted heavenwards, in a rapid litany of prayer. A shower of brilliant sparks swirled skywards from the moiling surface of the font, defying the darkness that was suffocating the light. In the cradle of his own terror, Alan saw the eyes appear. He knew this had been the last vision of poor Billy Foran. The eyes changed from moment to moment, the silvery blue-green of rancid flesh, the bloodcurdling rose of butchery, then a mad altercation, like a corrupted rainbow – and the glee, the horrible glee of its malice was invading their minds.

"I can't stop it! I have tried all I know. I can't stop it," Penny wailed.

"Read the inscription!" Alan heard his voice demanding it of her. For in the light from the spiralling water, the inscription stood out boldly.

"I can't. I don't know what it means. I have tried and I can't. You must try yourself, Alan. You're the one. It's your name that yoke is calling. It's you it's after."

How her words contracted his heart. Terrified him so that he could not concentrate on the ancient Ogham. Yet it had been his leadership that had brought them all here. In his consternation the eyes seemed to gather strength. He focused with all of his failing courage into the water in its half sphere of stone. What had those ancients known – the druids who had carved this font on the summit of Slievenamon?

Desperately, he tried to imagine what had gone through the minds of a people he had never known, people from a time he just didn't understand.

As if in contempt for his ignorance, the water spun in an increasing vortex, now turquoise, now the old gold of the torques about the throats of those ancient druids.

Duvaaalll! the voice seethed, a loathing so dreadful it vibrated in the rocks under his feet. *I will sunder you for my sport! I will break your bones open and suck the juices of the marrow.* Every syllable was caressed, as though the words gave it a carnal glee.

Alan took the spear from Sean's hand. Although his legs were jerking out of sheer terror, still he climbed on top of the table of stone. Now he stood there, his solitary figure braced with one foot on either side of the whirlpool of light, holding the spear of Lug aloft. In his Brooklyn accent, he shouted his defiance into the sky.

"Come on then, ya bastard! You might have frightened Billy Foran but ya don't scare me!"

Brave words, they scarcely hid his terror.

The eyes turned their full malevolent glare upon his defiant figure. The raised spear goaded it into an uncontrollable rage. Alan wilted a moment under the force of malice, yet he held his ground while those eyes descended upon him out of the tormented air. The eyes glared hatred on either side of leviathan jaws, lined with a thousand deadly fangs, dripping venom. Suddenly, crazily, Kate was on the summit beside him. His heart leaped with renewed courage at her love and boldness, as she wrapped her arm about his trembling shoulders. He waited until the maw was about to enclose them both, the eyes carmine with blood lust, and then, first immersing the blade in the foaming waters, with all of his might he hurled the spear into the nearest eye. The spear burrowed deep into that baleful furnace. With a roar of pain that shook the mountain, the monster shrank back into its lair.

But it wasn't over. And Alan knew exactly what was to follow.

He had seen it a hundred times in his nightmares, when it had caused him to wake up screaming. First the rise, far into the heavens and then the descending maw. Alan refused to look. In desperation, he studied the runes about the rim of the font. He knew from the shrieks of his friends that the abyss was descending, the fangs closing about them. He could not read the Ogham. How could he! In despair he turned from the spuming cauldron where the waters of the three sisters had been brought to consummation. His face was contorted by the terrible visions that were growing there…. He saw a battlefield long ago, on the edge of time, over which a storm-racked sky wheeled and tossed. He was the warrior who lay on the blood-soaked ground, his arm with its broken sword thrust into the heavens. His mouth was twisting into a final desperate cry – to the goddess to whom he dedicated his death. In the storm, his voice was a single quavering reed, anguished and broken.

"Mó-rí-gáááん!"

The demon had expanded a thousandfold, so that its throat was a valley of hell between the livid tors that were its fangs.

The anguished cry was rising, the death cry of the warrior was dying now on his own trembling mouth, its spiralling and receding into the ravening sky.

A pinpoint of sound was the dwindling of his summons. A condensing grey dot in the sky, wheeling and turning.

A voice colder than awe was whispering in his mind, a voice deeper than his terror, telling him the meaning of the runes… if only he could focus on that against the blank wall of terror.

A voice speaking from a great distance, as if across the eons of time and space. The impulse to incant its strange message became overwhelming.

He had no conscious control anymore, no deliberate thought kept him standing astride the cauldron, where he felt the spiralling motes of sacred light invade his flesh and glow fiercely within his very being.

With his face grotesque with urgency, he hurled the summons, the sound that was becoming substance, born from the name of Mórígán, the goddess of death and the battlefield, whose name he had cast into its midnight furnace.

"Tá an geann circleach!"

More than any human voice that ever issued from the clenched throat of terror, it echoed from the sky, like a distant, distorted peal of thunder. Tá an geann circleach: *the world is a circle.*

A statement of nothing, yet it encompassed all.

Alan stared up out of terrified eyes at the place where his call took form, grew and expanded, where it assumed a potent and frightening form. His eyes gaped as that focus began to darken, darker by far than the blackest cloud and proliferating until it became a great trapezoid of ebony, at the fore the cruel chisel of a beak the size of a mountain in a skull with pits of starlight where there should have been eyes. He stared in awe as the swelling took shape to either side until he could clearly see the slow beating of leviathan wings. In moments the shadow of an almighty raven grew so vast that it circumscribed the heavens.

Its cry was thunder, descending over the mountain like the winter of worlds.

In the umbrella of its wings, the children were protected, immune from malice. Though their tormentor snarled and lunged one final time, it was to no effect. Its threat was suddenly extinguished – utterly, as if it had never been.

Voices calling, voices beseeching him. A new voice in his mind, he did not recognize…

"Behold the Pass of Kloshe Lamah!"

Duval heard the note of its urgency, felt the tug of arms that were attempting to draw him back. He did not want to wake up. He wanted to stay in his memories, where a great stirring was expanding in his universe: *the gateway to another world.*

Yes – oh, yes, he understood now. He was the One. Only he had been intended to enter the gate. But Kate's courage and love for him had taken her with him. *Oh, Kate – Kate! You should not have come. You were a mistake.* He knew that now – he understood at last.

His lips moved as if to comfort Kate, although there could be no retreat… there never was any possibility of retreat.

As one miasma was drawn aside, it opened onto a still greater darkness. It seemed that for all of his life a single mind had been beckoning him to this moment: a voice of immense power, waiting for him behind that gateway into another world.

EIGHTEEN

THE VALE OF TAZAN

IT WAS THE voice of Qwenqwo Cuatzel he had heard, Qwenqwo's warning shout, still ringing out from high in the crow's nest.

"Behold the Pass of Kloshe Lamah! Behold if you dare the countenance of Magcyn Ré, Suzelz Tazan, the keeper of the Forest of the Undying and last overlord of the Fir Bolg whose spirit in truth yet guards it!"

Duval struggled to his feet, still feeling the beckoning of that voice of power. His mind only reluctantly clearing, he hurried forward over the deck, past the exhausted face of Siam – the chief had held the helm all night without rest – and onto the prow, where Kemtuk Lapeep stood like a sentinel, peering through the dawn mists at the extraordinary vision that confronted them.

The Isscan River had become deep and fast-moving where its great waters had been compressed to no more than sixty yards wide. Siam and his Olhyiu crew were piloting their way with painstaking care between the ragged crags and escarpments that reared on either side of them. And there – it seemed impossible, for the scale was beyond any human aspiration – yet suddenly there it was, towering above them, a great figure of stone, rising out of the deep and as much as a thousand feet high. It guarded the left gate of the pass in the gigantic figure of a man – a man seated not upon a dais but upon the shelf of rocky outcrop, his legs crossed at the ankles and his arms folded.

Behold the Pass of Kloshe Lamah!

Shocked to full wakefulness, Duval stared up at the massive sculpture. He was so awed he had to lean against the rail for support.

More than any other aspect, it was the head – a tumulus of granite as great as the entire Sphynx – that cast a brooding threat over their forward passage.

Square of face, the nose was broad, with prominent nostrils and flattened across the bridge, the eye-sockets caves of shadow. With redoubled shock, Duval saw the resemblance between the great head of stone and the features of Qwenqwo: they might have been brothers.

Duval's attention wheeled to the portal on his right, but there he saw only a vaguely human shape, though equally massive as that on his left. Some calamity more destructive than wind or rain had ruined the image – and recently too he judged. The upper portion was shattered into a confusion of broken ledges and sharp projections. Shards of rock had tumbled down over the shoulders and torso, masking the presence that had once towered opposite its companion across the pass.

Siam averted his gaze, murmuring to himself in a stricken whisper.

"What malignancy would dare to profane the guardian – surely we journey into a vortex of evil!"

As they dropped sail to slow their passage through the portals, a defiant if bedraggled femininity exuded from the desecrated right portal; so powerfully did he sense this that Duval had to assume that the ruined figure had been a representation of the queen.

With a grim set to his jaws Siam piloted the ship deeper, passing through Lamah's pass and into the blue-black shadows of the crooked throat, where the Isscan River became the Kiwa Hahn. Great cliffs overhung their passage, exuding menace – as if they were gigantic beasts that had slunk down to the water to drink. Even the Shee who stood guard upon the deck fell silent.

The air became still and dankly humid and it seemed that even the beating of their hearts echoed from the massive keeps to either side. For Duval, standing by the burly chief, it felt as if he had hardly dared to breathe for the hour or more that Siam picked his course, twisting and turning between these dreadful cliffs – and judging from the chief's expression, at every moment he expected the menace of those jaws to close about them and end it all in the splintering of oak and bone.

But then they were through the pass and a secret world opened before them.

The sails were once more hoisted to catch the moisture-laden winds that drenched the widening valley with a blustering rain. Lichens carpeted every rocky outcrop. A tributary rushed to join the river in a white-water furnace over timeworn rocks, its spray sending up clouds of water droplets in which a rainbow shimmered. Duval watched a pair of dippers, their grey-brown plumage dusted with a chalky blue, diving and bobbing in the curtain of droplets.

After the barren cold of their journey from the ice-bound lake, it was a wonderland.

Mile after mile its wonder extended.

The weather would change without warning. One minute a clear rain washed the view to a sparkling clarity. The next minute a wetting fog would close about them, plunging the day into twilight. They might have been entering the primeval forest at the beginnings of time. Duval's first glimpse of the trees was of great boughs, festooned with living curtains, over green-carpeted banks. Every branch and twig was so bearded with moss and lichens it was difficult to make out their forms. In places the saprophytic growths were so dense as to become gardens in the canopies. The giant green fingers of arboreal ferns proliferated in the sunlit openings.

In a whisper, Kemtuk spoke of a forest of giants and Duval nodded, awestruck. He had seen massive trees in the forests north of Isscan, but compared to these they had been no more than saplings.

Great boles of trunks soared into the distant sky, their upper reaches lost in the fusion of mist and canopy. He struggled to identify even a few of the species – Douglas fir perhaps, and Sitka spruce and cedar – only to be forced to withdraw his gaze with eyes dazzled by spears of sunlight striking down through gaps left by a falling snag.

Over the splintered caps of the encircling mountains to the northeast, smoke and fumes fed the discoloured clouds. He saw now that many of the peaks were volcanic calderas, and he heard the cracks and rumbles of their restless violence, even at this great distance. Partway up the slope, heated air rose from vents in the rocks, billowing steam that fell down into the forests and ran like a tidal race between the trees.

Hour after hour they watched in amazement as the great ship sailed deeper into the pass, past streams yellow with sulphur from the discharges in the distant peaks. Here and there age had thinned out the woodland, where bedraggled survivors of some natural calamity lay scattered about open spaces, supporting a profusion of saprophytes and parasitic mantles that created miniature gardens in their skeletons.

Then, as they rounded a bend into a sunlit valley, Duval's breath caught in his throat.

Rising, as if through immense struggle from the arid rock of the waterside, was an immense tree. Its roots were a gnarled battle of intertwining shapes, as ancient as the stones, and from that complex skein of roots, the trunk and branches were grotesquely twisted, their ends broken and repaired through the storms of thousands of bitter winters, until the golden heartwood was exposed, whorled and bent like the eddies of whirlpools.

Unable to take his eyes off the gnarled tree, Duval could only whisper his question to Kemtuk: "What do you call these trees?"

"Ah – such are the Oleone – revered as the most ancient of living spirits in all of Tír, the elders of the Forbidden Forest."

Duval recognized the species from his own world, where it

was also revered for its great longevity – a species known to live for six thousand years and more. Though broken and bent almost beyond recognition and taller and broader than any known on earth, he was looking at a bristle-cone pine.

Its significance overwhelmed him. He heard a sound of roaring in his ears and suddenly thunder boomed overhead and lightning crackled in the forest about them.

Kemtuk's voice – Kemtuk shaking him about the shoulders. "Desist, Lord – or the power of your passion will destroy us all!"

When Duval opened his eyes they were blank with grief. "These are the trees of my native land, Kemtuk."

"What land is this, Mage Lord, that it should arouse such passions?"

"America, Kemtuk. I have come home – to America in an alien world."

"A-me-ri-ka!" The Shaman tested the syllables, a look of astonishment on his wrinkled face.

Duval could not speak any more of it. His mouth was a dry cavern, his heart a hollow pounding that filled his chest and his throat.

He recognized other trees among these forest leviathans. The rust-coloured tannin of their barks was unmistakable. These were the giant redwoods called Sequioa. The river hinterland was dense with them, in tall upstanding coppices ramifying among the Douglas firs and spruce. If ever he had harboured any residual doubts, he believed it now.

Monisle! With moist eyes, he looked onto the mirror image of America in this sundered world.

After another day and a half's journey, the river expanded into a lake, several miles in width. Ahead of them the stream divided around a pinnacle of rock. As they sailed closer, Duval saw that it was the rocky edge of a spindle-shaped island and that the river was split into unequal tributaries about it.

The main stream flowed right while a lesser stream flowed left, through a shadowed inlet.

Closer still, he saw that the island was densely forested over its lower reaches and rising in a series of scarps to a broad plateau on which he glimpsed walls and buildings of crumbling stone. From the level of the plateau more scarps buttressed a tor that soared almost vertically upward, so steep and high he could hardly discern its peak in the mists of afternoon.

On that soaring pinnacle he glimpsed an architectural structure, a tower with a figure on its summit. At this distance, the tower appeared like an obstinate fist, and the figure a single finger raised against the sky.

"Dunéduezel is the island name from ancient times," said Kemtuk. "Such was it called in the tongue of those who first settled the valley. Though the meaning of the name is lost today, for it is an alien tongue no longer spoken anywhere in Monisle. But all who have occasion to sail under its shadow know it now as sanctuary of the Dark Queen."

"The Rath of Nantosueta!" breathed Qwenqwo, who had arrived beside Duval, Kemtuk, and Siam, his emerald eyes ablaze.

"On the plateau below the tower," the dwarf continued, speaking a little louder, though his voice still shook with awe, "you see what remains of the temples of her dark arts, elevated above forest and river, from where her witches coven could cast their spells over forest, mountain and river – and over the kingdom of men."

Siam was pulling hard on the wheel to direct the prow into the broader tributary, when a dreadful foreboding seized Duval.

"Stop! Don't head that way, Siam."

Siam turned round to confront Duval. "We cannot take the leftward channel. That way is obstructed by a causeway that connects the forbidden forest with the fortress of rock you see before you. If we enter there, we will be forced to stop under the very shadow of the Dark Queen's rath."

Duval sympathized with Siam's dismay, but the sense of danger waiting for them on the broader tributary was so over-whelming that the oraculum was pulsating strongly. He took a firm hold of the chief's shoulder.

"I'm sorry, Siam, but we have to turn aside! We're in great danger."

Duval wheeled round, already finding himself surrounded by panic-stricken eyes.

"Duval is right." It was the clear strong voice of Ainé that cut through the rising panic. "I too detect the trap that awaits us upon the greater channel of the river, beyond the rath."

Duval looked at the Kyra's brow and her oraculum was also pulsating strongly.

"But this way is also a trap," muttered Siam, with a bewildered shaking of his head. "We shall be forced to stop at the causeway!" With a groan of disbelief and a continuing shaking of his head, he nevertheless heeled the great ship about, so they were heading into the left channel. His face was haggard with worry.

As they drew nearer to the island it seemed a brooding apparition that drew mist about itself, as if to confirm Siam's cautions. Within half an hour of entering the narrow channel, Duval could make out a small alluvial plain that gave way almost immediately to the dense forest of bristle-cone pines and redwoods that cloaked the island's lower slopes: and now, when they were no more than thirty yards distant, the black rock broke out several hundred feet above them, shaking off its forestal coverings, and, in escarpments and buttes, towered over the river.

The only access to the buildings on the plateau above appeared to be an ancient staircase of stone steps, twisting and ascending into the coiling mists.

Now, peering aloft through gaps in the mist, Duval followed the twist and turn of those steps, rising almost vertically above him. A vast ascent took his gaze no higher than the broken ruins of the plateau – what Qwenqwo had derided as the temples of the "witches coven". A second staircase of stone began on the plateau and scaled the tor with its lofty tower that linked the river valley to the louring sky.

Then it was Mira who stood stiffly before them, her face racked with alarm. In a piping voice she warned them. "We must abandon the Temple Ship."

"Abandon the Temple Ship?" Duval heard the incredulous growl of Siam even as he felt the oraculum in his brow pulsate with increasing intensity. He saw a new alarm in Mira's eyes and he heard himself speak – and his words, driven by a sudden powerful instinct, caused a spasm of fear to grip his own heart.

"Mira is right, Siam. We must leave the ship."

"No – no, *no!* You cannot ask this of my people. I will do all that you ask of me, Duval, but do not compel us to leave our only sanctuary. And here –" His gaze turned up to the dark rath that towered over them.

"Siam – everybody! I understand your fears of leaving the safety of the ship. But you must trust me!"

Kemtuk's hand was gripping Duval's shoulder, as if supporting him against the resistance of the elders, now gathering about them in consternation.

"The Mage Lord demands that we abandon the ship," Siam groaned to the small sea of surrounding faces. "Here, in the very shadow of Dunéduezel."

Ainé stood erect to Duval's left side, with Kemtuk and Mira to his right.

"Never has danger so threatened us in this journey as it does now." The Kyra's deep voice rose above the clamour of debate. "Can you not sense eyes upon our every movement!"

"But if there is danger in the forest, we are safer leaving this place. We shall pole our way back up these quieter waters and find the greater tributary."

"Foolish people!" Ainé declared. "Do you not yet understand the peril that faces us in this accursed Vale of Tazan. A Legun has passed through the portals of Kloshe Lamah. What other force could sunder the image of the Queen, where she has guarded the gates for two thousand years. The Legun has created a deathmaw over the river. That is the peril that the Mage Lord has sensed ahead. Sail downstream and you will be drawn into its snare by the river's current."

A groan of fright went through those who heard her.

"What is a deathmaw?" Duval asked Ainé.

"It is a force invisible until you come up against it. Then it is deadly to flesh and spirit."

"Then we are doomed!" muttered Siam.

Ainé thundered: "We are not doomed. But we are certainly trapped here if we stay, since even here, in these sheltered waters, it seems that both Mira and the Mage Lord have foreseen the destruction of the Temple Ship. Take heed then of the gravity of our position. Dark forces close upon us from all sides. But at least for a time we are safe." Ainé lifted an arm to calm their terrified babbling. "A single course remains open to us. We must enter these forests and escape on foot – either that or wait on board the ship in this undefended harbour and make our final stand."

"Once in the forest – then what is to become of us?" an old woman wailed, taking hold of Duval's hand.

Duval insisted: "Listen to the advice of the Kyra. We can't stay aboard the ship."

"But darkness falls – it can be no more than a few hours at most!"

Ainé insisted: "Darkness will bring the attack we fear. We are losing time. We must go immediately. If we can hide ourselves in the forest, at least it will give us time to discover a new way to safety."

"It is a delusion that seizes the Kyra and Duval!" exclaimed Topgal. "I say return to the main stream and sail on. Take our chances in spite of these faint-hearts with their womanish forebodings."

"No!" Siam passed the helm to another so he could stand full square with Duval. Shaking his head, however bitterly and reluctantly, he declared: "Not one among you dreads these accursed forests more than I do, yet I trust this man more than I fear the forest. Is he not the Mage Lord, who has come to lead us to safety in Carfon! How can you even consider denying his counsel. Are we all to die against this forlorn shore because our courage has failed us?"

Duval nodded in gratitude for Siam's leadership. Then he turned to look across the causeway of boulders to the island, his face lifting to the temple plateau.

"We could cross the causeway and climb the tor. Those are defensive walls I can see above. There appear to be some buildings still intact that might give us shelter and a degree of protection."

But the Olhyiu responded with dismay. Qwenqwo was of one mind with Topgal and the other elders. Even Siam quailed, wringing his hat. Duval understood their fear of the rath. Once inside those defensive walls, they would come under a furious siege. There was no prospect of food to withstand such a siege, no going anywhere once the Death Legion had surrounded them. It would become another trap, with no prospect other than delaying the eventual slaughter. At least through the forests there was the possibility of avoiding conflict – perhaps even bypassing the deathmaw over the main tributary of the river. And no matter how difficult the progress southwards through the forest, there was the possibility of constructing rafts that could carry them to Carfon.

As much as he hated the prospect, he could see no choice but to abandon the ship beside the causeway and head inland, making best use of the remaining few hours of daylight.

The Shee spread themselves out, with Ainé leading and the others distributing themselves throughout the single hurrying column. Within minutes, they were under the gloom of the canopy.

Every heart was filled with dread as they struggled up the winding slopes, climbing in silence for the last few hours of daylight. Just as darkness fell they arrived at a wall of stone, at least fifty feet tall and a hundred yards long. It appeared part of a great building, now ruined and overgrown. The bulk of the people rested about tiny campfires under the wall while Duval and Kemtuk explored it further.

It was so dark they carried torches of flaming brushwood. They had to use machetes to force their way through dense undergrowth. At each angle, and high upon the walls, they saw gargoyles, straining monstrous jaws out over the surrounding forest. It seemed that the building had once been a pentagon, surmounting a paved base. On the crest of the pentagon stood the remains of a pinnacle of golden sandstone, suggesting that it had once had a religious function – a tantalizing hint of the sacred beliefs of a people long dead and forgotten.

In the scrub about the perimeter of the building, Duval came upon a stone monument, overgrown with creepers and ferns.

Between them they hacked away the ferns to discover a giant head carved in black quartz, which, though tilted askew and a quarter buried, still rose a good nine feet above the forest floor. The face of the head had the same squared features as Magcyn Ré. Back among the campfires, and while satisfying their hunger with salted fish, Duval discussed the significance of their discoveries with the others.

Kemtuk lit his pipe, talking reflectively. "I wonder about the people who cut these buildings. Here and there, in these marks upon the stones, I recognize an ancient calendar – a year marked by the eighteen months of the moon cycles and the sacred nature of the five days."

Duval considered Kemtuk's words. It was his guess that the tower on the island was also a pentagon. The two men had stood below the main entrance in the walls of the pentagon, where a stone staircase ascended to its summit. In the light of their torches the grandeur of the entrance had lifted their gazes to a band of petroglyphs that ran in a broad course above the entrance. They had been able to make out the forms of warriors fighting dragons.

The pipe-smoking Shaman broke through his thoughts: "Legends do tell of a fierce warrior race called the Fir Bolg, from the days before even the Olhyiu were known in this land. It may be that these people were the architects of these temples of stone."

Fir Bolg – Duval recalled the shout of Qwenqwo Cuatzel, from high in the crow's nest, as they had first approached the guardians: *Magcyn Ré… last overlord of the Fir Bolg, whose spirit in truth yet guards it!*

They camped for the night under the wall of the ancient ruins. Few could have slept soundly in the oppressive darkness, surrounded by the whispering of the forest. Duval woke in a nightmare from his distant childhood.

For the first time in many years, he had dreamed about the Brooklyn orphanage, before his Irish grandmother had rescued him: he saw the boy, a ragamuffin, in old torn jeans, and secondhand boots.

"*Your daddy is no loss to anybody! He's better off dead. When a guy dies at thirty-seven years old it's nothin' more than he deserves. Your daddy was a bum, just like your mommy was a tramp!*"

"No!" He mouthed the word again. *No!*

As dawn was breaking, Duval was back at the giant head, studying it closely.

The face was impassive while conveying an impression of power. There was no doubt about it – in the faint light, he confirmed the resemblance to the king, Magcyn Ré. But it equally resembled another head, with tousled red hair, and with that same profundity of gaze in those deep-set eyes of emerald.

Without turning, he spoke softly:

"I know you are there – that you have been following me – Qwenqwo Cuatzel, of the Fir Bolg."

The dwarf stepped out of the shadows. "You show the intelligence for which you were chosen. What service can I perform for you, Duval, Mage Lord. You only need to ask and it is yours."

"We are surrounded by dangers here, Qwenqwo – I believe we face the gravest threat we have met on this journey. I feel confused, full of uncertainty." He hesitated, looking down into the small man's eyes. "I need to ask questions that might cause you pain."

"What man does not gladly suffer pain when it may help a friend!"

Duval thought that the green eyes were now curious, gazing back at him with equal frankness.

"These people who guarded the forest, the Fir Bolg – tell me more about them."

"They were the bravest and the noblest of men."

"And you still have a link with the guardians of this forest?"

A fierce pride glowed in Qwenqwo's eyes for a moment and he dropped his head to conceal it. "I am the last of the Fir Bolg."

"And your talisman – the runestone with its emerald eye – that too was of Fir Bolg origins?"

"While you were examining it, I saw enlightenment shine in your face. I saw its light even in your eyes – I knew then that you had felt that weight of history. Yours are the only eyes with the wisdom to see there that old and terrible tragedy. My father was the Mage and lore-master to Magcyn Ré in his final great reign – he whose image keeps sentinel still over the entrance to this sacred valley. Most particularly did my father show me, and not through words alone, how the true worth of a man is measured not by his stature but by the courage and integrity of his spirit."

"How did your talisman lose its force?"

"What does a mortal man know of such things as the plotting and scheming of days so long ago? I retained the lore that was lodged within my mind and the result of my training. Yet the runestone – or always it seemed to me – promised more than was ever fulfilled. If there was a reason why I placed it in your keeping, it was in part selfish and in equal part unselfish.

If any might reawaken the power of the runestone, it must be you. For you shocked me to my very soul when you appeared in the chamber of the imposter bearing the Oraculum of the Trídédana on your brow. I had heard of such a thing but only in legend. And I will confess that the hope it kindled in my heart was so powerful that therein was born my selfish motive. I dared to pray that even the mere proximity of such power might reawaken the runestone to its calling. But even then – and this I swear – if you had resurrected the power of the Fir Bolg, I intended to place that power within your service – as now I pledge it."

Duval believed Qwenqwo. He was also certain that he knew more than he was saying of the loss of the power of the runestone, but Duval accepted this reticence. "Thank you for your honesty, Qwenqwo. Let's work together from now on. We might begin by examining this strange head with the advantage of your history and knowledge."

Together they inspected the brow of the great head of stone.

In the uncertain light, Duval saw a pit or depression there, though the crystal, or whatever jewel that should have adorned it, was long lost or stolen.

After a thoughtful hesitation, Qwenqwo spoke softly. "Perhaps you should look upon it through the lens of your own experiences. Is there not a common source of all power as you have already discovered?"

Duval was startled by these words. But Qwenqwo did not expand upon his explanation. Instead he maintained a look under that heavy brow which suggested Duval had been given an important reference. Then Duval could no longer see that great face of stone clearly because a dense bank of clouds was obscuring the sunrise. The forest about them had reverted to gloom.

"You haven't explained what it is about these forests that has kept the Death Legion from passing through them."

"Do not ask me this. I am not at liberty to disclose it."

"I must know, Qwenqwo. Even if it profanes a sacred trust.

Many lives may depend on it."

"I believe you, though you speak strange words here in the land of the Fir Bolg. I do not like to volunteer rumours."

"What do these rumours say?"

"It is said that these stones once harboured great power for good and evil. The pentagon was built over such a source of power, to harness and control it. Even, I will warrant, to challenge Nantosueta on her accursed rath." Qwenqwo's voice was trembling now as, after a hesitation to take control over his fears, he spoke again, softer than a whisper. "Yet it was her power in the end that triumphed."

"And it is her power still that preserves and protects the valley?"

"So it is believed."

"The Death Legion need only to pass through these forests along the river and they would reach the walls of Carfon. And Carfon is where the Council of the Women in Exile sits. I presume the city is well defended?"

"Carfon is a great city, rich in history and richer still in intrigues. But of military strength? I doubt that they could hold out in the long term against a sustained assault by the Death Legion. What defences could there be against such dreadful weapons and malengins as the Legion possess. Yet you are right – it is the greatest of mysteries that Carfon still stands, through twenty years in which the Legion have ravaged all else before them."

"I have to tell you, Qwenqwo, that I don't like mysteries."

"What is a world devoid of mysteries!" Qwenqwo smiled, a secret smile.

"Tell me why you think it has survived."

"It is said that Carfon is protected by an almighty power – so dangerous none will talk of it – not even the rebel council-woman, Milish. Yet this valley holds some link with that power – as if it were a key to its understanding."

Duval was silent a moment, pondering this further riddle. He considered also the cautious way in which Qwenqwo spoke of this source of power in Carfon. Duval remembered the warning of Granny Ddhu as they made their way down the icy valley. *Be silent, Duvaaal – even the sky has ears.*

On impulse, using the oraculum, he turned in a circle, scanning the forest. "I feel it, Qwenqwo," he murmured softly. "I sense that power buried in the very bowels of root and rock: as if a force greater than you or I could imagine still exists here."

"It is dangerous even to speak of certain things – yet surely Carfon's preservation and the rath of the Dark Queen are linked."

"How? I need to know."

The dwarf's head was shaking from side to side and his face fell into a brooding frown.

"You are a very persistent man," he murmured. "Yet it is true that some whisper behind their hands that when the Death Legion destroyed Ossierel a power remained in the land that would give a final hope. It is said that the De Danaan read the omens of her own downfall and withheld her force to preserve some priceless wonder."

His voice fell still further, to little above a whisper, though his face shone with the force of his concentration. "Mage Lord – if such rumours are based on fact, the greatest power in all of Tír is to be found in Carfon. If such a power should fall to the Tyrant, it would extinguish all hope."

Duval studied the dwarf's face. He studied those glittering green eyes. "What power?"

"Would you brush aside all caution and compel me to speak of it?"

"I must know, Qwenqwo."

"Very well then!" The dwarf ran a distracted hand through his tangled hair. He whispered: "If so I am compelled – the power I speak of is an inheritance beyond measure, the legacy of the Arünn themselves. I break every pledge of silence when I speak now to you of the great and sacred *Fáil,* the destiny of worlds."

Back at the camp, they had lit morning fires about which

people were washing their faces or preparing a hurried meal. The elders were clustered about one of the fires but Siam was not among them. Overhead clouds were thickening in an oppressive sky, as if a storm of rain threatened to deluge the troubled land. Duval found Siam at the edge of the forest, berating Mira, who was returning from a dawn foray, her arms full of herbs. Turkaya was missing. Earlier he had left the camp with Mira but had stayed in the forest when the girl had returned.

Duval placed his hand on Siam's shoulder to pacify him, then he squatted beside Mira, whose resentful eyes still brooded at the angry chief.

"We are preparing to leave, Mira. We can't afford to delay through waiting for Turkaya."

"Turkaya has gone deep into the forest," she replied with a shrug. "He seeks information on the enemy. None understands the wildwoods as he does. He will become our eyes and ears."

Duval had to restrain the chief again before he could beat Mira about her head with his hat. "That foolish boy! I despair of knowing what he will do next."

"Don't underestimate his spirit, Siam. Turkaya has already given you cause to be proud of him."

But Duval had to watch the angry Siam storm away, hitting out with his hat at imaginary insects.

He was so lost in his thoughts he had forgotten about Mira until her small hand tugged at his sleeve and suddenly he sensed her anxiety. He followed where she led him, several hundred yards deep into the shadows of the forest, until she pointed out the Kyra, standing upon a buttress of rock that protruded from the slope. Ainé held herself erect, as if standing to attention, then suddenly her position altered and she moved through ninety degrees and took up a similar position. Duval watched her closely for a while, wondering what the girl had sensed. The Kyra appeared to be sending out a signal, using her oraculum as a beacon.

Duval squatted down in the undergrowth, with Mira by his side.

"I know you are very worried about abandoning the Temple Ship."

"Yes, I am, Mira."

"Is all lost? Or is there hope for us still?"

Her question had the startling directness of a child's. So much so that for a moment or two Duval merely shook his head.

They needed to get back, but he put his arm about Mira's slender shoulder and cradled her head a few minutes against his chest while he listened to the sigh of the wind in the trees, the murmuring of the river far below them, the earth sounds. He was still conscious of Ainé, now sitting cross-legged on her stony platform, her eyes closed: he sensed the waves of her beacon striking out into the world. He understood now that Ainé was calling for reinforcements, any Shee that might be close enough and able to answer her call to arms.

It emphasized what he already knew. Their situation had never been so desperate. Yet what could he do?

"Here, in this brooding forest," he spoke softly to Mira, "there is a great power that has protected it for a very long time. I need to understand it. Perhaps if we can just find enough time for me to understand it, it can be made to help us. At the same time, I don't know what that power is – or what its real purpose is. I don't even know if the power is for good or for evil. Even if it is for good, I don't know if it has been worn away during the great length of time its temples have stood idle."

Yet, searching again with his oraculum, he sensed a brooding potency that was still active in this forest – but then, suddenly, he was aware of another presence, a second and more distant force, yet one of awesome power – a horribly malignant force that was also searching.

As if detecting his probing, it turned its awareness toward him.

Then he heard the sound of screaming. Immediately he was on his feet and running. A terrified Mira ran beside him.

NINETEEN

INTO BATTLE IN THE FORBIDDEN FOREST

A S THEY RAN back toward the camp, Duval could hear men shouting and children screaming. In the distance, at the bottom of the slope next to the island, a pillar of green fire rose into the sky, with a horrible crackling. A dense mushroom of smoke billowed out of the flames, gusting and spiralling over the surrounding slopes, carrying an acrid odour on the wind, that same rank smell he remembered from the ambush north of Isscan.

Duval's heart fell. The source could only have been the Temple Ship. If they hadn't escaped into the forest, none of them would have survived.

When he reached the turmoil of the camp, Siam was attempting to restore order. The embers of fires were being extinguished with handfuls of earth.

Milish reached out to hug the tearful Mira. With a look of barely concealed desperation she asked Duval: "The ship had a great force of protection within itself. What manner of weaponry could have so overwhelmed it?"

Duval didn't reply. He remembered the malice he had encountered in the Chamber of Dreams.

"We must escape this place," Siam's brother-in-law, Topgal, spoke decisively. "We are too few to resist any coordinated attack and these ruined walls offer no protection."

Ainé had also returned, but she made no mention of her signalling for help – Duval assumed that she wanted to avoid increasing the panic that was already overwhelming the frightened people.

He strode among the crowds of murmuring and gesticulating Olhyiu. "Don't allow yourself to be panicked into stupidity. We need to think logically about our situation. And you, Siam – I know that you haven't forgotten Turkaya."

Siam was wringing his hat in his hands. "So I have argued with them, Duval. And Kemtuk too. But the hairs on their necks speak louder than wisdom."

Their panic was easy to understand. Duval called out to capture everybody's attention. "It would be madness just to run without direction. We must find another way. Hide, perhaps. Until we can plan a more effective strategy."

"How do we hide so many people?"

Duval didn't know the answers himself. He needed more time to think.

A frail old man spoke, his voice trembling with conviction. "What is life but a bitter journey. Though these giants strike a chill in my heart, yet while we travel among them we still live."

"You fantasize in your dotage, Canim!" interrupted Kemtuk Lapeep. "All should listen to the advice of the Mage Lord. Is he not our guide through peril?"

The old man turned his wrinkled neck about, eliciting the support of others, all equally fearful.

It was Topgal who spoke now for the others. "The Olhyiu have prevailed in adversity throughout many generations because they have listened to their elders. The wisest among us sense the dead hand of history in this graveyard of stone. All are oppressed by it. We should depart this place immediately."

Duval turned to Topgal but saw only blind resistance in his eyes. *The dead hand of history?* Duval was startled by the notion.

"Don't just panic like this!" He shouted at them, twisting and turning so he could look as many as possible eye to eye. "If you don't believe me, trust the instinct of your own Shaman."

Siam stood uncomfortably, his hat running through his hands. He addressed Duval without making eye contact.

"Experience has shown that you possess powers of wonder. Yet this is not your world and even we, who belong here, feel threatened in this place of foreboding. Even the Kyra, with all of her wisdom and experience, does not openly disagree with us. There is little food left – barely enough for two days travel. Carfon is many weeks march if we must cross these accursed mountains on foot, yet there is food in the river's waters, and in the mountains – for we are fishermen and hunters. We do not wish to die of hunger among these walls."

With eyes that darted fearfully about them, the long column of people set off once more between the trees. Shadows swallowed them. Sparks of wintry sunlight pierced the canopy, every mote of light illuminating a splash of green needles or a half-seen edge, while flitting shadows hovered about their path or watched from only a few yards away in the stillness.

Soon they came upon another of the giant heads, half buried under a rotten tree that was festooned with the brilliant yellow crescents of fungi.

Despite the cold, the humidity brought out a sweat that trickled over Duval's skin, like sinister fingers.

During a subsequent halt about mid-morning, he watched Ainé pull down a creeper that coiled down from the canopy. He saw her hack it through with her sword and drink the water that pattered from its core. A family copied the Kyra, pulling at another tendril, the whites of their eyes showing as they slaked their thirst. Duval shivered, listening to the shudder of the wind in the canopy overhead.

Kemtuk materialized out of the gloom and stood by him in the small clearing. "You feel it as I do. We are not alone in this forest. Something other than the Black Legion stalks us."

As his eyes fell, Duval saw it, no more than yards from where he had halted.

Brooding over him, with those dark pits of eyes, he saw that their presence here was observed by another giant head.

Unlike the two he had already seen, this one had retained the insert in its brow. Attempting to examine it, they were joined by Siam, who threw his stout legs apart and tapped his shoulder. "Climb upon my back," he invited. Duval did so cautiously, bringing his face to the level of the eyes. The steam of his breath bathed his hand as he reached up to brush the embedded stone. Its surface was hard, like polished glass, yet, as best he could make out in the murky light, a dull, semi-opaque green.

"Jade, I think!"

He moved some foliage aside to examine the entire head. It had been capped with some other substance. Most had eroded away but there was a rim about the crown that resembled verdigris. There was no doubt about it. The head had been capped with copper.

They forced several more hours' march before pausing again at noon. Duval did not need to search for long before he found another of the heads. He called out for Milish to come and give her opinion.

"Look!" he exclaimed. "See if you agree with me!"

"The face is different."

"Yes! Each face is different."

It was so murky under these trees that Duval had to study the face in the light of a firebrand. The circular pit in the brow was empty but he assumed it had once been inset with jade. The helm of copper was also missing but he could see the mark where the head had been similarly capped. Duval figured that the heads were spaced at regular intervals, and very close intervals at that, considering the ease with which they had come across three. There appeared to be a vast number of them forming a grid through the forests.

After a brief rest, they struggled on to make the most of the afternoon daylight, the weak having to be supported or carried.

Resting later, with his tired back against the bole of a tree, he noticed that the Shee were increasingly anxious, peering into the crepuscular shadows. Duval glanced about him for Qwenqwo, but the dwarf had disappeared.

Three more hours of wearying march and they arrived at another wall of stone. Darkness had fallen and they had to proceed by the light of firebrands. They saw that much of its upper courses were worn away, yet what remained showed that same intricate masonry. Through a gate with sloping jambs, they entered a cluster of buildings, the ruins of a town now tumbled by time and lichened with age. Most of the buildings were in ruins but a few had retained their roofs. One of these was clearly a temple, its walls sculpted with those same menacing scenes of warriors fighting monsters.

It was enough to provoke renewed fears among the Olhyiu. No one would shelter inside the walls.

Topgal, with a half-crazy look about him, was gathering the elders around him.

"It is even worse than before," he murmured. "There is a malevolence here that withers the spirit. Surely this place is all one with those heads. Who among us does not feel their brooding evil, stalking us at every step we make. No – there can be no halt here. Exhausted as we are, we must discover a safer refuge."

While Siam was shaking his fallen head, Kemtuk cautioned against a further march. There were too many exhausted among them. But the Shaman had lost the respect of his people and his arguments convinced no-one.

Pressing deeper into the night, the diagonal way led by Topgal was much more difficult. They were soon sliding down slopes of leaves and bracken. Yet even in descending these difficult inclines, treacherous with the roots of trees, they discovered more stone heads. They slid and stumbled down the rock-strewn slurry to land in thorny scrub at the bottom. By the light of firebrands, they forced a meagre path through this, heading vaguely southward. After two more hours of halting progress they heard a distant thunder in the air. With every step the thundering became louder until they emerged from a screen of giant ferns to be confronted by an astonishing spectacle.

The noise came from a cataract spilling over the table of rock at the top of the slope. Catching the pallid light of an over-clouded moon, it dissolved in a curtain of mist and spray, falling like rain through the shadows of the cliff face. The thunder arose from the valley floor, where its violent impact threw up a mist of freezing vapour. A swamp of streams and tributaries ran downslope, fast flowing and bitterly cold. While the Shee and a few strong men might risk the uncertain crossing, for the majority it presented an impassible barrier.

Dismayed and exhausted, they gathered on the rocky shore, lost in the dark of night, buffeted by the wind and icy spray.

Approaching the waterfall, Duval's hair was immediately soaked, his clothes pressed against the outline of his flesh. Ainé stood beside him in a watchful silence.

Back on the shore, women sat on their bundles, some quietly weeping, or cuddling their fretful children.

Duval felt a dreadful premonition, as he turned to peer into the surrounding dark. He was convinced he heard it again, that same beating of leathery wings he had heard during the first river journey. He did not dare to consider their retreat up that steep and treacherous slope, a morass of rotting vegetation and fallen trees.

"Mage Lord," a despairing Siam cried out to warn him, "your brow is aflame."

Milish rushed up close to him. "The oraculum has awakened."

"We've got to get away from this place, Milish. Immediately! I sense great danger!"

"Hush! I sense it too – but do not speak of it here!" Her eyes glanced over at the frightened women and children and her voice quavered to silence.

"This creature that terrifies you – this Legun – tell me what you know about it."

But Milish was so tremulous she could not speak. It was Ainé who now replied: "The Tyrant has an inner circle, the

Septemvile, each a reflection of its own malevolence." Her fingers brushed the scarred left side of her face with a grim reflection. "The one who did this to me is known as the Captain. Its mask is death. Had it wished other than to torment me, my end would have been as certain as that of my sister-mother in the arena in Ghork Mega."

The voice of the Kyra, with all of her reserves of self-possession, hesitated a moment, as if even for her to speak of it caused fear and grief.

"When a Legun attacks, it may do so in spirit, as a bane of darkness, or it may attack as its incarnate self." Her alto voice lowered so as not to carry to the ears of the Olhyiu. "In spirit we may fight it." She spoke matter-of-factly as always but in her eyes Duval encountered a hardening of resolve. "If it attacks in the flesh no mortal force will prevail against it."

The villagers were huddled in exhausted and demoralized groups. A few men, under the direction of Kemtuk and Siam, were gathering brushwood. Duval heard their voices, eager to light a fire. Ainé's voice cut through this activity as a commanding bark: she forbade it, though they were as fearful of the dark as they were of an attack.

Duval shook his head. "We've got to get out of here at once, Ainé."

Suddenly there was a woman's high-pitched scream, followed by several more, then a tense and awful silence.

In the silence Duval could feel the drip of sweat from his beard onto his chest. He ran in the direction of the screams. His nostrils detected a heavy smell, which his instincts told him was blood – and then...

"Dear God!"

As he neared he was sickened by the sense of foulness. He gagged on the excremental stench.

An entire family had been annihilated. He caught glimpses of terror-stricken faces, he heard the patter of running foot-steps, the sobbing cries of terrified people.

Several were ignoring Ainé's warning and lighting bundles

of twigs. One had already thrown burning tinder into the undergrowth, causing more smoke than fire. In the confusion, Duval tripped over a smooth firm weight. He realized it must be a body. It was too dark to see but he felt the flesh still warm and slippery with blood. He moved his hands about, encountering a heavy leg, the exposed knee above a skintight boot. A Shee – dead. Inching forwards, he peered into the shadows and smoking brush. Another body, then another. As he touched one of them, there was a startle of life, as if the injured person were fighting him, cursing and aiming blows at his head.

"Easy – easy!" he whispered. "It's me, Duval."

"Duval, my friend!" sounded the answering whisper. "It is I, Qwenqwo Cuatzel! One of my arms is broken. Yet do not wait here. Danger is about me – I pray it does not find you."

"Lie still. I'll come back for you."

In the light from the brushfire, Duval was heartened by the fierce courage of the dwarf, his eyes blazing with outrage. "Do not worry about me. It takes more than a devil's disciple to make an end of the Fir Bolg!"

Even as Qwenqwo spoke there was a grotesque tearing, as of a rib cage being ripped apart, and it was accompanied by an anguished moaning from nearby in the tall rushes. Duval entered the reeds to find the old man, Canim, who had argued for flight into the forest. He lay bleeding and broken in the reeking undergrowth. The moaning stopped as Duval arrived by his side. Duval's nostrils recoiled from that stink again. His stomach rose. It was getting rapidly stronger. He was breathless with apprehension. He sensed the concentration of evil upon himself.

Duvaaalll!

He heard his name, like the malodorous bubbling of gas through slime, a guttural whisper from the surrounding darkness.

A rash of gooseflesh erupted over his spine. The proximity of malice was overwhelming.

Outside the clump of rushes, the night seemed to whirl and

glitter like an agitated vapour. Anticipation made the muscles in his legs tense, and rivulets of sweat ran from his brow, over the folds of his face, stinging the angles of his eyes. He could taste blood in the air like a thin salinity on the surface of his tongue.

A presence loomed, between the vague bulk of two trees. He watched it from his concealment and saw how it flickered as if metamorphosing between dimensions. It was loathesomely misshapen, yet rabid in its search for him. An extrusion of lividity began to coil and then expand toward him, licking at the air, following his scent like a snake's tongue.

In the past, rage had activated the oraculum. But now, in spite of his rising anger, he felt only a weak throbbing from his forehead. There was barely power enough to illuminate the shadows that tightened about him. Coming closer, only a little more substantial than the mist that wreathed the low ground, was a pale phosphorescence. It might have been a wraithlike face a long distance above the ground. With the touch of the light from the oraculum, it retracted in hesitation, as if repulsed by it. Abruptly, with what sounded like a roar in his mind, it had gone. The effect was so rapid, its disappearance so complete, he might have imagined it.

For a minute he just held his ground, staring into the grey darkness, gritting his teeth. Then he shouted for the Kyra.

"Ainé! If you're still alive!"

There was much shouting now in the background and running footsteps, then a torch flaring into life next to him. Ainé was examining him, from his face to his feet. "Trídédana be praised – can it be that you are without wound?"

"It was here. Then it fled."

The Kyra lifted the flame to peer into the shadows. With a shudder, she retracted from the stench.

"Never has it been known for a Legun to withdraw from its murderous purpose. It is not over. You must tell me all that happened here."

Duval explained what he had seen. "It spoke my name." He

shook his head, uncomprehendingly. "I tried to use the oraculum. I tried to probe it, but only managed a feeble beam."

"Then," she concluded, "it was only present in spirit, and weakened even at that, or so it seems." Wrinkling her brow in perplexity, she gazed about her at the impenetrable shadows. "There truly are forces at work in these forests more dire than even the legends have foretold." She took firm hold of Duval's arm. "Where is the dwarf mage?"

"His arm was broken during the attack."

Her eyes narrowed. She cried out rapidly, some words of command, ordering the survivors of the Shee to regroup and maintain their guard. Then she asked Duval to lead her to Qwenqwo. But before he could do so, she murmured as much to herself as to Duval. "A Legun never attacks randomly. There is a pattern to this. First it baits a deathmaw – but over the river some miles southward and not within the forest. Then it destroys the Temple Ship. Only then does it cast its spirit in search of us, and then its attack was directed not at you, its obvious rival in power, but at the Mage of Dreams."

"So what does it mean?"

"Who can say. Yet I wonder if this diminutive mage's lore runs deeper than he tells."

"I'll find Qwenqwo, Ainé. You have important tasks to organise. No matter how tired and frightened these people are, we must get away from this place. We made a mistake in coming here."

Shaking her head, she declared, "Bitterly do I regret leaving the island fortress, for it was constructed with defence in mind. Yet that mistake was largely mine. Now I see that pride of reason led us into this trap. The enemy has used me and my experience." Pressing the blazing torch into Duval's hand, Ainé was away instantly, hurling orders.

Duval hurried away to where he had left the dwarf. "Qwenqwo! Qwenqwo – damn you!" He turned in a circle, searching for him in the dark of the trees.

No answer. Only the silence and the dark. Duval hoped that

he had not abandoned the Mage of Dreams to his doom. His wandered the gloom, peering into shadows. He almost fell again over the body of the dead Shee. Now, inspecting its gruesome form with the torch, he saw the unfortunate woman had been bitten in two. Shivering with dread, he held out the brand against the encircling darkness, calling more loudly, "Qwenqwo! If you're alive, answer me."

"Can't a man take a quiet drink without the hounds baying?"

Duval heard the grumble, no more than yards away, from a cavity in the tangled roots of a tree. Then, as if he had appeared within a blink, the dwarf was propped against it, a flask uplifted against his lopsided mouth. "Had the monster not broken my sword arm, I would have left my mark upon its ugly neck." Qwenqwo chuckled, while his eyes protruded with bloodthirsty excitement. "If a neck it truly possessed!"

"You're drunk!"

"As well a man might be who discovers he owes the debt of his life to the witch-warrior lying yonder." He waved the bottle in the direction of the dead Shee. "Never in all my long life… and two thousand years is a mighty long life…!" He hiccuped, then took another swig.

Duval helped Qwenqwo from his cave among the roots and, ignoring his remonstrations, shouted for Milish to come and splint the broken bone. "It seems the Legun chose to attack you – as if it feared you more than it did any other of our company."

The splinting soon done, Duval took the dwarf by one shoulder, with Milish supporting the other, to search for Ainé. The Kyra was right. There was much that remained mysterious about this diminutive man.

"So you have lived two thousand years?" Duval managed a wry smile at the dwarf's drunken swagger.

Then he turned to the approaching Ainé. "Call the elders together. We need to talk. We have a hard night ahead of us."

As the Shee formed a protective ring about them where they had gathered about a single small fire, Duval spoke to a dozen or so apprehensive elders, including Kemtuk, Siam, his brother-in-law, Topgal, and the attentive Ainé and Milish.

"The Kyra is certain that the Legun will return." He paused, looking from one to another of their faces in the firelight. "Its target would appear to have been the Mage of Dreams. And that should tell us something – something that might help us more than our enemy realizes. Ainé has already noticed a pattern to its overall attack: first the deathmaw, then the ship, and now the Mage of Dreams. Perhaps it was necessary after all to wander in these forests. We may be learning a vital lesson. We should all think about those lessons to see if we can work out a plan of our own. Meanwhile all of my instincts tell me that we must turn back immediately – make our way, by whatever means we can, to the island fortress."

Topgal replied, with the air of a broken man.

"I am ashamed I doubted you when you told us to hide. And you, Kemtuk, the greatest Shaman among the Olhyiu. Forgive a foolish man his weakness, born of grief and anger. Yet none can lift his feet a league further, though the alternative is death in this accursed spot. All are exhausted. We have children and wounded among us."

Duval waited for Kemtuk to speak but he held his silence. Siam then spoke his mind:

"You have made me your leader and a leader has powers of command. So I do command it. I will allow a two-hour rest, but no more. We shall travel by night. The strong among us will bear the children and the wounded on their backs. We will crawl if necessary the final league until we reach the causeway."

"Then," Topgal replied, "though my heart may falter along the way, I will gladly accept my burden of wounded."

"Spoken like a true Olhyiu!" shouted Qwenqwo Cuatzel, who sprang to his feet with his arm in a sling.

His face broke into a crooked grin as, passing the last of his flask's contents to the contrite elder, the dwarf mage now came to sit beside Duval.

"Perhaps," spoke Kemtuk, offering a pipe to the dwarf, "the

Mage of Dreams has a story that might enlighten this company in the dark hours before we lead them into yet more peril?"

Duval glanced at Kemtuk's downturned eyes. Clever of him to follow Duval's own line of wondering. There was an appreciative glitter in the eyes of Qwenqwo, who shrugged, then smiled his crooked smile.

"Truly," he declared, filling his pipe to the brim, "the Shaman is the wisest of men, for he recognizes that the power of truth – a truth, both great and terrible, yet one I have long awaited – was ever a prize of circumstance. I will therefore tell you a little of past events that might give you heart in this time of peril."

A reflective silence prevailed over the company while the dwarf lit the pipe. Then, his voice a little more sobered, he began his story.

"These stone men – these idols of brooding evil, as some have mistaken them – are all that remains of the bravest warriors ever to take up arms in a righteous cause. It is true that you see their likeness in my face, for they were my people, the Fir Bolg. And now, in this moment of common peril, I will share with you a sacred knowledge I have shared with none, man or woman, for two times a thousand years.

"Here, in this brooding forest, you have sensed the dread hand of iniquity from a time so long ago that all but myself have forgotten it. I carry the burden of that history. For I am the custodian of the purpose that brought them here, a full army of fifty thousand warriors, into this accursed forest, where it was their tragic destiny never to return home."

"But what dread power could condemn so great an army?" demanded Siam, who was staring at Qwenqwo with his eyes wide with scepticism.

"What dread power, you ask?" Qwenqwo took the pipe from his lips to spit into the fire.

"You will see that I have more reason to fear the Dark Queen and her island rath than you. There is much that I could tell, if I had as many years as we have minutes, of the ways in which a heartless woman, though beautiful beyond men's dreams, plotted the destruction of a warrior nation! Ah, my friends – !" He paused, his face wreathed with tragedy. Then Duval nodded to Milish, who passed him a flask of Niyave, which was accepted with gratitude by the Mage of Dreams.

"I will confess that I was bonded by my father to an oath of trust I would have kept unto death. Yet such is the peril we face that I see with new eyes the terrible purpose of that wrathful queen." The dwarf drank deeply from the flask, before passing it back to Milish.

"At that time, when the army of the Fir Bolg came here, marching for months from a land far to the south, we were the princes of power in this continent. The Queen of the forest – Nantosueta, she called herself – bade us welcome, for even then her realm was threatened. You might not know that even in those distant times the forces of darkness had long been stirring in the wastelands across the Eastern Ocean. And had it not been for the courage of the Fir Bolg, that darkness would have been victorious long ago.

"But even after great slaughter of the forces of the enemy and terrible losses too among our own, our leaders knew that we were not fighting powers merely of flesh and blood. The powers of darkness had swept down on Monisle from the north, just as during the fall of Ossierel. And with them came an evil of corruption that would have laid waste even these ancient forests. Some say the Queen herself perished in the heat of the final battle and that it has been her spirit that has reigned ever more from the rath that stands upon the fastness of rock that bisects the great river.

"I do not know all, for I was but a child at that time, and it may be in consequence that my memory is prejudiced.

"Yet I know that then it was Nantosueta's wish that our warriors were given the choice, each man for himself, whether he returned home to the pleasures of family and beloved country, or to stay as guardian of this pass against the evil that overwhelmed it.

"My father cast the runes that foretold that the evil could not be crushed by mortal courage. So was Nantosueta's grim design made plain. From her vaunted pinnacle she laid the hand of death over the entire valley. So she did and so she watches still, making certain that all keep fealty with her terrible command."

The dwarf wept openly, waving away the flask, for no healing balm could assuage the sorrow that had long brooded in his heart.

"In this way," he continued, "was her treachery unveiled and a warrior race condemned not for life but for all eternity. And so here, in this Vale of Woe, all that survived of the Fir Bolg, fully thirty times a thousand warriors, shed their life's blood, each selfsworn to do so by his own hand. Every consecrated spot was marked by a stone head, inscribed of their living features. And on every grave the Dark Queen called upon Mórígán, the raven of death, to accept the sacrifice so that such a spirit of fealty would endure."

Qwenqwo wept inconsolably for a short time, so that those who sat on either side of him placed their arms about his shoulders and held him steady. Then, once recovered, in a voice of outrage, he continued:

"At the throat of the pass, Nantosueta, in her final act, moulded the very mountains to the figure and countenance of Magcyn Ré, the last king of the Fir Bolg. Yet – such was her arrogance – that, in spite of her treachery, upon the right hand pillar she married the figure of herself. As such they would forever guard the entrance to her valley, like some benighted King and Queen."

The dwarf drew a great sigh and he tamped the ashes of his pipe upon the makeshift hearth.

"And so now I arrive at the most painful confession of all. My father was none other than the Arch-Mage of the Fir Bolg, Urox Zel. After his name do I bear Cuat-zel, for I am the son and heir of Zel, the greatest Shaman of my race. The Mage of Dreams he made me in his stead before he became the last to spill his blood. Thus now, as you see me, with my heart and spirit broken, and my poor body upon the rack of my grief, did I accept this dreadful burden and bear it alone for two thousand years.

"So, I now answer the Mage Lord, Duval – so I tell him how in grief the oraculum of the Fir Bolg lost its power. And in telling it, I weep no more. For I thank the brave Olhyiu, and my friend Duval, you who have allowed me the privilege to unburden my grief at last. I ask only this of you, that when I fall my grave should be added to theirs, and so the sacrifice will be made complete."

There was a hushed silence of many minutes, during which the flames of the fire discovered the high points of eyes and cheeks. Not a man or a woman among their circle was other than stirred to a new courage by the story of the sacrifice of an entire nation.

Duval understood now the hatred the Legun felt for Qwenqwo. The Mage of Dreams remembered the history of an earlier conflict with the Tyrant's forces – a conflict the Tyrant did not win.

Siam stood erect in the centre of them, all scepticism banished and his face aglow. "I am proud that I have lived long enough to hear such a wonder. Now we know at what price security was purchased in days beyond memory. It is time to see how great is the answering courage of the Olhyiu people." Though Siam did not speak of it, Duval knew he was thinking of Turkaya. "We know that danger lurks in every shadow on the journey that lies ahead of us. Still let us all forget our wounds and our pains to share what little food and drink that remains among us. Let every man woman and child celebrate as best we can how precious is this liberty that we have come so far to win."

At Siam's command, the Olhyiu stood wearily to their feet and, with their dependents and wounded upon their backs, they began the arduous climb through roots and thorns. Progress was anguished. The children did not understand and in their exhaustion they cried out to their struggling parents.

Waiting for the last of the stragglers to clear the top of the slope, the party paused only to account for all before driving on again.

Though it was dark the scouts had little difficulty back-tracking their route, for many feet had trampled the undergrowth. Their lungs pained more at every mile, and their hearts palpitated with weariness; still as they arrived at one head and then another, they were encouraged where earlier they had been frightened.

One of the scouts sent ahead to check their path failed to return. Suddenly an explosion tore through the night. It came from behind them, perhaps no more than two or three miles distant. Duval felt a quickening, like a slight weakening of his remaining strength.

Qwenqwo shouted: "The Legion are destroying heads." His voice shaking, he added, "I cannot bear it." Still he took a deep breath and forced himself on.

A man's roar some distance away cut through his thoughts. Duval ran forward until he found Ainé.

"Five dead. Two men, two women, one child." She met his eyes, then carried on walking into the darkness.

"The Legun?"

"It is close," she replied tersely.

"It fears us," Duval muttered, with a growing conviction. "It fears what we have learnt from Qwenqwo about the forest."

Ainé soon called a halt to regroup. Her oraculum flared as she was issuing orders. There was a shuffling of feet as the Shee organized the people within their overstretched protection, filling the gaps in their ranks with the fittest of the Olhyiu men. The injured Qwenqwo, still thirsty for fighting, insisted on taking his stand among them. The remaining men and women formed a second circle of defence about the vulnerable children and wounded. Duval sensed the presence seconds before it attacked.

"It's coming," he roared.

A hissing frenzy cut through the trees, twenty yards to his left. For a fraction of a second the nacreous malignancy was visible. Then it was among them. Fast as she moved, the Shee blocking its attack was beheaded even before she could direct her weapon. Once inside the outer circle, it travelled parallel to the second defensive line of Shee, slaughtering as it moved. Suddenly a big man stood out to confront it, with his harpoon raised.

"Topgal!"

Duval heard the man's oath, even as he hefted his weapon with all of the strength in his two burly arms. "Feel Olhyiu steel, you vermin!" He struck down fiercely upon the presence, but the simple metal blade passed through it.

With hardly a pause in its progress, the Legun destroyed him, crushing his head with a single blow.

It destroyed everyone in its path until it stood before Duval, who had stepped out in front of the Olhyiu, with Mira shielded behind him. It saturated his nostrils with the stink of the grave, its baleful intelligence exploring him as it savoured the moment of its impending victory.

Ainé hurled herself in front of Duval. The glow on her brow spread until it illuminated her whole face from within. Her sword blazed with that same flickering matrix. With a great stroke, she slashed a line of brilliant green sparks through the spectre of evil. The power in her sword had hurt it. Duval felt it weaken, as those eyes, laden with hatred, still kept their focus upon him.

Protector of the throne of women! Dare you confront me upon the exalted plane!

The murderous hiss invaded his mind as it cut down another Shee, making its escape through the outer circle. Its sibilant threat echoed in his head as it twisted and turned, like a malignant serpent, past the dark pillars of the giant trees.

Ainé had saved his life. Yet there would be another attack.

The Kyra was already shouting at the terrified Olhyiu to take up their burdens again and struggle forward. Kemtuk's voice sounded out, also exhorting them. Ainé took Duval's arm, to press him onward. Milish was left to protect Mira while he hurried beside Ainé, deep in thought.

If the focus of the previous attack had been Qwenqwo, this time there could be no doubt that it was Duval.

It understands! he thought. *As if it reads my mind – it knows that I sense its fear of the forest!*

He knew that he had been useless in that last confrontation. Yet he had seen how the fiery matrix of Ainé's oraculum had extended power to her sword arm. He picked up the sword of one of the slaughtered Shee.

"It is a brave thought, Duval. But you have no warrior training. The speed of your strike will be too slow."

Perhaps Ainé was right, but he was determined he would not die without trying to defend these innocents.

Qwenqwo Cuatzel came forward to stay his arm. He took the sword from Duval and laid it awkwardly against his own side. "Accept a blade fitting to the Lord of Mages!" He handed Duval a long-bladed dagger with an elaborately cast handle of green bronze. The blade was wrought of many twisted and curved sinews of strange metals, lambent with spiritual charge.

"Since my own sword arm is useless, I have armed you with the blade of Magcyn Ré. This dagger was blessed twice, once by my father and again by the Witch-Mage, Nantosueta herself. If ever I preserved it through the long years it was for this moment."

It was a weapon designed for close-quarter fighting. Even while he was weighing the squat and heavy dagger in his hand, there was another deafening explosion, this time no more than a few hundred yards distant. The Legun had destroyed the next head along their line of passage. It confirmed Duval's line of thought. For some reason, the Legun must fear the heads. But the realization did not help their immediate danger. They were struggling on once more, a common fear weakening even the most redoubtable legs.

Although they altered course a little southward, no more than minutes later Ainé stopped abruptly and shouted to Duval. "It is coming."

For the first time since he had met her, he took firm hold of the Kyra's arm. Her fearless green eyes met the determination of his own.

In the faint light before dawn, Duval pushed through to stand at the head of the wedge facing the attack. Ainé took up her position by his side, her oraculum pulsating brightly. Duval waited with such a weight of apprehension, every muscle strained to alertness.

"Now!"

As if anticipating their tactics, the Legun did not rush at them with fury but approached at the pace of a cantering horse, little caring that could anticipate it. This attack was to be the final one.

Manly combat – I demand it of thee, Duvaaalll – gladiatorial confrontation in the exalted zone! He heard the susurration of its glee.

Bathed in the light of his oracular blaze, it reared, monstrous in form before him, flickering wildly through quicksilver and darkness. Duval felt his heart beat so hard, it expanded the entire cage of his chest with every throb. Sweat, which had never left his brow since the shore by the waterfall, poured in a stream from his face, descending in rivulets over his upper lip and beard.

This time, I shall devour thee. I covet thy torment. And after I have slain thee, I shall take my time to sport with these others until I gnaw the meat from their bones.

It preened its malevolence before him with a lubricious gloating. But then he heard Kemtuk lead the Olhyiu in their chant behind him.

The Shee also had joined the chanting, that same battle hymn they had sung as they fought the Black Wolves by the Tshis-Cole River. Duval felt comforted by that spiritual ritual.

"I am ready for you."

He heard his own voice, barely recognizable it was so huskily defiant. As he spoke, the light from the oraculum burst into a conflagration in which, for a moment, he could make out the Legun. The roinish grin was insane with evil, the spectral lips drawn back over salacious fangs, the arterial red of the hateful eyes dimmed by the brightness of the light from his own pulsating brow.

Die, Duval – spawn of woman!

As the Legun rushed toward him, Duval felt the avidity of its baleful eyes upon his skin. He was drowning in the sulphurous smell of its rank malignancy, but still he waited, taking courage from the communion of spirits behind him. He bore that terrible patience, touching the dagger against his brow until it began to burn with the brilliance of his oracular fire. Not until they were just feet apart did he move – and then, so quickly a movement it was almost instantaneous. He thrust forwards with all of his strength and allowed the rush of the monster to bury the incandescent blade of Magcyn Ré deep in its brow. He felt its malevolence bite upon his hands, his arms, until his mind and entire being were enveloped by its murderous will.

Here, in the foul effluvium of its spirit, it maddened to fight back, though the dagger was buried to the hilt between its eyes. Still he forced in the dagger, twisting and pressing it deeper still.

Its malice invaded his mind to torment him with a vision. In the gloating of its implacable hate, he saw the feral girl. The Legun's voice, fawning with glee, rasped in his mind: *The female is ours to use as we will. She has long been the plaything of my master!* He saw Kate as he was forced to abandon her in that vile backstreet in London. And now he was shown her fate. Kate was held prisoner in some horrible dungeon in a strange landscape of stinking vapours and twisted trees, in which a tower of bones in the shape of a skull protruded brokenly from the anguished ground. It could not possibly be a landscape on Earth. Kate was here – a prisoner somewhere on Tír. She lay bruised and beaten on the rancid dirt of the tower's dungeons.

Duval's heart faltered.

He remembered that single youthful kiss in Clonmel. The desperate reminder of that love in her tormented eyes in London. He retched, sickened by this vision of her capture and torment. Weakness overwhelmed him. He saw the dagger begin to withdraw slowly, though he still fought it all the way: a fraction, then half an inch, accelerating.…

No!

A new spirit joined his in the maelstrom.

It was not a voice he would have anticipated. Not that of his friend, Qwenqwo Cuatzel, nor the voice of the Kyra, but the girl, Mira.

True Believer - discover the guardians!

He was aware, as if in another dimension, that the Kyra was attacking. But a swipe from the Legun struck Ainé aside, her fall broken against the trunk of one of the huge trees.

Discover the Guardians!

Duval heard that tiny reed of voice again, mind to mind, as weak as the plaintive song of a bird, buffeted in a tempest of malice.

Again the Legun rasped with triumph. *Naive cur of a misbegotten race. Thou would'st confront my master!* His mind was violated by horrible laughter. *Know then that at every step, it was his design thou hast followed!*

Was this true? Had he been manipulated at every step by the Tyrant?

In his anguish, the dagger was dragging back. It was only half buried now in that spectral mask. Though he understood the message from Mira, yet still the power to discover the guardians eluded him. He heard the gasping breaths that must have been Ainé, lying injured in the dark, her voice stuttering yet insistent:

"Shee – attack!"

The order was a brave one but it could not succeed.

In those faltering moments, Duval sensed another presence, powerful and fearless. It was Kemtuk. He heard that incanting voice as it evoked A-kol-i and the coming of the changers. The Legun shuddered. He felt its focus move, as if a monstrous head were turning, carrying Duval and the inserted dagger upon its brow, as a troublesome wasp upon the mask of a tiger.

The Shaman was in terrible danger. Duval opened his mouth to shout his caution, but no sound came out. Through his mind he shouted the warning:

Kemtuk – get away! Save yourself.

But the old man's courage was resolute.

Duval saw him now as he had seen him over the lake of ice, that incandescent glow about his features. He heard the incantation continue, the psalm of beginnings. A-kol-i was gazing down upon the world of creation. And Granny Ddhu, the Earth Mother, was peopling the land with voice and song. Duval felt a new entry to the spiritual struggle, an alien aware-ness that seemed sluggish to awaken, a courage weakened through eons of slumber, as if sparks of anger rose through a withered matrix of time and space. A head – his instincts told him that it was one of the heads that was awakening. In desperation, his mind responded, reached out, made contact. With a growl of rage, the Legun diverted its attack to the Shaman. There was a horribly familiar sound, the cracking of bones. Duval's eyes closed as he felt a warm moistness drench his face and knew it was the blood of his friend.

Thunder pealed and lightning tore through the pallid glim-merings of dawn. He saw how it illuminated the shadows between the huge trees, from sky to earth and then from earth to earth.

Outrage coursed through Duval's arms and he plunged the dagger to the depths of his arms into the mind of evil. The oraculum sent an almighty discharge through the Fir Bolg blade.

The Legun screeched in a tormented fury before slithering away between the boles of the great trees. In its wake was a vaporous green trail, as if its spirit bled from a grievous wound.

TWENTY

BITTER RETREAT

OR SOME TIME he was so stricken with grief, Duval could not move. His friend Kemtuk Lapeep was dead. Kemtuk, who had given his life to buy time for him. And Kate captured – a prisoner in that place of torment!

As he knelt in this shocked state, Ainé stood over him, with blood seeping from deep parallel lacerations to her right shoulder. Duval climbed to his feet, then stumbled down into a nearby gorge, where a stream cascaded toward the distant river. He waded out into the water, kneeling down in it to wash away the blood of his friend. He pushed his head under, immersing his senses in its icy current. All the darkness that had haunted his life struck him now, in this terrible moment. He roared his anger through clenched teeth. "It's all a damned lie!" he shouted. "Hope is a lie!" Ramming his hand deep into the pocket of his saturated greatcoat, he extricated the harmonica. He looked at it as if it were an abomination, then hurled it away from him, far downstream. It was Siam who waded out to join him: Siam's dogged voice cutting through the murmuring of the wide-eyed onlookers.

"Though we are sorely injured and exhausted, we must leave this dangerous place."

Duval refused to be placated by Siam. He refused to change out of his wet clothes. The heat of anger would burn them dry. He waited in silence while Milish bathed and stitched the wounds to Ainé's shoulder and while the Olhyiu tended to their own casualties.

There was no time for the Shee to cremate their dead. The bodies of Olhyiu and Shee alike were hastily covered with loam and rocks, and abandoned there. Siam wept openly by Duval's side as the frightened company turned its face once more to wearisome retreat. They all shouldered their burdens and struggled on through the forbidding forest, Milish and Ainé staying clear of Duval, though both women kept a wary eye on him. It was Duval who forced the pace every perilous foot of the way, his fingernails clawing at the slope, his feet sliding down embankments, ignoring the stricken glances of elders, the sobbing of frightened children, and the furious look of Qwenqwo.

The Temple Ship destroyed! Kemtuk dead! The feral girl the plaything of the Tyrant! He himself, manipulated at every step!

What did it mean? What could it all mean?

He remembered Kate, the girl he had loved. He knew – he knew it absolutely – that the feral girl was his Kate from Clonmel. No matter how changed she looked, no matter the bizarre circumstances when she had saved his life in London. Kate, bruised and tormented, was a prisoner of the Tyrant in that godforsaken place.

The riddles and contradiction were enough to drive him insane. Despair was expanding in his mind like the mass of clouds that were invading the sky.

"No!" he roared his anger into the dark canopy of trees.

The people near to him had stopped walking. They were staring at him with bewildered eyes.

Somebody was trying to restrain him as he scrambled over the slippery scree of a new incline, but he tore the hands from his shoulders.

Milish's voice! She was calling him and he stared at her without comprehension, the anxiety in her dark eyes, her hands frantically signalling. His brow blazed. The pain in his head was such an agony he shook his body from side to side, fell onto his hands and knees and attempted to bury his head in the mulch of pine needles between the gnarled roots. Distantly he heard the shriek of a child. The hands of many were attempting to pull him to his feet, only for him to clench his fists with such a fury that he spun and slid down the slurry of the slope.

He would neither talk nor listen to anybody as he forced his aching feet to step onward again, stamping them into the ground in deliberate mortification. His head was so confused it seemed full of random electrical charges.

There was a sudden crack of lightning, strange lightning, a lurid red, as livid as blood.

It cast a sinister flare through the trees and left his eyes temporarily blinded. Then thunder shook the ground beneath their feet and left men moaning and the women and children screaming. At once the wind surged, howling through the forest. Duval saw a mother, with her clinging child, bowled over and then dragged along the ground, their lives only saved when they were blown against the trunk of a great tree. Bundles of clothing were being torn out of people's hands and carried off by the hurricane that bent the groaning branches and raged in the canopy.

Voices screaming, fingers clawing at him: he didn't give a damn. He didn't want to understand them.

The storm raged about him. The wind howled around him, flapping the clothes about his head and face, whipping at his exposed flesh. He clung with both hands to a massive root, ignoring the pain as shards of stinging debris tore into his skin. But the grip of his bloodied fingers was inexorably slipping when he felt the Kyra's powerful arm take hold of him and press him forward.

He caught glimpses of other Shee, sheltering the people who had fallen flat on the ground, looking for handholds on projecting roots or stones.

There was an almighty creaking and groaning, then a rumbling thunder. A giant sequoia on the edge of the embankment tore free of its roots. It crashed to the ground, its great trunk fragmenting into cylinders that went battering down the slope, uprooting other trees and crushing anything in their path. In the ravening gale he heard the spite of the Legun again, the glee with which it had shown him Kate's torment. A tempest raged in his heart and mind.

Then Ainé struck him.

He felt the blow on his face, like a numbing shock of icy cold water. It broke the madness that had invaded his senses. When Duval looked up into the face of the Kyra, he saw that it was illuminated by the fierce red flame of his own oraculum, reflected back at him in those hugely dilated pupils.

"The Earth Power, Duval! Control your passion before all are lost."

Duval looked into the vortex of storm and sky through the gap left behind by the fallen tree. He was responsible for it.

"Oh, God!"

Shaking his head, he struggled to think beyond his despair. He sat hunched, with his face in his hands while he regained his composure. Then he stood up on his reluctant feet, forced them to move onward again. He led the company in a renewed rhythm, forcing limbs that felt black with fatigue into a new stride, joints that tormented with every movement, minds that begged for sleep.

And so, as daylight dragged on into noon and noon into afternoon, they found themselves back once more on the shadowed walkways of the bristle-cone forest. Still they forced themselves to move on, too wearied to think, until the tangled masses of foliage merged with the inky dark of evening. On and on, they endured beyond exhaustion, each pace a further achievement, until the gloom darkened and they might have been threading their way through the depths of a cave. Torches had to be lit in the glimmer of which the twisted trunks were the merging of stalagmites and stalactites, so ancient they had fused into dense pillars that supported the roof of foliage.

The dark was so oppressive, it seemed to devour all life. Every breath pained deep in their lungs. Even Ainé, weakened by wounds and blood loss, appeared to stagger from time to time, as if the inertia of darkness were about to overcome her.

Still an iron in Duval's will drove them on.

Drawing on the human strength of his own anger, he ignored the moans of pain and frustration, the gasping breaths that lifted from hanging jaws to form clouds in the torchlight. At last they stopped, when they could not physically take another step. They had reached the great wall and lichen-encrusted ruins where they had camped on that first night after abandoning the Temple Ship. Other than Shee, Duval and Siam were the only ones still standing among the wrack of tormented bodies, collapsed about the stones.

Siam's eyes were hollowed with weariness. When he walked, as he walked now by Duval's side, it was with the stagger of a man with blistered feet. They halted next to one of the small fires that had been lit by the Shee to warm and comfort the exhausted people.

He murmured, "We would follow you, Duval, unto death itself. But here we must die then, since none will endure another journey."

Duval nodded in sympathy to the chief, whose black eyes reflected the orange glow of the fires. His voice was little above a whisper. "I know, Siam, that many of your people have given their lives."

"Perhaps as many as one of every five who began this journey. And other deaths will follow."

"The causeway is only a few hours' march, even for exhausted limbs, and downhill most of the way. If we can reach it and make a stand there! If we can only hold it, for a while! The Death Legion will have to cross the straits in single file."

Siam's calloused fingers rotated the crumpled hat he had preserved through gale and attack.

"It is asking more than we have to give. My people will never reach the river. They will die on the way or the few that survive will be easy prey as they cross the causeway – for I fear that it is also an obvious place for the enemy to bait a trap. So this is why I come to you. To beg on behalf of the Olhyiu people to halt this retreat – let us stay here and rest. And if die we must, then we die together in the dignity of these hallowed ruins."

Duval put his hand on the tensed shoulder of the chief.

"Siam – my friend! I have never deserved your courage or the sacrifices of your people. Go and tell them all to rest."

Within minutes Ainé also approached him. The Kyra had never shown any open display of emotion before, but now as he looked up into her eyes he could not mistake the desperation he saw there.

"You too must feel it, Duval. Moment by moment, danger gathers itself about us here."

"Yes." His tired limbs couldn't even tense. His eyes swept over the huddled masses of bruised and wounded people.

"Death Legion are approaching."

"I know. Take me to see Milish, Ainé." His voice was flat with resignation.

They found Milish, her hair muddied and awry, working with the seemingly indefatigable Mira. They were kneeling before a wounded mother. Duval could see that the woman was on the point of death. Her husband, a man of perhaps thirty, had carried his wife all the weary way.

Ainé drew him away from the scene of anguish, leaving Milish and Mira to comfort the man.

Walking on among the villagers, he watched the tired hands spreading their impoverished bundles about the fires. Others among the wounded had fallen into stupors, with ice crystals condensing on their cooling flesh. How many, Duval wondered, would ever wake up again? Even as he gazed down on them, there was another explosion in the forest. Duval's ears followed the sound to the pillar of fire that violated the night, closer to the river, perhaps two or three miles distant. The faint hot gust of it came seconds later, a rancorous breath sighing through the trees.

Another head.

Milish had left the distraught husband to follow him. The ambassador's sleeves were rolled up and her hands were caked with blood and dirt. She tugged at his arm, drawing him away from the others, so she could hold him alone eye to eye, as if weighing what he must be thinking.

"Do not despair, Duval. Consider what has been achieved. Nobody, not even the Shee, has ever defeated a Legun before."

"I needed help." He sighed. "I couldn't repeat that struggle now, Milish. If it attacked again –"

Her hand rested on his arm. "Yet you defeated it, inflicting a humiliating wound. And in wounding it so you gave us time to retreat. Then, too, it was your endurance that saved us all on that death march through the forest."

A squall of wind rattled the pine needles, as if it were a continuation of the mocking glee of the Legun.

Duval spoke softly, insistently. "The Legun will recover from its wound. As Ainé has warned us, it will attack again. It's hard to believe we will survive this night, Milish. I think the time has come for you and me to be a little more open with each other." He had to take a deep breath before continuing. "In the snowstorm, when Valéra was dying, I had a vision in which I spoke to a being of perfect light. I demanded answers to riddles. All I got were more riddles. I was told that the understanding I seek is power unlimited. It awaits me at Carfon – a place called the Gates of Eternity."

He stopped speaking to gauge her reaction. She stared back into his eyes in utter silence.

"I have also talked to Qwenqwo. I know about the *Fáil*, Milish – the fact that it is believed to hold all the answers!"

"Desist!" Fear caused Milish's pupils to grow, as if devouring the brown irises.

"No – I won't stop. I want you to tell me what it all means. I demand it – now. What is this power unlimited that stands at the Gates of Eternity?"

Milish was swaying on her feet. Duval had to take hold of her arms and hold her before she fainted. Yet still she shook her head at him, shook it again, with surprising violence, her exhausted eyes clenched.

"Why can't you answer my question?"

"I cannot. There are dangers more perilous even than Leguns."

Abruptly there was another explosion, and soon the acrid stink of the green fire reached their nostrils.

"They are speeding up their attack," she groaned, her weight falling against his body. "Can you not see the pattern to it! They are destroying those heads closest to the river. Soon they will have opened up a path into Carfon."

He clenched his teeth in frustration, staring sightlessly into the night. From the nearby forest came the clash of battle. It must have involved the small band of surviving Shee guarding the perimeter. Duval was already hurrying toward Siam, who had climbed once more onto his blistered feet.

"Arouse yourselves, warriors of the Tilikum Olhyiu!" Siam roared. He was staggering among them, driving them on to a final effort. "Let a proud people make a valiant stand!"

Duval had drawn the dagger of Magcyn Ré. The renewed throbbing of the oraculum was accompanied by a roaring in his ears. He heard Ainé's shouts of command. The Kyra too was injecting her determined leadership into what could only be a hopeless battle. And then, plaintively, he heard the brave chant of the Shee. But the chanting of so few voices was drowned by the explosion of legionary weaponry. The sky grew gangrenous with the flickering green fire. Duval felt the continuous flare of his oraculum as he listened, ears pricked in the direction of the nearby forest. It would not take long for the few surviving Shee to be overwhelmed. Then he heard the Shee battle hymn began again, but much louder – so powerfully it was more like the roar of a thunderous surf. It was impossible – yet hope fought the weariness in his limbs as he ran in the direction of Ainé's voice.

"Duval – Mage Lord!" Siam's voice, Siam's hand throwing his hat into the air. "See who it is! Turkaya – my son! He returns! And he has brought reinforcements."

Duval saw the gangling youth in the illumination of the

fires, the boy running toward his father – and Siam's hair was standing wild on his head, as the two shouting figures embraced.

And then the glinting of silver on the cape brooches was the first he saw of the new arrivals. An army of Shee flowed from the shadows of the trees into the firelit ruins, in a chanting wave. They came together from every direction, eyes darting about warily, as if searching for evidence of a trap. Their battle song overwhelmed that of Ainé and the small gathering of her companions who had survived the Legun's two attacks. From the weary Olhyiu, a great cheer broke the air, as bruised arms thrust their weapons aloft.

Duval spun about himself in amazement. He felt diminished by the stature of so many gigantic women. There appeared to be more than a hundred of them already within the encampment, those great capes twisting and turning, different faces, many bruised and bloodied from conflict, different colours of braided hair, different uniforms – and the glitter of weaponry at the ready.

He was facing a remarkable black woman.

Though she moved with the same stealth and grace as the other Shee, she was not quite as tall as the others and looked older. Her hair, braided over her left shoulder, was almost white.

"I am Bétaald," she spoke, in a clear, deep alto. "And you are Du-vaal! The Mage Lord, who bears the oraculum of the sacred Trídédana. I am honoured!"

Between Bétaald and Ainé he sensed a wordless communication.

Bétaald smiled. "I have heard how you defeated a Legun in spirit! It is the very air of legend I breathe."

Duval could only gaze into her eyes with astonishment – amber eyes, like those of a tigress.

Milish rescued him from his confusion, arriving at his side to take his arm. As he struggled to comprehend all that was happening, the black woman held a hand to the air as if to demand quiet and Duval realized that the sounds of battle had ceased. An ominous silence prevailed over the encircling forest.

"Fortunately we encountered only a scouting party of Death Legion. But they bore new weaponry, which may carry their foul discharge over great distances – and some with strange body forms, the like of which has not been seen before and the malevolence of which we cannot imagine. I fear there is a great force of them at large in the forest – many tens of thousands – and still more are arriving from Isscan by the river."

Duval accepted a welcome sip of the golden Niyave, provided by a wizened little woman among the newcomers, before returning his gaze to Bétaald.

Ainé treated the newcomer with great respect, though Bétaald herself carried no weaponry. He assumed she was their spiritual leader.

"Why," he asked Bétaald, "are the Death Legion destroying the stone heads?"

"I don't know. I too am puzzled about this curious behaviour. And led by a Legun incarnate!" Her gaze eye to eye with his own was frankly assessing. "This surely is the spearhead of the great invasion force we have long anticipated. It is the first step in what we presume is the plan to take Carfon. All of the city's food and supplies come from the hinterlands about the river." She paused, as if to emphasize the full gravity of what she was explaining.

"Then," declared an exhausted elder, "all is surely lost!"

"Not so! Something appears to hold them back. Why do they hesitate here? Why not immediately progress downriver? Instead they move with great stealth and patience, destroying these monuments with the ruthless efficiency they might otherwise devote to city walls."

Duval nodded. "Then Qwenqwo Cuatzel is right. For some reason, their purpose is threatened by the heads."

Bétaald lifted her eyebrows at the mention of the Mage of Dreams. "Surely it is true that there is a spiritual presence that guards the pass – as foretold by so many legends. In such a vortex of ancient forces it may be that their malengins of war do not function well – perhaps there truly is a force even greater than we suspect at large in this valley?"

"A force," agreed Duval, "that might still help our purpose!"

There was nothing more to be said and so Milish took them back to the circles of fires, where supplies of food and drink, and much-needed flasks of Niyave, were being distributed among the Olhyiu. Duval was impressed with the efficiency with which Bétaald organized this.

Siam, who seemed to need no more reviving than the safe return of Turkaya, had to be persuaded to take some food and Niyave. Others among the newcomers were busily treating the wounded and constructing biers for those unable to walk. Bétaald called these Aydes. The woman who had recently given Duval Niyave was one of these, a curious-looking people with leathery, almost scaly skin – very different from the Shee or the Olhyiu. Tiny and wizened, yet they seemed stronger and more nimble than their appearances would suggest, and they were clearly skilled as smiths, weapon's testers, and forgers. They seemed to include most of the cooks and scouts, all very necessary to support an army in the field.

Duval drank wine from a gourd and ate a welcome meal of meat, after which he found a warm corner to curl up and get some rest.

While the exhausted people slept, a scouting party of Shee moved down the slope to secure the causeway for the morning. Then, at first light, refreshed by hope as much as food and sleep, the Olhyiu ate a hot stew of herb-flavoured vegetables, provided by the Aydes, before gathering together their meagre possessions and setting out once more, the wounded carried on biers.

Duval estimated that at least three hundred reinforcements had swelled their numbers during the hours of darkness, of which most were warrior-Shee. So it was a growing army that now picked its way through the ankle traps of moss-encrusted roots and treacherous boggy ground glinting with frost over a decayed carpet of pine needles. By the time the sun was two hours clear of the Blue Mountains, south of the river – those same mountains that Siam had called the Mountains of Mourning – they had arrived at the last slope before the causeway. Here Ainé raised her left arm to halt their progress while she joined Bétaald in studying the panorama of river valley that appeared, like a startling vision, through the thinning screen of trees.

Duval also stared across at the formidable crag of rock that reared up through the morning mists, its lower slopes carpeted by dense woodland.

His gaze followed the winding staircase of stone that led up to the intermediate plateau, with its triple fortifications, roughly level with their present perch on the slope, where he could make out the broken walls of buildings. On the summit, soaring above the wheeling clouds, he saw the black fist of the tower. The pinnacle on which stood the statue of Nantosueta.

"Such omens does it conjure up within one's mind!" He heard the voice of Qwenqwo, who had made himself scarce until this moment.

For Duval too it seemed the very embodiment of awe.

"Now that we are alone, Qwenqwo, I must ask you to do something for me. When I was fourteen years old, a girl called Kate befriended me. Together with four other friends we climbed a mountain to find a gateway to another world. I now assume it was this world, Tír. Something terrible, perhaps something extraordinary, happened. Something, I believe, that was vital to my quest. But I don't remember it. I need to remember what happened."

In silence, Qwenqwo still stared at the towering pinnacle.

"I am asking you, the true Mage of Dreams, to enter my mind."

Duval saw how the dwarf flinched.

"I have both anticipated and dreaded this request. Give me the grace to accompany you until we reach the sanctuary of the third fosse with its temple complex. It can be no more than a half day's journey. There, my friend, when these brave people had found a greater degree of safety, shall I do as you bid me."

TWENTY-ONE

THE RATH OF NANTOSUETA

ASTENCH OF DEATH Legion weaponry still cut through the aroma of pine and earth, as they threaded their way down, between the great trees that grew dense on this portion of the slope. They spoke only rarely, aware that their progress was closely watched by unfriendly eyes. Although he knew that a party of Shee now guarded the causeway, Duval saw no sign of their presence until a tall figure, with sword at the ready, stepped out of the shadows as they came upon the shore.

Here they gazed in horror upon the ruin of the Temple Ship, the timbers of its superstructure reduced to cinders and its great mass sunken onto the shingle of the straits. Nobody could keep that image in their eyes for long, such a feeling of desolation hung about it.

The first to cross the channel was a party of warriors, led by Ainé, moving lithely in response to a low-pitched whistle from the other side. In a moment they were swallowed up by the trees. Then the Olhyiu carried the first wave of children and wounded across the great boulders that made up the stepping stones over the sombre waters. The silence was eerie. Not a single bird hailed the morning.

As they arrived at the great stairway, ascending to the rath, they found it hoary with age and overgrown with lichens. The passage of great age was evident in the saddle-shaped depressions in every stone. The steps twisted and turned, never straight in their course, delving at times under the canopies of the tall evergreens or bridging over swiftly running streams. At one twist they passed under a fall of water several hundred feet high that fanned their sweating faces with a refreshing rain. There were no handrails here, no warning signs of obstacles to come. To look down was to invite a giddy dizziness.

Soon they were high above the branching river, visibly exposed to any attack from the opposite slopes. Yet in the faces of every Olhyiu, and Qwenqwo too, there was a greater fear of what lay ahead.

A column of a hundred Shee now led them, and their steps were followed by all that remained of the Kyra's army after a hundred more had stayed behind to guard the causeway. More Shee were arriving in answer to the Kyra's summons. The army that ascended the vast climb of steps was at least eight hundred strong. It was an aching and breathless company that, after two hours of steady ascent, passed through the first of three great defensive fosses that reared out of the slopes before the plateau.

Although he was tired, Duval's eyes couldn't help marvelling at the cyclopian masonry of their construction, each stone an individually shaped boulder, skilfully shaped so that the convexity of one stone exactly met the concavity of its neighbour. The labouring file became a trickle here, passing through massive jambs that permitted only one at a time through the great rampart that merged into the rising shelf of the mountain. Through the second and third fosse, they arrived at the rath, with its temple complex, that Duval had glimpsed from the opposite slope.

It was a magnificent warren of ruins extending over several acres of the plateau.

To the south, he could make out vestiges of terracing, which suggested that the people who had once lived here had been self-sufficient in crops. He wished those crops were still here to feed the hungry mouths who might soon have to withstand a siege. There were walled enclosures that might have held animals and a parapet that jutted out over the abyss to the northeast. From here you could stand and look out over a fantastic view of the river as it approached through the meandering valley.

The Shee made them stop while they probed for any signs of an ambush in the cobbled alleys between broken walls. But they found nothing, only desolation. They checked out one ruin after another until, roughly central, they found a building large enough and sufficiently preserved to accommodate the entire company.

To Duval's gaze, the deep-carved entrance, flanked by the inwardly sloping jambs and surmounted by a great triangular lintel, evoked a prickling amazement. Inside, the single chamber was so large it must have been a hall of assembly. Outside the entrance, to the west and east, paved roads led to walled gardens and courtyards. Duval's eyes were drawn to another building, on a slightly higher level than the main complex of ruins. He made out the unmistakable grandeur of a temple, its roof intact. On one corner was a pentagonal tower with a single stellate window high above the plateau. The window appeared to be glazed, twinkling in the reflection of the wintry sunlight.

Nantosueta's temple!

Gooseflesh stood up on his back as he studied this structure: a pang of fear, mixed with awe, as if he found himself caught in an eye that looked out over the entire valley.

The Shee wasted no time. As soon as the wounded had been made comfortable, the Aydes, under the direction of the magisterial Bétaald, began a careful inspection of the defensive walls. Duval left them mapping out the breaks and weaknesses, while Ainé recruited the fitter of the Olhyiu men to bolster her army. He needed to make his own exploration through these ancient streets and passages, which formed a labyrinth on many levels, interconnected by stairways and tunnels.

The rath appeared to have been abandoned in antiquity, and judging from the dense growth of lichens, it had lain uninhabited ever since. Still that mixture of fear and awe had never left him – if anything it intensified as he explored deeper.

He was certain now that within this brooding complex lay the key to the power that had preserved this valley for two thousand years. The Legun had respected that power in its obsession with destroying the heads. But soon the Death Legion would attack this place. That was why the Shee were organizing. They would attack with an overwhelming advantage in numbers, led by the Legun. And when they did so, it would mean a fight to the death. He needed to understand the history that lay desolate around him. He needed to understand the power of the Queen.

Wandering alone through cobbled alleys and byways, he found himself climbing steadily to an upper level until he was standing before the temple with its corner tower and the single glazed window.

There was a modest doorway, its head shaped as a triradiate arch. Some of its facing had tumbled into the atrium inside. Over the arched lintel a pentagon was recessed into the stonework. Duval skirted the rubble to enter the atrium, where decayed marble facing had fallen away to expose ochre-coloured walls coated with islands of black fungus. A spiral of marble steps led higher.

With a rising nervousness, he began to climb. Step by anxious step, he ascended the first story to emerge into an elevated cloister. He had to shrink back from where tattered pediments hovered over an abyss. Peering about himself carefully, he could see that a section of outer wall had collapsed onto the fosse, exposing his gaze to the valley far below. He had to inch his way past the danger, passing through into a pentagonal loggia. This was lined by colonnaded arches, each double pillar of waisted marble, coral red and surmounted with carved reliefs. Every aspect of this inner architecture had an exquisite sophistication. With a stepwise increase in his fears, he padded along a narrow cloister, past openings that had once boasted doors, each leading to its individual cell. Each cell was illuminated by a single window, an unglazed filigree of floral design. The impression was evocative: a marriage of spirituality and denial. If this had been a convent community, reflecting the spirituality of the Dark Ages, it had also been spartan in its outlook.

Entering one of the cells, his instincts picked up an aura of violence.

Though there were no bones – time would have withered bones to dust – the floors were littered with green-encrusted bronzes, scattered and broken, too precious to have been abandoned. There had been a violent invasion of Nantosueta's religious order in this secret valley in the mountains with its brooding forests. It had all ended in bloodshed long ago!

He arrived at another entrance, cut deep into the wall at the end of the cloister. It was sealed by a bronzed door, thickly encrusted with green verdigris. The door was damaged, battered and broken on its hinges by what he presumed to have been that same violence long ago.

Duval could not stop here. He had to know what lay behind this battered portal.

He squeezed through the broken door to find himself ascending another spiral staircase of marble. He knew where this was leading him. He was inside the pentangular corner tower, where the window had flashed at him, like an eye watching over the valley.

After a further climb of perhaps sixty steps, he came to another bronze door, broken like the last, and leading into the summit chamber. Dust as white as a swan's breast carpeted the floor.

The dust was inches deep, so undisturbed through time its surface appeared to be patinated like frost. Duval's first impression was of an empty room, at least thirty feet in diameter. His gaze turned to the great stellate window, which was glazed with coloured panes. Though only a poor light penetrated the grimy window, colours glowed about the floor and walls, delightful shades of emerald and ruby, turquoise and gold, set in a pearly lambency.

There was a dance and dazzle to the play of light, a living feel.

His boots left deep impressions, as if he walked through virgin snow. The rising plumes of dust caught strange glints and gleams of light. He saw no evidence of the triumphalist carvings that had decorated the Fir Bolg ruins on the forested slopes. These walls, even to close inspection, were perfectly smooth, bone white marble. The work of the masons had been so exquisite he could hardly pick out the courses between the individual lining blocks.

All he could find by way of adornment were inserts in the walls, flush with the surface. Brushing away dust with his fingers, he could make out naturalistic filigrees of gold and silver that might have represented a contour map of the valley below.

The vault was an evening sky of blue-black marble. There was a scattered tiny glitter, which might have been crystals set into it to represent the rising constellations of the stars of Tír. The otherwise empty chamber was a great disappointment to Duval. He had hoped to learn something more about the queen. While standing in the dust, brooding on his disappointment, he sensed a presence outside the open door. There had been no sound, not even the faintest pad of a footfall. Yet he knew who had followed him here.

"Mira!"

"Yes, Al-an!"

The girl came into the chamber with a noiseless blur of footsteps. Now her eyes darted about the extraordinary walls before returning his questioning gaze directly.

"I think it is time we were honest with each other, don't you?" He hesitated, his voice gentle. "Who are you, Mira? What are you really doing here?"

"I am the voice of prophecy." That calm piping voice replied, without a moment's hesitation.

He shook his head, though he was a little startled at what she had said. "So tell me then – what does the prophet see in this empty chamber?"

"The shrine of Nantosueta is not empty."

Duval studied Mira's hollowed face for several seconds, yet there was no flicker of retraction in the eyes. "I don't understand."

With a dart as lithe as a young antelope, she sprang across the dust-laden floor and confronted the window. Then with a quick hop, her head inclined at an angle as if playing with him, she knelt on the sill and wiped the dust from a small portion of the stained glass. Duval's eye caught a sparkle of movement in the air, a rainbow diffraction of colours, before a series of what he initially took to be holograms took shape in the incident beam of light. But the images were too vivid for holograms. They seemed to be infused with life. With a grunt of surprise, he joined her at the window, wiping clear a greater portion.

Duval had mistaken the panes for stained glass. Now he saw that they were a strange hybrid of crystals – crystals of a myriad shapes and colours.

The sun was still above the horizon and the incandescent glow of its transillumination now pervaded the chamber. It thrilled the air with a flickering motion of reds and indigos, emeralds and gold. He stiffened, his heart beating violently, as suddenly there was a more powerful burst of light – as if the sun had come from behind a thin gauze of cloud.

In the dusty air of the chamber, Duval found himself looking into a delightful vignette of nature. Young saplings hung over a glittering stream. He could have reached out and plucked the flowers that grew on the gentle incline of the banks. He seemed to hear the burbling of the water, the faint sigh of the breeze through leaves and the trembling lances of reeds. Then, no matter how impossible it might be, he knew that he heard the birdsong. He could never have brought it from memory because the lilting notes were unfamiliar to him. He saw Mira laughing as she pirouetted among the slender trunks, as abandoned as a nymph, now dancing forward to take his hand and lead him down to the stream. He saw the pebbles through its rippling current. He felt the cool of the spray as he splashed it joyfully over his face.

It was an impossible idyll, a dream that could not be real. Yet it felt real.

Laughing hoarsely, his joy cutting through the disbelief of

reason, Duval threw off his boots to run with the girl through the soft meadow, the soft feel of the grass and loam under his feet.

"Behold the nemeton of the Queen of the Forest," the voice of Mira rung out through the wonder of the woodland scene.

Duval blinked several times in astonishment. Through an arbor of blossoming trees, he saw the great ascending spiral of stone steps as they must have appeared two thousand years ago, those steps above the temple plateau, climbing to the great pentagonal tower on the summit of the mountain. That tower, which in this vision had as yet no figure of stone standing on the pinnacle. All through these recent terrible days, Duval felt that he had been learning a difficult but important lesson. The legends of some ominous power that protected the valley, the vast numbers of stone heads among the trees, the story of the Fir Bolg told by Qwenqwo. Each was a clue, a complementary facet, adding up to an overall picture of a mystery. A mystery that had led him by the nose to this magical chamber.

What could he make of it all?

Duval tried reaching out through the oraculum. He recoiled from the answering caution of that strange potency.

He could not explore it with the oraculum: he would have to look at it more simply, logically. Long ago, two thousand years ago, Queen Nantosueta had faced a force of evil similar to that they faced today. A desperate war had been fought out – in the forests and on this plateau. The enemy forces had broken through into the cloisters and cells below this very chamber. They had murdered everybody and destroyed every-thing on the temple complex, then battered down the doors to get to Nantosueta herself. What must have gone through the mind of the Queen in those desperate moments?

Duval thought that he knew what Nantosueta would have considered. One last act of defiance.

The will to defeat those forces of evil had taken its final comfort in this very chamber. Something terrible, something extraordinary, had been invoked by Nantosueta in those final minutes, as the enemy battered their way through those bronze doors.

The clue lay in Qwenqwo's story about the great sacrifice of the Fir Bolg. Duval had felt the potency of a single waking head, during his desperate struggle with the Legun in the forest. There was a great lesson to be learned here: but the answer eluded him.

"You were always a step ahead of me, Mira. Help me now to understand."

Her dark eyes gazed up at him without replying. Then he could not tell if she was merely pointing or it was her delicate hand that conjured up the greatest thrill of all.

Duval was startled by the vision of a young woman who stood among the trees, still and silent, as if observing them. Her hair was a downy cataract of blue-black and she was dressed simply in gown and sandals. Her face, bare of adornment, was serene with purpose, her left hand splayed toward the ground and her right arm raised to the sky. Duval knew he was looking at the face of Nantosueta. On her brow she bore an oraculum, an inverted triangle of the Trídédana, similar to his own – but where his was red hers was as black as her hair.

He did not dare to blink, so arresting was the serenity of the face that had once soared over the right portal of the pass of Kloshe Lamah.

There was barely time to wonder about the meaning of those gesturing hands, the one, as it seemed, stretched to the heavens, and the other, with its widespread fingers and thumb, extended over her beloved valley – and then she was gone.

The sun had set. The image of the Nemeton blinked out at once. They stood once more in the thick dust, facing each other in the twilight, beside the crystal window in the empty chamber. Duval took Mira's shoulders between his hands. He knelt down so he could put his arms around her.

She hugged him back, like a frightened daughter.

"I don't know who or what you really are, Mira. I only know what my instincts tell me – that your purpose and my own are bound up together." He held her at arms length, so he could look down directly into her eyes. "What you said earlier – do you really have the gift of prophecy? If so, can you tell me what the future holds?"

Her answering voice was more adult, more knowing, than he had ever heard previously. "Your power is greater than you know. Yet darkness is fast growing in strength. Every life within these walls is imperilled. No outcome is certain."

Despite her precocity she seemed so vulnerable that Duval felt an overwhelming impulse to protect her. He hugged her to him again. He didn't want to let her go.

"There is something I have to do – something that will give me important information even though it might be dangerous. Tonight I am going to ask Qwenqwo to enter my mind."

Her head fell against his shoulder. Her whisper was the cry of a frightened child. "I don't want anything bad to happen to you."

"I have to do it, even though I'm a little frightened too. I believe that our future depends on it."

"Then what must be must be endured."

THE FALL OF OSSIEREL

With night already falling, it was with foreboding
that the others welcomed Duval and Mira to their
gathering about the open fire on the flagged floor of
the great hall. Duval felt a pang of grief at the absence of
Kemtuk, whose advice would have been so welcome in this
meeting.

Each took a drink from a porcelain cup provided by Bétaald:
a herbal tonic prepared by the Aydes to refresh and clear the
mind. Incense and aromatic spices were added to the flames to
banish the stale odours of the old building.

Qwenqwo explained Duval's intention of exploring his
hidden memories.

At this most of the eyes of the elders and leaders fell down
to reflect on the flames. Milish was the only one to look directly
into Duval's eyes, a hint of reproach, before even her head fell
onto her chest.

"The Mage Lord is faced with a grave and difficult problem."
Qwenqwo spoke clearly, but with his voice stiffened by inner
tension. "It would appear that he came to Tír once before, in
the company of a friend – a girl called Kate. He returned alone.
He cannot remember what happened to his friend in this
world. When he tries to remember, terror cloaks those memories from his mind. And therein lies the mystery.

"Why should his memories be cloaked with terror in this
way? Is it merely the shadow of terrible events that happened
then? Or is this a caution, placed around his memories for

reasons of his own safety?"

Swallowing with emotion, Qwenqwo seemed to hesitate, then hold his tongue, as if there were more he might have said.

Duval glanced at the Mage of Dreams, a look that valued his integrity and his concern for him. "I think you know how deeply I care for you all. I don't want to do anything that threatens your safety. But I need information on what happened to Kate all those years ago – I must find those answers that appear to be buried deep in my mind. I believe this is vital to my purpose here."

As if in response, Ainé lifted her green eyes to look at Duval. "There is, as this meeting infers, a way in which even the deepest secrets of your mind might be explored. Yet it worries me that you will insist upon this course. You are fatigued from battle and more wounded in spirit than you realize. The risk of what you contemplate is at best uncertain – it may be great."

"I have already asked the Mage of Dreams to explore my memories."

Bétaald spoke for the first time. "Is it not madness, Duval, to go against the counsel of those who have shared the dangers of this journey with you? For all its defences, this fortress may prove a fragile refuge. We are greatly outnumbered. The Legun incarnate is still within the forest armed with new malengins of war and strange new forces of legionary. If evil should befall you, the consequences would be grave indeed."

Duval nodded, accepting her concerns. Murmurs of agreement arose from others around the fire.

He lifted his gaze, until it was Mira's eyes that again held his. In that wordless communication, Duval felt selfish and ashamed.

Qwenqwo, who had seemed lost in concentration until now, spat out sharp words of rebuke at Ainé.

"What would a Shee-Witch know of anything! Has the Mage Lord not explained his reasons to you! Has he not explained that those hidden memories are vital to his quest?"

"Hark at the wisdom of a fallen mage!" Ainé's cold asperity

countered the angry glare of the dwarf. "Was your power not corrupted by the Warlock in Isscan, where you were held in its thrall for twenty years! How do we know you still retain the power of dreams? Worse still – how do we know that what small power you still retain has not been perverted by malign influence?"

"Ah – so there we have it!" Qwenqwo growled. "At last we hear the suspicions that have darkened your mind since we met. But then, who among us is surprised at your suspicions, Shee-Witch. Your vocation is ever to suspect others."

"Please – we must remain calm and united," urged Milish. "We must not allow internal divisions to distract us from our purpose."

"Well spoken!" growled the dwarf. "Since my power has been questioned let me assure you all that to reveal what is buried in the inner labyrinths of the mind remains within my lore. Yet –" His eyes roamed over the high vaulted roof as his voice softened and he confessed his fears. "Though I know the power rests still within the runestone, I freely admit that it is dimmed by long disuse – all the more so in such close proximity to the Dark Queen. I must marry my art with the power of the Mage Lord to release it." His eyes returned to stare obstinately into those of the Kyra.

Ainé barked, "All men are foolish, as is commonly witnessed, but a dwarf it seems has wits commensurate with his stature."

Qwenqwo jumped to his feet, livid with rage. "The basest woman will embrace a man but this one will brook no pleasure between her legs."

He slammed his foot down on the flagged ground and his eyes protruded round and glistening as he pointed with a stubby finger at Ainé, taller seated than he was on his toes. "The honour of your house was quickened in the valley of Gadhgorrah, where the ground is yet paved with valiant skulls!"

With a raised arm, Milish halted Ainé's angry reply. She

urged Qwenqwo to sit down. Then the diplomat spoke calmly, reassuring all around the fire.

"Not one among us is without duress. And this is not the time to quarrel among ourselves. There is none here us who wants Duval to suffer risk. We need to bear in mind that even if all goes well, he will be exhausted, physically and spiritually, by such sorcery. Yet we understand his reasons."

Qwenqwo turned to Duval directly: "Though I possess the lore to help you, I too am fearful of the danger you may face in consequence of it."

Even Milish could not stop herself from clutching Duval's arm with a final and mute urgency, shaking her head from side to side.

Duval spoke gently, his eyes moving in turn to meet directly the eyes of each of his companions in the circle around the fire.

"I really do appreciate your concerns for me. And believe me, I don't want to take any risks with my mind, any more than you do. But I have no choice. I have waited a very long time for this moment. Let's get started as quickly as possible."

As Qwenqwo left the company to gather the materials he needed, Duval took advantage of the pause to escape the continuing tensions around the fire. He walked out into the cold of night, finding a quiet refuge on the rampart that looked out over the uppermost fosse. Below him, silently as always, he knew there were Shee patrolling the walls. There would be no calls from the watch to declare that all was well.

Gazing down onto the winding valley, shadowed under a night sky and obscured by mist and cloud, he couldn't help but wonder at the nature of the ancient power that still lurked within the forested slopes.

Ainé was right. The encounters with the Legun had drained him spiritually, but he also felt a sense of elation since his visit to the shrine with Mira.

If only he understood the precise thinking of the Dark Queen long ago!

Milish came to bring him back to the fireside. Qwenqwo was ready. Into the fire he now placed a small bronze vessel, in which an object glinted and flashed with spectral potency.

"The preparations would normally require two full days of incantation and meditation," the dwarf grumbled, with the wild mop of his hair controlled by a cap of knitted golden thread he must have brought with him from Isscan. Qwenqwo's good hand stretched before the flame, as if shielding his eyes from its heat and light.

Then his fingers appeared to tremble and he hesitated for several seconds, as if allowing Duval a final chance to change his mind.

"Go ahead! Do this for me, Qwenqwo," Duval urged, perceiving the doubt that still harboured in the Mage's eyes. "I need to find my memories of Kate. She was my friend twenty years ago, in a town called Clonmel in a country called Ireland. We gathered, with four other friends, about a mountain called Slievenamon. This is the memory I want to go back to."

Duval focused upon Qwenqwo in his mind. He felt the oraculum begin to pulsate. He couldn't suppress an involuntary shiver, but he would not change his mind.

"Listen to me carefully, Qwenqwo – all of you. What we find may be frightening. You must not draw back, no matter what we find there."

His face now set with purpose, and ignoring the renewed murmurings of concern from the others gathered about the fire, Duval put his hand on the dwarf's shoulder. "I'm ready, Qwenqwo. Let's get on with it!"

No one could have missed the charge that entered Qwenqwo from the touch of Duval's arm. His wiry hair escaped his golden cap in a spray of random force, each strand individually catching the orange of the flames.

From the bronze pot, Qwenqwo lifted something heavy and wonderfully glowing, an object he treated with great reverence. In the firelight it sparkled a deep and perfect blue. Duval knew it was the runestone, though it was already changing in

Qwenqwo's hand. It metamorphosed in a way reminiscent of Granny Ddhu's handling of the whisky flask, to become a goblet, pentagonal in its outer surfaces above an ornately carved base, yet a perfect half globe in its interior.

Sybaritic shapes moved within the flask walls, as if bridling to escape their confines, eliciting gasps from the people sitting around the fire.

Even Ainé's eyes went wide with expectancy.

"Well you might whistle," Qwenqwo preened. "Such rapture is it to gaze into the chalice of Urox Zel, my father, and the Mage of the Fir Bolg. Witness then the power of mages from a time when wonder was commonplace."

The dwarf inhaled the aroma from the goblet's contents, an elixir that condensed the light like quicksilver and smelled of a pungently aromatic fragrance. Then, his will focused on the goblet, he chanted a series of incantations in which Duval caught a single word, which sounded like the name of a deity, then Qwenqwo added a pinch of powder, sniffing again, holding the goblet over the flames, mixing the elixir with a gentle rotation of his gnarled hand, until with a final sniff he was satisfied it was ready.

With a fierce pride in his eyes and bearing, he handed the goblet to Duval.

Duval did not take an immediate sip. Still there was an instinct that held him back. He stared down into the swirling ichor, reflecting the goblet walls so decorously and purely blue, the fabulous glowing blue of lapis lazuli.

No mortal hand could have carved the goblet, its beauty was so strange and fecund. He inhaled its heavy perfume, already falling under its hypnotic spell. The oraculum was pulsing powerfully. Suddenly a massive surge of power flashed from his brow and the goblet blazed in its rubicund glow. Then the goblet itself took fire. Its eldritch blue light poured out into the air about them, invading the minds of everybody gathered in the circle.

For a moment Duval glanced at Qwenqwo, his grip upon

reality more tenuous by the moment.

It startled him to see the tall spirit, handsome and proud, who gazed back at him from the place of the dwarf. Already the women were beginning to incant a strange benediction. Now he understood something he had not understood before. Though his was the mind that would be laid bare, the experience would be shared by all who sat around the fire.

He drank the contents in one swallow.

His eyelids closed and with them faded his awareness of present time and place. A feeling of great peace and tranquillity invaded his mind. Then it was as if someone previously blind, deaf, and insensate began by degrees to rediscover a heightened vision and perception.

He was aware of the day first: he had returned to that beautiful July morning, very early and quiet. The sky was that of a glorious summer, with scarcely a hint of cloud. It was refreshing, like walking out of darkness into brilliant sunshine, his face washed by a delicate dew of rain.

He was the boy again, straddling his bicycle, waiting for Kate outside the gates to the Doctor's House.

The Doctor's House!

He saw it again as the metamorphosing contours of a dream. The excitement rose in him, prickling with dread and wonder at the adventure they were about to undertake. He willed these experiences by, urgently, quickly. A glimpse of the six of them meeting in the old dairy at Sean's father's sawmill. The gathering of the sacred waters of the three rivers – the Sacred Sisters.... The final approach to Slievenamon!

The mountain had been the magnet, drawing them to its need. Expecting them since the moment each had been born. He knew now as he had never realized before that it had waited for them much longer than that, longer than it was rational to conceive. He understood now that a great plan was already conceived, a gamble of fate set in motion eons earlier, by powers much more knowing than he was. Still he was scrolling through the landscape of dreams, faster – though learning now with a mind more primed to understanding than the mind of the boy. He had reached the time of terror: the confrontation over the mound of stones. A thunder in the sky that was the growling of a monster. Peril descending in the form of leviathan jaws, lined by venomed fangs.... And then the spark of darkness that began high in the sky, from which the wings expanded into the awesome magnificence of that extraordinary shadow, the protection of the great battle raven he now knew was the manifestation of Mórígán, the Third Power and Goddess of Death, so immense its wingtips reached from horizon to horizon.

Voices calling, voices warning. Voices he recognized as the expression of mental fears: Milish, Ainé – Bétaald. Duval could hear the warning voices but he could not heed them. Their fears were attempting to draw him back from that brink into another time and world. But he spurned that relative sanctuary. A great stirring was expanding his universe.

His lips moved as if to reassure his companions but there could be no communication at this level.... And there was no longer any possibility of retreat.

As one fearful miasma was drawn aside, it opened upon a still greater darkness.

It seemed now that through all of their childish adventure a single mind had been beckoning them to this moment: and now, in that final moment, he recognized that as his youthful voice again incanted the runes – *Tá an geann circleach,* the world is round, the world is a circle, the world is infinity – it had been a single voice calling, a voice of suffering, a voice of immense power.

Scrolling now, faster and faster, leading to the one experience he was searching for, the source of the terror that lay in the landscape of his dreams....

In a twilight world, and under a sky of wrath, leaden bellied and crimson in its leading edges, a great citadel lay in desolation and plunder. Its wonderful towers and minarets were tumbling, its frescoed arts and domes, its hallowed walls: yet even in flames it evoked the memory of impossible beauty, the gardens of exotic flowers, the crowning achievement of three millenia of liberty and peace. Libraries of illuminated books and manuscripts, detailing the profounder mysteries of nature, burned in great pyres among the ruins: the history of peoples, the shock of contacts where invader encountered native, where culture married culture in a symbiosis of understanding.

A spiritual evolution had flourished here. The soul of the forest, of trees and flowers, bird and insect, the wisdom of exotic arts alien to material science. Where another tower collapsed, in a groaning protest of sparks and ash, the guiding principle had been love of nature, and the power derived from it. A sympathy with the natural world that went beyond the mechanistic models of Duval's own, beyond the physics and chemistry, beyond even the mathematics and cosmologies, to the very root of existence and being. Even to the incomprehending gazes of the two children, Alan and Kate, the desecration was a blasphemy against truth itself, a wickedness beyond understanding.

Brave Ossierel, whose guardian Shee lay dead in tens of thousands among the broken walls.

Blood and terror ran side by side in the ravaged libraries and courtyards, while an army of pitiless warriors, drunk with glee, glorified in its rape and ruin.

Alan and Kate stood appalled, their souls etiolated by terror so profound they could not comprehend their senses. Their guide, an old crone with a crumpled mouth and a staff of power, led them out of the burning ruins through an underground labyrinth to a place before the gates. Here she receded from them into the shadow of a grove of trees, with silvery seedpods chiming like alarm bells in the gale.

Their terrible duty, now it seemed, was to bear witness to the crime of crimes, the genocide of such a civilisation.

Every vestige, from cupola to sacred grove, from marble hall to the glory of the mosaics that extolled natural beauty in the floors, all were being torn down or ripped apart, so that stone would not rest upon stone, so that not even a fragment of foundation would remember what once was and take comfort from the history. All destroyed, burnt, trampled by a malice that knew neither pity nor reason.

All of a sudden, thunder cracked, a dreadful noise, like the tearing apart of mountains.

In a momentary silence between detonations, Alan caught the sound of Kate weeping, and his grip tightened on her hands, his eyes travelling upward, reluctantly drawn to a vision of tragedy.

A woman hung crucified before them. A giant woman, with white hair spread like the Medusa about her face, with limbs nailed to the decorated panels of massive gates, her blood running over the whorled and spiralling patterns of ancient silver laid upon black oak, its artwork as complex as the Book of Kells. She had a long, expressive face, tapering to an almost pointed chin under a wide, intelligent forehead. Her eyes were all-black, as if the pupil had expanded to devour the whites and irises. In the centre of her brow was a disc of power, an oraculum circular and silvery as a full moon and dappled like the lunar face. There was evidence of scourging upon her huge frame, with its tattered remnants of formal white dress, gilt-seamed; and streams of blood ran from multiple wounds to patter onto the cobbled entrance. Black bolts transfixed her arms in their outstretched posture, and similar nails bisected the bones above her ankles. But her weight would have ripped the iron bolts through the flesh had it not been for the gruesome shackles of spiked strapwork that pinioned her thighs and her trunk between the great thorax and abdomen, fettering her body to the gates.

All of Monisle knew her name: for she was Ussha De Danaan, the last High Architect of Ossierel. The greatest in understanding in the history of Monisle.

In mocking profanity, the crown of the spiritual capital had been impaled upon her brow, the emerald tiara, with its tall vertical crescent in a delicate filigree of gold, ending on either side with the two emeralds of state, myriad faceted and wrought as eagles' heads.

In the courtyard behind the gates, columns of women, wearing gowns of lime green, embroidered with silver, were compelled to kneel upon the despoiled marble with their heads bent. A dreadful creature, massive and bearing the face of doom, sat astride a giant battle charger, horselike in its form but with carnivorous fangs for teeth and a frame as powerful as an elephant's, with jet black coat and mane. Though its rider had the lean caricature of death, the spine of the charger was bent under its weight. A blare of trumpets, strident and alien sounding, and the sudden deep rumble of drums, and in a moment, as one, all of the women were beheaded, their blood anticipating their bodies to the desecrated ground.

Then the eyes of the crucified giantess flickered open once more to behold the demoniacal glee of her tormentor. There was another almighty crash of thunder that shook the foundations of the great wall in which the gates were embedded. Lightning tumbled in its wake, so charged it could not be extinguished through striking the ground, but crackled and spread in a fantastic mantle over the ruined gardens, igniting the trees in its path.

The creature upon the horse appeared to back away, as if fearful still of the power of the De Danaan, though she was visibly close to death.

As the burdened charger reared with eyes bulging in terror at another great thunderclap, its rider seemed unaware of the two children who huddled close together holding hands, confused by terror yet absorbed by pity, to keep their dreadful vigil at the foot of the crucifixion.

The black eyes of the giantess fell upon their faces. As they became the focus of that tormented gaze, a startle of intimate communication flickered through their minds and was sewn into their souls. Each she addressed in turn as "Chosen", as if in each heart of innocence she beheld a final window of hope. With a gentleness of caring behind that terrible gaze she warned them that perilous would be the quest she now implanted deep within them.

The adult mind knew what the child did not: that the creature on the charger was the Legun that had scarred Ainé's face, the Legun of Leguns: the Captain. Belatedly, it seemed, the Legun registered their presence and talons sprang from the extremities of its claws, clawing the sweat-streaked flesh of its steed, in a brutal determination to force it under control, and now the red glitter in its hateful eyes was directed toward them, as if with a ferocious urgency probing their minds.

Wave upon wave of ebbing power emanated from the crucified woman. Even as the spectre clawed its mount to leaping obedience, a vast shock wave struck the ground, accompanied by a tearing of the air and the discharge of multiple bolts of lightning, in the centre of which the children were cradled, as if at the protected eye of a hurricane. About the actinic cataract of power the prancing warsteed circled, goaded on by its snarling rider, whose countenance and skeletal frame were spectral in the reflection of the lightning: yet even that protective cage merely enraged it without the power to hold it back for long. The creature howled and roared as it beheld the summons of the dying woman, and the focus of her eyes.

Then, in an extraordinary effort, her great head rose again, as if to gather succour from the heavens, and in the silvery moon upon her brow a flickering matrix became powerfully alive. Her lustrous black eyes were upon Alan Duval alone. He heard her words in his mind, the gentle voice, deep and calm, if halting, through an agony of effort. *You then I forswear the True Believer. In you I place the greatest trust, though its very peril demands it should lie dormant until the time is chosen. Upon your shoulders then will rest the fate of worlds.*

Her scourged gaze fell into a repose of grief, as if she pitied him his future.

With a snarl of fury, the gibbous-faced creature sundered

the cage of lightning. It reared before the terrified children, close enough for them to gag on the suffocating stench of its presence. A monstrous claw reached out to rake Kate's delicate white throat with a single talon, leaving a trickle of venom burning, like acid, upon her breast. In a moment, Kate was unconscious. Alan fell down onto his knees beside her, calling her name, trying to revive her. The dreadful creature did not wait to relish the effects of its venom. Immediately its rage was redirected to the dying woman as, baring its fangs in a monstrous roar, it hurled its spear, with huge black blade livid with a loathsome green opalescence, into her heart.

Terror so great, it overwhelmed the will. Terror such as no youthful heart could bear nor mind recall. As the heroic figure upon the gates sighed and her head began to fall, a voice that was no longer human, a command that had become the elemental winds, carried omens no human ear could hear nor mind understand. An immense shock struck the ground, sweeping outward in a grievous ripple, as if a tidal wave of uncertainty were threatening the universe.

The hammer blow of such a stroke knocked her tormentor backward, cast down from its steed onto the quivering earth, yet still those red pits of eyes were turned on her in irredeemable hatred. A sudden agony, as if his being were disintegrating in the grip of almighty forces. He knew from instinct he was being sent back through the gate. He was leaving and Kate was staying. *No!* He struggled against it. He wanted to deny it, even as his consciousness was fading. *Nooooooooo...!* But already there was an ominous susurration, as if a great wind were rising, and in his mind's eye was an equally ominous vision: as if all over this terrifying and barbarous world the leaves were falling from the trees.

— TWENTY-THREE —

THE LEGUN INCARNATE

OMETHING WAS WRONG... something horribly wrong with the world.

Tossing his head, with tightly clenched jaws, from side to side, he demanded to know what was so horribly wrong with the world.

Duval seemed to be back in the nightmare of the Arctic wilderness. Agony racked his bones and joints, ravaged his flesh, excoriated every mote of his physical and spiritual being. Nobody could survive such pain. Yet a part of him whispered that this was not real, this was the past. He had survived that agony. He was surviving still. With his teeth bared in a rictus of determination, he roared his defiance with the last crushed breath of his tormented lungs:

I will survive!

Then, as if from a great distance away, he heard a new voice, a new voice whispering. His confused mind seized on that voice. He heard other sounds from far away in the distance, sounds carrying from where there should be no sounds. Desperate shouts, moans... screams. Who could be screaming in this Arctic wilderness? Who could possibly be enduring this same hell?

"Al-an! Al-an!"

Kate... *Kate!* Was it Kate calling him? No – impossible! Kate was a memory. His eyes were blinded by madness still. His arms were curled against his chest, his fists clenched so hard his palms must be bleeding. He was shaking his head furiously from side to side, shaking his head in another world. A world racked by moans and screams. But was Kate truly just a memory? A memory cut deep into his brain by the terror… the terror that was so great….

"Al-an! Believer!"

"Oh God!"

With an immense effort of will, he forced the terror out of his mind, the nightmare visions out of his eyes. With his head weak on his wobbly neck, he peered around from where he found himself, on his back in the dirt, only yards from the great hall on the temple plateau – where he had left his friends around the fire.

"Believer!"

He saw her now, her timid form hugging the contours of the ground, her hand touching him, brushing the sweat from his eyes.

"Mira!" He sighed with relief at finding her close to him.

Highlighted by flames, her face was anxious and drawn, thinner, if such were possible, than when he had last seen her. She sat up to look at him, her lustrous eyes peering out of a mask of soot. While she crouched beside him in the shadow of the great hall, a thunderous explosion peppered them with fragments of stone. They both coughed in its wake of dust.

"How did I get here? What's happened?"

"They attacked, Al-an. While you were still lost to us in your dreams."

They had to shout to each other just to be heard above the fury of battle.

"How long … how long was I lost?"

She crouched down again, frightened by another explosion. "All night," she said, "and through this morning."

Duval's head fell back in extreme exhaustion. It must be early afternoon, although it seemed like twilight because of the smoke. He had no memory at all of being brought out here, no memory of that entire night and morning. Above him a tempestuous sky tossed and howled over the shadowy outlines of the ancient sanctuary, and the acrid smell of fire and smoke choked his nostrils.

The plateau was in tumult.

Every few seconds the shadows were lit up by flares of foulsome green. Even the sky about the perimeter of the island danced and glowed as if illuminated by flickering searchlights. It took several moments of reorientation before he realized that the light came from the forests burning. Currents of hot wind lashed his skin, accompanied by the harsh detonations of exploding missiles, the crackling and splitting of masonry; and everywhere his nostrils registered the dank musky odour of slaughter.

"Ainé! Siam! Milish –"

Tears filled Mira's eyes as he took hold of her arm.

"All out there – fighting!"

With a groan of pain, he lifted himself onto one arm, found a better position to look around. He had to wipe dust and splinters of stone from his face and eyelids.

Then, through a gap in the smoke and flames, he glimpsed the unmistakable forms of Death Legionaries. But there was something else nearby. A menace he could not see although its presence assaulted his senses. In his brow, the oraculum flared, sending a thrill of alarm throughout every nerve of his body. Barely recovered enough to stagger to his feet, he knew what he was sensing: the awesome malevolence of a Legun incarnate.

The attack was so violent that the air glowed with that foul green lividity as Duval turned slowly about to probe the confusion of battle with the oraculum.

No clear sign of the Legun but he could still sense its loathsome presence. It mocked him from the forested slopes on the southern bank opposite to the island. This was where most of the missiles were coming from. But there were legionaries here among them who must have broken through the defences at the causeway – even the triple fosse itself.

He realized what must have been the heavy cost of such breaches. Yet still every sacrifice would be for nothing if the assault succeeded. He had to force his own recovery – to help.

"How long since the attack began?"

"At first light this morning."

Their voices were torn away by the hot wind of another cannonade, then the clamour of a fresh attack, the defiant battle hymn of the Shee rising above the crackling of the flames.

Ainé, if she survived, must be there, at the very heart of it, holding what she could of the breach in the face of over-whelming odds.

Suddenly there was a lull, in which he could hear the broken stonework crackling. Mira's voice fell to a whisper. "Is it the dark one from the Wastelands who is making you sick?"

Duval looked at her with uncertain eyes. Was she able to perceive the Legun? A chill invaded his mind at the sight of that small, grimy face now puckered in concentration, her lip trembling. He shook his head, attempted to clear his mind of bewilderment, aware of a shadow approaching, relieved when the shadow revealed itself to be a smoke-begrimed Milish. There was no time for words of concern. Milish was kneeling by him now, her hand clasping his shoulder as she lifted the flask of Niyave to his lips.

With gratitude, Duval accepted the elixir. His eyes returned to the face of Mira, the force of concentration there, as her fingers brushed the brow of her doll. He felt the sudden re-viving of his strength and spirits.

In the renewed thunder of battle, Milish was shouting into his ear.

"We face a dreadful disadvantage in forces... such grotesques at large in the forest. We are besieged not only by tens of thousands of legionaries but also by monsters from the darkest pits of the Tyrant's malice. Gargs!" she groaned, as if the term were terrifying to her. "And new malengins of war the like of which neither Bétaald nor Ainé have previously witnessed. The forest about the southern slopes is in conflagration. Soon the entire Vale of Tazan will be consumed." For a moment, she shuddered, her distraught gaze faltering. "We should find some means of helping you to escape. All is lost here."

"I'm not going to abandon you, Milish."

"Then help Ainé. If she falls, the Shee will have lost their leader."

What Milish said made sense. Duval felt at his waist for the dagger of Magcyn Ré, but it was gone. He presumed that Qwenqwo had taken it back. Then abruptly, glancing at Mira, he sensed a growing wonder about the girl. There was a compelling force in the childish features, a power emanating from that downturned face, the eyes hidden by the fallen lashes. He hesitated in the act of leaving them, watching Mira as, with a touch like thistledown, she held up her hand and pressed it against his sweating brow. All confusion cleared from his mind.

Milish had stopped remonstrating with him. She too was staring at Mira.

The girl's face now glimmered with reflection, as if some inner force was radiating moonlight. Duval gazed in wonder at the glowing face of the child healer.

"At every confrontation earlier," he shouted to Milish, "it was Mira who guided me! I know now that it was her voice I heard in my mind, telling me to discover the guardians when I was fighting the Legun." His eyes, in parting glance, met those in Milish's tensed and dust-grimed face. "Take care of her, Milish."

Picking up the steel-bladed harpoon of a dead Olhyiu, he stumbled toward the fury of battle. The sulphurous blast of the explosions had taken down a whole section of the third defensive fosse. If Ainé was anywhere, it must be here.

Arriving at the breach, the spectacle took his breath from his lungs. It extended for at least thirty yards through the broken wall, a wrack of bloodied bodies, fallen masonry and spluttering flames. Duval recognized here and there men of the Olhyiu fighting alongside the dazzling artistry of the Shee.

As he looked about him, sickened by the gore and stench, a huge detonation struck close enough for his face to burn and for the breath to be whipped from his lungs. It was followed by a screeching sound, as if the air was being tormented by the passage of the incandescent mass that tore an arc thirty yards over his head. The missile exploded with a thunderous impact against the side wall of the great hall.

The building was tottering, already pitted with huge holes. Where were the vulnerable, the elderly and wounded? Where were the children?

Duval shook his head, not wanting to imagine the injuries and terror confined within those ancient walls.

"Ainé!" he shouted.

An unseen Shee, bloodied from several wounds, sprang to intercept a shadow that appeared suddenly from the smoke to descend upon his head. Duval stepped back from a grotesque shape that fluttered through the air, suspended on vast leathery wings.

He stumbled and nearly fell over a decapitated body, his mind wrenched back to Milish's conversation. *Monsters from the darkest pit of the Tyrant's malice.* Fleetingly, he recalled the impression he had had on more than one occasion of being watched from the forests, followed by the sound of leathery wings beating.

The bat-creature had gigantic brown wings, stretched in sinewy membranes across attenuated fingers. Its skeleton was drawn out to grotesque proportions, with a powerful scaly tail, so it could not only glide but fly, with great flapping movements through the tormented air. In that vision, he had glimpsed a grotesque face equipped with fangs, and hugely elongated feet and toes, from which needle-sharp talons extended, livid with poison. He presumed that this was the creature Milish had called a Garg. The Garg would have clawed his eyes out if the Shee had not taken it by one leathery wing and smashed its skull against the broken fosse.

Duval barely had time to recover from his shock before the

same Shee was fighting hand to hand with a massive legionary.

The soldier's helmet had been partially cloven in some earlier confrontation yet still he snarled at the woman, with bestial canines bared under the fanaticism in his coal black eyes. Taking advantage of her distraction with the Garg, the legionary had taken a fierce grip of the Shee from behind, his hands encircling her throat and his fingers burying themselves deep in her flesh, rooting for arteries and windpipe.

Duval plunged the harpoon into the legionary's side, but only managed to wound him. With a blood-flecked howl, he continued his attack upon the Shee. Duval twisted the blade deeper even as, with a deft twist and side step, the Shee brought her sword backward and upward, and at a seemingly impossible angle pierced the legionary's throat. Without waiting for the corpse to fall, she stepped forward to place her body before Duval's as another shrieking Garg plummeted down through the air, preceded by two taloned feet that were directed at his heart.

The strike was lightning quick, with no time for the Shee to protect herself. She took the venomous thrust, beheading the monster with her sword even as she was killed.

Stumbling sideways, so he didn't make such an easy target, Duval was knocked backward by another unequal struggle. A lone Shee fought two legionaries, striking sparks from their swords with her glowing blade.

With a roar, Duval struck the harpoon against the helmet of one of the legionaries, but his strike rebounded with barely a dent in the matte black metal. At the same time as the Shee gutted the legionary in front of her, the second brought his short sword upward in a two-handed lunge, piercing the woman in the small of the back and then tearing, rending, bisecting bone, flesh and spinal cord, yet still revelling in the upward lunge, tormenting the Shee in the very moments of her death with its hacking, ever deepening wound. Duval took more careful aim with the tip of his weapon, directing its point into the gap where the base of the helmet overlapped the neck of the mail shirt. He thrust the blade through the crevice, then plunged deeper. With a throaty moan, the legionary collapsed, killed as the harpoon transected the base of his brain.

Snatching up the green-bladed sword of the dead Shee, Duval was stumbling, running, gaining strength with every step as the oraculum blazed to white power, the swell of his anger ramifying and spreading into his muscles.

Dead bodies of Shee lay scattered about him now, inter-woven with lesser numbers of the Olhyiu, their flesh overrun by the green-glowing slime, which flickered and danced over their wounds as it devoured them. The oraculum registered Ainé somewhere to his left. He spun in that direction, through rubble and carnage and the oppressive closeness of monstrous evil.

Before he had taken twenty paces, he heard the screeching of tormented air as another sulphurous missile cast its foetid arc to crash into the ancient walls somewhere behind him. He cast a wave of power to avert the concussion of thunder and flames from his face.

Two legionaries had materialized out of the smoke to challenge him. Duval touched his sword against the oraculum in his brow. He felt the shock wave as the amplification of the power descended into his arm and infused white anger into the glowing blade. In a blur of motion that was his own sword arm, the legionaries' heads rolled from their shoulders. Finding a small mound of broken wall, he sprang up onto it, standing above the drifting smoke and flames, and he peered about him through the screams of the dying and the continuing clash of sword and armour.

An old Aydes woman, with a twisted spine, reached up to offer him Niyave. A moment later she uttered a dull cry and fell like a sack of bones, half her chest destroyed. He saw how her body was already oozing the slimy glow of the Legion's poison. Rage deepened in him, rage took possession of him, roaring through his mind and honing the speed of his thinking.

Duval held the Shee sword aloft, its effulgence burning like a sun. Through its brilliant aura, he searched for Ainé and Qwenqwo, the two other oraculum-bearers, finding them, surprisingly, side by side. There was no time to interpret the meaning of this, only to realize that they were trapped within a ring of a dozen or so legionaries, so that no matter how bravely they fought they were doomed.

With the battle rage now coursing through him, he sprang back down onto the battleground and ran in their direction.

As if through a surge of his mind, Duval made contact, power for power, with the Oraculum of Brí on Ainé's brow. He used it to lead his attack to her, sweeping the white-blazing sword through the cordon of enemies. The flame of his rage consumed them, danced in an instant from helmet to helmet, passing through shields, through the black meld of iron and silicate that fashioned their helmets. Their bodies exploded into pyres of flame.

With shocked eyes, Ainé and Qwenqwo peered about them, unable to believe what had happened: then they sprang to join him, where his sword was still burning brightly over the burning corpses.

The weariness of Duval's limbs was forgotten as he grasped the dwarf's gnarled shoulder, the bloodied dagger of Magcyn Ré trailing from Qwenqwo's hand. Tears of friendship sparkled in those green eyes as Qwenqwo sheathed the dagger to return Duval's fierce grip of welcome. Ainé stood back, staring at him in open astonishment. He felt the quick probing of her oraculum, assessing the power that must be visibly glowing on his brow. Then she did him the greatest honour. She offered him the fleeting wrist and arm embrace, in the manner of intimate Shee greeting.

"Our cause is desperate. Already there are a great many injured and dead. Our scouts believe that all the southern battalions of the Death Legion are close by in the forest and on either bank of the river. If so, our enemies number a hundred thousand."

Then Qwenqwo, his face purple with fury, could hold his tongue no longer. "There has been treachery here, Duval. What else but treachery could have allowed the Tyrant's vanguard to penetrate the triple fosse. Before we knew it they were among us."

The Kyra stood, bloodied and silent, her posture and bearing tensed.

What was Qwenqwo implying? That traitors had concealed themselves among the large numbers of Aydes that had arrived with Bétaald?

Duval did not believe it.

The answer to that treachery lay with that ominous presence he detected nearby.

"One more cannon hit," growled Ainé, "and the hall will be destroyed."

Into his consciousness came a desperate foreboding. Before he could see it through the green pyres and the smoke and the stench of death, he heard its obscene growl, as if the veil of light and air had been rent apart and something dreadful were willing itself into form.

Duuuvaaalll!

A storm of evil purpose flickered and swirled about the smoking ruin that surrounded them. Ainé began the chanting battle hymn of the Shee, calling back the survivors of her scattered army through the breach.

Duuuvaaalll! I, the humble servant of my immortal master, challenge thy feeble powers in combat!

Duval turned to Qwenqwo, who was standing to his right, with his feet wide apart, the dagger of Magcyn Ré outstretched. "Go! Run! I want no foolish sacrifices here. Find Milish. Help her escape with Mira."

For just a fraction of a second the disgruntled face of the dwarf glared back, furious at being dismissed from the field of battle. Then he disappeared, as if the smoke had swallowed him. Ainé remained, crouched to his left, with her oraculum blazing power to her sword arm. In a moment, the malevolence of the Legun was nearby, probing his inadequate defences.

It reared in front of him, half emerging from the flames and ruin. A monstrous shadow, fifteen feet tall, it was only vaguely human in form. An immensity of malice and power glimmered about its edges as if a dark sun were continually reforming out of the voids of space. There was a head of sorts, vague and grisly, with those malevolent eyes but no discernible face. The Legun reared again, then appeared closer. In its approach it seemed to amplify in power and darkness, as if from moment to moment it recreated the malice of its existence from the corruption of its surroundings. Splinters of loathing, like dying stars, glittered in the pits of its eyes.

Duval was forced to step back, lifting his head to confront it.

Through the white flare of his oraculum, Duval searched the immense enemy for the vestige of a human heart. But he found none. This malevolence had never been human.

From this close, the issuing voice was an assault upon his hearing, a harsh hiss, like red-molten slag polluting fresh water. *Put aside thy venal moralising for the castrated priests of thy kind. Thou cannot comprehend my master. He is the left arm of eternity.*

Ainé took advantage of its focus on Duval to attack. With a great cry, "De Danaan!", she sprang high into the air, her sword extended, every ounce of strength in her tall frame directed at the shadowy region of its throat. But the blade, even though glowing with all of her power, made little wound in this evil. It sliced through darkness with a blaze of green sparks, but there was no pause, not even a shudder in her terrible enemy. The Legun struck out while she was still in flight, catching her shoulder with an immense dark reach. Duval saw blood spurt from the previously healing wounds, then with a growl of glee, it gripped her by the hair in its other reach, dangling her body above them as if she were a figure of straw, then cut deep, with an extended talon, reopening the scars on the left side of her face.

I tire of such trivial sport. Again I challenge thee, Duuuvaaalll, spawn of Earth and vain hope of the Great Witch of Ossierel, to mortal combat upon the exalted plane.

The remorselessness of its fury struck all of Duval's senses at once, an assault that struck at the limits of normal space and time.

Duval's oraculum blazed through spectra beyond the visible. He no longer needed rage to activate it. Assuming the First and Second Powers, he held steady against a second wave of its fury, directing his own powers through his left arm and into the sword of the Shee, so that it metamorphosed to a weapon beyond physical substance. It became the force of his will.

"I do not fear you, though I know your capacity for malice. Go back to your obsequious veneration of the foulness you call your master."

The two powers expanded in Duval, finding a common consummation, ramifying to fill his being. With all of his force, he struck out at the figure of darkness. The flame of his anger exploded to the right of its chest, below the shoulder that held Ainé's battered body aloft, the point of impact shimmering in a strange implosion, issuing wave after wave of aftershock into darkness, as if being had encountered unbeing. The impact shattered his sword, the reaction reeling like a tide of agony through Duval's body.

With an almighty roar, the Legun dropped Ainé. But Duval could see that even though he had attacked it with all of his power, he had not seriously weakened it.

Thou darest profane the almighty one!

The words rent the air as if tearing apart a mountain. *Know then that he is the perfection of all that is sinister, the boundless seed of malign destiny. Thou art no more than a speck of dirt in his eye. He will not deign to pit wits against the irritation that is thee.*

The reach above the point of penetration struck back, a glancing stroke of effortless ease. Duval attempted to parry it with his force, but he hadn't the strength to deflect it. A crushing pain exploded in his chest and abdomen. He was tossed backward, landing with a bone-jarring concussion upon the misshapen pile of broken stone and bloodied shapes. The Legun expanded even more until it became a thunderhead of dark power, devouring the light. A rancid laughter perverted the air, echoing above the din of battle.

Be assured I have a relish and a patience for inflicting pain that is beyond thy reckoning. On thy knees and pray for death to release thy torment.

The triumph of malice was unbearable. Duval was choking with the stench of putrefaction. Yet still he must somehow play for time.

Ainé needed to recover from the concussion. Her instincts then must be to flee the battle, search the ruins for Mira and Milish – save them. He struggled back onto shaky legs, yet challenging it still, keeping its murderous focus upon himself.

"A power without pity has no foundation. Your master will not prevail."

A horrible laughter, like the slithering of serpents ravening with lust. *Is this thy measure, Duuuvaaallll – insufferable True Believer. I might have extinguished thy mortal existence at a stroke, but thou hast insulted my liege, so I am inclined to sport with thee. I shall scourge thee first through those thou fawnest over, so my ultimate satisfaction will be all the sweeter.*

So saying, the monstrous form reached out and, picking up the still unconscious Kyra, it extended two great talons at her eyes.

"Stay thy malice, Septemvile!"

Through a mist of pain, Duval saw the slim form of Mira insinuate herself between the Legun and himself. Her piping voice had fallen an octave, yet still it was childish in its intonation. With a new intensity of interest, the Legun moved its focus to the girl. Duval also felt the immense force of that piping command and he remembered feeling it once before, when the head had awakened.

"Mira – get out of here! Go back – save yourself!"

Her show of force was foolishly brave in these desperate circumstances. Mira could not hope to defeat the immense power of a Legun incarnate.

What pretty spoil art thou?

Mira's face was spectral with light. "I am the one your master covets – I am the Arünn reborn, the Heralded One who will come out of the wilderness."

Ahhhhhh!

Duval was ignored as the gigantic shape shifted its focus to the diminutive figure of the girl.

"Let him live. Let them all live and I will come willingly with you."

"No! Mira! Better that all of us die than you surrender yourself to the Tyrant."

Thrusting all that remained of his faltering power between them, once more he was struck aside, hurled against the stone wall, the Legun barely registering his intervention, so absorbed was it in the challenge of Mira. The Legun made no attempt at a physical attack on her. Duval felt it probe the small figure at once, both in the Dromenon and in the flesh. He sensed its desire, covetous beyond limit.

Why would I bargain with thee, little sparrow. Thy strength is but a sigh in the storm of my malice. I shall take thee and sport with them also.

Rage blazed in Mira's eyes. The Legun drew back from the challenge, as though reconsidering the nature of this new threat. In shock, Duval heard Mira's words invade his mind: "I have power only to hold it briefly. Flee, Al-an – escape this doomed world!"

TWENTY-FOUR

THE THIRD POWER

DUVAL WOULD NOT abandon Mira. Instead a desperate idea took shape in his mind.

"I accept your challenge." He hurled his defiance at the Legun with all the power of the oraculum. "Combat to the death, then! But not here on this field of common blood. Up there – where the tower meets the sky!"

While the Legun exulted in this vanity, Duval forced himself away from the dreadful stalemate between the Legun and Mira. "Come on then!" He attempted to distract its attention, drawing it after him.

Gathering strength as he drew in distance from the Legun, he broke into a run, hammering the ground with his booted feet as he climbed above the broken fosse and the buildings, and above the fierce battle that continued over the plateau. A roar of fury from the Legun revealed that he had succeeded in dividing it in its purpose. It relished the sport while it would not allow either of them to escape.

Turning his face high overhead, Duval gazed up at the pentagonal tower raised like a fist above the tor. The upper staircase!

Immediately he sprang to the ascent.

As he climbed the first dozen steps of fissured stone, the malevolent reek followed him. The monstrous enemy, even while still confronting Mira, could still cast its malice in a second direction. With a chill of foreboding, Duval realised what this implied. The Legun had reasoned that his was the weaker challenge. It had only cast its spiritual malice against him, holding back its incarnate presence to confront Mira. Already he sensed it probing his mind. It was attempting to control him.

Unbidden, into his memory came the image of the old Aydes woman who had died while offering him Niyave. A test. And he couldn't hide the sorrow he had felt at witnessing her death.

It had taken the Legun no time at all to discover a source of weakness.

At once, into his consciousness was inserted a new image of wounding evil. But this was the evil of human inflicted upon human. Even as the images tormented him, Duval knew these were all too real. History was littered with examples like this: and no century had been more cruel than his own. He shook his head from side to side, in a vain effort to clear his mind of the images.

Still he continued to climb.

The rasping voice of the Legun echoed inside his mind. *Deny then that darkness rules thy kind, Duuuvaaalll!*

"I do – I deny it!"

He played its game, he played for time, wondering why the monster did not tear him bodily from the rock.

Mira must somehow still be holding it, absorbing the greater part of its malice so that it was sufficiently weakened for him to oppose it. As if enraged by his perception, it strengthened its assault. It forced him to witness the darkest moments in human history, the brutality of armies, the massacres and pitiless extermination. Duval could smell the blood: his nostrils were drowning in the smell of slaughter. His eyes could not see the rock in front of him. He could barely feel the staircase on which he willed his flagging limbs to climb.

He forced himself to think about the other side of humanity, the essential good nature of people. He focused on family values. Caring. The wonder of human love.

The Legun brushed his feelings aside. It had the power to

shock him deeper, dissecting apart the scenes of slaughter to penetrate the terrible experiences of individual grief. He felt the paralysis of fear in the victim as if he looked out through the victim's own eyes on the tormentor: he felt also the cruel glee in the pit of his belly, as if he were the murderer or torturer; and then back again, to feel those torments visited upon his own struggling body.

My master need not teach thy kind. The darkness is there already, Duuuvaaalll. Does it not lie at the very root of thy species!

"Not true!" he shouted.

The answering stench of wickedness, of the putrefaction of its hate, almost threw him into the abyss.

As its malice wore at him, the Legun-in-spirit was swelling in power, a storm of doom about the lonely figure climbing the steps. Still he opposed its malice, focusing every shred of his will in opposing it, keeping his face turned into the mountain, his legs climbing… climbing. Against the fury of its spite, he was hopelessly exposed. But his concern for his friends drove him onward. He thought about his love for Kate. He focused on the memory of her face, her eyes… *the green of evening light on a meadow!* He remembered the kiss, with the bicycle between their youthful bodies. He felt his friendship with Mira, Ainé, Siam, and Turkaya – people to whom he owed so much. In his love and friendship he found the strength to endure the torment that clawed at every lift of his agonized ankles and the scorn that tore at the flesh of his back upon every step until it felt as if his hair were being ripped from his head and his flesh were being flayed from his ribs.

What do these wretches mean to thee, fighting their miserable skirmishes in this alien world? Reflect – reflect! How easy it would be to relieve thy pain!

Duval wrenched his head up to stare up at the looming pinnacle. Closer. A couple of hundred feet at most. But so distant still! And the light was ebbing from the afternoon, as if a terrible darkness beckoned.

The flailing wind numbed his fingers so they could not feel

the roughest stone, and his feet had lost their sense of position. Through the oraculum his mind struggled for a purchase. While a spark of hope remained, he would fight on. Upward he climbed, more wearily and slowly than ever, while a tormented world spun and shrieked about him and in his mind the malignant probe dissected and pried, hunting for the secret places, reaching back into the memories of the maturing boy, discovering the pain that harboured there in his saddest memories: the brutalized orphan after the death of his father.

Immediately, a dreadful debility contracted over his heart and he fell against the cold stone, he felt its edges bite into his body, tear at the flesh of his hands and his knees. *Your daddy was a drunken bum – your mommy was a tramp!* The belt rose, hesitated at the top of its arc, descended over his naked skin. Pain consumed him. Pain and humiliation and fear. The pain and the fear that would leach into his soul, where it would haunt him for the rest of his life.

"No!" Every breath was a groan. "They cared for me. They loved me!" He had stopped, striking his forehead against the rock.

Yeeesss – Duuuvaaaalll! Thou hast seen thy species' own iniquity. Bear witness and accept its downfall.

He had to cling dizzily to where he had stopped, while evil crowed its hegemony over him.

Staring back over his shoulder again, unable to resist the impulse that was being fomented in his mind, there was no doubting the allure of letting go, of allowing his pain that final release in the tumble, that sheer fall through crackling wind and howling abyss, to end his life on the rocks below.

The Legun had expanded to a tempest of malignant force about his weary and tormented body. The triumph in his mind crackled with glee.

A single step into the embrace of darkness. There shall thou discover the end thou cravest.

Duval's head lifted to the wheeling clouds, to the few steps above as they turned abruptly leftward, the final ascent. Above him was the pentagonal tower, a black monolith, thrust into the spuming caldera that had become the sky. His teeth chattered together in a bitter exhaustion yet still his will stood firm.

"Go to hell!"

In a supreme effort of will, his left hand became a claw and into those clawed fingers he thrust every ounce of the force that remained within him. He smashed through pain to force himself onward, to cling to the next step, pulled his shuddering frame eighteen inches higher, though the pitch of the staircase seemed almost a vertical climb, with no handholds other than the cutting edges of the steps themselves.

The yawning chasm spun below him, giddy and nauseating, drawing his will back, pulling at every limb to drag him off the face.

He felt a sudden intense stab of despair. He knew this could only mean that Mira's strength was giving way. For all the time he had been climbing, she had endured a more terrible struggle than he had. She had withstood all of the malice of the Legun incarnate – she couldn't hold on much longer. And he was so worn he was climbing on hands and knees. Blood oozed from around his fingernails and mixed with sweat so that his hands slipped with ever increasing difficulty on the fractured stone. Groaning aloud, he forced himself on.

Suddenly, the going was easier and he almost fell over the topmost step, so determined were his pain-racked limbs to continue climbing when at last the climb was over.

The Legun roared so violently it shook the tor. Duval felt the stones shift and grind under him, as if they had been struck by an earthquake. With his back still bent, he staggered through the inwardly sloping jambs of the ancient portal, into a wide atrium of storm-weathered stone, paved, walled, and vaulted with that same dark granite. And there he felt a welcome respite. The fury of the Legun battered the outside walls of the tower, but it did not dare to enter here.

A twist of staircase led up into the projecting pentagon of the tower.

Shambling, stumbling, ignoring the battering of his heart and wheezing of his lungs, he ascended the staircase until he emerged under the vault of the sky. He stood on a flat pinnacle, surrounded by a low wall beyond which the Vale of Tazan stretched in a dizzying panorama from horizon to horizon. Here, in the howling of the wind, so high the tempestuous sky seem to press down upon him like a ceiling, his nostrils were washed free of the overwhelming stench of evil. He slumped against the wall, looking down into the despoiled valley, at the pall of smoke and ruin rising from the temple complex far beneath him. Islands of orange flame licked among the great sweep of forests, feeding the black mantle of smoke that rose upon the tormented air.

Out of the smoking ruin on the northern slope, a grey speckled mist was rising, as if the leaves of the forest were ascending into the sky. He realized what it was: thousands upon thousands of the Gargs rising, a vast storm of terror, soon to hurl itself against the survivors in the ruins below.

His limbs trembling with exhaustion, he turned to look up at the colossus that surmounted this pentagonal rath: a single figure, great and tall, yet it was not the queen he had expected. He remembered the radiantly beautiful woman in the woodland grove. But this sculpture was ten times life size, struck from the same enduring granite as the tower that bore it. Sombre as the elements that had fought to conquer it over the ages, its countenance was cold and grim, the eyes without pupils and the brow, with its incised black triangle, ragged with fury. For a moment the risks of the gamble he now contemplated sapped his will.

Abruptly, he felt a new force intervene, a force he had not anticipated. With gritted teeth and his eyes clenched shut, he resisted that force with every shred of his will, resisted the feeling of dislocation as he was torn away from this stony platform on top of the tower, away from the mortal world of Tír.

When he opened his eyes, he was back in the labyrinth of caves where Granny Ddhu had introduced him to the Trídédana. In his nostrils was the faint reek of sulphur, from the nearby lava lake, enclosed by its wall of emerald. From this strange magma the triangular oraculum had been forged, its ruby gleam casting light before him as it seemed to draw his resisting limbs onward.

Before him, nascent with foreboding, was the circle of petrified trees, in the heart of which stood the brooding figure. Drawn toward its triple cowled and shadowed form, his lungs seemed to hunger for air as he gazed once more at the whorled surface that glittered and metamorphosed in the flickering matrix of its extraordinary being.

His limbs still trembled as he drew near, thrown onto his knees on the dirt before the immense power of those three heads. Duval struggled back onto his feet, determined to stand with his head unbowed.

"I don't know the mantras of incantation," he spoke with difficulty, through cracked and broken lips. "But I ask you, although I don't understand the nature of your power, to help me."

Communion exploded again in his mind. His eyes widened to the wonder of the awakening being. He forced himself to stagger forward, embracing the lined and weathered surface. His bleeding fingers fumbled for the runes. The oraculum on his brow touched the incandescence of the first head and her being metamorphosed before him, the image of the mature woman. He was surprised to sense, though only a shadow of her previous presence, the cautioning figure of Granny Ddhu nearby in the dust. Watching over him still, her warnings reached out to him, like ghostly whispers in his mind. But Duval had no time for wondering about the meanings of things, any more than he had time for caution: within a moment the face had changed and he was gazing at the mask of bone.

So, Duval – would you now embrace me?

"No!" A more experienced Duval faced the Mórígán than in

their first encounter, but still he held back.

The voice of death was as low as a great fall of water, breaking over stones. *What craven spirit bears the mark of power upon his brow? What fear draws this timorous one back from the challenge that the De Danaan died for?*

"I am not worthy of this power you would give me."

Not worthy! The voice, colder than the wastes of eternity, echoed, fading slowly as if into a waiting pool, deep with stillness. *Foolish man! No mortal could be worthy. That power is mine alone to confer. Yet with this power I would make you immortal.*

"When I was a prisoner of the Storm Wolves, I saw what I would become if I embraced you." Duval recalled with horror the ash white fury in the clearing by the river. "Maybe I am foolish – but at least I am humanly foolish."

You will not sacrifice your petty humanity – even if in doing so, you would save the lives of your friends?

"I would accept any sacrifice if that was all that was expected of me. But I know that once made, its benefit would end there. I have seen the example of Nantosueta, who made that same sacrifice long ago. Once her sanctuary was destroyed by the same forces of darkness that threaten us today. Two thousand years ago, she embraced you. She was willing to pay that price to save her valley. Yet the Tyrant was not destroyed. It was only a temporary victory. And now darkness has returned, more powerful than before. If I repeat that mistake, my quest is lost."

A pause, in which that dread countenance appeared to assess him anew.

Two powers were bestowed upon you, the First Power, of the Land and its elements, and the Second Power, born from forces of Creation. Such powers have you still. Would you fail in your quest for want of using them?

Then, as if to scorn him further, he was shown a pinpoint of light and the darkness that seethed about it, determined to fetter it. A terrible despair cut through his awareness: a voice that rose, like a plaintive cry, on the wind. "I am lost, Al-an!

Abandon me!"

"Mira!" His throat choked with concern for her.

Duval had heard her confirm her true identity to the Legun. She was the Arünn reborn. That was why the Legun had focused on her and diverted his attentions during his climb up the stone staircase. But even with Mira captured, the Legun would allow nobody to live. It would kill them all for the sport of it as much as to prevent them telling of the girl and the potential she carried. He remembered how Mira had tried to help him. How, with great prescience, she had indicated all he needed to know. She had shown him the most vital clue in the nemeton: the black triangle on the brow of the queen – had he not seen that same triangle carved deep into the brow of the terrible figure on the summit of the pentagonal tower.

He spoke huskily, urgently, "I must gamble on the fact that even Death knows pity. One deserving of your pity could help me. I ask for your help in awakening Nantosueta."

You eschew what is in your own will to do, yet you would reawaken another whose courage exceeded your own in ages past?

"I have the First and Second Powers. Nantosueta has the Third. Between us we possess all three."

There was a moment's pause, as if she were considering his blasphemy. He waited in that terrible silence, laden with fore-boding. Then he felt a powerful throbbing from his forehead which spread so that his whole mind seemed probed. There was a quickening in him, as if his strength were flowing back. Immediately he found himself cast out of the labyrinth.

Back on the pinnacle, he saw how the Legun had expanded in power. The entire sky was a pit of darkness, ravaged by light-ning, and the very granite of the encircling mountains crackled and split with new volcanic eruptions in the grinding force of its rage. Immediately Duval stared up, with oraculum blazing, the Earth Power flowing out of him and into the figure of stone that surmounted the tower. A phosphorescence of ruby light lit up the figure of Nantosueta, like a terrible sun being born out of the chaos. A second conflagration and the creative force of the Second Power also blazed from his brow, compelling the figure to draw life from him, marbling its surface with luminescence, which sparkled and cascaded in a dense web of runnels and matrices throughout the crystals of the rock.

Moment by moment, as the figure grew ever more incandescent, a coldness invaded Duval's heart, a dispiriting gloom so bleak and dreary it was an anguish to bear it. His eyes quailed to face her: for the beautiful maiden he had thrilled to witness in her woodland grove had assumed the gibbous mask of the Third Head.

Still he held himself erect as the fierce light of the two powers continued to pulse from his brow.

And moment by moment, the Dark Queen blazed brighter: as if the crystals of granite took fire from his own life-giving sun. When she spoke, it sounded like the rattling of a sea of bones.

Speak, bearer of the oraculum of the Holy Trídédana – and quickly ere you invoke my wrath. To what design do you profane my age-old slumber?

"My purpose is your own." He had to hurl his words with all of his strength from mind to mind and even then they sounded like a whisper against the battening storm of force that whipped and tossed about the tor. On legs braced with resolve, Duval turned to indicate the Legun and the raging battle below. "Look beyond even that malice to what has become of your valley!" His arms extended against the battening chaos to encompass it. "You see the desecration of your sacred forests. And there below, on your temple plateau, the innocents who took sanctuary there are being destroyed by the same forces of evil you recognize from long ago."

Weariness again, in a great wave of sorrow, swept through the very atoms of his spirit as that great head turned in a thunder of movement.

Know you well that once invoked, my wrath has no limit unto completion. Though bitter has been my restraint, yet unrestrained all would perish, from the eagle that commands the skies to the very ant that burrows in the earth. Take care what you would ask of me!

Duval faced the adamantine pits of her eyes. "I saw your loveliness, in your youth. I must put my life and trust in the goodness of that image. There are innocents on the plateau whose lives must be preserved. To save them I ask for consummation with you, body with body, and spirit with spirit."

His teeth were clenched from the horror of what he was asking, yet he refused to avert his gaze from those terrible eyes now beholding him from their ivory brow, shuddering to sense the judgment that brooded within the sharp-rimmed orbits as she beheld the ruin of her sacred valley. He spoke again, with undisguised compassion: "If what I now observe is the price of the Third Power, I pity you your loneliness."

Pity! the voice thundered, the susurration of that dreadful ocean buffeted his soul. Yet still she paused, as if in bitter reflection. *Is it through pity then that you would persuade me? Would that I too could feel pity, oraculum-bearer. Yet to mingle thus with a sentient heart, though brief unto a single moment, would be such sweetness. Great anger at injustice was my undoing. Pride became my blood and it hardened my heart to stone. Thus wrath has become my fate and I must endure it until the end of time. Yet you would risk such a consummation?*

"I would gladly risk it."

Be one with me then. And avert your senses unless dread rather than pity is the memory you would keep of me.

He felt his physical presence dissolve into the molecules that made it – and beyond that, to the energy of the atoms, and even beyond that to the forces beyond time and space that could create a universe out of nothing in the blink of an eye.

In that same blink of an eye, that force melded him into consummation, masculine with feminine, mind for mind and heart for heart, into a spiritual union that was agony and ecstasy, enraptured and entwined beyond any sense or emotion he had ever experienced, or dreamed.

Those unblinking eyes became one with his own as the right

arm drew its awful force down out of the heavens and that single white-marbled left arm extended, with the fingers splayed to a spider-shape of bleached and deadly ivory. Suddenly, those fingers exploded in blue-white lightning. The accompanying words were a whisper in a language older than time, a proclamation of absolute command that bent the universal laws to their bidding. The dreadful summons swept far and wide over mountain and river and through the forests, a command such as had been seen only once before since the first creation of worlds.

Warriors of doom awaken!

All that lived below froze in its being, hushed in the very act of breathing, thrown down upon the uncertain earth with stopped heart and horror-struck eyes.

Great cataracts of lightning fell through the air, crushing from existence the matrices of storm and wind that had been summoned by the Legun, falling in luminescent rainbows over the landscape, even as the rivulets of silvery light expanded and fused in the Dark Queen's substance, so her figure was transformed into a furnace of light. Duval observed how the avalanche of lightning separated into a myriad feelers and rivulets as it spread its deadly impact over the ground. The thunderous resonations seemed to go on and on. A terrible constellation of stars began to glow in their own spectral luminescence in the war-ravaged valley. Duval had felt the great destructive force of a single head in his struggle with the Legun: now all of the valley's heads awoke into avenging life, their regular intervals searing the forested slopes on either side of the great river. The call of annihilation expanded until it was a tidal wave sweeping through the valley.

Duval was united in body and spirit with the awful supremacy of death.

There was no time in that single moment for the screams and tormented cries of slaughter. Breath was taken and heartbeat with it, then the very soul and the spirit that was the essence of life. All in a moment. Other than the trees, and the wild life that lived their lives in intimate union with them, nothing survived that annihilating wrath. Yet still it was not over. As yet, because Duval willed it, the plateau had been spared.

Now he accepted the burden of slaughter from his spiritual partner as she willed into existence a new and dreadful constellation of stars. If innocent life were to be saved, his power alone must control these stars of death as, in a second and more selected wave, they spiralled down over the temple plateau, sparing his friends while darting through the hearts of the Death Legion and their monstrous allies. Tiny motes, icy and brilliant, scoured the interrupted conflict, unerring and pitiless. In this more protracted extermination, there was more opportunity for screams and terror. Then, in a few harrowing moments, it was over. The Legun incarnatewas destroyed.

Duval sensed that its deadly existence had not been entirely extinguished, no matter how dreadful the force of their combined wills. Its immortality, only a step down in power from the Tyrant of the Wastelands, had saved some miserable shred of its spiritual form, even as, ravaged and scourged, it fled to the wrath of its malevolent master.

As to its servants, there could be no doubt of their fate. They had perished in their tens of thousands, either in the great extinction upon the forested slopes or the wretched few moments, writhing in the attack of the deadly stars upon the temple plateau.

TWENTY-FIVE

ON THE WINGS OF
ANGELS

H E STOOD ON the elevated platform of Nantosueta's
tower, blind to his predicament, deaf to the great yet
gentle wind that was blowing from the southeast, from
Carfon and the sea. How long he had stood there in that
stupefied state he did not know. Yet the wind of change was
blowing too in the landscapes of his mind.

The battle was over.

Now the dreadful implications of it sighed in his soul,
educating him, as the splinters of icy light had flickered in the
limpid reaches of those wholly black eyes.

"Duval – Mage Lord!" Powerful hands were gripping his
shoulders, a slap on the flesh of his cheeks, the press of burning
liquid against his frozen lips.

Ainé's face – Ainé, herself wounded, forcing drop by drop
the Niyave past his clenched teeth even as he became gradually
aware of the sky, the hard high green sky of early evening, with
its wrack of clouds, wheeling over him. His jaws were still
clenched in a grimace of anger as he gazed first at the Kyra's face
and then away from her, above them both, to the face of stone
on the figure that towered above him.

"Mira?"

"She lives."

"And Milish?"

"Milish is well."

She lives. Milish was well but Mira merely lived. What was
Ainé hinting at?

He saw Mira in that sad moment in Nantosueta's chamber when, as he now understood, she had faced her future, knowing she must confront the Legun: *What must be, must be endured!*

Grief rose in him a moment, boiled within him like a madness. The grief was there but he was no longer afraid. The fear that had lain in the deepest, darkest reaches of his soul had left him. Ainé preceded him down the winding staircase cut into the sheer face of the rock until finally they emerged onto the battlefield of the temple plateau. Here, the calls of the wounded filled his ears and the smell of death hung in his nostrils. She took him to Mira, who lay where he had left her at the heart of the battle, being nursed by Milish. He knelt beside her. With gentle hands he touched the emaciated face, the matted black hair that was dank with sweat.

Milish's whisper in his ear. "She will live. There are others, more desperate, who need assistance."

She was right. The need for ministering to the survivors overrode all others. He stood shakily erect to face the Kyra, her two arms stained with her own blood and with the old scars reopened on her face. His eyes met hers in a weary affection and gratitude. "You must accept help from Bétaald for your own wounds."

"My sister, Beetaald, is herself wounded." The Kyra's eyes searched his own as if she too were confused by grief. "A great many of those who answered my call to arms lie dead among these accursed stones."

So he was made aware of the gravity of the catastrophe that surrounded him: in addition to the losses of the defending Shee, many of the Olhyiu were also dead. And a large number of the survivors lay injured from the legionary's weaponry – with wounds that ran deep and poisonous. Even the survivors, haunted by grief and loss, faced an uncertain future. Where would they go now that the Temple Ship had been destroyed?

Then, unable to face the pain that still confronted him in her eyes, he left Ainé standing there, her eyes following his departing figure.

He was determined to walk among the wounded and the dead, to witness the price paid by those who had sacrificed so much to help him. He didn't have far to wander. At every step, pools of blood, broken bodies, and worse met his gaze. The groans of the injured scourged his ears as, one by one, he came upon their pain-racked figures, often in small huddles, blood-soaked and pitted by the green fire of the Death Legion. On and on he wandered among them, absorbing the blankness of shock on their faces, the ebbing of life from their eyes.

A hardening of purpose was taking place in Duval on this cold and bitter evening.

He stood aside to allow two survivors to pick up one of the dying Shee noviciates. He watched them carry her through the wisps of smoking ruin, heading for some surviving chamber, where the mother-sister would devote her failing heartbeats to the tiny beat within, to the daughter-sister yet to be born.

A rank pestilence still seeped from the blasted earth, as if the darkness still struggled to seed itself everywhere. Although all of its servants had been destroyed, the shadow of their forms were etched in black ash upon the fire-raddled stones. They mocked him still with this vision of murdered innocence, of so many faces that had once smiled at him, looked to him for hope and protection, the precious life now taken from them. Where walls had stood a thousand years, now little remained other than crumbling outlines and scorched rubble.

It was difficult to conceive that any of the more vulnerable had survived such a spiteful assault. Yet desperate arms were opening up avenues into subterranean passages and cellars, from which the surviving children and elderly were being assisted into the crepuscular light. Others were pulling aside the rubble to discover still more dead and wounded.

The exhausted Milish had left Mira with others to seek him out. Now she walked the bitter way beside him.

"The wounds caused by sword and arrow we can repair. The Aydes will stitch sinew to sinew, or set broken bones. And

Niyave will support the loss of blood and the shock of scorched flesh, even that resulting from the fell flames of the Death Legion. It was chosen and ever modified through the herb lore of the Aydes to achieve such ends. But not all that lie here were struck down by sword or the foul green flame of their weaponry." There was a new tremble of outrage in the diplomat's voice. "No wound has been more grievous than what you will see here!"

She led Duval down into one of the underground chambers, where they had found a dozen of the youngest children, hidden from the conflict for their safety: they all lay dreadfully still on the ground, pallid and feverish.

"One of the Gargs, so great and powerful it may have been their leader, forced entry here, though the door was guarded to the death by three of our bravest. You see its shadow in ash over half the flagstones. Although one star of wrath discovered its dreadful purpose before fang or claw could destroy such innocence, yet in the very moment of its death it exhaled its poison into the refuge."

Milish wept tears that no other barbarity had wrung from her exhausted and battle-weary spirit.

"These are all of the younger children that still live. If only you, in your wisdom and power, can discover the means to save but a few of them."

Duval examined them where they lay upon the blackened piles, eyes glazed and red-rimmed, the cherry red lividity on their lips, that same glow aflame in their cold flesh: in it he saw a false promise of death in the guise of hope.

In that terrible chamber he realized the selfishness of his own despondency. All about the plateau were other survivors among those poisoned by the claws, fangs or breath of the Gargs.

One of these innocents he recognized: it was Poppy, the little girl who had danced to his harmonica and pulled his beard.

He knelt beside her, pulled down the lids to see the bright red injected eyes, touched the livid lips with his finger, then parted the rags of clothing to discover the same carmine poison as it rooted and branched throughout her pallid flesh.

Duval sighed through clenched teeth.

Did even a shred of his oracular powers remain? If it did, what skill could he put to work to help these dying innocents?

He recalled how Granny Ddhu had healed him when he had been wounded beyond hope. She had used the Earth Power – a power not of thinking or even of seeing, but feeling. Could any sight have evoked more feelings of compassion than this dying child? He allowed that sense of caring to expand until it coursed his arteries and veins. Then he picked the child up and held her limp form in his arms.

The oraculum pulsed weakly. Examining her through its faintly flickering light, he saw her as pallid as death. He allowed his compassion to flood his senses and the image became more solid, yet still as pallid as if he saw her under moonlight. He felt his way in through her eyes, through the dully clouding humours and into the raddle of brilliant red vessels that lay behind. Further he entered, and finer his gaze became, until he was within the walls of her feebly pulsating arteries and from there his vision moved ever more centrally until he was within the chambers of her faltering heart.

And here he saw it. Coating the fine cells that lined every chamber he saw the poison, like a mould of the grave, with a myriad roots, invading the very muscle of the pumping chambers, squeezing the strength of contraction from them, and thereby starving her body of oxygen and life. As if he were cleaning an obscenity of graffiti, he scoured the chambers of her heart clean of the sepulchral fungus with the force of his will. He continued that intense focus until it had all shrivelled up and peeled away.

Bathed in sweat, Duval opened his eyes to look down upon the still unconscious face. With tensed fingers he felt her pulse – stronger, stronger by the moment!

Milish, whose own trembling hands accepted the child from his, looked at him with widened eyes. "Duval – oh, Mage Lord!"

His voice was husky, little above a whisper. "There are others who are similarly poisoned in this chamber – and outside, among the Olhyiu and the Shee, Bétaald among them." His eyes were burning as he took a gentle grip of her arm. "Bring them all here to me, Milish."

Through what remained of the evening and all through the night, he used the Earth Power to heal them, child and adult, as Granny Ddhu had once used it to heal himself. He refused to rest until the last had been treated.

In the first glimmer of dawn, Duval wandered alone to the easternmost reaches of the third fosse, where a thousand feet of sheer cliff face bolstered the defensive ramparts. The air was cold and reviving. The cyclopian stones of the fosse – their concavities of geometry hinged to withstand the ravages of earthquake – supported him as he leaned on them, standing high on a promontory and gazing out over the spectacular panorama.

The Vale of Tazan yawned before him, too colossal in its wandering valleys and soar of mountains to be encompassed by his tired eyes. How serene it must have appeared in the bright eyes of the young queen before war and death had invaded that tranquil scene.

The disturbed elements still coursed the ravaged forests. Thunder rolled among the distant calderas, charging the air with casts of lightning. A storm of icy rain squalled among the trees, quenching any remaining flames. On his face it felt cleansing, washing away the reek of death. In the rumbling detonations that still shook the tor under his white-knuckled fingers, he sensed relief in the very rock.

Evil was receding, though its defeat could only be temporary: and even this small victory had been bought at so great a price.

Kate was somewhere out there – a plaything of the Tyrant's malice. Yet even in that situation there was hope. The Tyrant had some purpose in keeping her alive for twenty years. That purpose, in whatever evil scheme or plan, would not have changed. That purpose was all that still kept her alive. On Duval's brow the oraculum pulsed, anxiously yet purposefully. He had no way of knowing if she could hear him as, far and wide, he cast his promise, carried upon his pent-up anger into the universe of morning. *Only survive. Soon, I promise, I shall come for you!* And patiently waiting, hoping, he thought he detected from far away the tiniest echo of a responding intelligence: like the faintest pinpoint of a morning star.

Duval was still standing there at full daybreak when a battered and bloodied Qwenqwo came upon him.

"My friend," he said, his voice hushed. "A man's drink."

Duval was too grief-stricken still to turn to look at Qwenqwo. He remained gazing eastward, seaward – beyond the Eastern Ocean to the Wastelands, to where a Tyrant schemed. His feet felt frozen to the great rampart of stone, his mind still locked in the direction of that faded star. Qwenqwo squeezed the flask into his fingers, and he felt its glow rise to his face and eyes. As he lifted it to drink, barely conscious of what he was doing, a sparkling of colours danced about its rim, and the interior glowed with a bright golden light. Duval's spirit was revived by the potency of friendship as much as the refreshing alcohol.

The dwarf spoke gently, yet insistently. "Though our losses are great, still there are the living to grieve them. Bétaald will live – making you still more of a legend among the Shee. You must save the child, Mira – though a darkness broods within her very spirit."

Qwenqwo was right. During the long night, Duval had treated Mira as he had treated the others. He had tried to cure her and failed. There was something different about her illness, as if the Legun had wounded her deeper than Duval could remedy. No probing of her heart or blood had revealed an invading evil that could be destroyed through the vision of his oraculum. Milish had revived her physically with kindness and regular sips of

Niyave. But in spirit she remained withdrawn from him, unresponsive – as if in that terrible confrontation some vital spark had been taken from her.

That morning they began the descent to the causeway. There were so many injured and sick among them that Ainé had to organize two escorted passages.

Duval waited on the Temple Plateau with Mira, her face wasted almost to a skull, while Milish led the first descent, ferrying half the sick and injured, including the children. He came down with the second passage, carrying Mira's slender frame himself. Down the interminable cascade of stones they picked their laboured way, while the mist-wreathed grandeur of the valley wept in its desolation about them. At last Duval could see the wreck of the Temple Ship below them, charcoal black, as he had first seen it after its destruction, its great masts reduced to stumps, and its timbers and decks despoiled under a coat of ash.

The stench of burning was still acrid in their nostrils as they crossed the causeway to join the others, with the recovering children laid upon the ground by the shore. All watched Duval in a fearful silence as, having placed Mira in the care of Milish, he approached the withered hulk, where it had been moored against the valley shore. The Death Legion had not dared to set foot upon its hallowed decks. Instead, raining down their green fire upon every inch of its undefended superstructure, they had poured their hate as much as the destructive fire of their malengins into the effort to annihilate it.

From close behind him Duval heard the cry of Turkaya, a piping hymn of woe from the new Shaman, so reminiscent in its cadences of Kemtuk on the frozen lake. And then the youth was by his side – taking a handful of embers. Ash spilled from his fist, forming a sorrowful plume in the gusting air, drifting down and about the pebbled shore and the lapping water.

The ruined ship lay unnaturally low in the water, as if at the end it had sought some small comfort from burrowing into the river bottom.

Siam's voice, from his other side, was breaking with emotion. "Surely, we may attempt to rebuild her. Is this not the greatest forest in all the land?"

"No, Siam," he spoke to the man, who was pressing his right arm, as if to persuade him. "Nantosueta has been woken from her sleep. She guards her forests again, and long may she do so!"

"Then all is lost. For the ship cannot be made sailworthy – yet with so many sick and wounded we cannot travel overland."

Duval turned to Siam, noticing the left arm and shoulder bloody with wounds, and still that old hat was twirling about in his hands. Siam had been drinking. Duval had a fair idea where Siam had got hold of alcohol. Qwenqwo! The Mage of Dreams seemed able to conjure up alcohol from nowhere. Duval smiled wryly at the source of that comfort. Minute by minute, people began to gather round him, the exhausted Olhyiu at the centre and even the surviving Shee. Then it was the dwarf who pressed his way to stand before him. Facing him with pride, he took something from his trousers pocket and he pressed it into the astonished Duval's hands. It was his father's harmonica. Even during the chaos of Duval's despair, Qwenqwo must have taken the trouble to rescue it from the mountain stream.

Dropping his head, Duval was so overcome with emotion, he was unable to thank Qwenqwo.

But then he lifted his face to smile at his friend, before turning to address them all. "I'm not one for making speeches." He spoke hesitantly, gruffly. "But I want to thank you all. I don't know how to begin – how to say how much I owe you – or how much I admire you all." He shook his head, unable to say more.

Siam replaced his hat and with a defiant stance he turned to face the survivors of his people.

"In his modesty, we see the brave heart of Duval, our friend and Mage Lord, clearer than he sees it himself. What if we had stayed among the Whitestar Mountains – what then would have become of us? Had we not sacrificed all dignity and hope when we surrendered our fleet to that desolate place. What else but a slow and bitter humiliation lay before us. The Mage Lord came from another world, yet he suffered to lead us out of winter. Twice, in so many days, he has destroyed the malice of a Legun. Would we not follow this man, the Chosen One of the De Danaan, to the gates of Ghork Mega itself."

Duval was embarrassed then by Siam's lofting of his battered hat and by the strained cheer that sounded from these brave and injured people.

"Though our sacrifice has been great, we thank you, Mage Lord. For you have saved the children. Yet what greater purpose might befall the Olhyiu people than to help you in such a quest. And that quest has not ended. It still leads us to Carfon by the Eastern Ocean. And there, if I have to drag this hulk by its keel along the bed of the great river, is where we shall take you."

Taking the example of that determination Duval addressed them all in reply.

"Siam is right. We must make the best of whatever presents itself to help us. The courage of your chief will be our guide."

They prepared a meal from what was left of the salted fish and they ate it on the bank, in the shadow of the hulk. Over this frugal fare, they debated what to do. The only hope, no matter how desperate, remained with the Temple Ship.

They needed to know if it could be made to float, rudderless, like a raft. Ropes were passed about the trunks of the bankside trees so that, using this leverage, they could drag the hulk into the deep water of the central stream. A party of Olhyiu went out into the forest and returned with long poles, taken only from dead trees. If it was a hope at all, it was a very slender one. Even if they succeeded in refloating the ship, a Herculian task awaited them. If the hulk would float, they would still have to pole their way upstream around the island before they could take advantage of the current, which would carry them, with only the poles for rudders, all the way to Carfon.

Some of the fitter men took up key positions, a leg clinging

to a beam or inside a crumbling porthole. Shouts of encouragement willed on the tired limbs and sweat-drenched brows.
They strained and pulled with every ounce of strength, until
the muscles of their arms and shoulders bunched like the
gnarled roots of the encroaching trees and the veins on their
brows swelled like hawsers.

But the massive ruin would not budge an inch: it was stuck
fast, resistant to every effort.

The labour continued until the midday sun broke through
the wintery mists that still bathed the valley. Seeing their
exhaustion, Duval climbed onto the deck, watching for the
slightest sign of hope.

"One more time!" He heard Siam's half-strangled shout, the
chief at the thick of the struggling figures.

But this time, though the hulk was as obstinate as ever,
Duval sensed the faintest tremor deep within the bowels of
the ship.

His hands tightened on the gritty charcoal that had been the
stout rail of the fo'c'sle. Then, picking a cautious path over the
deck, he probed here and there, as if listening with his mind as
well as his ears. Suddenly, there was a muffled roar as part of
the superstructure fell in, showering them in charcoal and ash.
Those on the deck gaped with horror, fearful the remaining
structure was about to collapse. It was Siam who again stood
fast.

"What," he demanded, "has become of the proud Olhyiu,
who respond to every groan and shiver with startled eyes! Is the
Mage Lord not here among us? Have you so soon forgotten his
words of mere hours past? Above all we must keep our faith."

But it wasn't easy to keep faith against the groans of reset-
tlement that were taking place around them. Every eye was
fixed upon the region where the superstructure had collapsed.
Yawning there into the dusty light was a gaping portal. Probing
it with the oraculum, again Duval sensed a responding
shudder: like a moan issuing from deep below. Approaching
the hole, he peered inside. Nothing beyond the immediate

opening – yet he sensed that a natural passage lay there, as irregular in its lining as a mountain cave. Then, astonishingly, in the gloom beyond, he glimpsed a staircase.

"A torch – somebody!"

It was Siam down on the bank who produced a firebrand.

"I shall be your torchbearer," shouted Siam, who was already climbing aloft the makeshift ladders.

Duval shook his head, taking the firebrand from Siam's hand. "Go back to the bank. Tell everybody else to stay clear of the ship. It may be dangerous. I must go in alone."

He was barely a step inside the portal when Duval recoiled from the odour of mildewed decay. He was glad of the breeze that entered with him: fresh air rushed in, as if to fill a vacuum, fluttering the firebrand as he held it aloft before him. He took a second step into the throat of darkness.

There really was a staircase. He descended it, spiralling down ten or twelve feet, to a level where the lower main hold of a normal ship might be. But this was no normal ship. Here a cobweb-encrusted door obstructed his passage. Yet when he pressed its surface to test the locks, its substance dissolved into dust. Beyond the door wraiths of darkness swallowed the light, as if darkness had become a force here, a fearful passion borne out of misery.

Caution ignited the oraculum so that it added the rubicund glow of its light to that of the firebrand as, with tentative steps, he continued his passage onward.

An eerie silence pervaded the gloom beyond the doorway. Side entrances confronted him as he held the firebrand aloft to inspect their organic walls. They might have been the internal passages of some vast dragon, with ridges at intervals like the rings of cartilage supporting a gigantic trachea – but one that had long since ceased its expansion and contraction with the act of breathing the primal air.

The main throat – for throat was how he now thought of this passage – twisted and turned on itself, with many diverging branches, often multiple, opening to either side, or to above and below, so that he had to be careful to circumvent the pitfalls. He grasped what he could of the wall or ceiling with his free hand. Yet though he had wandered a hundred paces into this labyrinth, still nothing became familiar. It seemed to defy real dimension. He counted his paces from that point and soon registered another hundred, yet as he could easily determine from the absence of footprints in the grimy floor, he had never once retraced his steps. Stumbling to his knees over a protruding rib, he sensed how darkness closed about him, as if to devour him.

Panic so profound, it took his breath: yet, gaining his feet again, steadying the firebrand so that it glowed brighter again, he paused to regain his composure. He was certain now of that answering tremor.

Answering to me – to my innermost thoughts… to my feelings.

Now and then he detected new odours: sometimes pleasant, the scents of flowers, at other times unpleasant, of bog tars and sulphur – or the clashing sounds of almighty if distant upheaval, as if he were close to the embryonic forces at the creation of the universe. A distortion of distance that could not be possible: a shudder in the heart of the ship – if "ship" was a pertinent word for the real nature of this mystery. There was a feeling of being watched. He almost shouted aloud, it so overwhelmed him. Yet there could be no need to shout, even to whisper, only to think. *Sorrow,* he thought it aloud, *more than injury, has scourged your timbers.* Then immediately, as if it had sensed his thrill of communication, welcomed and shared it, new hope tensed its labyrinth. Slowly, almost imperceptibly, he felt the metamorphosis of its elements, though, from moment to moment, there was little perceptible change.

If what I sense is true, then it is wonderful beyond belief. I want to believe it. Give me a sign that I am not mistaken.

How could he not be reminded of it: this was the same feeling he had had during the passage with Granny Ddhu through the stone heart of the snowcapped mountains. A journey into a place that did not exist in normal space or time:

a sanctum within a sanctum. The clue, the clue of clues that had been placed before him not once but twice, was hammering for admission to his mind.

Could it be that science far in advance of his own had created this?

A level of understanding of the universe far beyond the mechanical observation of his own world? A kind of science? *My God* – he hardly dared to think it!

Question after question thrilled his mind. But there was one he hardly dared to articulate out of sheer wonder. Then he asked it, excitedly, falteringly, through the window in his brow: *Let me ask a single question, then: are you sentient?*

Silence for several charged moments, and then, through the oraculum, he first detected the change. An answer not in words but in the metamorphosis of substance, his mind numbed by the awe of a perception that hinted at explanation.

Although he had not moved another step, he found himself within a chamber with walls that glittered as if made of gold. But their surface was too soft for metal. When he reached out to touch them they had a heavy liquid feel, as if he were pressing into a lake of mercury. There was no clear reflection in this glittering substance, not even when he shone the firebrand's light against it. It absorbed light as he assumed it must absorb all energy that was directed toward it – yet still it glowed with a soft and ancient light.

What are you? Are you a construction or a living entity? Or, at your level of being, does the distinction no longer matter?

No reply, yet he sensed the communication still stronger.

He ran his fingers over the giving surface of the walls – the liquid softness of organic being – uncertain if they were changing even as he looked at them, while observing for the first time that in cross section they formed a pentagon. The ceiling was faceted also, the natural drawing together of the lines of the pentagon.

You grieve as I do and for the selfsame reasons – I know you do. I sense it.

He took a further instinctive step and then, abandoning all defences, he opened his mind completely, through the oraculum.

The sense of a listening being was overwhelming. But a being that was not evil or mischievous. The Second Power: it was calling on him to use the Second Power.

Oh my God! Communication!

Extraordinary sensitivity combined with power. Not the patronizing voice of command he had anticipated but the sense of sharing, the invitation to discover. A wave of new vigour tingled through his mind and body.

With all of his mental strength, he poured the Second Power into the gold pentagon. The tingling surge was so exhilarating he was forced to clench his teeth – otherwise he would have shouted out like a drunken man. Healing! He was healing the Temple Ship. The wonder of it coursed through his mind, the joy of it. And in return it gave him what he had wanted ever since coming to this world. He knew it was no more than the first lesson, yet it gave it to him with such joy – more freely than he could ever have hoped for or dreamed.

Understanding!

Duval ran, stumbling and shouting, as he retraced his steps through the dusty labyrinth, slipping around the pitfalls, until he emerged, blinking with the intensity of daylight. He did not look back as the portal closed itself off behind him. It didn't surprise him. Rushing to the foredeck, he waved his arms at the startled faces that had been standing around, confused and anxious, waiting for him.

He saw how their expressions changed from fear to awe, sensing the change in him.

"Siam!" he shouted, his voice ringing with elation. "Gather everybody together and bring them up on deck. And Ainé!" His eyes scoured the uplifted faces until they found her. "The Shee too – everybody must come up onto the deck. Bring the wounded. I have something important to tell you all."

With caution still, the recovering wounded were lifted up the makeshift ladders onto the fire-ravaged main deck. A Shee carried Mira on board, then left her to Milish, who was overseeing a bed of furs in a sheltered corner among the other sick and wounded.

Suddenly a woman screamed as the cinders of an oak bulwark a few yards away disintegrated in a shower of dust. "The ghost of the ship will devour us. See there its very bones are gleaming!"

And in the gap it seemed that she was right: the skeleton of the ancient vessel did seem to protrude through the ash, like a rib of ivory.

"Stay calm! No harm will come to you!" Duval could hardly contain the joy that glistened in his eyes.

He stood in silence, feeling the charge of power that amplified and crackled about him. He knew that the Mage of Dreams had come to stand beside him, his face rapt with questions.

"What is it, Duval? What did you see in the depths of the ship?"

He looked Qwenqwo directly in the eyes. "A hint of a mystery so profound I haven't yet got to grips with its implications! A glimpse of power, Qwenqwo. Power beyond the imagination."

"Tell me more – or I shall die from the curiosity of it on these blasted decks!"

The look on Qwenqwo's face was so pleading, Duval couldn't help but laugh and then to wrap his arm about those gnarled shoulders. "Patience! We have won a hard and terrible battle but not the war. We're going to need all of your courage in the new battles that lie ahead if the sacrifice of the Fir Bolg is to be avenged."

"Ah – so sweet would such a thing be! I shall get drunk a hundred days and nights just to celebrate the thought of it."

Duval's smiling eyes met those of the dwarf, and he remembered as he did so the figure he had seen grow out of that tormented frame as Qwenqwo had invoked the rite of dreams.

"Mage Lord!" It was Siam who now approached him, Siam whose eyes were wide with shock, his jaw trembling as he waved around the groaning superstructure with his hat. "Your hair stands on end and you bear such a look in your eyes. You speak of wonders yet I cannot see how we are to escape this prison of ash and peril."

Duval took hold of Siam's shoulder and he strode with him across the quarterdeck to the ruined stairs of what had been the fo'c'sle. Together they climbed onto the second step so Duval could be seen and heard by everyone gathered on the decks.

"Don't be afraid of the changes you are about to see in the Temple Ship."

More cries were sounding out. Yet excitement surged ever higher within him, his heart hammering so much with new understanding that he struggled for breath. For with a shimmer about the very molecules of its structure, the ship was metamorphosing. "Look about you," he shouted to them. "The ship is healing itself."

He could feel his own sense of wonder spread, like a joy, among them.

"I am struggling to put into words the miracle I have witnessed. Throughout this difficult journey the Temple Ship has been more than our refuge. Don't be afraid when I tell you that it is alive. This is no vessel constructed out of oak but a living intelligence, beyond our understanding. It feels joy and it knows despair. It mourns those we also mourn for."

"Yet how are we to make headway in this sunken wreck the hundred leagues of distance that still separate us from Carfon?" It was the doubting Siam, standing beside him, who was still demanding answers.

Duval threw his arms about Siam's shoulders and hugged him, then turned to the equally incredulous Milish, who had left Mira to come and listen to him. He smiled at Milish, then hugged her too. "For the moment, it isn't necessary to understand, only to believe that it will happen." Then, with rising excitement, he watched how the ash was peeling from the underlying ivory: it was showering skyward, contrary to wind or gravity.

"Trust the Temple Ship. It will care for us during this journey." He nodded to Milish, adding in a softer voice, "Now bring Mira to me."

Duval accepted the limp body of the girl into his arms. He remembered Qwenqwo's words in the tale of beginnings: he had called the ship the Ark of the Arünn. It seemed that none of them had heard Mira's words as she challenged the Legun. *I am the Arünn reborn.* Ark and Arünn: he was just beginning to understand. No human healing could cure Mira! Mira was not human. The Legun had not damaged her physically. The Legun had attacked her spiritually. And the powers, of Earth, of Creation – how stupid he had been. He should have realized. He had been shown all he needed to know in the cave of the Trídédana. Now, as they watched him, the entire company spellbound, Duval's whole body assumed the light and power of the oraculum. He made contact again with the ship, being to being: his figure radiated light.

Beyond the lap of the water, they heard a faint keening; comforting as the response in music of a great soul. With much whispering and nervousness, they rushed about the decks or gathered in protective clusters about the wounded, as moment by moment the ship responded anew to the creative spark of Duval's communication. The oraculum flashed from Duval to the ship, a glory of power that took form in the Daughters of Mab, spiralling and revelling like living angels about the superstructure. In the Cave of Creation, he had witnessed their seduction and in the forest clearing he had seen what terror their rage might bring. But now he perceived them as a new vision. In their rainbow of light was the delight in form and colour, in their voices the birdsong symphony of spring, in their fragrance the intoxication of a child dancing through a summer meadow dense with wildflowers, in the touch and taste of their kisses the caress of beginnings, the carnal exultation in the seed of life. They flooded his every sense until in the whole was the miracle of life.

"You are beautiful!" he exclaimed, the sceptical scientist compelled to wheel and turn, bedazzled in the glory of their being.

The playful forms consummated to a single focus that became the form of Mab with the impossible voluptuousness of the Second Face, shimmering in the air before searching out the figure in Duval's arms. With a curve of great tenderness, her body stooped until her lips brushed Mira's brow. For a moment, the child's body took on the same healing radiance as Duval's. In that moment, he sensed the spirit revive in her, just as he had sensed it in the ship. Mira's eyes opened and she looked up into his smiling face. Gently, he passed her back into the trembling arms of Milish.

Moments later, the whole ship shuddered, then lifted a foot or more out of the water, and almost immediately began to inch away from the shore. Slowly, haltingly – as if needing to accustom itself to its new form and purpose – it assumed a new course against the centre stream.

For the first ten miles or so it gathered a slow and steady pace, as if they were heading back to Isscan. All the while the cloud of ashes billowed from the dissolving timbers, following in their trail like a plume of smoke. Then, on the port side it first became manifest, a spar as if the bud of a great wing, extended outward, sparkling over its ivory surface like starlight.

"It is as a bird – see even the prow has become a great beak!" one man exclaimed.

But little by little, as the forested slopes glided by in regal farewell, the form of the Temple Ship emerged more clearly and it was not as a bird but the delta shape of a great manta ray, with vast, winglike extensions of its pectoral fins. The prow assumed a dome and then a streamlined head, the breadth of its wings brushing the waterside foliage of the narrow channel at either upswept tip and sweeping round to fashion the living quarters within twin-horned cephalic fins to either side of its head, some thirty feet above the waterline.

Past the divergence of the waters about the island and into the great swell of the river, there was a new urgency to the ship's movements. A quickening of pace, as if it strained to leave this haunted valley in the cradle of its smouldering mountains.

All but the severely wounded stood on deck to watch the Rath of Nantosueta pass them by on their port side and then recede into the mists of afternoon, the reek of battle still pungent over the water and a lambent energy still flickering about the dreadful tor, as if in passionate farewell.

Meanwhile structures continued to evolve over the smooth hill of body behind the head, rearing high, as gill slits, then arching over until they became shelters for the convalescing wounded.

There were no doors or portholes any more, no masts or spars for sails, no bell tower or staircases that led below. Instead downy combs grew down, like living stalactites under these beautiful roofs, raining down a gentle mist of sweet-tasting nectar. The Olhyiu women tasted it on their fingers and then they began to gather it up in vessels and hats, so parched lips could be refreshed by it. The men began to construct primitive nets from what cord and material they had retained. They cast these makeshift nets from the stern and drew them in, heavy with fish. As the great mountains moved by once more on either side, they were so overcome with awe, they didn't cheer. They merely watched in reverential silence as Tazan's formidable valley closed its fist behind them, as they passed out of a second winding pass of cliffs that soared above them and echoed their passage.

Past the cliffs, they felt the slowing of current as the river widened again and the cliffs by degrees broke down into smaller pinnacles, a broadening valley of rocks in place of the giant redwoods.

By first light the next morning, they were moving swiftly south along the great Carfon River.

A creative ambience trilled the air, as if the ship communicated its joy of recovery with the mountains and the thinning trees, with the water that moved slower than they did in its swirling currents. The first of the seabirds wheeled overhead, delighting in the chase of their passage.

On the fifth day of their journey downriver, the late-afternoon sky cleared to a beautiful high blue from which a light fall of glittering snowflakes imbued the air with a fairy-tale loveliness.

Mira joined Duval on the prow of the ship, still watched assiduously by the caring Milish. Physically, as with all of the other sick and wounded on board, she had improved sufficiently to stand on deck with his arm supporting her. Time had worn a fantastic geometry of stone and sand in which delicate shades of lilac, gold, and lavender curled about the natural sculptures: cones and pyramids of stone, gorgeous shades and shapes, as if they had been moulded from the primal landscape by the playful hands of God's children. There were thousands of configurations – tens of thousands. They shimmered and sparkled in the setting sun, like mother of pearl.

"What do they call this place?" Duval asked Milish.

"In Carfon they call it the Painted Desert. But others know it as the Sea of Illusions."

The following morning, like the ghost of a bygone age, the broken dome of a great vault rose out of the haze of scrub and sand: a monolith at least two hundred feet high, by its left side a single wall survived of what must have been a great hall of stone, with level upon level of pillared porticos and romantic arches, surviving, through obstinacy, the millenia of dust-blown time. It seemed much older and finer than the walls of Isscan. Duval, who found himself alone on the prow, wondered at the great antiquity of the civilizations of Monisle and the city state they were now approaching. About its hinterland he saw clusters of beehive shapes, tiny in the distance, yet they must be two stories high and of the same hues as the rocks.

Milish joined him a little later, standing silently for many minutes, as if she were deep in contemplation.

Something is troubling her, he thought to himself.

Duval kept his own silence for a while as the ship hummed to itself, against the complex rhythms of its bow-wave against the rocks.

"Carfon," she spoke at length, "will appear a strange city to you. Of all the city states, it was the most ancient in its lineage and so the most elect within its boundaries. The fall of Ossierel changed everything. It made Carfon the final repository of the philosophy and logic that was our world."

Something is frightening her!

Duval watched how mists coiled from the bow spray over the water and, like sprites of mystery, still seemed to follow their passage.

It was many minutes before she spoke again. "In Carfon, the ruling families cannot help but resent the transformation. First the Council in Exile demanded territory within the oldest walls – and in arriving there became a power within a power, subject to no laws of Chamber. Since then a generation of refugees has swelled its population to eight million."

"I'm no politician," Duval replied. "I'll look to you for advice."

Another hesitation, to digest this. "I may be less useful than you anticipate. And politics may prove unavoidable for you."

Next day, the passing landscape gave way to the great alluvial plain that fed the city and its hinterlands. Piñon and juniper scrub took root in the desert, and then trees. Broadleaf trees. To Duval they looked familiar, but sufficiently different to be vaguely alien. He recognized oaks but with golden yellow leaves instead of green. At first these appeared in scrabbly knots but they soon became denser, coppices, and then woodlands: the relics of great forests that had once cloaked the land. Soon they came upon the first evidence of cultivation, a warmer land with fields of spring corn, like great rugs laid out to dry in the warming sun.

It was in the second week after leaving the forbidden valley that people came out to welcome them in the waters below.

They approached them in small boats or canoes and tossed garlands of flowers aloft or fresh loaves of bread. Others threw lines, at the end of which were baskets of fruit and vegetables. The food lifted everybody's spirits, since they had tired of the monotonous diet of fish. Still the great winged shape, the ivory of its coat taking on the rose of sunset or the gold of morning, coursed swiftly along the centre stream as the crowds became ever more numerous along the banks, as if word of their coming preceded them in every hamlet.

And soon a cry was heard from the banks to either side, the same phrase, like a hymn of thanks for their safecoming: "The Angel Ship – the Angel Ship!"

It was another day before they first glimpsed the city walls, straddling the great estuary of the Carfon River. Reflecting the low sun of evening, they soared a hundred feet above the rocky shore. Crowds lined the battlements. They were holding lighted candles in their hands and, as the ship drew level with them, people performed a ritual, fashioning a triangle from right to left shoulder and down to the inverted apex of heart.

Milish took her place on his left side, dressed in the formal regalia of silver plume and ornate gown and dress. Mira, with head bowed, hunched silently to his right.

The Temple Ship coursed by a deeply recessed and ancient gate in the highest walls. It appeared a half-pentangular arch within an arch, with above it a tablet of stone carved with runes about the edges of its weathered stones. The gate and the walls that enclosed it gave the impression of great antiquity, older by far than the cyclopian walls of Isscan – older even than the Rath of the Dark Queen in the Vale of Tazan.

"Why are you so tense, Milish?"

She hesitated before replying, as if accepting the fact that he sensed her every mood.

"It is the Water Gate, which leads into the Old City. It troubles me that the High Council in Exile has kept it closed against us. Do not underestimate their capacity for mischief."

He looked up with interest at the massive walls, and at the

people with their lighted candles. "My quest has brought me to these walls, Milish. I sense the power inside them, stronger than any force I have ever felt through the oraculum."

"Hush – hush! I beg you. Do not speak openly thus. It is blasphemy even to speak of it. Yet," her voice fell to a whisper, her presence suddenly frail and vulnerable beside him, "you sense the closeness of the *Fáil*."

"I feel its presence – as if I were sensitive to its calling in every particle of my being." He put his arm around Mira's shoulder and hugged her to him.

"For all your wisdom, will you not heed my counsel! Do not talk of such things in this unguarded circumstance! Do not even think them!"

But how could he not think of the *Fáil* when he knew that it held the answers to the quest entrusted to him by the High Architect as she lay dying. He reflected on that warning at the moment he lay wounded in London, as the atoms that made him were being torn apart to permit his journey here. *The emissaries of malice have already entered your world.* The others were also in danger. Liam, Sean, Penny and Maureen. All of his friends from long ago. There was much he needed to do. Plans he needed to make.

Meanwhile, the greatest quest of all now faced him. Soon, though it might be the most dangerous force in the universe, he would have to face the *Fáil*. And Milish was right: even thinking about it, he felt its terrible awareness focus on him.

"First we rest," he said, quietly, calmly. "Then we organize."

Milish's dark eyes assessed him, as if for the first time in his eyes she saw the new Duval, the man hardened by experience – the flowering of the seed that the De Danaan had chosen. "For the moment let us give thanks that fate has preserved us. Let us not look grim and whisper." Milish lifted her arm to wave and her face was smiling at the fluttering ribbons and the dancing lights.

The Temple Ship then heeled about a buttressed corner of the ancient walls, where a tall tower hovered a hundred and fifty feet above them, and it approached a second gate, more openly constructed than the Water Gate.

"This is the Harbour Gate," said Milish. "Yet even this is ancient in a city that knows only intrigues. Pay heed to my words. Knowledge more dangerous than you might dream opens now before you."

The Temple Ship halted a hundred yards out, in deeper water.

Soon a barque of state, of gilded and tapestried finery, emerged through the wide-flung gates and many oars dipped and pulled in perfect harmony as its shallow draught skimmed over the waves. A great cheer sounded from the Shee and the Olhyiu on board, and it was answered by the thousands of people holding aloft their candles of welcome.

On the dock, as if disdaining to join those aboard the approaching vessel, Duval sensed a powerful mind. He searched the distant mass of figures until he found its source: an old woman who stood alone in the shadows of the gate, her toothless mouth collapsed and wrinkled, her back stooped and bent over a staff of power. For a moment he was too shocked by an alarming ewcognition to sense her warning:

Beware the object of your quest. It may prove a poisoned chalice.

A thrill of alarm pulsed in the oraculum. Duval shook his head, dismissing it from mind. He put his other arm around the shoulders of Milish.

Let whatever danger come, he would face it when it arose. Today Carfon welcomed them like the buds of spring after a famine winter.

GLOSSARY

Aydes (Eye-dees): The helpers, healers and workers who accompany the Shee into battle.

Ainé (Eye-nay): The Kyra, or leader, of the Shee.

Arünn (A-rinn): The original inhabitants of Tír, who created the Fáil.

Brí (Bree): The oval-shaped oraculum of the Kyra of the Shee.

Carfon: The great city south of Isscan on the shore of the Eastern Ocean.

Cuan na Hanam: The harbour of souls.

Dana, Bave (Baa-vay) and **Mórígán** (Mow-ree-gawn): the triple goddess, or Trídédana.

Deathmaw: A force of elemental destruction that only the Tyrant or a Legun can generate.

Doras Vawish: the portal of death.

Dromenon: The infinite plain. An exalted level of existence, beyond normal space and time. Amongst other things it enables transmigration between worlds.

The *Fáil* (Faw-il): the great and dangerous legacy of the Arünn - a structure of infinite power that exists simultaneously in all worlds and all times.

Ghork-Mega: The capital and sprawling megapolis of the Wastelands, which covers a hundred miles radius, including the mouths of the Foul Trinity of rivers, Nega, Brukh and Kaal.

Granny Ddhu (Granny Dew): the Earth Mother.

Guhttan Mountains: The homeland of the Shee, rugged landscape in the southwest, where the Shee daughters are educated and taught the martial arts, including their inheritance of the history of their maternal line.

Hul-o-ima: Olhyiu for stranger.

Hyas Di-aub: Olhyiu for the great devil, the Tyrant of the Wastelands.

Inion-Baha: the sister-daughter of the Shee.

Isscan: The ancient trading city on the meeting of the Tshis-Cole (Snow-Melt) River and the Ezel (East) River.

Kloshe Lamah (Klo-shay Lah-mah): tactical military leader of the Fir Bolg of long ago, after whom the pass into the Vale of Tazan is named.

Kyra (Kye-rah): The great leader of the Shee. Bears the oraculum of Brí upon her brow.

Lañans: Sophisticated city dwellers, from the Western coastal cities. These are the government administrators and the communicators.

Léanov Fashakk (Lay-an-ov Fashakk): the Child of the Wilderness.

Leloo Kwale (Leh-loo Kwa-lay): Olhyiu for the Storm Wolves.

Magcyn Ré (Mag-syn Ray): Last High King of the Fir Bolg and Suzelz Tazan, or Lord of the valley of Tazan.

Neevrashvahar: immortality in the language of the Shee.

Niyave (Nee-yave): the gold coloured healing elixir of the Shee.

Nimue Guinevere (Nim-way Gwin-e-vere): The white shadow, a goddess of lakes and lakesides. Her symbol is the moon.

Ossierel: the ancient spiritual capital of Tír, where the Highs-Architects of Monisle ruled.

Qurun (Koo-runn): the word that means both woman and queen in the most ancient language of both Earth and Tír.

Septemvile (Sep-tem-veel-eh): The seven deadly members of the Tyrant's inner circle.

Tilikum Olhyiu: The children of the Sea (literally means people who live like seals).

Tír (Teer): the mirror world of Earth.

Tshis-Cole: The Snow Melt river arising in the Whitestar Mountains to the far north of Ulisswe.

Ulisswe: The great Eastern province of Continental Monisle.

Would you like to know more about Frank Ryan and his other books – or what he is planning next for Alan Duval and his friends? Why not pay him a visit at the website:

www.swiftpublishers.com